THE DEBT

THE DEBT

Glenn Cooper

severn
House

This first world edition published 2019
in Great Britain and the USA by
SEVERN HOUSE PUBLISHERS LTD of
Eardley House, 4 Uxbridge Street, London W8 7SY.
Trade paperback edition first published
in Great Britain and the USA 2019 by
SEVERN HOUSE PUBLISHERS LTD.

British Library Cataloguing in Publication Data
A CIP catalogue record for this title is available from the British Library.

ISBN-13: 978-0-7278-8859-4 (cased)
ISBN-13: 978-1-84751-985-6 (trade paper)
ISBN-13: 978-1-4483-0197-3 (e-book)

All Severn House titles are printed on acid-free paper.

Severn House Publishers support the Forest Stewardship Council™ [FSC™],
the leading international forest certification organisation.
All our titles that are printed on FSC certified paper carry the FSC logo.

Typeset by Palimpsest Book Production Ltd.,
Falkirk, Stirlingshire, Scotland.
Printed and bound in Great Britain by
TJ International, Padstow, Cornwall.

ONE

H is eyes were blue. Not a watery blue but vivid, the color of lapis lazuli, and she was transfixed by their unblinking focus on her face as he made love to her.

'Don't stop, Jean, please don't stop.'

'Nothing could make me stop,' he gasped, and he didn't until in a shudder he let his weight fall on to her.

He was slim and sinewy, without a trace of fat. It would be at least a decade before he would be expected to succumb to family traits transforming his body into the sleek corpulence of the moneyed class. But for now he was a hungry twenty-seven. Hungry for opportunity, hungry to prove himself, hungry for this dark-haired girl with buttermilk skin.

Ricca's hair was a wonder to him, black as a moonless night, falling all the way to the small of her back, thick with plenty of bouncy curls to occupy his hands. Lying in her arms and playing with her tresses he caught his ring.

She yelped but before he could apologize there was the sound of rifle fire in the distance.

He pushed himself up and swung his feet on to the rough floorboards. Naked, he pulled back the curtain. The morning sun was bright enough to flood even these grimy windows and tinge the room yellow. The Roman Ghetto, the Jewish enclave in the Sant' Angelo district, was notoriously crowded and dark owing to its narrow streets and tall dwellings. But their room faced east on the very top floor of an eighteenth-century addition, and though it was a squalid affair, its morning sunlight was priceless. The ghetto walls had prevented outward expansion of the quarter but the city fathers of Rome had long turned blind eyes to vertical growth. If and when a shoddily constructed building collapsed – well, only Jewish lives would be lost.

Jean pushed the window open to figure out which direction the shots were coming from but there was a lull and all he heard was a husband and wife arguing inside the ground-level butcher shop.

'I think they're shooting near the river, but I'm not sure.'

The girl became upset and began throwing on clothes. At first, he thought it was because the resumption of street fighting had clouded her mood but she set him straight.

'Why didn't you wake me?' she cried.

'That's exactly what I thought I'd done. Didn't you like the way I did it?'

'That's not what I mean! My God, it's late. My father will kill me.'

'If he lays a hand on you he'll have to deal with me.'

'That's not helpful, Jean.'

She had him turn away while she used the chamber pot and when she was finished he announced a plan.

'I'll go into his shop looking for you and while I'm at it I'll buy some bread and a few buns, you know, a complicated order to give you time to sneak up the back stairs and get to your room. When he goes to fetch you, tell him you couldn't rise because of a fever or a bad throat or any excuse you like. Don't worry, the plan will work a treat.'

The way he said it didn't quite work in Italian, his third language. She corrected him, as she often did. He was born in Paris and had lived in London for a decade before coming to Venice on a mission to expand the family business into the prosperous, merchant-friendly city. But after a promising start, a series of setbacks had sent him packing. Rather than turning tail back to England and admitting defeat to an imperious father, he had decided to try his luck in Rome. The modest office he rented was across the street from Ricca's father's shop. It had been all but inevitable that they would meet.

Her father, an impoverished fifth-generation baker, salivated at the prospect of marrying off his daughter to a rich man's son but Jean knew that his own father would be far from pleased.

The rifle shots resumed. One volley, then another.

'Republicans,' Jean spat. 'Revolutions are bad for business. When will it end? First France, then Germany. Hungary. Poland. Galicia. And now Italy.'

'People only wish to be free,' she said.

'This so-called freedom is for the Christians,' he said, pulling up his trousers, 'not us Jews. They'll always find ways to control us.'

She slipped on her shoes. 'I think this new pope is a good man. The ghetto walls are coming down slowly but surely, you can't deny it.'

He changed the subject to something more to his liking. 'When can I see you again?'

'Let's see if I survive this day,' she said.

He grabbed her for a last kiss. 'How about tomorrow night?'

She pulled away and said, 'How about we get married? Then you can have me every night of the week and you won't have to rent this drab room anymore. And I'll be an honest woman again.'

'Tomorrow night it is,' he said brightly, dodging her entreaties. 'Already, I can't wait.'

He opened the door and waited for her to follow. At first, the sound of footsteps coming up the stairs didn't concern him. After all, a family lived in the rooms below. But when the footsteps continued up to their level he went numb. Had someone found his love nest? Ricca's father? Her brothers?

Before he could shut the door a man came into view, then two more. They had daggers.

'Jean Sassoon! Stop there!'

Jean slammed the door and bolted it.

'What's happening?' Ricca cried.

'I don't know. Get under the bed, quickly.'

After he ignored two urgent demands to open up, the men forced the door, showering the room with splinters.

'Jean Sassoon,' a burly man in civilian clothes said, his fist curled around a lethal dagger, 'I order you to come with us.'

'Where?' Jean said, trying hard to sound brave.

The reply ricocheted back. 'To the Vatican.'

Another one-word question formed in Jean's mind. 'Why?'

'A man with a red hat wants to see you.'

TWO

The Vatican, present day

Pascal Lauriat didn't much look like a modern man. Perhaps it was his rather dainty, graying goatee and thin mustache and his insistence on always wearing all the entitled regalia of his position as cardinal secretary of state that made him look little different from all the old portraits of cardinals of past centuries that lined the Vatican walls. As soon as he returned to his office following his private meeting with Pope Celestine VI he summoned three of his colleagues for a debriefing. Cardinals Malucchi and Cassar arrived first followed several minutes later by Cardinal Leoncino, the influential Prefecture for the Economic Affairs of the Holy See, who entered and closed the heavy doors.

Mario Leoncino had patches of vitiligo on his face, and flushed as he was from his brisk walk across the Vatican grounds, the pale patches seemed whiter than usual.

'Well?' he demanded. 'How did it go?'

'He was quite animated,' Lauriat said. The other men laughed at the way the Frenchman puckered his mouth, as if he'd just sucked on a very sour lemon. It wasn't that Lauriat disliked the pope. On the contrary, on a personal level he had always found him charming and indeed quite disarming. They had been peers, of course, not so very long ago. Cardinal Aspromonte had been at the helm of the Secretariat of State when Lauriat was the Prefect of the Congregation for the Doctrine of Faith. In those roles, the two men had gotten along famously, often sharing meals and Curia gossip. Lauriat had thought that he had known the man and had, in fact, voted for Aspromonte in each of the ballots at the conclave that elevated him to the throne of St Peter. Beyond that he had lobbied for him. Aspromonte had, in turn, rewarded the French prelate with a promotion into his old job.

'Worse than we feared?' Cardinal Cassar asked. The unsmiling archbishop of Malta was fit and trim, a competent golfer who always seemed to be on the verge of locking his hands and simulating a swing.

'I'd say so,' Lauriat said. 'He had a new report from the auditors he plans to preview with the C10 and then formally present to the economic council. He ranted and raved about it. He even waved it over his head like a banner. He has a flair for the dramatic.'

Malucchi, the vicar-general for the Diocese of Rome, was well on the way to becoming as corpulent as the pope. He lowered himself on to one of Lauriat's good chairs and began to grumble. 'The auditors,' he spat, saying the word as if it were a venereal disease. 'They're more pious than the priests. The Church faces unprecedented challenges and here is the pope obsessed with money. Always profit and losses, assets and liabilities, these infernal balance sheets. In every instance he imagines the worst. To him all is corrupt. What he doesn't understand, he sees malfeasance. This obsession seems to take precedence over bedrock concerns about tradition and faith. You'd think we elected him head accountant, not Vicar of Christ.'

'Where did all this come from?' Leoncino asked in exasperation. 'Does he really wish to turn our Church over to green-visored men at counting tables? Our friend, Aspromonte, did a marvelous job hiding his true tendencies from us all these years, even when he occupied this very office. I never would have voted for him if I'd known.'

'Well I didn't vote for him, not even on the final ballot,' Cassar sniffed. 'You had my votes, Pascal.'

Lauriat tilted his head and returned something of a smile. 'What's done is done. We have our pope and we must do what cardinals in the Curia have always done. We must be a buffer against unhealthy tendencies. We must blunt the damage. Celestine is not infallible in matters of governance and administration. He is but a man all too liable to fumble in the dark. He has neither the time nor the aptitude to fully understand the intricacies of all our financial institutions and practices and their historical role providing ballast for the ship of state. It will take longer than his lifetime for his new councils and commissions to penetrate all the veils. Remember, we have seats on the economic council and Mario and I were able to wheedle ourselves on to the C8, his council of cronies, and turn it into the C10. Nothing happens without our knowledge. When Celestine is gone, we will turn the page. The papacy is self-righting. The pendulum will swing.'

'God willing,' Malucchi said, reaching for a pastry.

THREE

Cal Donovan was used to stares and sly comments whenever he strode through the reading rooms of the Vatican Secret Archives.

Occasionally he heard some of the cranky whispers from other academics who were planted at assigned places.

'That's Donovan.'

'Lucky bastard.'

'He looks pretty damned smug.'

A Vatican archivist would serve him up a knowing smile and let him pass through the private entrance doors into the areas restricted to staff. And then he would be on his own, free to wander from floor to floor, free to stop at any cabinet or shelf and peruse any item in the archive, the only exceptions being the modern documents from the past seventy-five years that remained under absolute quarantine to outsiders.

For all other researchers, the archives were ostensibly 'open', although it was the definition of open that was the rub. A qualified academic had to make a written request to use the Secret Archives or the adjacent Vatican Apostolic Library. Some fifteen hundred researchers a year qualified for admittance but there was a catch. They had to make specific requests for books or documents contained within the collections and to do so, they had to rely on imperfect catalogues and indexes and deal with the very real possibility that a document had been accidentally or purposefully misplaced sometime in the past. Requested documents were delivered to them in one of the reading rooms and returned to the stacks when their work was done.

The first time Cal ever used his golden library card, his sole purpose had been to take a very long walk through twelve centuries of history. He had started at the top floor, the frescoed Tower of the Winds, built in the sixteenth century as a solar observatory by Pope Gregory XIII. Then he had breathed in the musty air of the second level, the so-called Diplomatic Floor, commissioned in the seventeenth century by Pope Alexander VII as a central depository of the complete diplomatic correspondence of Holy See legates, nuncios, and other agents. All the written communication between the Vatican and the states of the *ancien régime* were still stored, bound or loose, in the same wooden cabinets that Alexander had constructed, an archive spanning the fifteenth century to the Napoleonic era.

His next stop had been the thirteen kilometers of documents housed in the long gallery built in the early twentieth century to the west of the Cortile del Belvedere. Dubbed by insiders the Gallery of Metal Shelves, the documents stored there included the archival material of the Curial offices, various Vatican commissions, and papers from the papal household. Nearby was another archive, the so-called Soffittoni, built after the Second World War above the gallery of geographical maps in the Vatican Museum, containing the documentary history of the Congregation for Bishops and other Vatican congregations.

Finally, he had descended to the basement to explore the most recently added archival space, affectionately known to insiders as the Bunker. There, under the Cortile della Pigna of the Vatican Museums, were forty-three kilometers of shelving dedicated by Pope John Paul II in 1980, a fireproof, two-story reinforced-concrete structure, carefully climate and humidity-controlled. The Bunker housed a huge array of documents ancient and modern, ranging from the archives of the most important families of the Vatican City States to various institutions of the Roman Curia and its councils, from the Congregation of the Rights to the near-modern archives of the Secretariat of State. To Cal's delight, he had even been allowed to enter the most secure storerooms adjacent to the Bunker that contained the greatest treasures of the archives such as the letter from English noblemen to Pope Clement VII concerning the 'Great Matter' of Henry VIII's divorce, the Edict of Worms with the signature of Emperor Charles, and the bull excommunicating Martin Luther. Giddy and with aching feet, Cal had emerged from his inaugural visit to the Secret Archives and had headed for the nearest café for a large celebratory drink.

On this day he checked in at the reception desk and was pleased to see an old acquaintance, the assistant archivist, Maurizio Orlando, the number two official on the professional staff, emerge from the back office to greet him.

'Professor Donovan!' Orlando said, his eyeglasses dangling

from a neck holder. 'I heard you were coming today. I hope you are well.'

Cal shook his hand and exchanged pleasantries before the archivist asked if he could be of service.

'Well, maybe you could tell me if I'm heading to the right place.'

'Of course. What is the nature of your research?'

'Ever hear of a cardinal named Luigi Lambruschini?'

'Yes, yes, I'm sure. He came close to being elected pope in the mid-nineteenth century, I believe.'

'You know your cardinals, Maurizio. He was Pope Gregory XVI's secretary of state and came within a hair's breadth of getting the big job at the 1846 conclave. He was a central figure in the 1848 revolutions in the Italian states. I'm writing a paper on his role in suppressing the revolts by enlisting the support of the French so I'm looking for primary documents. Thinking about starting on the Diplomatic Floor.'

Nodding, Orlando said, 'I would do the same. Let's see, 1848. That's the reign of Pope Pius IX. The official correspondence of the Curia with his ambassadors in the court of Napoleon III and senior clerics in Paris, Marseilles, Lyon, and other key cities might be fertile ground.'

'Maurizio, you're a scholar and a gentleman.'

Orlando beamed. 'Happy hunting, Professor. Ring my office if you need any further assistance.'

'I'll do that.'

Orlando's expression suddenly became serious. It looked like he wanted to say something else, so Cal gave him an opportunity by staying put.

'I hesitate to bring this up, Professor, but I received an awkward phone call a few days ago from your department chairman at Harvard, Professor Daniels.'

'Really? Awkward in what way?'

'He – how shall I say – strenuously requested the same privileges as the archive affords to you. He said that as your chairman it was only right and proper.'

Cal's blood began to boil. 'And how did you respond, if I could ask?'

'I merely told him that your privileges were unique and personally afforded to you by Pope Celestine, not the archive staff or even the cardinal librarian. I explained that there was nothing I could do.'

'And how did he take it?'

'He was rather irate.'

Cal shook his head. 'I'll bet he was.'

One week earlier

Cal's sneakers squeaked noisily on the hardwood basketball court of Harvard's Hemenway Gym. The player guarding him was no ordinary opponent. He was Cal's boss, if tenured full professors – a highly protected species – could be said to have bosses. More accurately, Gil Daniels was Cal's dean, a distinguished professor of theology at the Harvard Divinity School. The two of them were always a bit yin and yang and it was only fitting that they dueled periodically on opposing faculty sports teams. Daniels was a flinty Brit with an academic career centered on the history of the synoptic gospels, a topic that overlapped a tad with Cal's areas of expertise. Daniels was a decade older, and more importantly for the moment, he was freakishly tall, a full head taller than Cal, a six-footer himself. And while Cal had always been just a pick-up game type of player, Daniels had been a member of a championship men's team at Oxford University.

Cal had been pressed into an unaccustomed role as center because his teammates who turned out on the day were all on the short side.

'Where the hell is Cromer?' he had asked the team captain, an English literature professor, about their usual center.

'I think he's getting some kind of geophysics award.'

'Daniels is going to be a problem,' Cal had said.

'You'll run around him as if he were but a rooted tree.'

'Nicely put, Harold. You should do something with words one day.'

The captain had been correct. Cal was quicker and handled the ball better. He'd outscored Daniels two-to-one in the first half. When the second half began, Daniels unleashed a new strategy. He started draping himself over Cal like a new suit of clothes.

Since it was only a club game with a bunch of faculty duffers there was no referee; they relied on self-calling fouls and collegial acknowledgements of transgressions. But Cal didn't much go in for shouting, 'Foul! You fouled me!' He preferred letting the mild infractions slide and settling the major ones with quiet retaliation.

The ethos had come from his father, a strict disciplinarian and very much a man's man, who had taught his only child to deal with bullies and tough kids, not by tattling to the teachers, but by bloodying a nose or two. His mortified mother would handle the call from the principal's office by sending Cal into his father's paneled inner sanctum.

From behind his big desk, his father, the famed archeologist Hiram Donovan, would listen to the boy's account of the fight and would say, 'Get ready to scream really loudly,' and he would thump his desk hard with a book.

The smiling boy would say, 'Ow!' and his father would reach into a cigar box in one of the desk drawers and give Cal a worn Roman coin for his collection.

'Now get out of here and look miserable. For your mother.'

When Cal made a move to the basket, Daniel's long arm reached around Cal's neck and blocked his shooting arm. The ball bounced out of bounds.

Cal's captain called 'foul' but Daniels sported a what-did I-do look and said, 'It's Cal's call to make, Harold, not yours.'

'You calling it, Cal?' Harold asked.

Cal shook his head, wiped sweat from his eyes, and went on defense, whispering to Daniels, 'Gil, what's it going to take for you to play fair?'

Daniels grinned and said, 'I'm scrupulously fair, Cal. Everyone knows that.'

On the next possession, Cal took a pass and dribbled past the flat-footed Daniels to the top of the key where he set for a jump shot. As his arms went up he was rocked from behind by Daniel's chest. Off balance, he tucked the ball in his left arm and furiously delivered his right elbow into Daniel's breastbone, sending the taller man reeling backwards.

'Foul!' Daniels cried when he regained his balance.

'You fouled him first,' Cal's captain responded. 'You've been fouling him all day.'

'Christ, Cal, that hurt,' Daniels said, rubbing his chest.

'When you play dirty, that's what you get,' Cal seethed.

'I'm playing you tight, goddamn it,' Daniels protested, 'not dirty. An elbow is dirty.'

Cal wasn't backing down. 'I know dirty when I see it.'

A member of Daniel's team, a young economics professor, laughed and said, 'Easy, Cal. He's your dean.'

Cal gave the guy a withering look. 'We're all equal on the court.'

Another player tried to defuse the situation with this comment: 'Good thing you guys are at the divinity school. If you were in the government department there'd be blood on the floor.'

Harold suggested a five-minute break and the two teams parted to opposite sidelines. There was a single spectator in the stands, a young, compact man with a receding hairline, dancing eyes, and a clerical collar.

'Somewhat surprising,' the priest said with his Galway accent when Cal joined him.

Cal wiped at his forehead with a towel. 'What's surprising?'

'I expect fisticuffs when I go to your boxing matches. Always thought basketball was tamer.'

'Boys being boys.'

'Is that what it is? Still it gladdens my heart.'

'Why's that?'

The priest deadpanned, 'If you can do that to your chief, I'm free to imagine what I might do to you.'

For the rest of the game Daniels behaved and Cal's team won by eight points. Afterwards, Daniels came up to him and said, 'Hey buddy, no hard feelings.'

'Of course not, Gil.'

'Gotta play hard, play to win, right?'

'Words to live by,' Cal said unconvincingly.

Cal sat down on the bench to pack up his gear and Daniels did the same.

'I hear you're off to Rome,' Daniels said.

'Day after tomorrow.'

Every year like clockwork Cal spent two weeks in Rome during the Christmas break and a further month or more in the summer doing research on whatever project was on the front burner.

'Going to hang out at the Vatican?'

'Is the pope Catholic?'

Daniels chuckled and zipped his sports bag.

'I suppose you'll be using your golden library card.'

Cal could have predicted the comment. The resentment was

palpable. As a reward for Cal's extraordinary service to the Vatican on the matter of the stigmatic priest, Giovanni Berardini, Pope Celestine had granted him a unique and singular privilege coveted by every ecclesiastical scholar in the world. Cal was now the first outside academic in history to have unfettered browsing rights at the Vatican Library and the Vatican Secret Archives. Cal could wander the endless stacks and pluck out anything that caught his fancy. Any manuscript. Any book. Any stack of letters. Any financial ledger. Any papal bull and proclamation. Cal never advertised it or boasted about his unique status but these things get out and envy – some good-natured, some not – began rolling his way. Daniels had a penchant for laying it on thick, laced with his irritating brand of sarcasm.

'What are you working on?' Daniels asked.

'Cardinal Luigi Lambruschini. Ever hear of him?'

'Can't say that I have.'

'Early nineteenth century. He's on the obscure side.'

'Well, if you need someone to sharpen your pencils or your quills, give me a call.'

'You're a man of many talents, Gil.'

Daniels shouldered his bag and got ready to leave.

'And don't get lost in there. I've read the archives are pretty endless.'

'About eighty-five kilometers.'

Daniels whistled. 'If you don't make it back we'll send a St Bernard with a cask of brandy.'

'Fill it with ice-cold vodka and I'll make sure I get lost.'

Father Murphy was still in the stands, waiting to walk with Cal back to their offices on Divinity Avenue. Daniels spotted him and said, 'That's Joe Murphy, isn't it?'

Cal was sure that Daniels knew exactly who he was. Cal had showcased Murphy at a recent faculty symposium that Daniels had attended. The priest had given a talk about the subject of his successful Ph.D. thesis on new insights into Pope Gregory's chronicles of St Benedict. Now that Murphy had his degree, Cal was pushing for his appointment as a junior faculty member. Not that there were quotas, but Cal thought a Jesuit priest would make a good addition to the Divinity School and Murphy unquestionably had become an accomplished young scholar.

'It is,' Cal said. 'You've had his folder for a while. Any thoughts?'

'Honestly, I've been swamped. Maybe I'll have a chance to look at his paperwork over the break. I'll be stuck in Cambridge. No golden library card for me.'

Cal slipped on sweatpants and a sweatshirt for the snowy walk through the campus. The priest had to motor to keep up with Cal's long-legged strides and he had to fight to light his cigarette on the fly.

'I thought you were quitting?' Cal said.

'I thought so too.'

'Sinning in public.'

The smoke coming out of his lungs mixed with snowflakes. 'Well, you know what St Benedict said about that: a priest must not hide from his abbot the evil thoughts that enter his heart or the sins he commits in secret.'

'Didn't know I was your abbot.'

'One's academic advisor is not light years away. Let's call you my secular abbot. You had a word with Daniels about me, didn't you?'

'Either you've got amazing hearing or you're a lip reader.'

'The latter. When I was growing up I had a deaf friend. I learned it for solidarity.'

'He said he hasn't reviewed your application yet.'

'Believe him?'

'Not sure.'

'Time for a back-up plan?' the priest asked. 'I might have to dust off the old bench in the confessional back home.'

'That's not going to happen. I know for a fact that you could get an appointment at Boston College or Notre Dame in a heartbeat. We've got time. I want you here, Joe. Leave it in my hands.'

Cal shrugged off his irritation over Gil Daniels and breathed in the musty air of the Diplomatic Floor. He had it all to himself. The large wooden cabinets that lined the walls were unlabeled and even though he had done prior research there, it was hit or miss to find the right ones. Fortunately they were generally in chronological order. Once he located the cabinets containing diplomatic correspondence between 1848, when Pope Pius IX was chased into exile by revolutionaries, and mid-1849, when he was escorted back to the Vatican under the protection of French troops, he began climbing a tripod ladder to pull down thick bound volumes.

It was slow going wading through densely lettered documents written in Italian and French, looking for any mention of Cardinal Lambruschini. The hours dragged on and he began to feel the effects of jet lag compounded by the discomfort of the unpadded straight-backed benches, the only places to sit. The quest proved largely fruitless; he found only a single oblique mention of the cardinal in one communiqué. Cal wasn't particularly surprised. Most of the relevant correspondence from that period revolved around the sitting secretary of state, Cardinal Gabriele Ferretti. Lambruschini, having left the high office in 1846, would have been a quieter presence in Pope Pius's regime, whispering in the liberal pontiff's ear, advocating for an iron-fisted approach to deal with upstart revolutionaries. Had the conservative Lambruschini prevailed in the 1846 conclave and become pope the Vatican would surely have taken an earlier and more militant approach to the nascent republican revolution and history may have been altered. But even though Lambruschini was no longer secretary of state during the revolution, he still possessed a powerful anti-rebel voice and for that, the republicans hated him with a passion. His house in Rome was sacked and he had to flee for his life.

Cal's stomach began to rumble and thoughts turned to coffee and a sandwich. Still, he pressed on into the 1840s until he finally made it to the critical year of 1848, the year of the Italian Revolution. There were no fewer than five hefty volumes covering that fateful year. By the time he got to the last of the five, his backside was sore from the wretched bench so he took to the floor, sitting cross-legged against a cabinet, the heavy book resting on his lap. It was then that one of the young assistant librarians happened upon him and tried to suppress a grin. He had seen her before and her name came to him just in time.

'How are you, Mariagrazia? I expect you're wondering what I'm doing down here.'

She was dark and pretty, perhaps thirty, probably not quite. 'In fact I *was* wondering, Professor.'

'The benches were killing me.'

'I could bring the books down to the reading room for you. The chairs aren't great but they're better than these benches.'

'I prefer it up here. It's quiet.'

'As you wish. I'll leave you to it then.'

She wasn't wearing a ring; he noticed these things. He considered asking her out for lunch or maybe a drink after work. Maybe one thing would lead to another – one never knew.

A wicked daydream sped through his mind. He was in his mother's apartment, high over Central Park.

'Mother, I'd like you to meet my new wife, Mariagrazia. Yes, she's very young but so were you when you married Father. Did I tell you that she's a good Catholic girl? Mother, what's the matter? Are you all right?'

Two days before Cal left for Rome he had stopped at Manhattan for an obligatory visit with his mother. Bess Donovan was a formidable woman. Upon the occasion of her seventy-fifth birthday party at an old-line, swanky Manhattan restaurant, Cal had risen to deliver a toast to a hundred of her intimates. He had begun his remarks by describing his mother with a single word: Indomitable. Everyone understood exactly where he was going. Nothing had ever defeated her, or to be more precise, she had never publicly admitted to any defeat, large or small. She had overcome breast cancer and was currently battling her chronic leukemia to a draw. She had plowed through the emotional upheaval over the loss of her husband, who had died in mysterious circumstances during a dig in the Middle East. After she buried Hiram Donovan in Boston she had moved back to her native New York, where she had become a major player in philanthropy for the arts.

When Cal had finished his warm and slightly irreverent remarks, his mother had followed him to the podium and a little tipsy from champagne had said, 'I want to thank my son, Calvin, for his speech. Isn't he gorgeous, ladies? He's like a young Cary Grant or Gregory Peck, don't you think?'

A friend, equally tipsy had shouted from her table, 'You're showing your age, Bess. I think he looks like John Hamm from *Mad Men*.'

'Now that's a gorgeous man too,' Bess had said. 'But seriously ladies, from one Jewish mother to another, he's not a doctor or a lawyer but he's a Harvard professor like my late husband and he's still single, not even divorced. So email me the names and bona fides of your eligible daughters, nieces, or, for my really old friends, your granddaughters, so we can make a match. And I know what you're thinking – never married, in his forties, but no, he's not gay! Ask his old girlfriends.'

During his visit Cal had taken tea with her in the sitting room of her Park Avenue apartment against the muffled soundtrack of honking taxis far below. She was dressed to the nines, caked in makeup, her hair a lacquered fortress. He didn't think he'd ever seen her natural complexion or her hair in rollers, even as a boy. These days she had become frail, her skin translucent, her hands covered in liver spots. She walked with a cane. Not a drugstore cane, mind you, but a splendid ebony and mother-of-pearl antique, made practical by the addition of a new rubber grip. When she lifted the tea to her mouth her tremor had become more pronounced. Her maid had made a compensatory adjustment by only half-filling the china cup.

'So you're off tomorrow, is that right?' she had said.

'Early flight.'

'To where did you say?'

'Rome. The Vatican.'

'Again? You seem to spend an inordinate amount of time there. I do wish you'd spread your wings a bit more. You're not getting younger.'

He had half-smiled. 'Are we going to be having that conversation again?'

'Which conversation is that?'

She had known full well, of course. The religion conversation. The heritage and identity conversation. The marriage conversation.

'Willie Sutton robbed banks because that's where the money was,' he had said. 'A professor of history of religion goes to the Vatican because that's where the documents are.'

'They have documents in Israel too.'

He had tried to keep it on an even keel. 'I travel to Israel with some regularity. You know that.'

She had put her cup down, rattling it on the saucer. 'I want grandchildren, Cal. You're the only one who can make that happen. I want Jewish grandchildren, not Catholic ones. The amount of time you spend in Italy. I know what's going to happen. You're going to marry a Catholic.'

'Just like you did,' he had said, looking her in her milky eyes.

She had been undeterred. 'I know you say you identify as Catholic, Cal. It's hardly a surprise given the larger-than-life effect your father had on you but by law – Jewish law – you're a Jew because I'm a Jew.'

'As you know, or conveniently disregard, I've taken it rather further than identifying as a Catholic, mother. I'm baptized, confirmed, and have received the Eucharist. Hook, line, and sinker as they say.'

'I don't even know what all that mumbo-jumbo means.'

He had glanced at one of her priceless table clocks. 'Look at the time. We'd better get going if we're going to make our lunch reservation.'

Cal blinked at the young librarian and hoped his daydream hadn't lasted more than a second.

'You have a great day, Mariagrazia. *Ciao* for now.'

He buried himself back in the book and nearly halfway through it, his eye caught Lambruschini's name at the top of a page. It was a letter addressed to him, written in reddish-brown ink in a neat scrawl. He began to read the short letter, hoping it might salvage an unproductive morning.

It took only a few moments for Cal's day to become considerably more interesting.

29 November 1848

My Dear C. Lambruschini
We arrived safely. True to his word King Ferdinand has been gracious and has afforded us sanctuary. However I write you in urgent warning concerning information passed to us by a Neapolitan spy. The republicans are said to target you in an assassination plot. The Holy Father wishes that you leave Rome immediately to join the papal party. Furthermore you are to bring the banker with you. The Holy Father has expressed that apart from your well being nothing is more important to him than the safety of the banker.
C. Antonelli

Cal took a deep breath of that intoxicating, stale air. Who the hell is this banker? he wondered.

FOUR

Rome, 1848

Giacomo Antonelli was young for a cardinal secretary of state, only forty-two. Long-serving functionaries within the Apostolic Palace were still having difficulty wrapping their minds around the notion of a cardinal deacon with nary a single strand of gray hair. He was a sober man, a natural administrator who had managed to advance his career, first under the conservative administration of Pope Gregory XVI, and then under the decidedly more liberal tenure of the new pope, Pius IX. However, two turbulent, war-filled years had turned Pope Pius away from his liberal tendencies and had turned him into a heavy-handed ruler. Now the young Antonelli would need every bit of his even temperament and administrative skills to navigate the present crisis swirling around the Eternal City.

The cardinal hurried through the halls of the palace at an unbecoming pace, his leather-soled slippers slipping on marble floors as if they were sheets of ice. With each clap of distant gunfire his pace quickened until he was practically running. If he had paused to look through the windows of the corridor he would have seen the sea of cobblestones of St Peter's Square, wetted from nighttime rain and glistening in the morning sunshine, and he would have noticed that the square was empty save for a small number of determined, cloaked pilgrims making their way up to the great doors of the majestic basilica. Ordinarily, by this time of day, the square would be thick with the faithful, but two days after the assassination, most Romans were staying indoors to avoid the unpredictable danger of public spaces.

Pellegrino Rossi, the pope's minister of the interior, had been stabbed to death on the stairs of the parliament by a republican sympathizer, an act of violence that was reverberating throughout the Vatican. If a papal minister could be killed by the mob, why not the pope himself?

The pope was working in the office he used whenever he

travelled to the Vatican from his residence at the Quirinale Palace. Until recently, the pontiff almost always appeared serene, but stress had creased his patrician face into a fixed frown and his skin had turned blotchy. His downy white hair, usually well kempt under his red skullcap, looked unruly, like a neglected garden.

The pope was at his writing desk by the window. 'Thank you for coming. Did you sleep?' he asked, putting down his dipping pen.

'Very little, Your Holiness,' Antonelli said. 'Did you fare any better?'

The pope blew on fresh ink and pushed away from the desk. 'Hardly a wink. The gunfire, you know. There was no let-up.'

They huddled by a small fire. It was mid-November and the palace was chilly.

'Do you feel as you did yesterday?' the pope asked.

'I do. Rome is not safe for you,' the cardinal said. 'The fighting in the city is only the beginning. More revolutionaries are on the march and Rome is their destination. Garibaldi's legion is coming. The Polish legion from Lombardy is coming. Others too. We are defenseless. The Swiss Guards, as you know, have been disarmed and confined to barracks by the rabble. My plans for your escape are not yet set in stone. However, within days, perhaps a week at most, we will remove your person from the Vatican to a safe location away from Rome, away from the Papal States.'

'To where do you think?'

'Gaeta seems best.'

Antonelli did not wish to burden the pontiff with the complex diplomacy involving the Bavarian and French ambassadors who would arrange for safe passage to Gaeta, only a day's carriage-ride from Rome but safely within the Kingdom of Naples. From there, if the pope wished, a Spanish ship would take his party to the Balearic Islands until the revolution, God-willing, burned itself out.

'Gaeta . . .'

The pope's sadness touched Antonelli. He wished he could provide comfort but it was not his role to be a friend or confessor. He was a fixer and there was much to be fixed. The fire that had begun in France was burning throughout Europe and the flames were threatening the very heart of the Church.

The pope was staring at his own small flames, dancing through a pile of logs. 'Before we depart there is an urgent matter, Giacomo.'

'Yes, Your Holiness?'

'There is no money.'

'Perhaps that is an overstatement,' the cardinal said. 'We are not completely bereft of resources. The contents of the treasury will be sent to Gaeta. I am making the arrangements.'

'It is only a matter of time before we are bankrupt, and not a great deal of time,' the pope said wearily. 'I have a stack of letters from governors of the Papal States requesting emergency funds. And now to make things worse we will have to fund a government in exile. I thought the situation under Gregory's reign was dire. This is worse.'

When his predecessor, Gregory, was made pope the Vatican cupboards had been almost bare. The economic woes traced to before the turn of the century when Napoleon came to power and demanded the Vatican pay enormous tributes to France. When the Vatican could no longer make contributions he sent troops to Italy to rob churches and cathedrals of anything of value, shipping the loot back to Paris. Compounding the problem, Vatican real-estate revenues had tumbled after Napoleon nationalized Church properties throughout France. The situation was hardly better elsewhere in Europe as rulers in Austria, England, Scandinavia, and Germany diverted Vatican-bound rents to their own treasuries.

The newly minted Pope Gregory had to deal with the crisis from the moment he took office. With full knowledge of the inevitable outcry, he turned to the Jews for help. And not just any Jewish moneylender, not some Court Jew who loaned a few thousand pounds or francs here and there, but the Rothschilds, the pre-eminent European banking dynasty. The Rothschilds were lenders to monarchs, saviors to governments, for who else had deep enough pockets to prop up a state?

It was Carl Rothschild, brother of James de Rothschild, the head of the family enterprise, who had travelled back and forth between Naples and Rome, negotiating the terms of a regime-saving deal, pumping hard currency into the Vatican treasury in the nick of time. Gregory had suffered the slings and arrows of anti-Semitic sentiment, but he got his money and disaster had been averted.

'What would you have us do?' Antonelli asked.

'We must secure a loan.'

'How large?'

The number shocked the cardinal.

'For a sum of this magnitude, we must go back to the Rothschilds,' Antonelli replied. 'I can draft a letter to Carl Rothschild and have a courier ride to Naples.'

'No! We cannot go back to the Rothschilds!' the pope shouted, surprising the cardinal with the seismic eruption. 'They will know we are in dire straits. We have no leverage with them. They will exploit their advantage and we will be forced into predatory, even crippling terms. They are like sharks with blood in the water. No, not the Rothschilds.'

'Who then?'

'There are other bankers, other Jews. I have in mind a grasping family who would aspire to elevate themselves to the heights of the Rothschild clan. Our friend, Lambruschini, knows them from his years in Venice. I speak of the Sassoons, particularly the Sassoon son who represented the family interests in Venice but is now in Rome.'

'Do they have the resources to satisfy a loan of this size?'

'They have the funds on hand, if Lambruschini's information is sound.'

Cardinal Lambruschini had been Antonelli's predecessor as secretary of state. An archconservative and conclave rival, Pius had marginalized him in favor of the more palatable Antonelli. But as the pope's attitudes had hardened, Lambruschini had been brought back into the fold. In ordinary times, Antonelli might have been annoyed that the old cardinal was whispering in Pius's ear but he had far too much on his plate to worry about Vatican politics.

'There is an impediment, I believe,' Antonelli said. 'The previous loan contract with the Rothschilds stipulated that we are obligated to return to them, and them alone, should we require future lending.'

'Then we must compel complete secrecy from the Sassoons so that the Rothschilds remain unaware.'

'It is no easy thing to keep a large papal loan secret,' the cardinal said.

'Lambruschini assures me we can accomplish this,' the pope said enigmatically. 'Of course, I want more than secrecy.'

'What more?'

'I want excellent terms,' he replied. 'Truly excellent terms.'

'If we go to them with a begging cup, how are we to extract good terms from these Jews?' the cardinal asked.

The pope smiled for the first time that day. 'Leverage, Giacomo. Leverage. I know a thing or two about these Sassoons and I will not hesitate to – how shall I say it – nail them to a cross.'

'Then we must approach this Sassoon. I presume he operates from the ghetto. I will send my secretary to locate him.'

'No need for that,' the pope said, pushing himself out of his chair. 'You can find Jean Sassoon closer to home. Lambruschini has him locked inside a cell in the basement of the Sistine Chapel.'

FIVE

The morning after the discovery of the enigmatic letter from Cardinal Antonelli to Cardinal Lambruschini, Cal was back at the archives, about to make his way through the reading room and up to the Diplomatic Floor. As he was heading toward the staff entrance he turned to wave at Maurizio Orlando who was leaving his office. Just then Cal almost collided with a nun in a black habit who was leaving the stacks.

They traded hasty apologies. Ordinarily he paid more attention to a nun's habit than her face – he was fairly adept at identifying a religious order by the garb. But this face surprised him and he found himself staring to the point of embarrassment.

She was stunning, on par with the most beautiful women he had ever seen, and he fancied himself somewhat of an expert on that score.

For her part, she lingered for a long moment, fixing him with what he thought was a flicker of interest.

When she disappeared he went over to Orlando and asked, 'Who is that? I think I just made an ass of myself.'

Orlando laughed. 'You are not alone in that regard, Professor. That is Sister Elisabetta Celestino. She is no ordinary nun. She is the secretary of the Pontifical Commission for Sacred Archaeology, the first woman to hold this position. She has a very interesting background, but as you like to find things out for yourself, I will leave you to your own devices to learn about her.'

Cal tucked his curiosity away and headed straight for the Lambruschini papers on the Diplomatic Floor. He had left off at 1848. The cardinal died in 1854 so the task at hand was not exhaustive – six years of the cardinal's papers spread out over three volumes. He dove in looking for any further information about this mysterious banker.

For the most part the correspondence and documents in the folios were banal, the work product of an elderly prelate no longer grasping the reins of power. Cal hadn't completely lost interest in his original mission of finding new, relevant information about

Lambruschini's involvement in the revolution but there was a critical gap in material during the nine months in 1848 and into 1849 when Lambruschini was in exile with Pope Pius. When the cardinal returned to Rome, Cal could detect a certain apathy in his writings, as if the great events had taken a toll on his spirit, if not his physical health.

Sitting cross-legged on the floor, Cal was getting to the end of the exercise. Only a few pages remained of the last volume. It was fast approaching noon and Cal had a luncheon appointment with his friend, the archbishop of Boston, Cardinal Da Silva, and he quickened his pace and rapidly turned each page after only a cursory scan.

Cal felt the last two pieces of paper between his thumb and forefinger. The penultimate document, written a month before Lambruschini's death, was a polite letter to the cardinal from a Roman store requesting payment on a past-due bill for wine and olive oil. He came to the last page. It was a letter in the cardinal's distinctive handwriting, but the script was uncharacteristically sloppy and loose, the lines written at a downward slope. Within ten days the man would be dead. Cal could almost visualize the ill prelate limply holding a dipping pen, perhaps sitting in bed with a lap desk, drawing the pen unsteadily over the paper.

Cal raced through the short letter and the reply, written in a steady, bold hand in the empty space at the bottom of the page. As he read it, he felt the sting of adrenaline prickling his skin.

2 May 1854

My Dear C. Antonelli,
I know you are aware that my health is rapidly failing me. I am endeavoring to address the last of my worldly business. Among them is the matter of the Sassoon loan. I had intended to deal with the matter four years hence upon its maturity but alas I will no longer be an earthly presence at that time. If the loan is not repaid there will be consequences. I regret that it will be left to you to attend to them. Might I suggest that when the moment arrives you enlist the assistance of Duke Tizziani? He is a friend who possesses the ability to deal with the bankers in Venice and their foreign offices. And now a final request. Please pray for my soul,
    Lambruschini

My Dear Luigi,
Do not trouble yourself any longer. Consider your burden
passed to my shoulders. The Holy Father prayed for you this
very evening and I too fervently pray for your eternal soul.
  Giacomo

Cardinal Da Silva was momentarily distracted by the arrival of a
large plate of pasta.

'My goodness, Cal! Would you look at that? Magnificent. You
might want to reconsider.'

Cal tasted his salad. 'This will do me fine, thanks, but your
carbonara does look good.'

The café, a popular spot for Vatican staffers, was a short walk
from the walls of the city state. Da Silva, short and roly-poly,
never disguised his love of eating; it was his self-declared sole
vice. As he lowered his head to twirl a forkful of buttery fettuc-
cine, his scarlet zucchetto shifted forward over his bald dome
forcing him to reposition it with his other hand.

'This really is superb,' he said. 'Here, you must have a taste.'

Cal obediently forked himself a few strands and rendered an
approving verdict.

He had known Da Silva a long time. They had first met years
earlier when the Portuguese-American was bishop of Providence,
Rhode Island and the two appeared on the same panel discussing
the history of the Catholic Church in Portugal. Cal had given a
talk on the two Portuguese popes and Da Silva had spoken about
the dissolution of the monasteries after the Portuguese Civil War.
Afterwards they had become friendly and Cal was a personal
guest at Da Silva's investiture as cardinal in Rome. The modest
and self-effacing prelate, whose face seemed to be in a state of
perpetual mirth, was one of those cardinals always mentioned in
articles about future papal candidates. Lionized by liberals,
demonized by hardline conservatives, Pope Celestine counted him
as one of his closest advisors, appointing him to his kitchen
cabinet.

'How long will you be in Rome?' Cal asked.

'Only till Thursday. The C10 meets tomorrow and then I have
a series of additional meetings. My calendar has no white spaces,
I'm afraid.'

'I'm glad you made time for lunch.'

'This is my recreation, Cal. Seeing an old friend is always a pleasure. Tell me, will you see the pope during your visit?'

'I don't want to bother him. I doubt he knows I'm here.'

'I'm sure he does. Nothing at the Vatican escapes Monsignor Moller.'

'Is he well?'

'I'd say so. Physically he is strong. Emotionally – well, the job takes its toll. He's been much involved with finances. It's a job too large for one man and he hasn't enough true allies to lean upon. The C10 will try to lend its support but there is only so much we can do.'

'I've read the articles. Cleaning up the Vatican financial mess is like Hercules mucking out the Augean Stables. Mythic quantities of manure.'

'Ha! You're right about that. Well, he views this as part of his legacy. We shall see how he does but he's certainly up for the good fight. So tell me, what are you working on? You're always chasing something interesting.'

'I was doing research on Pope Gregory's secretary of state, Luigi Lambruschini, a prominent anti-revolutionary figure during the Italian Revolution.'

'I note the past tense.'

'That's the beauty of having browsing rights. I happened upon something potentially more interesting.'

'Come on then, let the cat out of the bag!'

As Cal spoke about what he had found, Da Silva made a good dent in his mound of pasta.

'Is there no record of this loan to the Vatican?' the cardinal asked.

Cal tried to catch up on his salad. 'Not that I'm aware of. The Rothschilds made some sizable loans to Pope Gregory in the 1830s. I wrote a paper about papal lending and usury laws several years ago but I'm no expert. I only found this letter from Lambruschini to Antonelli mentioning the loan an hour ago. I need to run it to the ground to see if there's any mention of it in the historical record. As far as I know, there's a Sassoon Bank that's still in business. Whether it's the same one – I don't know yet. Anyway, I'll be back in the archives after lunch. If I'm lucky, at the end of the rainbow I'll have a nice paper to publish.'

'Well, Cal, your excitement is contagious. Promise me you'll keep me informed. I love a good mystery.'

*   *   *

Cardinal Antonelli's papers were far more voluminous than Lambruschini's since his tenure as cardinal secretary spanned almost a full three decades to his death in 1876. Diving in, Cal's first observation was that the correspondence and documents were meatier than Lambruschini's, reflecting an administrator in his prime dealing with the tumult of a turbulent period. During his tenure, the Vatican had tried desperately to hold on to the Papal States in the midst of the Risorgimento, the unification movement that would eventually succeed in creating the new Italy.

Cal hadn't been at it for more than an hour when he found a tantalizing breadcrumb in a note dated 18 September 1858 from a Monsignor Parizo to Cardinal Antonelli.

> *I have received a rather sharp letter from the banker regarding the loan. I have been in communication with the Duke and have provided him with the documents he requires. When he is done he will return them and I will have them destroyed. The Duke assures me that we need not concern ourselves with the outcome. In my opinion the matter is in capable hands.*

Cal pulled out his notebook and copied the letter in its original Italian. He presumed that the duke was Tizziani, the fixer recommended by Lambruschini. He resumed his search, finishing the 1858 papers and making it all the way through the end of 1860 without another mention of loans, Sassoons, or the duke.

Sensing a presence, he looked up from his spot on the floor to see Maurizio Orlando standing over him.

'I'm sorry, Professor. I didn't mean to startle you. I was just passing and thought I'd say hello.'

'Good to see you, Maurizio,' he said, standing up and stretching his lower back.

'Please, I don't wish to interrupt.'

'Not a problem. I think I've reached the end of the road here. Actually, you can help me, if you've got a minute.'

'Of course.'

Cal opened his notebook. 'Have a look at these. They're transcriptions of some letters I found. I need advice where to go next.'

Orlando read the series of letters and said, 'So, you've shifted the focus of your research.'

Cal smiled. 'I think I may have a bit of a case of attention-deficit disorder. I often read something and head off in another direction. I want to see if I can find out more about this loan. Where would you go next?'

'Well, I don't recognize the name Sassoon,' Orlando said, 'I'm not completely certain but I don't believe we have a folio on anyone by that name. As you likely know, it wasn't unusual for the Vatican to take loans from merchant bankers in those days.'

Cal nodded. 'I've written a couple of papers on the techniques the Church used to circumvent usury laws on its borrowings.'

'I am always impressed at the breadth and depth of your knowledge, Professor.'

'I wasn't fishing for compliments.'

Orlando nodded, slightly embarrassed. 'If the lender were the Rothschild family I could point you to an abundance of archival material,' he said. 'Likewise, I don't recognize this Monsignor Parizo. So many faceless bureaucrats over the centuries. Now this Duke Tizziani. I shouldn't imagine we have all that much on him as I don't believe he was a major player. Most of the material on noble families from this period is kept at the State Archive of Rome, not here. However, we might be in possession of corres- pondence or documents sent *to* the Vatican from this Tizziani. I suggest you go to the Bunker to the section devoted to nineteenth- century nobility. We can assist you further, but I suspect you will wish to use your own resourcefulness.'

'Trolling the stacks is half the fun, Maurizio.'

Orlando patted his sleeveless sweater over his small paunch. 'Also excellent exercise.'

Well into the afternoon, Cal was regretting turning down Orlando's offer of help. The Bunker was a vast basement space of endless metal bookcases and it was all too easy losing one's way in its sameness. Simply finding the right shelves was devilishly difficult but waving the white flag wasn't his style.

It was four-thirty, a half-hour before closing, when he finally found two comparatively slender volumes on the Tizziani family, seemingly misfiled as they bore no alphabetical or temporal rela- tionship to the other books on the shelf. The label on one spine was faded so that only a *Ti* was visible and its companion volume had no label at all. He almost hadn't discovered them before closing time because when he passed by a massive section on the illustrious Borghese family, he had almost succumbed to its gravitational pull.

Now with the first Tizziani volume in hand he stood, flipping pages, in the narrow space between two rows of shelving. They were extremely uninteresting, concerning seemingly minor legal disputes for which Duke Tizziani was enlisting Vatican support. But one of the last documents in the book was far different. It was a letter from the duke to Monsignor Parizo dated 2 September 1858. He read it slowly, particularly this one paragraph.

> *I am in receipt of your gracious letter. Please assure the Cardinal that I am willing to assist in this delicate matter. I understand that I am to persuade the Sassoons using any means at my disposal that it is not in their best interests to call in the loan. I further understand that I will endeavor to obtain their signed copy of the loan contract and its annex. Once the documents are in my possession I will put them to the fire. As you suggest I will require your copy of the loan contracts so that my agents may know they have located the correct documents. When the matter is closed I will return the Vatican copies per your instructions. Finally please tell the Cardinal that I appreciate his kind offer that I might receive a blessing from the Holy Father when the task is concluded.*

Cal grunted in frustration. So all copies of this enigmatic loan were probably destroyed. Pity. There might have been something interesting at the end of the rainbow but now he'd probably never learn more. Historians were used to that. Not every inquiry led to an answer. On the bright side, he'd only blown two days chasing the goose. Tomorrow he'd get back to work on his original topic. He transcribed the letter into his notebook then thumbed the last pages in the volume before putting it back on the shelf. He almost didn't bother with the companion volume but he thought better of it and with only a few minutes until the archives closed, he began skimming the remaining pages.

Late that night Cal was back at his room at the Grand Hotel de la Minerve, his favorite haunt in Rome, partly because it was right next to the Pantheon, partly because it was an elegant old converted palazzo that suited his taste. His mind had been racing ever since he'd left the archives and draining the minibar hadn't remotely slowed it down. He was online, furiously working his keyboard, when at ten o'clock Cardinal Da Silva finally returned his call.

'Cal, I just got your message,' the cardinal said. 'I hope it's not too late. I was at a reception. Excellent, excellent veal dish. Is everything all right?'

'I'm fine, thanks. I was only calling because I promised I'd let you know if I found anything more about that loan. I have. It's interesting stuff – I mean really interesting – but it can wait. I know you've got a busy day tomorrow.'

'Nonsense. I'm back at the guesthouse now with my shoes off and my feet up. Tell me what you found.'

'That's great,' Cal said, 'because I've been dying to tell someone.'

An hour later Cal's room phone rang again. He thought it might be the cardinal with one more question but it was a voice he didn't recognize.

'Good evening, is this Professor Donovan?'

'It is.'

'This is Monsignor Moller, Professor. I hope I haven't woken you.'

'I'm very much awake.'

'Very well then. Could you please hold for Pope Celestine?'

SIX

Rome, 1848

'We leave in an hour,' Monsignor Campo announced to the prisoner. 'Have your breakfast and prepare yourself for a journey,'

Jean Sassoon was lying on his thin mattress, his arms tightly folded across his chest, the posture of defiance he assumed whenever he heard the iron lock clunking open. He had been at Cardinal Lambruschini's house in Rome for a week. When he had demanded to know why he had been moved from the Vatican, the reply – 'for your safety' – had been unsatisfactory. But now he was reluctantly becoming accustomed to his fate resting in the hands of others. The dour priest at the doorway was carrying a tray of food. He found room for it at the foot of the bed.

Cardinal Lambruschini had chosen Gaetano Campo as his private secretary a few years before the 1846 conclave, elevating him from the obscurity of rank and file ambitious young men who populated the Apostolic Palace. He had become aware that Campo shared his anti-republican political views and that the eager Tuscan priest, when in the employ of his previous bishop, had developed a reputation for loyalty and discretion. Lambruschini was secretary of state at the time and one of the papabile cardinals. Had he prevailed, Campo would have had a clear path to a glittering career. But Lambruschini, the conservative choice of the conclave, fell short and the liberal and arguably glamorous Cardinal Mastai-Ferretti had become Pope Pius IX. Campo had been left to tend to an aging cardinal whose best days were behind him.

'Where are we going?' Jean asked Campo.

'You will know when we arrive.'

'How long is the journey?'

'Less than a day but who knows? I understand the roads are treacherous.'

Jean stared at the priest. His black cassock was scraping the top of his well-polished shoes although in his haste one of the thirty-three buttons was undone. The two men were similar in age, both devout in their faiths, but they were a world apart.

'You look scared,' Jean said. 'I can hear the gunfire perfectly well. They are coming for you, I think. The republicans.'

Campo turned away. 'One hour, no more.'

The priest locked the door and hurried to the cardinal's study to finish bundling up Lambruschini's papers. For all he knew the mob would be inside the house by nightfall and the last thing the Church needed was for confidential papers to land in the hands of the rabble. The housekeepers were nailing the lids on the filled crates to be carted to the Apostolic Palace for safekeeping. Campo cleared the top of the desk then tackled the desk drawer. Inside was the letter they had received the day before from Cardinal Antonelli.

Nothing is more important to him than the safety of the banker.

He put the letter into the last crate and heard the sound of hammering before proceeding to the cardinal's chamber to assist him with final packing.

They worked together, they ate together, they prayed together. Their houses in Cannon Street in London shared a common wall. Behind their backs their employees wondered wickedly whether brothers Claude and Mayer Sassoon slept in the same bedroom, leaving their wives to sort things out for themselves.

Inside the counting room of the Sassoon Bank the brothers faced each other at opposing standing desks. Chairs were banned at the firm. Far too slothful. Claude was older by a mere eleven months but that sliver of time meant all the difference. Mayer was argu-ably better looking, had a better head for numbers, was a better schmoozer, but oh those eleven months.

There was no denying that they were born to be bankers. Their father, Herschel, had founded the bank in Paris some fifty years earlier in the aftermath of the French Revolution. His principal competitor had been the Rothschild Bank, which had gotten an earlier start and an earlier foothold in European banking, handling payments from Britain to hire Hessian mercenaries in its war against France. Although Mayer had been his father's favorite – his name was a nod to his father's great rival, the founder of the

Rothschild Bank – it was Claude, in his position as first-born, who inherited the majority of the equity, precisely fifty-two percent. The Sassoon Bank had thrived but in the troubled aftermath of the French Revolution of 1830 the brothers decided to pick up stakes and move to the more stable environs of London, opening their business a short distance from St Swithin's Lane, the head-quarters of the Rothschilds.

To the aspirational Sassoons, the Rothschilds were their North Star. They were far wealthier, their bank far better capitalized. After all, it was a hundred years older. While the Rothschilds were able to make loans to nations of millions of pounds, the Sassoons had never lent more than half a million to one party. The Rothschilds, despite the impediment of their religion, had managed to crack into the aristocracy and had become proper Jewish Englishmen. The Sassoons had not achieved that level of distinc-tion and lived unassimilated lives steeped in Jewish rituals.

The two brothers wore almost identical single-breasted frock coats and black neckties. Claude's muttonchops were as gray as the ashes in the fireplace and his hair had largely receded, leaving a few tufted patches like insignificant islands in a lake. Mayer's features were finer – he might have passed for an Anglican – and his head of hair was thick and curly with only a smattering of gray. His reading spectacles pinched the end of his narrow nose and he removed them to rub at the red indentations.

He waved the letter in his hand and said loudly, 'This is an outrage, Claude! An unlawful seizure and imprisonment.'

His brother had opened the letter only a few minutes earlier and was clutching the desk to support his wobbly legs.

'My son, my son,' Claude wailed and the men in the counting room who understood French could only presume that a calamity had befallen the house of Sassoon.

'I never supported the Italian venture,' Mayer said. 'There is plenty enough business here. Birmingham or Liverpool, yes. Venice and Rome, no. Italy is a nest of vipers and the pope is, well, you know what he is.'

'Would you be quiet, Mayer!' Claude shouted. 'It is but wasted talk. All that matters is that we must secure Jean's release.'

SEVEN

Monsignor Ludwig Moller, first private secretary to the pope and prefect of the papal household, left his office, a converted guest room across the hall from the pontiff's rooms, to greet Cal at the reception area of the Sanctae Marthae guesthouse.

'Professor, it's good to see you. Let me take you down the hall. The Holy Father is running a little late.'

Moller, an Austrian cleric in his early fifties who was said to be an excellent violinist, had been at the pope's side from his first days at the secretariat of state. Moller was lean and athletic, although in a priest's loose cassock his physique was well hidden.

Cal had met him on a few occasions and addressed him warmly. 'I trust you've been well, Monsignor Moller.'

'Very well, thank you. Busy as always. But I'm sure you've been quite busy too. Happy hunting in the archives?'

'I'm like a kid in a candy store.'

Arriving at the pope's office adjoining his bedroom, Moller assured Cal that the wait would be short. 'I'd offer you a coffee, Professor, but we wouldn't want to spoil the Holy Father's pleasure, would we?'

Cal knew exactly what he was talking about.

The very fact that the pope lived and worked in the Vatican guesthouse, an establishment that had it been a public hotel would only garner two, maybe three stars, told some of this pope's story.

In the view of many who had known Aspromonte before his elevation, the cardinal who had chosen the name Celestine VI had changed the moment the ring of the fisherman slipped on to his finger. The seemingly sober and measured churchman had become something of a bomb-thrower.

The first small signs of Celestine's coming radicalism occurred within the confines of the vestment room next to the Room of Tears, the plain chamber where new popes, fresh from their election, pause to pray and contemplate their fates prior to showing themselves to the faithful. The master of ceremonies had come to fit Aspromonte with garments to accommodate his more than ample frame and it was there that the new pope rejected the red mozetta, the traditional papal shoulder cape, and declared he would wear only a simple white cassock. Then viewing an assortment of red slippers, he mumbled that his brown crepe-soled shoes would do just fine. Appearing at the balustrade over St Peter's Square he spoke plainly, using homespun language, and uttered variations of the word charity multiple times in his brief remarks.

In the days that followed he had set tongues wagging in the Curia by eschewing the papal apartment and moving into a tiny two-room suite on the second floor of the Sanctae Marthae guesthouse and ditching the papal fleet of stately sedan cars for an economy Fiat with thirty thousand kilometers on the clock.

Of course, the Curia had learned quickly enough that these public-relations gestures, as some called them, were the tip of the iceberg. Celestine had bigger fish to fry.

When the pope arrived he greeted Cal with a soft clasp to both shoulders. Moller found a chair in the corner and sat motionless like an obedient hound awaiting his master's orders.

'I have to tell you, Professor, I am so delighted Da Silva called me last night,' the pope said in Italian, remembering Cal's fluency. 'I am pleased to find these few minutes to speak with you. I'm sorry I kept you waiting.'

Cal returned the sentiment and the pope offered him a chair.

'You should have told me you were coming to Rome. I would have made room for a dinner but alas I have so many engagements and so little time. Would you like a coffee?'

Cal knew from experience that Celestine would want him to say yes so that he could make a show of putting the capsules in the machine himself and making coffees for the both of them. He would be only half-shocked if, at the end of the day, the pontiff washed the cups himself.

'I would love one,' Cal said.

The pope happily pushed the buttons on the espresso machine and served Cal before dropping back into his desk chair and folding his hands over his prodigious belly. His desk was plain, the kind that schoolteachers use, but the chair was incongruous, a modern Aeron model donated by a local supplier to soothe his balky back.

'I think the sisters count the number of spent capsules every

day and report back to my doctor,' he said. 'My blood pressure,
you know. Do they count the capsules, Moller?'

The monsignor replied, 'Certainly not, Holy Father.'

'Well, Professor, I have to tell you this: a man in my position
has many acquaintances but few friends,' the pope continued. 'Yes,
I have some true friends from my youth in Naples, but they seem
to be dying off and those that remain – well, I cannot see them
very often. That is why I greatly value our friendship. It was
providence that brought you to me when I needed your help with
our dearly departed stigmatic, Father Berardino.'

Cal felt his face flush. 'I feel the same way, Holy Father. It's
an honor to be called your friend.'

'So, I am eager to hear about your latest project,' the pope said.
'Da Silva tells me you started to explore one topic but have shifted
to another.'

'The power of serendipity, I suppose. I came to the archives to
do research on Cardinal Lambruschini, the secretary of state under
Pope Gregory XVI.'

'And what was it that interested you about this cardinal?'

'In 1848 he was an arch-foe of the revolutionaries and encouraged the French to intervene in the conflict. To put it mildly, he
wasn't one of the heroes of the revolution. I was looking for fresh
material on his activities.'

'And did you find fresh material?'

'None whatsoever.'

'And instead you've discovered an enigmatic loan.'

'I have indeed. It seems that Lambruschini was involved in
securing a sizable loan during the reign of Pope Pius IX – three
hundred thousand pounds sterling.'

'A considerable amount in those days.'

'Very considerable. Do you know much about the Church's
history of borrowing money?'

'Only that it was done,' the pope said, his eyes twinkling with
interest. 'I hope you'll enlighten me.'

'Well, I'm not a bona fide expert but I'm familiar with the
subject. Over the centuries the Church borrowed money with some
regularity to meet its obligations. I've published two papers on
Vatican borrowing. If I'm lucky, I'll have a third.'

'Ah, publications. The mother's milk of academia.'

'Exactly that.'

'Da Silva tells me you don't believe this loan was ever repaid. How is that possible?'

'I really don't know. One of the transactions I wrote about is a loan made in 1831, during Gregory's pontificate, by the Rothschild Bank. It was for an even larger amount, four hundred thousand pounds sterling. That's about fifty million euros in today's currency. Gregory had inherited a massive fiscal deficit and needed a loan to prop up the Vatican. By turning to a Jewish banker, inevitably, he became the target of criticism. Carl Rothschild, the brother of the head of the bank, was summoned from Naples to a papal audience to discuss the terms of the loan and afterwards a well-known Lutheran wrote, "A Jew kisses the pope's hand while a poor Christian kisses the pope's feet."'

The pope's chuckle was slightly wicked. 'Was *this* loan repaid?'

'It was. The historical record is clear.'

'But not your loan.'

'I don't think so. What I found yesterday, contained within the papers of an obscure noble, Duke Tizziani of Romagna, is a contract, signed by Cardinal Antonelli, Pius's secretary of state. It's dated 1848 and lays out the loan amount and various nonfinancial understandings between the parties. The document is countersigned by someone named Claude Sassoon. There's a reference in the document to an annex to the contract that provides the repayment terms.'

'Da Silva tells me you almost didn't explore this duke's final book of papers.'

'I was losing steam, I admit, but I guess it pays to be on the compulsive side.'

'Why would there be a need for an annex?'

'This was typically done to maintain the farce that the papacy wasn't violating the usury laws that prohibited charging or paying interest on loans. It gave the Vatican an element of deniability because the repayment terms weren't in the main contract. It was a bit of Kabuki theater, really.' Cal reached into his briefcase. 'I transcribed the loan document, if you'd like to see it.'

Celestine took the lined notepaper and waving off Moller, who sprang from his chair, he managed to find his pair of reading glasses himself. 'Interesting,' he murmured several times before giving the notepaper back.

Cal gave him another few sheets. 'These are my transcriptions of letters written by Lambruschini, Antonelli, and Antonelli's secretary, Parizo. They provide some context.'

When Celestine was done with the pages he said, 'There seems to have been a remarkable display of cloak and dagger behavior.'

'I couldn't agree more.'

'It is curious,' the pope said. 'The secretary wrote that all copies of the contract were to be destroyed, yet you found this loan contract very much intact.'

'Only the main contract. For whatever reason it seems that the Vatican's copy was not destroyed. But there was no sign of the annex.'

'I see.'

'I knew I'd never heard of this loan,' Cal said, 'but as I mentioned, I'm not an authority on Vatican debt. I spent last night searching online and couldn't find any records for this or any other loan between the Vatican and the Sassoon Bank, which was owned by another Jewish family not as prominent as the Rothschilds. This morning I called someone who's a real expert, a professor of finance from the Wharton School in Philadelphia. He also had never heard of the loan or its repayment. It seems to have vanished into the mists of history.'

'A lovely way to put it. Does this Sassoon Bank still exist?' the pontiff asked.

'It does. The Sassoons are still less grand than the Rothschilds but from what I've read, it's a significant merchant bank.'

'So I put to you this question,' the pope said. 'Is there a possibility the loan is still valid?'

Cal had wondered the same thing but admitted he had no way of knowing.

The pope looked pensive as he refolded his arms over his cassock. 'If it carried interest that continued to accumulate, I would imagine it would be worth a considerable amount today.'

'I imagine so but without knowing the terms in the annex it's only guesswork.'

'Would you do something for me?' Celestine asked after an unusually long pause.

'I'm at your disposal, Holy Father.'

'It may be a difficult task if, as this Monsignor Parizo had requested, the Sassoon copies of the loan were destroyed, but I would like you to see if a signed copy of the annex exists. Do you think it could be possible?'

'I suppose so but we don't know if Tizziani succeeded in finding and burning the Sassoon copy. We also don't know if the Vatican destroyed its copy. I'll spend more time in the Secret Archives and if that doesn't pay off, I may have some other ideas.'

'Please have the archivists deliver to me the original documents you found, if you would be so kind.'

'I'll do that immediately.' He wondered if the question was appropriate but he couldn't restrain himself. 'Could I ask why you're interested?'

The pope passed his reading glasses from one hand to another, seemingly deep in thought until he said, 'These days I have been immersed in an examination of Vatican finances. There is, how shall I say, a lack of transparency in some departments but I can tell you we are not on a strong footing. A sizable loan such as the one you've discovered, if unpaid and valid, could be precarious to our current situation.'

'I can see that,' Cal said.

'Yes, very precarious. If you were able to find this loan, others could find it as well. Isn't that so?'

'I got lucky but I'm not the only one in the world who likes to crawl around archives. The loan contracts could be anywhere.'

'I would prefer that someone such as yourself, a friend of the Vatican, find the annex, rather than an individual with adversarial tendencies. That way we might have the time to thoroughly engage with our legal advisors on the issue of validity and prepare the appropriate defenses.'

'I understand,' Cal said, his hopes of a timely publication fading.

'Very well, then,' the pontiff said, rising. 'Please keep me informed of your progress.'

Cal and Monsignor Moller stood in unison.

'Actually, Moller,' the pope said. 'I wonder if you could give me a moment in private with the professor. I have a personal matter I wish to discuss with him.'

EIGHT

London, 1848

Claude and Mayer Sassoon argued into the evening.

'Listen, my brother,' Mayer said, 'what the pope is proposing is not a loan. It is a demand for ransom. Holding Jean on the pretext of violating usury laws is a joke! Nobody violates usury laws more than the papists themselves. We cannot bend to this blackmail.'

'What choice do we have?' Claude moaned.

'What choice? We don't pay.'

'And then what? Wait for them to kill my son?'

'This Cardinal Lambruschini doesn't say kill. He talks of unfortunate consequences, whatever that may mean.'

'It means that they will kill my eldest son. Tell me, what would you do if it were Edouard?'

'I didn't send *my* son to Italy. I sent him to Manchester.'

Claude hatefully stared across his desk, prompting Mayer to apologize.

'I should not have said that. But look at these terms they propose. Unacceptable! Insane!'

'We have no choice. We have the liquidity.'

'I cannot support this,' Mayer said. 'I love my nephew but we will set this bank back years, decades perhaps. If there is a downturn in business, we might not even survive. Yes, you have a responsibility to Jean but also to young Andre and the rest of your family and my family too. At least let us endeavor to negotiate. We should propose a flotation of Vatican bonds rather than an outright loan. Standard terms, not this insanity.'

Claude asked for the letter back and referred to it. 'You read what they wrote: "The existence of this loan must remain an absolute secret." There is nothing secret about a bond flotation. You know why they demand this, no?'

'Of course I know,' Mayer said, pointing in the general direction of St Swithin's Lane. 'It is an open secret that the Rothschilds slipped a clever provision into their 1831 loan to Pope Gregory. What was it, four hundred thousand pounds? The Vatican was prohibited from going to any other bank for their next loan. The penalty was rumored to be one hundred thousand pounds. If the Rothschilds find out that Pope Pius went around them, they would sue and they would win. The Vatican is being clever and ruthless, Claude. The pope has been run out of Rome by the mob. There is no possible market for Vatican bonds for the foreseeable future. The Rothschilds would never do a bond deal in the midst of a revolution and they would never do a deal with the structure the Vatican has proposed. Ever. So the pope kidnaps the son of another banker.'

'They call themselves men of faith,' Claude said weakly.

'At least let me negotiate with them.'

'I want my son back. What will I tell his mother?'

'Are you saying you would accept these terms?'

'I cannot take the risk otherwise.'

'My God, Claude. I must object.'

Claude folded the letter, replaced it inside the envelope, and stepped away from his desk. 'It is my decision. I have the majority.'

'Always the majority,' his brother said bitterly. 'All right, Mr Majority, at least let me have our lawyer draw the contract to our liking.'

Claude walked toward the Cannon Street exit.

Mayer called after him, 'Do you agree?'

Without turning around, Claude said, 'Do it.'

When Claude was gone Mayer muttered, 'Like hell I will.'

He was weary to the marrow but Genoa was his home and even though he couldn't let his guard down it was better to be a hunted man in his own city than an exile in a foreign country.

Earlier, his mother, once a glorious beauty, had come to see him in the small house by the docks he had rented under an assumed name.

'Giuseppe, how thin you are. How tired you look. Please stay in Genoa for a while and rest. And eat. I will come every day to bring you more food.'

Mazzini looked more like a university professor than a revolutionary. The middle-aged lawyer had a high forehead unattractively accentuated by a severely receding hairline. His clothes were of good quality, London-bought, but at this point they were worn through and almost shabby. After all, he was perpetually on the run and short of resources. Only a week before he had been flushed out of his safe haven in Switzerland after the Austrians attacked.

'I will not be able to stay long,' he had said, accepting a piece of fruit. 'I have some urgent business here and then must move along.'

'Where will you go?'

'It is best you do not know.'

She had been sad but had understood. After all, she could hardly criticize the life he had chosen to lead. When he was only twenty-nine she had helped found the secret society, Young Italy, the banned organization that called for a united Italy and the insurrection to cast off the yoke of the Austrian occupiers in the north. Now her son was a hunted man.

Shortly after she left there was a light knock on the door. One of Mazzini's associates parted a curtain to see who was there. It was dark but there was a nearby streetlight and the man's features were distinctive enough. Satisfied, he let him in.

'Is he here?' the visitor asked.

'He's at work.'

Mazzini was in the chilly dining room seated at a long table. A pair of candelabras illuminated his writing papers.

'General,' the man said.

'General,' Mazzini replied. Both men laughed and embraced.

Giuseppe Garibaldi was forty-one, the younger of the two by five years. He moved across the room with an athletic, loose-limbed fluidity, tutting at the paltry fire and bending to stoke it with the skill of a man who knew his way around a campsite. While Mazzini was the intellectual, Garibaldi was the man of action, an accomplished, unafraid soldier. Brains and brawn, they were, bookends of a revolutionary movement. They had both been made generals this year. Garibaldi, appointed to the rank by the provisional government of Milan, Mazzini, by the Lombard Army, although the lawyer insisted his rank was merely honorary. The two men had not been apart for long; both had shared recent exile at Bergamo.

Garibaldi was in civilian garb with a concealing, wide-brimmed hat. Wearing his brigade shirt around the city would have been like waving a red cape at the King of Sardinia's men.

'No problems getting here?' Garibaldi asked.

'Nothing too extraordinary. You?'

'A skirmish or two. We lost one man. My brigade is camped in a thicket on the outskirts of the city.'

'How many?'

'Some four hundred.'

Mazzini fished a sheet from his stack of papers. 'Have a drink and read this letter.'

'Who is it from?'

'A Jewish banker I knew from my years in London. The letter was sent to Bergamo and was delivered here by one of our men. I think you will find it interesting.'

Garibaldi poured himself a brandy and read it by the light of the improved fire. He tossed the letter back on to the table and had more brandy. 'So what?' he said, dismissively. 'The son of a banker gets in trouble with the pope and they expect us to help? We have our own troubles.'

Mazzini agreed but added, 'One of our troubles is a dire lack of funds. You told me yourself how you struggle to provision your brigade. A revolution needs money like a man needs food. When I was in London I approached the bank for loans for Young Italy. This man, Mayer Sassoon, was cordial but the question was always, what is your collateral? We had no collateral then and we have none now. Do you see what he writes? Free my brother's son and you will have all the credit you require on good terms. It is a godsend, Giuseppe.'

'I am unsure whether this entreaty comes from God or the Devil. Still, tell me what you want me to do.'

'Send a party of men to Gaeta to free Jean Sassoon. Then let us fill our coffers and get on with our revolution.'

The Angevine-Aragonese Castle at Gaeta was an ancient, ponderous structure of almost colorless stone. Although it was squat and utilitarian, it commanded a breathtaking, panoramic view of the green-blue waters of the Tyrrhenian Sea. From where it sat it was a strategic part of the defenses of the Kingdom of Naples.

Jean Sassoon could not take in the natural beauty of the promontory. He had arrived at night and was held in a windowless, medieval cell, dank and dirty. All he could do to stave off boredom and worry was to pace in a tight, squared-off pattern while waiting for word to arrive from London whether his father would accede to the pope's demands.

One of his jailers, a lowly officer in King Ferdinand's army, always seemed to be on a short leash, held back like a vicious hound. If he hadn't been under strict instructions not to harm the young Frenchman his natural inclination surely would have been to inflict daily beatings. On this evening, while waiting for his meager supper to arrive, Jean heard sustained, muffled volleys of gunfire penetrating the thick castle walls. He reckoned the shooting had to be quite close. Could it be that the republicans were on a southerly march from Rome? If the castle fell, might he be freed?

The sadistic jailer appeared with a wooden tray and set it down hard, spilling half the watered-down wine.

'What was the gunfire?' Jean asked.

'Didn't I tell you that I don't talk to Jews,' the officer said. Then a smile crossed his face when he seemed to find a way to defy his orders to keep quiet about the fighting, albeit obliquely. 'But if I did talk to the likes of you, you'd know that you're not going anywhere.'

'What does that mean?' Jean demanded, but the jailer left, laughing and hurling curses. When the door slammed shut Jean screamed after him, 'What the devil is going on?'

Cardinals Lambruschini and Antonelli went to the pope's modest apartment on a middle floor of the castle. They didn't know if he was still awake but they found him seated in a chair by a small fire, a rather coarse blanket on his lap.

'Holy Father,' Antonelli said. 'We are sorry to disturb you.'

'I heard the gunfire. Was it the Red Shirts?'

Lambruschini nodded. 'The information we received from the spy in Garibaldi's brigade was correct. A band of some twenty-five Red Shirts was met by the superior force of Ferdinand's men lying in wait for them on the castle road. The threat is no more.'

'Thank God,' the pope said. 'Now let us see what the Sassoons will do.'

Garibaldi received the news at his camp the following afternoon but waited until the cover of darkness to visit Mazzini's house.

'Slaughtered,' he told his sad-eyed colleague.

'All of them?'

'Every last man.'

'Bad luck or treachery?' Mazzini asked.

'It remains to be seen. We may have a spy in our midst.'

Mazzini had become hardened by their struggles but he fought to hold back tears. 'Their blood is on my hands. They died because I wanted money.'

'I refuse to allow you to be hard on yourself,' Garibaldi said. 'In war a commander is obligated to make hard decisions. Win or lose, we move forward and keep fighting. This affair is over but you will find other ways of raising funds to support our cause. Battles will be lost but the war will be won. Remember what you always say. There will come a day when there will be one Italy.'

Claude Sassoon was lit up with rage. He charged unannounced into his brother's house to find Mayer taking supper with his wife and his son, a pale young man a few years older than Jean.

'Claude, what a surprise,' Mayer said. 'We did not expect you. Look, Edouard has come from Manchester. Rachel, set another place. Join us.'

Claude was in no mood for socializing. He took a letter from his pocket and tossed it on to Mayer's plate of food. 'What do you know of this?' he demanded.

Without reading it, Mayer said, 'Claude, it is the Sabbath. We cannot discuss business.'

'You told me you were writing to accept the terms of the loan and were sending a contract but instead, you tried to make a deal with Mazzini. You went behind my back. You have jeopardized the life of my son. The plot failed and now I have this threatening letter from this cardinal giving us an ultimatum of one week. I will not forgive you for this.'

Mayer stood and tried to get Claude to come into the library but his brother stood firm. 'If my plan had worked you would have had your son back,' Mayer said, 'and the bank would not be faced with ruin.'

Claude shook a long finger at Mayer and said, 'It is my turn to write a letter. That letter will say that I agree to the loan terms and that the money will be sent. I have a majority! You should know that I was considering a change in my last will and testament so that Jean and Edouard would have equal shares. Now I tell you: that will never happen. My side of the family will always have a majority!'

'Claude, please!'

'I am sorry to say this over your Sabbath meal, Rachel, but Mayer, you can go to hell.'

NINE

There was no advance agenda for the meeting but the cardinals in attendance knew exactly what would be discussed. Cardinal Lauriat had made sure of that. The C10 had met earlier in the day and Pope Celestine had previewed his concerns with his closest colleagues. Lauriat along with Cardinal Leoncino were the bridging members of the two groups. Lauriat, as secretary of state, chaired the session today of the Council for the Economy, one of the pope's new initiatives to wrestle thorny Vatican economic issues to the ground.

'Prepare yourself,' Lauriat had warned the council's cardinals in rapid-fire calls. 'He's on the warpath.'

The pope had, in a cursory manner, raised another topic at the C10 meeting – he had briefed his advisors on what he knew about Cal Donovan's loan.

'I am informing you of this situation,' he had said, 'because in the event the professor finds the loan papers I would not want you to be surprised. Potentially, we might be facing a huge liability and we would need to mount our legal defenses to protect our solvency.'

'Can't you just shut down Donovan's search?' Lauriat had asked.

'Would you prefer instead that an enemy of the Vatican find it one day?' the pope had countered.

'Certainly not,' Lauriat had agreed, 'but if Donovan is successful we would need to bury this loan in a very deep hole.'

The pope had joked, 'Surely, Pascal, that is the type of thing lawyers do for a living.'

The economic council members had arrived at the third floor of the Apostolic Palace and had filtered into the Sala Bologna, an ornate and frescoed sixteenth-century hall strategically located between the traditional papal apartments the pontiff had chosen to eschew and the sumptuous chambers of the secretariat of state. Awaiting the commencement of the meeting, the cardinal members chatted amiably with the lay members, an international group of esteemed Catholics skilled in business, finance, auditing, and economics.

One of these men, the Canadian chairman of an international consulting company, buttonholed Cardinal Malucchi and said, 'I don't know if it was an oversight but I received no preparatory materials.'

'It was no oversight,' Malucchi said. 'The pope wished to address the council on a delicate matter and did not want to disseminate his thoughts in advance.'

'The pope is personally attending?' the wide-eyed businessman asked.

Just then, two tall Swiss Guards wearing the Medici colors of blue, red, and yellow took up positions at the entrance of the Sala Bologna whereupon the pope entered. He urged everyone to take his place and looking around, asked Lauriat where he should sit.

To polite laughter the French cardinal replied that the Holy Father could sit wherever he wished.

Celestine chose a chair in the middle of the long table and placed before him a thin red-leather portfolio adorned with the papal seal. When the room was quiet he began his remarks in English, the common language of the assembly.

'You may be wondering what the pope is doing crashing your meeting. With the kind indulgence of your chairman I wanted to speak with you today on a matter of some urgency. You sit on this council because you are experts in economic matters. Well, I should say that you lay members are the true experts but the cardinals are recognized as running rather efficient financial operations within their home dioceses. I wish I could tell you that the Holy See and the Vatican City State also have efficient financial operations. They do not. I formed this council to help us navigate stormy seas. You all know from your first meetings that our finances are a mess.' His voice suddenly soared and he slammed the table with his palm in a flash of anger. 'A complete mess!'

To a man, they all stared incredulously, some at the pontiff, others at their pads of paper. In public he was the picture of a mild-mannered, jovial uncle, a calm, beatific presence in a turbulent world. None, save Lauriat, had seen this combustible side, and the secretary of state had witnessed it only when the pope struggled with Vatican finances.

'I have here a new report from our international auditors,' the pope said, his hand patting the red portfolio. 'It is a damning report. When I leave you may read it. In this room only! I have made no copies because I don't want to see it in the press. I trust you but I cannot trust every member of your staffs. Some leak Vatican documents because they wish to help us. Others wish to harm us. Leaks are unconscionable. We must make our analyses and deliberations in private. That is the dignified way.'

He paused to take in the nodding heads.

'So, what does this report say?' the pope asked. 'It says we are running severe deficits within the Holy See. At least ten million euros per year, although the number could be much higher owing to the auditor's inability to get accurate information from several departments. One doesn't know if these black holes arise from deliberate obfuscation or incompetence. The profit and loss statement of the Governorate is more stable, owing to the revenues we receive from tourists visiting the museum, buying stamps at the post office, and so on, but again, some of the departmental figures are difficult to verify. And why do we have these deficits? We have too many employees! We are bloated. We have many, many employees who are paid a lot to do little or nothing. We have enormous pension obligations that arise from all these retired employees who are living longer and longer these days. Another thing. We don't have consistent bidding for contracts. Often there are no bids at all. We pay too much for our construction, our maintenance, our printing. Without accountability. We spent half a million euros on our Christmas tree! It was a very nice tree but not that nice! Some suppliers dump their useless and outdated products on us knowing that they can do so with impunity and do you know what happens? We have to buy them again! We are poor landlords. We often do not charge fair-market prices for apartments we own in Rome and elsewhere. Some renters get below-market rates. I was astounded to learn that hundreds of accounts are marked as *Affito 0*. No rent at all! Others get their flats for one hundred euros per year! Why does this occur? I cannot prove that graft and kickbacks exist but in my heart I truly suspect these dark practices. Then there is the peculiar phenomenon of funds entering into some especially notorious black holes never to be seen again. Actually, I prefer the term rat holes but Cardinal Lauriat admonishes me for pejorative language. I speak, for example, of the Congregation for the Causes of Saints where we collect an average of five hundred thousand euros from sponsors to support a single inquiry into sainthood, although in some complex cases the sum exceeds a million. That money – tens of millions of euros – is intended to support research into matters of sainthood, medical consultants, printing costs, but there is no audit of how these funds are spent. Again, no accountability. Money vanishes. Where does it go? Now let us consider the Vatican Bank, where we continue to have murky accounts and persistent allegations of money-laundering.'

Malucchi had been squirming in his seat. 'Surely there have been improvements there, Holy Father,' he interjected.

'You are correct, Domenico,' the pope said, nodding his large head. 'We have closed down many bad accounts but the auditors are not convinced everything is clean. A bigger problem is bad investments and too much speculation. We put money into these private hedge funds in America that make decisions about which direction the yen is heading and other things I can't even imagine. Last year we had big losses. This is the Vatican's money. This is the money of the faithful. We should not be losing their money in operations little better than a casino. We must be conservative and prudent. Then there is significant mismanagement of our real-estate holdings. I could go on and on but one finding of the report drove me to tears. Yes, I cried when I read it. Peter's Pence. Last year we received nearly one hundred million euros from the faithful – men, women, and children all over the world who put their hard-earned money into collection plates. Why do they pay Peter's Pence? Because they are moved by the spirit of charity within their hearts to help the poor, believing, as I did, that the money was going to support Catholic missions to aid the hungry and the sick and victims of disasters. Do you know what the auditors discovered? Only eighteen million euros went to the poor. The rest? It seems we have been using Peter's Pence as a slush fund to cover our administrative deficits. What if the faithful knew their donations were going to Christmas trees and pension liabilities, rather than the poor? Always it is the poor who suffer. And here the suffering is at our own hands. One hundred million euros is a great deal of money, but it is only a drop in the bucket of world-wide poverty and misery. We do not do enough! And now because of mismanagement we do even less? It breaks my heart.'

The only American in the room, Cardinal Sprague from Baltimore, said through a pained expression, 'What would you like us to do, Your Holiness?'

The pope leaned forward, indenting his midsection against the edge of the table. 'I want your help. I need your help. The pope cannot accomplish sweeping reforms alone. He is not a one-man band. I spend too much time on our finances! My predecessors, all worthy and revered stewards of our great Church, spent too little time on them and now we find ourselves in this mess. In the first moments after my election to St Peter's throne, I imagined that I might be able to use my pulpit for the betterment of humanity. I imagined that I might devote my days to promoting initiatives for our brothers and sisters who are suffering, to succor them not only spiritually but physically, for people need food and clean water and shelter and freedom from fear so that the seeds of faith may have fertile soil in which to grow. Not so many days into my pontificate I innocently turned over a financial rock and then another – rocks I freely admit I should have turned over when I was cardinal secretary – until I decided I could no longer turn a blind eye. I formed this council and empowered the auditors and here we are today. We need reforms, we need accountability. For once and for all, we need to purge our house of fraud, waste, and abuse of power. We need to wipe away corruption, eliminate the deficits, properly fund our liabilities, and free ourselves to focus on our mission: supporting the spiritual and physical well-being of our flock.'

Cardinal Cassar of Malta said, 'We can help repair the foundations, Holy Father, but to accomplish everything you cite, this will take some time. Considerable time.'

The pope softly repeated the words 'considerable time', and then said wearily, 'I'm an old man, Joseph. My time on this earth is limited. It is certainly not considerable. Please, all of you, please help me in my mission.'

Cassar was about to reply when Lauriat nodded vigorously and said, 'As chairman of the council, I pledge my help and the help of the members, Holy Father. We will carefully examine the auditor's report and we will continue our work as expeditiously as is possible.'

Cassar would not be still. 'I only wished to inject a sense of realism into the proceedings. Rome was not built in a day.'

Celestine impatiently drummed his fingers on his portfolio. 'I'll tell you what can be done in a day!' he said, his voice rising. Then he seemed to stop himself. His chest heaved with a sigh. 'No, I'll say no more,' he said. His sudden sadness was palpable.

A silence fell upon the room. None of the laymen seemed inclined to break it.

It was Cardinal Leoncino who chose to speak. 'Holy Father, I wish to assure you that this council will do its job as expeditiously as is humanly possible.'

The pope pushed back his chair and stood, prompting the others to rise. Forcing a smile he said, 'Thank you, Mario. I will let you do your job. But I beg you, gentlemen, proceed with a sense of urgency.'

TEN

C al left his meeting with the pope and headed straight for the Vatican Secret Archives, where he sought out Maurizio Orlando and informed him of the pope's wish to have the original copies of Cal's transcribed documents delivered to his office.

'To my knowledge this is the first time the Holy Father has requested texts from us,' Orlando said, his sweater swelling with pride. 'I will bring them to him personally.'

Cal told him he needed to try and find the annex mentioned in Monsignor Parizo's letter to Duke Tizziani. With a wave, Orlando led Cal into a small research room with a staff computer terminal. Cal stood, peering over his shoulder, while Orlando queried the database looking for any mention of the Sassoon family. The name didn't register.

'I'm sorry, Cal. This confirms my initial impression. There isn't a single catalogue reference to the Sassoon surname in general or to a Jean Sassoon in particular.'

'Too bad.'

'Of course, that doesn't mean that there are individual documents related to the Sassoons contained within other volumes, such as the ones you found amidst the Lambruschini, Antonelli, and Tizziani papers. Let me try Parizo.'

Again, there were no hits.

'Do you want my recommendation?' Orlando asked and after Cal eagerly said he did, he said, 'Let me lend you one of my secret weapons as a Vatican archivist: the consistories of cardinals, the rolls of all the papal appointments. They are invaluable tools.' He opened a large metal filing cabinet on one wall and found a particular leather-bound book. 'Here's the aggregate of all the consistories from the nineteenth century. Cardinal Lambruschini died in 1854. You might want to concern yourself with other cardinals, post-1854, who worked at the Vatican in lesser capacities than Antonelli, who might have been delegated matters such as dealing with loans. The bulk of their papers would be on the Diplomatic Floor.'

Cal took the book and thanked Orlando.

'The other idea I would offer is to go through the Rothschild material in the Bunker. You never know. Perhaps they purchased the Sassoon loan. A big fish swallowing a smaller fish, the way of the world.'

The list of mid-nineteenth-century cardinals who worked at the Vatican was long. Gazzoli. Mattei. Fieschi. Ugolini. Ciacchi. Tosti. Casoni. Corsi. Piccolomini. Marini. Roberti. Savelli. It took Cal the entire day to locate and work through the private papers for just half of them. By five o'clock, all he had to show for the effort was a sore backside and a throbbing headache.

The following day he returned and polished off the other half of the list. Again he failed to find a single mention or reference to loans, Sassoon or otherwise.

The weekend arrived and with it came a break from the grind. It was quite cold and on the Saturday snow flurries slicked the Roman streets and snarled the traffic. Cal slept in then waded through a series of planned social engagements – lunches, dinners, and drinks with friends and colleagues from the Sapienza University and the American University of Rome. On Saturday night, an Italian professor of religious studies and his wife brought along to dinner a vivacious graduate student. He liked her enough to invite her back to his hotel.

She was a talker, and by the time she had consumed half a bottle of Prosecco and had climbed naked upon the bed, her mouth was running as fast as a boat propeller. Cal was hardly listening but in his own vodka haze she seemed to be motoring on about the philosopher Wittgenstein.

'Did you know that Wittgenstein once said that a serious and good work of philosophy could be written consisting entirely of jokes?' she asked.

He dove on to the bed like an Olympian. 'I did not know that.'

When their frantic bit of sex was done, from somewhere far away he could have sworn that the same rapid-fire voice was talking about the metabolism of hummingbirds.

When he awoke, the light was filtering through the gauze curtains gusting in the frigid air. From the open windows he heard the sound of tourists milling around Bernini's elephant-topped obelisk in the Piazza della Minerva. His head pounded like a hammer beating on an anvil and then he remembered salient elements of the previous night. The bed was otherwise empty. He called her name then worried that he'd gotten it wrong. Was it Laura or Loredana? The bathroom too was empty but written in pink lipstick on the mirror was a very nice heart. A desperate call to room service followed asking them to hurry along a pot of coffee.

By the time Monday rolled around he was wearier than when the weekend had started but anxious to get back to work. He spent the morning buried in the Bunker at the section dedicated to the Rothschilds. It was slow going owing to the nature of the documents, rather densely and obtusely worded financial statements and agreements. By lunchtime Cal was satisfied that he hadn't missed a reference to the Sassoon Bank. When he was done, he stopped by the offices to thank Maurizio Orlando for all his help and moved on to Plan B.

The State Archive of Rome was located only a very short walk from his hotel. On the way he stopped for a cappuccino at Sant' Eustachio Il Caffé, one of the best coffee bars in Rome in Cal's humble opinion. Fortified, he arrived at the Palazzo della Sapienza. The building, commissioned in the fifteenth century by Pope Alexander VI, had been one of the early sites of the University of Rome. He traversed the grassy courtyard designed by Borromini with its porticoes on three sides and the church of Sant'Ivo on the fourth. With the slight rush of excitement he still experienced at the threshold of an old library, he entered.

The archive had been founded in the nineteenth century to conserve the documents of the Pontifical State for the period surrounding the Italian unification. As a practical matter documents later than 1870 were housed elsewhere in Rome, at the Central Archives of the State. Cal had been here many times but he was hardly a regular. He recognized no one in the index room, a large chamber with a classical mosaic floor and an elaborate coffered ceiling.

Within these archives Cal was a mere mortal, treated like every other academic who had to submit research requests in writing and patiently wait at tables in the index or reading rooms until the material was delivered. There were strict rules. A researcher could receive only three books or documents at a time with a daily limit of six.

Cal signed in with his Harvard credentials and went to the index bookshelves to search for any material related to Duke Francesco Tizziani of Romagna. The index books were all handwritten ledgers of some antiquity themselves, generally organized by family name. In time he found an entry for Tizziani that simply indicated the presence of various papers, 1757–1869.

Almost an hour after submitting his request, stipulating his interest in mid-nineteenth-century material, a young, pimply fellow shuffled into the reading room with three large boxes and plunked them down with a thud. Cal looked up from his phone he'd been using for emails.

'Were there more?' Cal asked.

The young man seemed surprised that Cal spoke Italian and replied that there were three additional boxes of papers related to his request.

'The magic number,' Cal said.

'What do you mean?'

'Six. Six units of material per day, isn't that correct?'

'You are permitted only six.'

An older man seated across from Cal had been eavesdropping and when the young man left he said, 'I think the boy is a temporary worker. Don't get a bad impression. The staff here is very sharp.'

Each box contained a thick stack of loose papers tied with a thin pink ribbon. The first box consisted of material too early for interest, pertaining to Francesco Tizziani's father. He dispatched that one quickly and opened the second box. It proved more relevant to his search. It didn't take him long to confirm his earlier impression that Francesco Tizziani seemed to have lived his life in constant legal battles with family members and neighboring nobles over land rights, rights to taxation revenues, and the share of profits from various agricultural ventures. The documents were, for the most part, obtuse and remarkably uninteresting and when he was done with this and the next box, he had no choice but to order up the next three.

When the dull young man returned with these, Cal knew better than to engage him in small talk.

It was midday when he finished reading through the next three boxes. There was nothing to show for his efforts. The word loan hadn't appeared in a single document. The day was still young but he had exhausted his quota. He decided to pay another visit to the index shelves on the remote chance that there was something on the Sassoons. From what he had read on the Internet, the Sassoon Bank, during its nineteenth-century tenure in Italy, had operated from Venice. The Republic of Venice had never been a member of the Papal States so this was the wrong archive for Venetian material. If push came to shove he'd be obligated to make a trip to the Venetian State Archives, or at least examine their online index.

He browsed the relevant index book while absently thinking about some trivial bit of academic nonsense stirred up by one of the emails he'd read earlier.

But there it was: the Sassoon name.

A notation sent him flying back to the staff counter.

Contains papers of J. Sassoon found among the papers of F. Tizziani.

His heart pounded out of his chest while he waited in a short queue manned by a female archivist. A second archivist, a man, became free first but Cal stayed put, thinking he might have more luck with the lady.

The archivist looked rather imperious, her hair pulled back so tightly it suggested a touch of masochism.

'I wonder if you could help me?' Cal asked, smiling as sweetly as he could.

She neutralized him with a sour once-over and waited for him to say more.

'I'm Professor Donovan from Harvard University. I understand and greatly appreciate your six-unit daily limit but I have to return to America and only need to look at a few more units of material. Is there any way you could make an exception for me?'

As she fixed him with a death stare he began to think about how he'd bide his time before returning in the morning.

Then she surprised him. 'Professor Calvin Donovan?'

'That's right.'

It wasn't exactly a show of warmth but her face became less scary. 'My colleague at the Vatican Archives, Maurizio Orlando, told me about you. You have special privileges there.'

'I do. It's a great honor.'

'How many additional units?'

'It's rather hard to tell from the index. Hopefully not too many.'

'Let me see the request.'

He slid the form across the desk.

'We'll see what we can do.'

'You're a saint,' he said.

She finally let herself go, flashing the most rapidly extinguishing smile he'd ever seen. 'I know I am,' she said, returning to form.

He spent another hour doing work on his phone all the while trying to imagine why Duke Tizziani had come to possess the Sassoon papers. Finally, the pimply clerk appeared, straining under the comically teetering weight of many more boxes.

'Seven, eight, nine, ten, eleven, twelve, thirteen' the young man said. 'I don't know how you managed to have your request granted.'

'I've got friends in high places. Is this all there were?'

'Only these. Any others and you would have exceeded the limit by even more.'

The spines of each box were embossed with a single name, Sassoon.

He opened them in quick order, untying ribbons and quickly getting the lay of the land. Most of the loose letters, contracts, and ledgers were written by Jean Sassoon. The earliest documents carried dates from the early 1840s and seemed to deal with matters originating at the Venetian office of the Sassoon Bank. The second and third boxes contained more of the same. Box four had material from 1846 to 1848; it appeared that during this period the bank was operating from Rome. The final three boxes revealed that the offices of the bank had returned to Venice. Documents and correspondence from these were dated from 1848 to 1858.

He returned to the first box and began reading through scores of mundane lending agreements, all for relatively piddling sums, mostly denominated in scudos, the currency of the Papal States.

He was moving through pages at a fair clip when midway through the second box, his eye caught a different handwriting from Jean Sassoon's. While most of the other documents that were in Italian, this one was in French. He paused to read it carefully and within a few seconds he knew he had come closer to the mother lode.

28 January 1849

My son,
I have received word that you have safely returned to Rome.
You will know that I have agreed to the egregious terms of

the Vatican loan and that the gold sovereigns have been delivered to the pope. Needless to say your uncle was unhappy with the transaction but I have the majority. Need I say more? It is incumbent upon me to share with you the terms of the loan contract so that you will understand the challenges the firm must overcome in the future. The principal was three hundred thousand pounds sterling representing a great deal of our available capital. We are not permitted to lay off our risk with a flotation of bonds to investors in London or Paris as would be the norm in a loan of this magnitude. The pope has his reasons for keeping the loan secret. We may surmise these relate to certain prior understandings with the Rothschilds. The duration of the loan is ten years with a rate of interest of seven percent compounded annually. Here is the rub. Since we were unable to recoup the funds through a bond flotation and were likewise unable to secure collateral we are vulnerable if at the end of the ten years we are not repaid. The loan rolls over into perpetual extensions until a date uncertain when the Vatican is able to repay the principal and interest. The cold comfort for us is that for loan balances exceeding ten years they agreed to a seven percent interest rate that will be compounded monthly. Why you may ask did I agree to these abhorrent terms where a repayment date was not fixed? It is because I feared for your life, my son. Now I would have you leave this barbaric country and return to your loving parents in London. Let us rebuild our capital together.
   Father

It was dark when Cal left the archive. He had transcribed the letter from father to son and then had moved laboriously through all the boxes until coming to the very last document in the very last box. Dated November 1858, it was a pedestrian letter sent to Jean Sassoon from a Venetian merchant about obtaining credit to expand a glass-blowing workshop. Walking briskly through the throng of tourists taking photos at the Pantheon, Cal reflected on a good but imperfect day at the office. He now knew the terms for this extraordinary Vatican loan but that's as far as it went. The Sassoon papers had not included a copy of the loan annex and there was still no definitive evidence whether the loan had ever been repaid.

His phone rang and he smiled at the caller ID.

'Joe! How are you?'

'I'm fine, Professor,' Father Murphy said. 'Am I catching you at a good time? Sounds like you're in a crowd.'

'Perfect time. Let me get away from this gaggle of tourists.'

'How's your research going?' Murphy asked.

'It's taken an unexpected turn, as research is wont to do. What's going on back at the ranch?'

'I was just wondering if you'd heard anything from Professor Daniels? You see, I ran into Marty Gordon. He told me he understood I wasn't getting the position.'

Gordon was an assistant professor at the Divinity School, a protégé of Daniels.

Cal swore at the news. 'I haven't heard a goddamn peep. Marty's obviously in a position to know a thing or two about what goes on in Daniels's world but it would be staggeringly bad form not to let me know about a negative decision or give me a chance to appeal. Hang in there. I'll try to reach Daniels and get back to you as soon as I have more info.'

With the phone back in his pocket, Cal let out a loud 'Son-of-a-bitch!' and scared some pigeons into flight.

Back in his hotel, Cal reclined on his bed and made some calls. All of Gil Daniels' numbers rang through to voicemail and Cal left the same message on each.

The next call was to Monsignor Moller to let him know that he had found more information about the topic of interest to Celestine. Moller promised to get back to Cal as soon as he'd had a chance to speak to the pope.

The final call was to one of his occasional basketball teammates, Frank Epstein, a renowned professor of finance at the Harvard Business School, who picked up on the first ring.

'Epstein.'

'Frank. It's Cal Donovan.'

'How the hell're you doing, Cal? Having a good holiday?'

'Better than you,' Cal said. 'I'm in Rome and you're in your office.'

'We're leaving for our place in Hawaii tomorrow. Can't wait.'

'I don't want to hold you up but you got a minute to help me with a question?'

'Not before I take the opportunity to congratulate you?'

'For what?'

There was a longish silence.

'Shit, Cal. Forget I said anything. I hate it when I step in it.'

Cal had no idea what he was talking about but just laughed it off, whatever *it* was.

'I need to figure out how much a very old loan would be worth if it were repaid today. It's for a research project.'

'OK, I'd need to know the amount of the loan, the age of the loan in years, months, and days, the interest rate, and the compounding schedule.'

'I've got all of those.'

'All right, shoot.'

Epstein took down the data then told Cal to wait a second while he opened a spreadsheet on his computer. Through the phone Cal heard the keystrokes, then Epstein coming back matter-of-factly with a number that made Cal's eyes water.

'You're kidding.'

'Nope. I never joke about loans. What you're seeing is the magic of compounding, especially monthly compounding for a hundred-sixty of the hundred-seventy years. Of course, there's another factor to consider. You could make an argument that it might be appropriate to inflation-adjust the three-hundred-thousand-pound loan into present-day pounds sterling. If you compounded an inflation-adjusted loan value, the principal plus interest owed today would be a few orders of magnitude larger than what I just gave you. Now that's a big-ass number. I could do the math for you but it seems to me, if you're the guy owed the money you'd probably be pleased as punch to get the first figure I quoted. Just saying.'

ELEVEN

The pope took almost all his meals at the modest cafeteria of the Sanctae Marthae guesthouse, sitting with staff or visiting clerics. He usually took a place at one of the communal tables but this morning he chose a private one in the corner.

'Have anything, Professor,' he told Cal. 'The food is quite good.'

When the waiter came, Cal grinned and said, 'I'll have what he's having,' sending the pope into titters of laughter.

'Then I hope you like dry toast, a bit of fruit, and coffee,' the pope said.

'Maybe you could also bring me some butter and jam,' Cal said hopefully.

When they were alone, Celestine said in a low voice, 'So, Moller says you have something to share with me. Did you find the annex?'

'Unfortunately no, but I did find a letter from Jean Sassoon's father laying out the terms of the loan. I have a photocopy. Do you read French?'

'Passably.'

The pope studied it and said, 'When I was a schoolboy, mathematics was not my best subject. I would need someone to tell me what it would take to repay this loan today.'

'It's a big number,' Cal said.

'Is it? How big?'

The toast and fruit arrived and Cal waited for the server to leave before answering.

'About twenty-five billion euros, roughly twenty-seven billion dollars.'

'Heavens!' the pope said, slowly lowering his coffee cup to avoid spilling. 'A great deal of money. And you've found nothing more to shed light on the ultimate fate of this debt?'

'Nothing. I still can't find a single mention of the loan in the historical record. Perhaps it was forgiven but what banker in his right mind would write off a loan of that size? From what I've read about the Sassoon Bank it wasn't large enough to absorb this kind of loss voluntarily. Even the Rothschilds Bank, the largest of its day, would have been under pressure. When we met before, I believe I told you about the four-hundred-thousand-pound loan the Rothschilds made to Pope Gregory in 1831. They structured it to avoid running afoul of the usury laws but also to avoid taking a bath if the Vatican couldn't repay it. The Vatican got three hundred thousand pounds from the bank and turned around and sold four hundred thousand pounds in bonds back to the bank. Then the Rothschilds sold off all the Vatican bonds to investors who liked the juicy interest they paid, pocketing one hundred thousand pounds for their trouble and locking in their profit.'

The pope followed closely, nodding his understanding.

'As you saw from the Sassoon letter, the Vatican didn't allow the Sassoons to do a bond sale and didn't give them any collateral on the loan.'

'It's quite shocking, Professor. Really shameful. This seems to be a case of kidnapping and extortion, something you'd see from a criminal organization, not the Holy Church. The elder Sassoon used the word barbaric. I would agree with him.'

'It's not an excuse but I imagine the Vatican was desperate,' Cal said. 'The Papal States were under attack by the revolutionaries, tax revenues were collapsing, the pope was in exile, trying to mount a defense with no money to pay for it. No one was going to make a conventional loan to a bankrupt Vatican so Cardinal Lambruschini or someone in the administration came up with a plan and the Sassoons were the victims.'

'So you don't think the loan was ever repaid?' the pope asked.

'I don't believe they ever intended to repay it.' Then Cal caught himself. 'I'm sorry, that's speculation. A good historian ought to rely on facts.'

'But it's not an unreasonable assumption,' the pope said, munching his toast.

'Well, that's it, Your Holiness. I'm afraid that's all I have to report.'

The pope shook his head. 'But what of the annex? Is there no way to see if a copy exists?'

'I really don't know where else to look,' Cal said. 'As far as I can tell, the Sassoon Bank only operated in Italy for about fifteen years. After 1858 they had no presence here. The State Archives of Rome seemed to have a collection of papers that spanned their entire Italian experience. Just to be complete I scanned the web portal for the State Archives of Venice and there wasn't a single mention of Sassoon. You never know if some documents might be tucked away in a private collection or in a not-so-obvious library or archive but there's no systemic way of dealing with that kind of historical problem. So, that's the end of the line.' Cal stopped abruptly, highjacked by a thought, and hesitated to utter the next word because he really needed to head back home. 'Unless . . .'

'Unless what?' the pope asked.

'Unless the Sassoon Bank has a private archive. The Rothschilds Bank maintains its own archive based in London. I've gotten permission in the past to use it. Do you mind if I quickly Google it to see if they have one?' Cal asked removing his phone from his sport coat.

'I have no objection,' the pope said. 'Look around. Half the diners are staring into their little screens.'

Before Cal could do his search, his phone rang. Gil Daniels was finally returning the call.

'I'm sorry,' Cal said, quickly silencing the ringer. 'It's my department chairman.'

'You must take his call,' the pope said, smiling. 'Go ahead, Professor. I'll finish my fruit.'

'You're sure?'

He laughed. 'You have my blessing.'

'Hi, Gil,' Cal said, answering the call. 'Thanks for getting back to me. It's one a.m. in Cambridge!'

'I'm working late. Christ, Cal, you left messages on every phone I've got.'

'Like I said I wanted to talk about Joe Murphy but I'm going to have to call you back. I'm kind of occupied.'

'You wanted me and here I am,' Daniels said testily.

'I'm having breakfast with Pope Celestine, if you must know.'

'Don't bullshit me, Cal.'

'I'm serious, Gil. He's right here.'

The pope was merrily rolling his eyes at Cal's side of the exchange.

'Give me the phone,' he insisted.

Cal gulped and handed it over. This was going to be one of those anecdotes he'd be telling for the rest of his life.

The pontiff pressed the phone to his ear and said in English in his instantly recognizable voice, 'Professor Donovan was speaking the truth. This is Pope Celestine. You are the professor's chairman at Harvard?'

After an uncomfortably long pause during which Daniels was probably trying to figure out if he was being pranked, he answered. 'My God, it's an honor to meet you, Your Holiness.'

'The same, I'm sure. You are fortunate to have a man like Calvin Donovan in your department. I am returning the phone to him now. Good day.'

'Hi Gil,' Cal said. 'So is it OK if I call you back?'

A rather smaller voice answered. 'Any time.'

'Now, back to the annex,' the pope said when Cal rang off.

Cal did a quick, fruitless Google search looking for anything relating to a Sassoon Bank archive and told Celestine that he'd have to call the bank directly.

'I hesitate to impose on you further.'

Cal assured him it was no trouble.

'And professor, unless it becomes necessary for someone to know the general nature of your inquiries, I would ask that you keep the existence of this loan to yourself. Consider it our secret. And keep me informed. Monsignor Moller knows that he is to put you through immediately, provided I am not at prayer. God comes first. You come second.'

TWELVE

'Would you mind telling me why I had to drop everything? What's so urgent?' Malucchi asked.

'My flight to Malta is in three hours,' Cassar complained. 'I don't want to miss it, Pascal.'

'Perhaps we should let our friend get a word in edgewise,' Leoncino said, raising his hands in the air.

Cardinal Lauriat took a seat behind his desk, thanked his three colleagues for coming at short notice, and assured them he had a good reason for the hasty summons.

'In five minutes, the pope will hold a conference call with the members of the original C8,' Lauriat said.

'How do you know?' Cassar asked.

'I just do.'

'The C10 only just met,' Malucchi said. 'Was there a discussion of convening a smaller group?'

'None whatsoever,' Leoncino said.

'Why would the pope deliberately exclude you and Pascal?' Malucchi asked.

'It's obvious,' Leoncino said. 'He doesn't trust us.'

'What do you think he's up to?' Cassar asked.

Lauriat checked his Rolex. 'I believe we'll find out in three minutes.'

Cal had been kept waiting on hold for a long time. The only consolation was that he didn't have to endure canned music; the line was mercifully silent. He was in his hotel room, his feet on an ottoman, his computer on his lap, the phone cradled on his shoulder. He was scrolling through the biographies of key employees on the Sassoon Bank website when a voice came on asking him to hold for Mr Sassoon.

He had asked to speak to the chairman of the bank, Henry Sassoon, but the man who finally picked up identified himself as Marcus Sassoon. Thanks to the biographies, Cal knew he was the vice-chairman.

The voice was impatient, as if he had been the one kept waiting. 'What is this in regard to, Mr Donovan?'

Cal explained that he was a historian doing research on the nineteenth-century Sassoon Bank in Italy and wondered whether the bank kept an archive of its historical documents.

'We have an archive in New York but it's private.'

'Do you ever admit outside researchers?'

'No.'

'And is it possible you might make an exception?'

Again, no.

Cal decided to play the pope card.

'Actually, Mr Sassoon, Pope Celestine is personally interested in this line of research. If it would be persuasive, I can arrange for him to send you a personal request.'

Sassoon's comeback was icy. 'If the bank were owned by Catholics, that might have some sway, but it isn't.'

There was nothing to lose at this point. 'I see,' Cal said, 'Is it possible that your chairman might have a different view?'

'You've got some nerve, Mr Donovan. Where did you say you were from?'

'Harvard.'

'Oh yeah? Which department?'

'Joint appointments at the Divinity School and the Department of Anthropology.'

'You sound young. What are you, an assistant professor?'

'Full professor. Named chair.'

The tone changed. 'I went to Brandeis. Wasn't the world's greatest student. My son is applying to Harvard. My cousin's kid is at Harvard Business School.'

'That's great,' Cal said, sensing an opening.

'If I let you into the archive would you write a letter for my kid?'

'I'd be happy to sit down and talk to him about his interests. We could take it from there.'

'Let me pass you back to my assistant and she can set something up.'

Lauriat removed a slip of paper from his desk with a telephone number and an access code. He explained that he would be muting the line and even if someone asked who was joining, they would remain on mute. Cassar asked how he had obtained the call-in numbers but all he would say was that it was his job to know certain things.

'How else can I protect the integrity of the Vatican?' he asked. 'In times past, I imagine cardinals put cups against the walls to listen to a scheming pope. Now we do this.'

'Won't there be a log of those who dialed into the conference?' Malucchi asked.

'Apparently so,' Lauriat said, 'but it is never checked. It's worth the small risk. In any event, it would indicate my line. You would be quite anonymous. If any of you are squeamish about my tactics, I urge you to leave now.'

All of them remained.

Lauriat waited until the top of the hour to punch in the numbers and the swarm of blips on the line indicated that multiple participants were connecting simultaneously. Their blip was lost in the mix. Monsignor Moller took a roll call and cardinals announced their presence from Europe, the United States, South America, Africa, and Asia. When everyone was on the line, Moller waited for the pope to join the call before signing off himself.

A sonorous Celestine came on, thanking the group for making the time. 'I do realize we met only last week but I would like you, my friends, to provide me with some advice concerning the matter of the loan we recently discussed.'

The archbishop of Lima asked why two members of the C10, Cardinals Lauriat and Leoncino, were absent.

'Let us just say that I desire feedback from those nearest to my heart,' the pope said.

Cardinal Da Silva spoke up from Boston, where he had just returned. 'Then by all means, Holy Father, we are at your disposal.'

The pope continued, 'Professor Donovan has made some additional discoveries about this loan. He has found a letter that laid out the terms.'

'A letter from whom?' the archbishop of Abidjan in Côte d'Ivoire asked.

'The owner of the bank, a gentleman named Claude Sassoon, written to his son, Jean, the man who was held against his will by the Vatican.'

'And what are the terms of this loan?' the archbishop of Manila asked.

'It was meant to have a duration of ten years,' the pope said. 'However, if it was not repaid at that time there was a provision that would perpetually extend the repayment provided that the interest on the loan continued to be applied. I believe the technical term is compounded.'

'This loan is about one hundred-seventy years old,' the bishop of Mainz, Germany said. 'What is its value today?'

'This is the astonishing news,' the pope said. 'The figure is twenty-five billion euros.'

No one spoke for several seconds. It was the cardinal of Mexico City who broke the silence by asking whether the Sassoon Bank was still in business and if so, whether they were aware of the existence of such an ancient and valuable loan.

'They are a modern, thriving bank, I am told,' Celestine said. 'The professor doubts they know of the loan but this has not been established. Now, the situation is not quite as clear as I may have led you to believe. The loan has two parts. The Secret Archives had a signed copy of the first part but we do not have a copy of the second part, the annex containing the various loan terms. We merely know these terms from the letter. That is why I have asked Professor Donovan to try to locate the missing annex.'

To what end? the German cardinal asked. Another added, whether it might not be better to sweep this kind of information under the rug, as Cardinal Lauriat had suggested at the C10. A third reminded the others what the pope had said about getting their legal ducks in order, rather than have an unfriendly third party find the document in the future.

'This is why I wanted to hear your opinions,' Celestine said. 'We cannot know at present whether a full and valid set of documents exists but if they do, it seems to me we may have a God-sent opportunity.'

'Opportunity?' the archbishop of Toledo, Spain said. 'I see only a monumental liability that could destroy us.'

'I have a confession to make,' the pope said. 'When Professor Donovan first told me about the existence of the loan my first thought was about a dream of mine. I thought about our potential to do good.'

The bishop of Mainz interrupted, 'But Holy Father, the other day you spoke of the need to get our lawyers to thwart a claim.'

'That is true, Hans. There were other ears in the room. I did not wish to speak of my dream in front of them. Not even Moller. This dream – it feels to me like a delicate flower that might be crushed under an unfriendly boot. That is why I wanted to speak only to you, my closest confidants. You all know my frustration at the corruption, the laxity, the incompetence that seem to define our financial situation. Spending as much time as I do working on our tortured finances, I have become increasingly despondent about how far we seem to have strayed from Christ's simple teachings of charity and humility passed down to us in the Gospels. The business of the Church is not business. It is helping our flock, particularly those who do not have the ability to help themselves. Can you imagine how much good we could do with twenty-five billion euros? We could provide not only food and shelter but a pathway to dignity in the spirit of Christ's noblest teachings.'

The Nigerian was the first to respond, asking the question that all of them had to be thinking. 'But, Holy Father, you are speaking of monies we may owe, not monies we may receive.'

'Yes, of course, you are right, Henry, but what I am proposing – again, in the event the loan is valid – is to approach the Sassoon family, for this remains a family-owned bank, and make an arrangement with them. We will pay this loan, not to the bank, but to a foundation to support grand, humanitarian causes.'

Da Silva chimed in. 'Holy Father, why would they agree to this? Surely a bank would take the position that they were entitled to these billions. Why would they be dictated to on the use of the proceeds?'

The pope replied, 'I have had a confidential conversation with one of our top outside legal advisors in Rome about this hypothetical situation. He assured me, without reviewing specific documents, that the Vatican would, at a minimum, have the ability to tie up any repayment obligation in courts for years, perhaps decades. And a more likely scenario is that a defect in such ancient loan agreements would be discovered and that the courts would dismiss the obligation. Therefore, we can say to these people, look, let's join forces for the common good. We will volunteer to forego legal challenges but only if the money goes to charity.'

The archbishop of Manila said, 'I follow your logic, Holy Father, and admire your charitable inclinations, but isn't this a moot point? I know nothing about the liquid assets of the Vatican but I am sure that they are a far cry from twenty-five billion euros. There is simply no way to pay money we do not possess.'

'Leave it to me, my friend. I have some ideas.'

Cardinal Lauriat hung up simultaneously with the other participants. None of the four cardinals had uttered a word among themselves during the lengthy telecon. Their offense was too great, their distrust of the simple technology of the mute button too palpable, their fear of the consequences of being unmasked too monumental. Even with the phone line dead they kept their mouths shut for a while longer in a stunned silence.

It was Cassar who broke the ice, rising and nervously extending his arms to simulate a chip shot.

'I think I'm going to miss my flight.'

'Is that all you can say?' Leoncino asked. 'We've just witnessed a call for the financial destruction of the Church and you're complaining about your flight.'

'I think he was joking,' Malucchi said. 'Were you joking, Joseph?'

'Yes, I was joking. The pope is out of his mind.'

Lauriat was on his feet, making his way to the window. Gazing at the dome of St Peter's the eavesdropper said, 'This is a monumental betrayal of trust,' seemingly unaware of the irony. 'He lied to us about his intentions.'

'Did you hear all the yes-men, sucking up to him,' Malucchi asked. 'Nauseating. Twenty-five billion! Where will he find this money? He says he has some ideas. What ideas? If and when the time comes, our voices of dissent must be heard. But what can we do? He is the pope.'

Leoncino said, 'It's a pity. When a corporation makes a mistake and selects the wrong chief executive, they can correct the mistake with a few strokes of the pen. When the Church selects the wrong pope it is usually obliged to wait for his passing to make a change.'

Lauriat returned to his desk, reached for a pen, and angrily threw it down. It skittered off the desk and when Cassar went to retrieve it, the secretary of state told him to leave it.

'No! I will not simply resign myself to a bad situation or wait for God to claim him,' he said in a near shout. 'If Celestine thinks I will stand by and let him weaken or destroy our sacred Church to aid this neo-liberal thinking he seems to have embraced he is sadly mistaken. This shall not pass, gentlemen, it shall not pass.'

THIRTEEN

There was something awfully insulting about the way Cal's meeting at the Sassoon Bank was playing out. Before he was allowed to set foot inside their Manhattan offices he was obliged to interview Marcus Sassoon's son, as if he couldn't be trusted to follow through on his promise if the sequence were reversed.

After a good night's sleep at the Pierre Hotel – he'd slipped into town without notifying his mother – he met the kid at the appointed place, an Italian restaurant chosen by the bank. After a week in Rome, he had hoped against hope for a change of cuisine. Steven Sassoon was already there, waiting at a table, glued to his phone and sporting a semi-bored expression. He was tall for sixteen going on seventeen, with a bunch of gelled, unruly hair. His blue blazer looked crisp and new.

Cal extended a hand and the kid took it without getting up.

It became quickly apparent that there wasn't going to be a lot of small-talk coming his way so Cal kicked things off after passing on a proper drink and opting for a diet soda.

'So your father tells me you're interested in Harvard.'

'Yeah, I guess.'

Somehow lunch instantly reminded Cal of pulling latrine duty in the army.

He asked Steven to talk about himself and after some coaxing a picture emerged of a privileged, spoiled kid who was expected to follow a preordained path from prep school to college to business school to prime the pump on his arrival at the family business. His cousin, Julian, was six years ahead of him, a second-year student at Harvard Business School.

'What do you like to do?' Cal asked.

'You know, the usual stuff. Sports, girls, hang out with friends.'

'Which sports?'

'Golf and tennis mostly. I'm good at tennis. What's Harvard's team like?'

'I think they're always competitive in the Ivy League. You think you're good enough to make the team?'

'I play number one singles at Dalton. Other than me the team kind of sucks.'

'OK. What do you think you want to study at college?'

'I don't know, something that'll help me get into business school. What do you teach?'

'History of religion and biblical archeology mainly.'

'Not that.'

Mercifully, the food arrived, slowing the conversation and speeding the time until the chore was completed. Cal decided to turn the remainder of the meal to his advantage by extracting information about the Sassoon family.

'So your father and his cousin, Henry, work together?'

'They always have.'

'Tell me about your Henry.'

'He's been sick a lot. He doesn't come in much anymore.'

'What's wrong with him?'

'Something with his lungs. Not sure. He's on oxygen.'

'So your dad is pretty much running things?'

'I guess so. I mean he's got people who've been there a long time and my brother's a vice-president.'

'Albert.'

'How'd you know his name?'

'It's on the website.'

'Henry's wife has been coming in too, I hear.'

'Is your mother involved?' Cal asked.

'Not a chance. She's a lady who lunches. Can we skip dessert? I've got tennis practice in half an hour.'

Cal smiled in relief. 'I'll get the waiter to bring the check.'

'It's paid for,' the kid said. 'We've got an account.'

It wasn't a stretch to imagine Steven Sassoon morphing into his father in forty years. Marcus was flat-ass lanky and tall, his suit hanging more loosely than modernity dictated, his almost colorless hair cut short back and sides. His eyeglasses too were from an earlier generation – flesh-colored, plastic frames with thick lenses that made his eyes seem far away.

He greeted Cal and ushered him into his office on the second floor of the East 73rd Street row of townhouses that served as the bank offices. From the window the seasonally bare trees looked forlorn but inside the décor was opulent and inviting – lots of dark paneling and good rugs. Very old-world European.

Cal declined a beverage and sat across from his host in his conversation area by a bay window.

'So you met Steven.'

'Just came from there.'

'What did you think?'

Cal was expecting the question. He lied. 'He's an impressive young man. He told me he's got good grades and test scores. The tennis doesn't hurt. Also, Dalton's a reliable feeder school for Harvard.'

'A lot of his classmates are legacies at Harvard. That's a problem, isn't it?'

'Not necessarily. Where'd Henry's son, Julian, go?'

'Columbia. No help there. Will you be able to write the letter?'

Cal nodded. 'Where should I send it?'

The banker gave Cal his card and without so much as a thank you, moved on. 'OK, Professor. Your turn. Henry's wife, Gail, wanted to join us. Do you mind?'

'Of course not.'

Gail Sassoon was much younger than he expected. He knew from the web bios that her husband was pushing seventy. This woman was in her late forties at most, stylish in a designer suit that clung to her curves and matched the color of her eyes. She looked uber-fit, like she worked at it conscientiously. And she was attractive enough that he had to force himself not to stare too long. But her girl-next-door beauty and blonde shoulder-length hair that bounced when she walked defeated him. She seemed to notice that he was checking her out and her smile became ever so slightly coquettish.

When she spoke she seemed genuinely interested in him and mentioned something about hearing him talk once. Before he could ask where, Marcus interrupted because seemingly, like his son, he wasn't given to chitchat.

'OK, Mr Donovan, you've got the floor,' he said, putting an end to the light banter.

'Marcus, he's not a mister,' she said sharply. 'The professor has a Ph.D.'

Marcus sounded annoyed. 'OK, whatever. Professor. Doctor. Go for it.'

Cal tried to defuse the tension by saying, 'You can call me anything you like if you let me into your archives. Here's the story. As I told Mr Sassoon on the phone, I was doing some research at the Vatican that has caught the interest of Pope Celestine. I'm here on his behest.'

'Go on,' Marcus said.

'What I found is this: it appears that the Sassoon Bank made a loan to the Vatican at the time of the 1848 Italian Revolution.'

Marcus interrupted. 'Didn't know the Italians had one.'

'There were revolutions happening all over Europe during that period,' Cal said.

'What's the size of the loan?'

Gail got testy. 'Marcus, would you please let Professor Donovan tell his story?'

The banker looked at the ceiling once, in a gesture of seeking divine intervention, then sank back into his chair in a forced silence, leaving Cal to wonder which one of these Sassoons was more in charge.

'The loan was for three hundred thousand pounds sterling. It originated in London – I believe it was Claude Sassoon who controlled the bank at that time – but the Italian branch of the bank, represented by his son, Jean Sassoon, was involved. Specifically, I found an executed loan contract, signed by Claude Sassoon and a Vatican cardinal named Antonelli, but the specific terms of the contract were spelled out in an annex to the contract that I haven't found.'

'Don't jump down my throat, Gail, but let me ask why the contract was a two-parter,' Marcus said.

She surprised Cal by answering for him.

'Usury laws, Marcus. That's the way a lot of contracts were structured in Europe back then. It gave the parties plausible deniability on usury.'

'That's right,' Cal said, nodding and smiling. 'Not too many people know that.'

'Gail's a fancy lawyer,' Marcus said. 'Harvard Law.'

'I'm rusty on modern law,' she said, 'but I remember old, useless things.'

'Not so useless in the current situation,' Cal said. 'Even without the annex we believe we know the terms of the loan from a letter written to Jean by Claude. Unusually, it was a non-collateralized loan with a ten-year term, carrying a seven percent interest rate that rolled over into perpetuity if was unpaid at the end of the term. Here's the thing. There's nothing in the historical record to indicate that the loan was ever repaid.'

This seemed to get Marcus's attention. He moved to the edge of his chair and leaned in toward Cal.

'Was this a compounded loan?' he asked.

'It was. Annually for the first ten years then monthly thereafter.'

Cal could almost imagine gears turning inside the banker's head. He got up to grab a calculator off his desk but Cal told him not to bother – he had the present loan value. He delivered the figure cleanly, like an arrow shot into the bullseye.

'I'm sorry,' Gail said, 'did you say twenty-seven billion dollars?'

'Approximately.'

Marcus was good for a 'Holy shit,' before leaning back again, a crooked smile creasing his face. 'So that's why you want to search our archive? To find the other half of the contract?'

Cal nodded. 'I've pretty much exhausted my options for finding the Vatican's copy. Maybe it was misfiled in their archives. Maybe it was destroyed.'

'I'm sorry,' Gail said, sipping at a glass of sparkling water. 'Back then three hundred thousand pounds was a great deal of money. Why would the Sassoon Bank have ever agreed to a non-collateralized loan? And wasn't the practice in those days to package the loan into a public bond offering?'

Cal was even more impressed. She knew her stuff. 'From what we can tell from a surviving letter, the Vatican pressured the Sassoon family by holding Jean Sassoon hostage. It looks like the loan was made under duress.'

'Do you think there was ever an intention to make good on it?' she asked.

'I don't know,' Cal said. 'Maybe yes, maybe no, but it looks like everything was done on the quiet.'

She pressed on with her lawyerly cross-examination. 'Why wouldn't the bank raise holy hell – excuse the expression – when the loan matured and payment wasn't forthcoming?'

'I don't know the answer to that either.'

'I'm sorry to keep peppering you with questions,' she said, 'but why on earth would the Vatican want to bring this enormous obligation to light? Surely it's very much against its self-interest.'

Marcus took on a look of pain. 'Why ask? If they want to find a way to pass us twenty-seven billion dollars, I say, let's show this man into the archive and let him have at it.'

Gail might as well have crowned Marcus with a dunce cap by saying, 'I'm quite sure their reasons are a little more nuanced than that.'

Cal pointed at her playfully. 'More than you could possibly guess. Pope Celestine is an interesting man.'

Gail's chauffeur-driven Bentley was waiting at the curb outside the bank. After the meeting she had asked Cal if he had time to see her husband, Henry, at their residence and Cal had readily agreed. Marcus wasn't exactly Cal's cup of tea and the less time spent with him the better. And Henry, though an unknown quantity, was the chairman. While Cal waited Gail had phoned ahead to make the arrangements for the visit.

'Do you live far?' Cal asked her as the big car eased into traffic.

'Just a few blocks away on Park.'

'Must be fairly close to where my mother lives.'

'Bess Donovan. I know.'

He did a double take. 'You know my mother?'

'Fairly well. We haunt the same philanthropic circles. That's where I heard you talk, at her birthday luncheon a few years ago. I thought your remarks were charming.'

'Quite a small town, this New York City,' he said.

'So Henry will be ready by the time we arrive. I should tell you, he hasn't been well. He's got pulmonary fibrosis. There's no cure. The steroids have altered his appearance. But mentally he's as strong as ever.'

Their apartment was only three blocks from his mother's. He hadn't planned on looking her up on this leg, but on the chance he might be outed by Gail Sassoon, he realized he'd have to call her. Bess Donovan's apartment, as regal as it was, could have fit in half of one floor of the Sassoon's penthouse triplex. The scale of everything was grandiose, especially for a New York high-rise, and Cal was struck by the design aesthetic, a rather clever blend of traditional and modern. From the entrance hall to the grand sitting room, the high ceilings and expansive walls allowed for oversize pieces of contemporary art. Rothko, Pollack, de Kooning, Hockney, Picasso, Botero, and Cal's eyes jumped around crazily.

'Are you interested in art?' she asked.

'Earlier stuff. Medieval, Renaissance mainly, work that dovetailed with the history of European Christianity.'

'As you can see, we're mired in the twentieth century,' she said. 'We haven't had the fortitude to understand really modern trends. I've just had a text from his nurse. Henry will receive you in his upstairs study.'

They took an internal staircase – the wall lined with more museum-quality paintings – up to another large reception room. At the far end, through a set of open double doors, they came to a library where a bloated figure was slumped in a wheelchair.

There were no flesh tones. Henry Sassoon had the grayest skin Cal had ever seen. It was dusky, almost like slate. A plastic tube snaked from an oxygen generator to nasal prongs. Cal knew he was seventy-two, but his illness saddled him with the appearance of a much older man. Whether he was self-conscious of baldness or simply cold, he sported a Yankees baseball cap. It looked like he had been hastily dressed because his trouser fly was wide open and Gail, noticing this, went over and gave the zipper a tug while pecking him on the cheek.

'Henry, this is Professor Calvin Donovan of Harvard.'

It took some effort for him to say, 'How are you?'

'I'm good, Mr Sassoon. Please call me Cal.'

'Then you should call me Henry,' was the breathy response.

Cal followed Gail's suit by sitting opposite Henry. She told her husband that the conversation at the bank had been so interesting she felt he needed to be personally informed right away.

'All right,' Henry wheezed.

She asked Cal to summarize the history of the loan for her husband, what was known about it, and what was unknown. When Cal was done Henry asked the same question his wife had asked earlier.

He labored at it haltingly, fighting breathlessness. 'Why – does Pope Celestine – want to bankrupt the Vatican – to pay back some Jewish bankers – on a loan they didn't even know – they were owed? It's wacky.'

'It is on the unusual side,' Cal said. 'I'll tell you what I told your cousin but I have to ask you as I asked him, that this conversation be kept confidential.'

With a wave of a hand, Henry assented.

'If we're able to find the contract, assuming it's signed by both sides and valid, the pope has instructed me to tell you that he wants to satisfy the obligation to the full amount due, principal plus interest. However, he does not wish to make the payment to your bank. He wants to pay it to a charitable foundation, perhaps under some kind of joint management between the Vatican and the Sassoon family – details to be hammered out, of course – for the benefit of the poor and needy of the world.'

Henry's eyelids fluttered. 'Only for Catholics?'

'The pope believes the foundation should be inter-faith,' Cal said. 'Again, this is only high-concept at this stage.'

'Doesn't that sound wonderful, Henry?' Gail said. Then turning to Cal, she added, 'Henry and I have a family foundation, you know.'

'You told my cousin this? That we were owed – twenty-seven billion?' Henry asked.

Cal told him he had.

'And what did he say?'

Cal wasn't anxious to step into the middle of family affairs and Gail came to the rescue.

'Oh, you know Marcus,' she said. 'He said he had no interest in the idea. If the bank was owed money, the bank should get the money.'

Henry's sputtering laugh became a cough and the cough a paroxysm that turned him the color of a ripe eggplant. Gail shouted for the nurse who came running with a suction catheter. Cal was asked to wait in the adjoining room while she worked on Henry. Before long, he was called back.

'It's dangerous to laugh – in my condition,' Henry rasped. 'Marcus is a piece of work – isn't he?'

Cal smiled and offered only a 'no comment'.

'But what's to say the bank – couldn't demand payment for a good – loan?' Henry asked. 'Marcus won't fold his tent easily.'

'The pope has had his lawyers look at this – on a hypothetical basis, of course – and they've told him that a loan of this age, with jurisdictions that don't even exist anymore, likely negotiated under duress, would be tied up in court until the other side of forever and probably would never be payable.'

'Unless the pope wants to pay it,' Gail said.

'Exactly,' Cal said.

'How would he pay?' Henry asked. 'I'm no expert – but I can't believe the Vatican – has that kind of liquidity.'

'He's got some ideas,' Cal said cryptically.

'So look, I'm not going to make – any promises here,' Henry said. 'My wife's smarter than me. She'll be able to tell you – all the upsides and the downsides to this idea. But there's time for that.' He paused to take a sip of water through a straw. 'First things first. If you need to get into – the Sassoon archives – you have my permission.'

The pale young man was kinetic with excitement.

'Are you shitting me? Are you shitting me?' was all he could say as his father, Marcus Sassoon, debriefed him on the extraordinary conversation he'd had earlier in the afternoon.

Albert Sassoon was in his late twenties and had been made a vice-president after only two years at the bank, a promotion that caused other young employees, some far more qualified, to howl, 'naked nepotism,' behind his back, of course.

'I am not shitting you,' Marcus said.

'This is the answer to our prayers,' Albert said.

'Be quiet,' Marcus said. 'Grab your coat. Let's take a walk.'

Outside on the tree-lined street, the wind kicked up what few autumn leaves remained. It hadn't yet snowed in New York City but there was a threatening chill to the air.

'I told you I'm worried about listening devices,' Marcus groused.

'You swept your office last month,' Albert said.

'That was last month. I don't trust Gail as far as I can throw her.'

'OK, we're good now,' Albert said. 'About our problems. Twenty-seven-fucking-billion dollars! One little spadeful of that fills in the two-hundred-million-dollar hole in our books. The rest of that truckload of cash turns us into one of the best-capitalized merchant banks in the world. Always wanted to join the club. Never figured to get there.'

'What club?'

'Nine zeroes.'

'What's that?'

'Get with it. Billionaires.'

'Don't count your chickens,' Marcus said. 'This Donovan character's got to find the contract first.'

'If we need to, we ought to send every damn employee into the basement to help him.'

'Maybe you should roll up your sleeves too,' Marcus said. 'He's starting tonight.'

The young man thought that was amusing. 'C'mon, Dad. I'm your son, not a damn worker bee.'

FOURTEEN

T he private archive of the Sassoon Bank spanned the inter-connected basements of three townhouses. The offices that Cal had visited that afternoon were in the middle townhouse that comprised the executive offices. The two that flanked it were packed to the rafters with lower-level employees.

When Cal arrived in the early evening to begin his work he was met by a woman named Consuela Gomes who introduced herself as the Sassoon archivist. Gomes, short and brassy, explained that hers was only a part-time position as there wasn't all that much to do. Her day job was as an associate librarian at New York University. Years earlier she had seen an advertisement for the position in a library journal, and needing some extra income, she'd applied.

'Honestly, I don't spend more than ten hours a month uptown,' she told him. 'When I took over from their previous archivist, the job required more time because the systems and procedures needed upgrading. I mean there wasn't even a good fire-suppression system in place and there was mold. Nuts and bolts type of things. I made it a little more state-of-the art but once that was done, it's only a matter of sorting through new documents every month and deciding what to keep and where to put them.'

'How many archivists have there been?'

'It was Henry's grandfather who decided to make some sense of all the documents that had been consolidated in New York from Sassoon offices in London and Paris. He hired quite a notable man, Conrad Wilkins, who got his start at the JP Morgan Library in the 1920s. Wilkins was the one who sorted through all the initial material and organized it. Let's see, there've been four others between Wilkins and me. I'm the first woman, for what it's worth.'

She summoned an elevator at the rear of the building and took it to the basement level. The elevator door opened to darkness and Gomes hit a switch that turned on row after row of overhead lighting. They waded through the stacks until they arrived at an open-plan space at the front of the building.

'Command central,' she said, pointing to her desk and computer terminal. 'The bathroom's over there. In the unlikely event the power goes out, there's survival gear in the top right drawer of my desk: a flashlight and a bottle of scotch. If you drink any, please replace it.'

'You're not staying?' Cal asked.

'I've got to make dinner for my helpless husband who thinks an oven is as complicated as a nuclear reactor and make sure my girls do their homework and don't scratch their eyes out. Typical night at the Gomes house.'

'I'm sorry to put you out.'

'Not a problem. I've got to run but let me give you a quick lay of the land. I'll be back after ten to see how you're getting on.'

The organization of the archive was straightforward. The oldest documents were in basement shelves farthest to the west, the newer ones in the middle and east basements. The floor-to-ceiling shelving was industrial steel, the kind used in warehouses, with fairly narrow spacing between sets of shelves. Once Gomes left, Cal headed to the oldest section to get his bearings.

He knew that the bank had been founded in 1794 by Herschel Sassoon, the son of a Parisian textile broker. Out of curiosity he opened the first box of documents labeled for that year. Immediately he saw a memo from the archivist, Conrad Wilson, dated 1927, addressed to the chairman of the bank, George Sassoon. It flagged the letter as the earliest known correspondence related to the Sassoon Bank, and noted that the letter's author was none other than the founder of the Rothschilds Bank, Mayer Amschel Rothschild. The letter itself was curt. Rothschild appeared to be responding to a letter written to him by his smaller rival, Herschel Sassoon, requesting an introduction to the paymaster in the army of Napoleon Bonaparte. The request was declined in a courtly brush-off, implying that the Sassoon Bank should make its own way in the world.

Moving forward in time, Cal soon found himself in the mid-nineteenth century, the era of brothers Claude and Mayer Sassoon. Unfortunately, the material was voluminous and Cal became further perturbed when he discovered that the document boxes were rife with chronological misfilings. He'd have to work his way through nearly two full rows of shelving. One thing quickly became abundantly clear. The bank was extremely busy during this period.

There were hundreds upon hundreds of loan contracts and letters of credit, all for much smaller denominations than the Vatican loan.

Since the loan contracts he sought were from 1848 Cal concentrated on that period, carefully sorting through ledger books and file boxes from the late 1840s until he began to note something disturbing. A number of the documents from this period showed signs of fire damage – charred edges, half-burned and curled pages – and were tainted by the faint but noxious odor of ancient smoke.

An hour into the search he'd found no sign of what he was looking for. Then, sitting on the wooden chair he'd been dragging around from shelf to shelf, reading through a box of papers, he thought he heard something toward the rear of the basement.

He listened hard but heard nothing more until something different materialized, the sound of footsteps.

'Hello?' he called out. Hearing no reply, he tried calling louder. 'Hello?'

A husky voice replied. 'Hello, where are you? Professor Donovan?'

'I'm over here.'

A man in a black sports jacket appeared, Gail's chauffeur.

'Mrs Sassoon asks if you would care to join her for dinner,' the man said. 'She's waiting in the car.'

'She knows I'm working,' Cal said, checking the time.

'She does and she apologizes for the interruption. She told me to tell you it was entirely optional.'

There was little question he had to accept so he placed the file box on the chair, left a note for Gomes in case she returned before him, and followed the chauffeur to the elevator.

The restaurant she chose was Milos Café, a quick drive at this time of night. The maître d' greeted Gail unctuously and showed them to a high-profile table where she continued her apologies.

'Really, it's not a problem,' he said again.

When he helped her with her coat he saw she was showing a lot of cleavage. He had thought he'd smelled a whiff of alcohol on her breath in the car and the impression was confirmed when he got closer. This was feeling more like a date night than a business dinner, but he was here and there wasn't anything he could do but keep it professional.

She ordered a Manhattan and he went for his usual, vodka on the rocks.

'The seafood here is amazing,' she said.

'If it was another Italian restaurant, I was going to shoot myself,' he said.

'Yes, of course. You were just in Italy.'

'Actually I was more referring to the place I went to lunch today with Marcus's son.'

'You had lunch with Steven?'

'Yep.'

'Why?'

'It was presented as a *sine qua non*. I'm supposed to write a letter of recommendation to Harvard.'

She showed her shock in a charmingly theatric sort of way. 'You met Steven and you'll still be able to write a letter?'

'Over the years I've become something of a letter-of-recommendation machine. He will be cast in as positive a light as humanly possible. I will honorably fulfill my promise to Marcus.'

'Marcus is such a pig, isn't he?'

'Not going there,' Cal said.

She took a good hit of her drink, with a blithe, 'Cheers,' the instant the waiter put it down. 'Well he is,' she said, 'and Steven is a creep. I'm so glad Henry's son – well, our son, Julian, turned out well.'

'Julian's from an earlier marriage?' Cal asked, gingerly wading into her domestic life.

'Henry was married once before. Julian was an only child. He's twenty-six now, only a little younger than I was when I met Henry. Hard to believe. I was only three years out of law school, an associate at Skadden in their corporate department. One of our clients was the Sassoon Bank and even though I was pretty junior on the team, Henry noticed me and made the partner include me on the important matters. You'd have to see pictures of him when he was in his fifties to understand how handsome and vigorous he was. There hardly seemed to be an age difference. Not like now.'

'He looks pretty ill,' Cal said.

'It's sad but it's progressed slowly enough that we've all come to grips with it. He's made his peace with the world, even made his peace with me.'

Cal wasn't about to ask her to explain but she chose to keep going, pausing only long enough to order another drink. To be polite, he did the same, though he needed to pace himself if he was going to do more work after dinner.

'After he got his divorce and we got married he never wanted me to work. All my training went down the drain. I think he wanted more children but I couldn't, and he didn't have any interest in adopting or doing the surrogate thing. So all I had to do was be a part-time mother to Julian, whose mother had joint custody. She was bitter as hell and she poisoned the well. Julian and I never had a great relationship, although it improved after she died. He was fourteen and he moved in with us, of course. Anyway, where was I? Boredom. Being wealthy in this city is such a bore. Same functions, same charity balls and silent auctions, same people on same boards.'

'I've heard my mother say similar things.'

'Well, she's delightful. I hope I'm half as well put together at her age. Sorry, I've lost the plot again.'

'Boredom.'

'Yes, boredom, thanks. So one thing one can do when one is bored is to fool around and I strayed from time to time in our marriage. That's what Henry and I came to peace about. I haven't been much of a nurse but I've become a dutiful wife and I've really thrown myself into the work of the Henry Sassoon Foundation, soon to be renamed the Henry and Gail Sassoon Foundation.'

'Congratulations.'

'Thank you. It's not huge – only about fifty million – but we do important work. That's why Henry and I are thrilled with the idea of Pope Celestine's proposal. I wanted to have dinner with you, so you'd understand the depth of our interest.'

'I'll be sure to tell him.'

'How is it you're close to the pope? You're not even Catholic.'

'What makes you think that?'

'Your mother, Cal. Remember the nice Jewish lady?'

'My father was Catholic. I converted.'

She let out a tipsy giggle.

'What so amusing?' he asked.

'I converted too. I was a good little Protestant miss from Pennsylvania. There was no way Henry was going to get married unless I converted. But I'm guessing yours wasn't forced. Why'd you do it?'

'Occupational hazard,' he joked. 'I spent so much time in churches as part of my job it kind of crept up on me.'

'No seriously, why?'

'I think the tradition spoke to me, this two-thousand-year sweep of history that began with an itinerant preacher with a small following and grew to become a great religious and cultural force that shaped the world as we know it.'

'Judaism has a tradition too. A longer one.'

'It does but it's decentralized. There's no single person at the helm of the ship. I guess I was attracted to the idea of a central father figure guiding the spiritual priorities of over a billion people.'

'Your mother told me you lost your father at a young age.'

She was tipsy, wasn't she? A little too personal considering the length of their acquaintance. 'Thank you, Dr Freud.'

That did the trick; she said she was sorry but asked instead, 'What about faith? Are you a believer?'

'Some days, more than others. What about you?'

'I have a vague sense of God and I expect he's only got a vague sense of me. You didn't tell me how you got close to Pope Celestine.'

'I did a consult for him. It involved a priest with the bleeding wounds of Christ. I'd written about stigmata.'

'I remember the story. You were part of that?'

He was telling her about it when the waiter came to take their order. When the waiter left, Cal said, 'Anyway, the pope trusted my work and we've maintained a friendship of sorts, if one can be friendly in a conventional sense with a pope.'

'What's he like?'

'He's warm, he's genuine, and most strikingly, he deeply cares about the little guy who no one else gives a damn about. What's not to like about that?'

'Well, I'm only a little fish in a very big pond but I'd like to think that our foundation does some good too.'

'I'm sure it does. You mentioned your husband was enthusiastic about the pope's idea for a large foundation. What about Marcus? Does he have any connections with your foundation or other charitable ventures?'

'Heavens no. Marcus is only about business.'

'Wouldn't he be an obstacle to doing a deal with the Vatican?'

'Henry holds a majority interest in the firm. End of story. Not that there wouldn't be concerns. But those could be overcome.'

'What kind of concerns?'

'The Sassoon Bank has a reputation for privacy. Our clients demand that. We're not a commercial bank or an investment bank. We're a merchant bank. Our clients are largely transnational, private entities that value our advisory and credit services and our ability to service them rapidly and discreetly. A major philanthropic association with the Vatican would surely thrust the bank into the spotlight so we'd have to think this through carefully. Still, I imagine that Julian will be supportive, and that would be important to Henry.'

The food came and another round of drinks. When the plates were cleared, Cal begged off the dessert menu and said he still wanted to get in a few more hours of work.

'You're a hard taskmaster,' she said, 'on yourself.'

'I'm on a tight schedule. I need to get back to Cambridge one of these days.'

She paid the check and when they rose to leave she swayed enough that he thought it wise to steady her with an arm around the waist.

'Sorry,' she said. She was glassy-eyed from the Manhattans and whatever she'd had before she picked him up.

'Not a problem.'

The intimacy of his arm seemed to embolden her.

'If you like I could drop you off at your hotel. We could have another drink. The archive will still be there tomorrow.'

'That's very kind of you,' he said, letting go of her and checking to see if she stayed upright, 'but I really need to get back to it.'

The chauffeur let Cal back into the townhouse, where he descended to the basement. It was past ten o'clock but it didn't look like Gomes had arrived yet; his note was still on her desk. He resumed where he'd left off and before long he finished the 1840s documents and moved into the 1850s, finding a similar scattering of fire-blackened papers. All of the material from this decade related to business originating in the Sassoon offices in London and Manchester. He kept his antennae out for any letters or contracts written by Jean Sassoon. After sorting through Jean's papers in the state archives in Rome he was sure he'd recognize his hand-writing in an instant. There were none.

He couldn't place precisely where, but there was a faint rustling sound coming from somewhere in the direction of the elevator.

'Hello? Mrs Gomes?'

There was no reply. When he heard nothing further he chalked it up to the ventilation system blowing a piece of paper around, or maybe mice, not the best of creatures for an archive.

The closer he got toward the end of the 1850s, the papers had a greater frequency and extent of fire damage, so much so that he had to take care in turning some pages to prevent crumbling.

There were several bound ledger books covering the latter months of 1858 but precious few loose documents. However, one of them was a signed letter from Mayer Sassoon that he gulped down like a desert wanderer offered a flask of cool water.

18 November 1858

My dear Edouard,
You must return from Manchester without delay. As your father it is my duty to inform you that the greatest calamity has befallen the bank. I will endeavour to provide you here with the bald particulars in order that you might appreciate the magnitude of the crisis. When you are safe to my bosom I will provide you with details. Although the events you will read here are traumatic you must prepare yourself to assume a new role at the firm, one where our side of the family may finally enjoy a true and equal partnership at the Sassoon Bank.

FIFTEEN

Rome, 1858

Cardinal Antonelli had known this day was coming but the letter still came as a shock. It wasn't as if he had been watching the calendar for the reckoning. Other affairs were uppermost on his mind. It had been a year of chaos and uncertainty within a decade of upheaval. In 1849 Mazzini had entered Rome and had declared a Roman Republic, complete with a constitution. But the heady days of the revolution soon came crashing down when the French intervened to cast out the republicans and restore the papacy. Mazzini, Garibaldi, and their compatriots were once again thrown into exile and Pope Pius, Antonelli, and their entourage returned from Gaeta to the Vatican. The years that followed were far from peaceful. The Papal States were restive and pockets of revolutionary zeal popped up here and there, requiring a military response. Then in 1857, Pisacane and Nicotera, followers of Mazzini and Garibaldi, mounted an invasion of the Kingdom of the Two Sicilies. The revolution was coming to a boil once again and tensions within the Vatican were high. Was history repeating itself so soon? Would the leadership of the Vatican once again be forced into exile?

And now this. A demand letter from this vile nonentity, Jean Sassoon. The nerve of the fellow! The insolence!

1 November 1858

Esteemed Cardinal Secretary,
I write to you on behalf of the Sassoon Bank. The loan we provided you in 1848 is coming due and we wish to arrange for repayment of the principal plus interest that has accrued over these ten years. By my calculations, should the loan be repaid on the date of its tenth anniversary, we would be owed the 300,000 pounds sterling principal plus interest payments of 290,145 pounds sterling for a grand total of 590,145 pounds sterling. My offices are in Venice but I will gladly

*come to Rome to take possession of the bullion. I would
remind you that under the terms of our contract, should
payment not be made by the tenth anniversary, the interest
would begin to compound on a monthly basis. It suits the
bank and I venture to say that it should suit the Vatican to
see to your obligations now so as to avoid costly interest
payments in the future. Please reply at your earliest convenience with the particulars of the arrangements. Timely payment
is a matter of some importance to the bank. My father who
is the chairman of our firm has instructed me to inform you
that he had never revealed the existence of the loan to the
public. However, if prompt repayment is not made he believes
he would no longer have the obligation of silence. I am aware
that Cardinal Lambruschini died some years ago, but it will
be a pleasure to see you again after so long an absence.*

Your faithful servant,

J. Sassoon

Antonelli read the letter again. A pleasure to see you again, he
wrote! The last time the cardinal had laid eyes on the man had
been on the day of the banker's release from the dungeons at Gaeta
Castle. Sarcasm! Sassoon had the gall to engage in sarcasm.

He had received the letter the prior day and had elected to sleep
on the matter rather than run headlong to the pope. Now, with his
recommendation formulated, he headed for Pius's office in the
Apostolic Palace, where the pontiff had come after celebrating
Mass at the basilica.

The pope had lost some weight these recent years and he had
a perpetually unhealthy pallor. Whether his diet was the culprit or
some occult condition, or whether it was simply the product of
stress, no one, including his doctors, knew for sure. He was sorting
through papers at his desk when Antonelli entered and saw that
his latest malady, a fine tremor of his writing hand, was on full
display. Some uneaten food was on a side table. The air was stale
and the cardinal took it upon himself to crack open one of the tall
windows overlooking the great piazza to air it out.

'Your Holiness, I have received a letter from the banker, Jean
Sassoon. Would you care to read it?'

The pope looked at the letter in Antonelli's hand as if he was
holding a dead animal.

'Tell me what it says.'

'He demands repayment.'

'How much?' the pope asked, his expression sour.

'Approximately five hundred and ninety thousand pounds.'

'But the loan was for three hundred thousand!'

'The interest payments, Your Holiness.'

The pope nodded ruefully.

Antonelli continued. 'The letter goes on to suggest that we might not wish to extend the loan beyond its term to avoid the harsher effects of monthly interest compounding.'

'Is that very bad?' the pope asked. 'You know I have no facility for these things.'

'It is quite disadvantageous to us. There is more. The letter contains a threat of sorts.'

'What threat?'

'He cautions that if repayment is not made then his father might see fit to divulge the existence of the loan to the general public.'

The pope thrust his hands straight out as if he were trying to stop an invisible force.

'Enough! This is too much. We cannot pay five hundred and ninety thousand. We cannot pay three hundred thousand. We hardly have enough in the treasury to maintain ourselves at a meager level. And now they would get the Rothschilds involved? They will demand payment for violating their agreement. The situation is intolerable, Antonelli.'

'There is a way we might proceed to rid us of this matter,' the cardinal said quietly.

'Yes? How?'

'It is better you do not know, Your Holiness. Before he died, Cardinal Lambruschini recommended that if and when this day came that we engage the services of a certain gentleman.'

As he said this, Antonelli made a show of crumpling the Sassoon letter and tossing it into the fireplace. He missed and the cardinal had to kick it the rest of the way.

'You are correct,' the pope said, picking up his pen and gazing at his shaking hand for a moment. 'I do not wish to know of what you speak.'

Duke Francesco Tizziani was small but physically powerful with a barrel of a chest and bowed legs that gave the appearance of his being on horseback even when he was not. He was certainly not handsome. He endeavored to hide a weak chin under a cropped beard. His overly long nose was set between closely spaced eyes. Nevertheless, he fancied himself a ladies' man, oblivious to the fact that his conquests were exclusively the result of rank and wealth. His ancestral estates in Romagna were lavish, particularly his palace a half-day's ride from Bologna. That is where he received the letter from Cardinal Antonelli, hand-delivered by a Vatican horseman.

His great room was drafty and cold, an inefficient space to heat on a cold late-November day but Tizziani liked its grand proportions and the view from its windows over manicured lawns and rolling horse meadows. After dismissing the rider and instructing his manservant to give him food and lodging, the duke went to his desk and pulled out the previous letter from Monsignor Parizo that had come only a week earlier.

This new letter was a fat one and when Tizziani broke the wax seal, it practically burst open. The top sheet was a short note from Parizo thanking the duke for his reply and stating that the documents were being delivered as promised. The duke knew full well that the cardinal secretary was a studiously careful man. It would have been unwise to send the first, explanatory letter and the contracts together lest they fell into the wrong hands. At this time, Tizziani would only make a cursory inspection of the contract and its annex; he had no interest in reading legal documents. His brain wasn't made for this kind of activity. It was made for scheming and fighting, hunting and whoring.

Tizziani knew Antonelli in passing. His true friend in the Vatican had been Lambruschini. The two men, in concert with the governor of Romagna, had made a killing in preferential trade deals with Rome. As the duke surveyed the new realities of 1858 he could see the handwriting on the wall. The old order was crumbling. Italian nationalism was on the rise. The Papal States might not survive for long. If the Vatican lost them, the Church would recede as a political power. Why should he stick his neck out to help a cardinal who could be shot any time by one of Garibaldi's lot? On the other hand, Antonelli was still in power and the favor he sought didn't seem overly dangerous. On this matter he would continue to be the pope's faithful servant and hope for the best.

The men he summoned were like a pair of obedient hounds –

muscular, silent young men who were smart enough for this kind of work but not so intelligent as to elaborately scheme on their own account. Each had literally grown up on his estate, sons of retainers, and their allegiance to the duke was absolute.

'Piero, Angelo, I have work for you.'

'Anything, my lord,' they said in a near unison.

'Can either of you read?' the duke asked.

One pointed to the other. 'Piero can.'

'Then Piero, you take these papers. The work you must do for me is in Venice.'

They were married now – Ricca, the baker's daughter, and Jean Sassoon, the banker's son – and they had a son, Ephraim, a four-year-old study in continuous motion. Perhaps it had been Jean's lonely incarceration in Gaeta that had persuaded him that life was but a gossamer fabric, all too easy to rend and destroy, and that he would do well to marry the woman he loved rather than someone his father thought suitable. Upon his return to Rome he had gone to the ghetto bakery and asked Ricca's father for her hand with the proviso that he no longer felt safe doing business in Rome. He would return to Venice, far from the grasp of the Vatican, and make a life with Ricca there.

Business had been good. The Venetian offices of the Sassoon Bank were in the Cannaregio, the section of the city where the Jewish ghetto was located. Even though Napoleon Bonaparte had abolished the separation of the ghetto from the rest of the city when he conquered Venice in 1797, old habits died hard and Jews still tended to congregate there. Jean Sassoon had established himself as a reliable lender to the glass and mirror artisans and the middlemen who plied the eastern trade routes. Furthermore, the turmoil that had spawned the 1848 revolution was still creating waves of opportunity. Every Italian army garrison, every militia it seemed, needed fresh arms and ammunition and Sassoon letters of credit were popping up across Europe.

The Sassoons lived above the bank in a narrow pink house on the Campo della Maddalena. To discourage thieves Jean posted a wholly truthful note in a front window stating that there was no money on the premises. To a merchant, his letters of credit were as good as hard currency and should silver or gold be needed for a transaction, arrangements could be made quickly enough.

Upstairs, there were three comfortable rooms, a luxurious amount of space for such a small family.

Jean and Ricca had put Ephraim to bed and were enjoying a quiet chat in their parlor when they heard an insistent knocking at the front door.

'Who could that be?' Ricca asked. 'Ephraim will wake up.'

'God forbid,' Jean said for it was no easy thing getting the energetic boy to go to sleep.

He put down his small glass of fortified wine and peered out the window, trying without success to get a view of the doorway below. However, he could see the piazza clearly enough and though it was dark, he was quite sure it was otherwise empty. When the knocking persisted, Jean feared the boy would surely begin to fuss, so he opened a shutter and leaned out. As he looked down, two strangers looked up.

'Jean Sassoon?' one of them said.

'Yes, what do you want?'

'We need to speak with you.'

'Is it a business matter?'

'It is.'

'Then I beg you to return in the morning. I am retired for the night.'

'It is urgent.'

'Could you kindly state the nature of this urgency?'

'It is private. We cannot let the entire city know our business.'

'Very well, I can give you five minutes. Ten at most.'

He told his wife he would be back shortly and went down the stairs to the office where he lit a kerosene lamp and unlocked the door. It was then that he saw that each cloaked man was holding identical pistols, together, a matching pair of Glisenti pinfire revolvers, valuable weapons supplied by their employer, Duke Tizziani.

Jean backed away with a horrifying memory of the day, ten years earlier, when men had appeared at the door of his love nest.

'I do not keep money here. Everyone knows this.'

Piero entered first. 'We don't want money,' he said. 'Who else is in the house?'

'Just my wife and child.'

Angelo came in and shut the door. 'Be silent,' he said, 'and no one will be hurt.'

'If this isn't a robbery, what is it?' Jean asked, his hands hanging heavily. They were useless to him right now. He wasn't a fighter. These hands of his were made for holding pens and paper.

Piero had the contracts in a small leather shoulder bag.

'Do you recognize these?' he asked, showing them to the banker.

Jean glanced at them by the light of the oil lamp. A pathetic, high-pitched sigh came from deep in his chest. So that's what this is about, he thought. He rapidly played out the possible scenarios in his mind and none of them ended well. Whatever happened, he had to protect Ricca and Ephraim.

He tried to sound unafraid. 'They are loan contracts. How did you come to possess them?'

Piero was the apparent spokesman. 'Never mind that. We want your copies.'

Jean understood what was happening. The Vatican was behind this, he had no doubt. If the contracts disappeared, if he disappeared, then the loan would disappear.

'Who has sent you? Cardinal Antonelli?'

'Don't know any cardinals. Where are your copies?'

'I don't have them.'

'I don't believe you.'

'I'm telling the truth.'

The shelves in the spacious room were stacked with papers, hundreds of contracts and letters of credit. Piero kept his pistol trained on Jean while he walked the perimeter of the space, brushing at papers with his free hand.

'It will take me all night to look through this lot,' Piero said. 'We don't want to stay all night, do we, Angelo?'

'We do not,' his compatriot answered. 'Let me break his fingers. That will loosen his tongue.'

'I have a better idea,' Piero said. 'Bring his wife and child down here.'

'No!' Jean cried. 'Don't touch them!' It was a cold night but he was sweating now. 'The contracts are kept at the London office of the bank. I only keep the smaller, local contracts here.'

Piero laughed at that and asked if he really expected them to simply take him at his word and piss off into the night.

'I am begging you to believe me because it is the truth,' Jean said.

'Bring them down, Angelo,' Piero ordered and when Jean tried to block the young man he brought the butt of the pistol down on his head, opening up a gusher that Jean tried to staunch with the flat of his hand.

Jean heard Ricca scream and when he began to rise up from his kneeling position, Piero pointed his gun and told him to stay down. Soon, Ricca was on the stairs, holding the boy's hand, Angelo at their rear.

'Jean, what's happening? They've hurt you,' she said. 'Is this a robbery?'

He shook his head sadly. 'They want a contract.'

'A contract? Then give it to them. They're scaring Ephraim. They're scaring me.'

'I would if I could,' Jean said. 'The contract they want is in London.'

'Did you tell them?'

'They refuse to believe me.'

The boy was staring at the pistol. 'Is that a real gun?' he asked.

'It is indeed,' Piero said. 'A very powerful gun. Banker, if you don't want a demonstration of its power you need to hand over the contract.'

'How can I convince you that it is not here?' Jean croaked.

'There is only one way,' Piero said, putting the pistol to Ricca's temple. 'I will count to ten. Show me the contract before my count is done and the gun will stay silent. One . . .'

Ricca tried to say Jean's name but her mouth was too dry.

'As God is my witness,' Jean cried, 'the documents are in London!'

'Five . . .'

Jean rose to his feet and lurched toward the shelves to make a show of looking for what he knew was not there.

'Seven . . .'

'Running out of time,' Angelo warned.

'Nine . . .'

'Stop counting!' Jean cried, throwing a handful of papers into the air.

He didn't hear Piero say ten. He only heard the hideous thunderclap and the high-pitched scream of his son whose small hand was no longer clutching his mother's. Ricca was on the floor, her eyes open but blind, the blood flowing from her head.

'I don't think the contract is here,' Angelo said to Piero.

'Perhaps not, but we have to be sure. One, two, three . . .'

The pistol was pointed at Ephraim now.

With no warning and no plan, Jean charged Piero with a guttural roar. He made it within striking distance of the large man when one of Angelo's bullets pierced his side, spinning him half a turn and sending him crashing to the floor. Ricca was close. He reached out to touch her and said, 'Please, no,' when, inexplicably he became aware that Piero was counting again.

'Eight. Nine. Ten.'

The small body fell between him and Ricca.

Jean could only manage one word. 'Ephraim.'

Mercifully, a moment later, a bullet tore into his brain too, ending his agony.

'Now what?' Angelo asked, peering nervously out the window into the dark, empty piazza.

'Now I will have to look through all the damnable papers in this room.'

'How long will it take? Someone could have heard the shots.'

'I don't know. Look at all of them,' Piero said. 'It could take all night.'

Angelo objected. 'It would be dangerous to stay that long.'

Piero glanced around the room and found the rear door. 'Wait here,' he said.

Angelo stayed inside trying not to look at the bloody bodies of the woman and child. When Piero returned he was carrying a wooden crate.

'There's a stack of them down the alley behind a dry-goods merchant. We'll load up the papers, steal a boat, and find a wagon on the mainland. Tizziani can personally go through them. It won't be our problem.'

SIXTEEN

By the time Cal finished reading Mayer Sassoon's account of the murder of Jean Sassoon and his young family, the effects of his boozy dinner were gone. He had never felt so sober in his life. He knew what Mayer Sassoon knew, which was not a lot. Who had done such a heinous thing, annihilating an entire young family? Thieves? A disgruntled merchant? Jew-haters? Or was there something even more nefarious? Could the Vatican have been involved? After all, the debt had disappeared from the annals of history.

Murders in Venice.

Signs of a fire at the Sassoon Bank.

Were the two related?

He got up and walked the stacks to burn off nervous energy. He no longer felt an ounce of fatigue. If he needed to pull an all-nighter, he'd be able to sail through.

Returning to the 1850s section he polished off the year 1858. There was nothing of consequence in the few remaining documents although many showed fire damage.

But he found a bombshell in the very first document in the volume marking the beginning of 1859.

Glued to a page of plain white paper was a yellowed newspaper clipping from *The Times* of London, a story dated 17 November 1858.

Cal read the clipping then looked up, blinking his eyes in disbelief.

Accident, my ass, he thought. The bastards couldn't find the loan contracts in Venice so they came to London.

London, 1858

It was the coldest November anyone could remember and the streets of London reeked from the coal fires burning in most every hearth. It was late evening and most shops and offices were dark and cold, but the premises of the Sassoon Bank on Cannon Street were awash in the light of gas pendant lamps and the roaring central fireplace.

Mayer Sassoon had left the office hours earlier but Claude had refused to go home for supper. A single employee stayed by his side of the bank chairman as he stubbornly pored over his accounts.

'Could I fetch you a plate of food, sir?' the employee asked. 'The cook has laid it in the warming oven.'

Claude peered over his spectacles. 'I'm not hungry.'

'It's frightfully late. Won't your wife be needing your company?'

Claude barely concealed his irritation. 'My wife is my concern, not yours. Look, man, why don't you leave? I can shift for myself.'

The fellow didn't need to be asked again.

'Very well, sir,' he said, taking his coat down from a peg. 'And once again, please accept my heartfelt condolences.'

The moment the door closed behind him, Claude Sassoon broke down and sobbed, gripping the sides of his standing desk to keep his wavering frame upright.

The letter had arrived two days earlier, penned by a Venetian rabbi in rudimentary English.

Claude had opened it at his desk and had collapsed, shrieking on the floor. That had been his one and only public display of grief.

The Italian rabbi had offered the bald particulars. He supposed Jean and his family had been the victims of a robbery. He didn't think they had suffered. Those responsible had not yet been apprehended. The burials had been done in accordance with Jewish law. The congregation of the synagogue had borne the expense. If Claude came to Venice, the rabbi would take him to the family gravesite.

Now alone, he peeled off his spectacles and cried, 'Oh, my son, my son. What shall I do without you?' Then he looked up, as if there were no ceiling, only heaven above. 'Why have you forsaken me, Lord? Am I too great a sinner? Is this my punishment? Why did you not take me? I am an old man. Jean was too young to die. And Ephraim who I never met . . .'

A knock on the door brought his sobbing to an end. He supposed his clerk had forgotten something and as he approached the door, he dried his eyes then blew his nose into a handkerchief.

But it was not his clerk.

There were three callers, one at the door, a smallish man

smothered by his greatcoat, two taller men at his heels in more fitted, Continental jackets.

The smaller man had the accent of a commoner. 'Excuse me, sir, might we have a word?'

Claude had no interest in an interruption. 'These offices are not open to the public,' he said, swinging the door shut.

The three men advanced on him, pushing him backwards. He tripped on his own heels and stumbled to the floor, shouting at them to leave at once.

The commoner produced a long sheath knife and advised him to keep quiet if he knew what was good for him while his two compatriots closed the door then fanned out to see if anyone else was about. Claude heard them talking to each other in a foreign tongue; it took him several seconds to place it but when he did he picked himself off the floor and angrily addressed them.

'Italians!' he spat. 'You men, you hear me. Were you the scoundrels in Venice? Did you kill my son?'

The commoner grinned. 'They don't speak much in the way of English. They give me a nice purse and your address. What their business is, what they did or didn't do, I've no notion. But I'd say they're ruthless sorts, if you know what I mean. They've got that look, don't they?'

Claude shouted for help but only managed to say it once before the small man punched him in the gut with his free hand, sending him back to the floor, gasping and retching.

'Now I could've hit you with me knife hand,' the man said. 'That would've caused you considerable more distress. Say one more thing and it'll be your last, that I can promise you.'

Claude closed his eyes and grimaced in pain. When he opened them again he saw the piece of paper thrust in his face.

Piero said in broken English, 'This. Where this? You say me.'

Without his spectacles, Claude struggled to read the paper but a hard squint brought it into enough focus to know what it was – the copy of the Vatican loan document.

He began to shake with rage.

'You bastards murdered my son and grandson because of this infernal loan.'

The small man glanced through the dark windows. There were too many houses for comfort close by. 'I told you to be quiet,' he said. 'I warned you.'

'You can go to hell,' Claude shouted. 'The Vatican can go to hell. The pope can go to . . .'

Angelo plunged a knife into the old man's flank once, and then a second time for good measure.

'Hell,' was the last word to pass Claude's lips, sounding like a rush of air escaping from a punctured bladder.

Piero asked his friend in Italian, 'Why did you do that?'

'He wouldn't shut up,' Angelo said. 'I don't want to wind up in an English prison or worse – my neck in an English noose.'

The small man swore and mumbled that he hadn't signed up to do murder. While the two Italians argued, he bolted out of the door and disappeared into the cold night.

'How are we going to find the papers now?' Piero said, surveying shelf after shelf of documents and ledger books.

'I don't know but we can't spend any time looking. Someone could have heard all the shouting.'

'What then?' Piero asked.

Angelo snatched a sheaf of papers from the banker's desk and took them to the nearest gas lamp. 'This,' he said. He lit them and began walking through the office, touching the flames to books and papers. For good measure he threw a few dozen ledger books on to Claude's still-warm body and set them on fire too.

Piero tucked his copies of the loan contracts inside his jacket and said, 'Very well then, let's go home straight away and tell the duke we found them and burned them, which I expect will be the truth. I hate this damned country anyway.'

As the two Italians fled the scene, a tipsy fellow was turning on to Cannon Street heading home from a nearby public house. His first impression was that the bank offices were looking rather festive and bright on such a bleak night but then he realized what was happening.

'Fire! Fire! Help, fire!'

There were thirteen firehouses in London, all of them under the umbrella of the London Fire Engine Establishment, a private firm owned by the city's insurance companies. The Rothschilds' Bank, located around the corner from the Sassoon Bank on St Swithin's Lane, was a significant investor in the largest insurance company and the Rothschilds had seen to it that one of these firehouses was installed close to their premises. It was a company of men from that very firehouse that responded to the alarm with a modern, horse-drawn pumper that doused the structure and saved the building. Hours later, in the harsh light of the frosty morning, Mayer Sassoon used his walking stick to push at the charred and soggy debris. He stopped at the spot where his brother's body had been found, the scorched floorboards stained with blood.

Claude's clerk came up to him and said, 'I never should have left him alone. Till the day I die, I shall regret doing so.'

'The ruffians who did this would have killed you too. They were a determined lot. First Jean, now Claude.'

'But who were they and why would they do this? Whatever was to be gained? As far as I can tell, nothing was stolen.'

'Don't you see?' Mayer said bitterly. 'It's the accursed Vatican debt. We never should have made the loan. I didn't want to do it but Claude had the majority. Now he's paid the price.'

'What will you do about it?' the clerk asked.

'Do? Why, I shall do nothing. If I were to press for repayment I have no doubt that my son, Edouard, and I, and Claude's son, Andre, would all find ourselves in the graveyard. I will not forgive the debt. No, that I will not do. But I will never speak of it again. Now, collect all the documents that are not burned beyond recognition and place them in crates. We will rebuild these offices. The Sassoon Bank will survive and my side of the family will finally be equal partners.'

Emanuel Spiegelman was a study in probity. From his austere rooms on Threadneedle Street, to his starched collar and immaculately clean black frock coat, to his perfectly cropped muttonchops and his measured elocution, he was every inch the successful London lawyer.

Mayer Sassoon had always trod carefully around him. While he respected his judgment and the opinions he rendered on behalf of the firm, it was always clear where Spiegelman's allegiances lay. He was Claude's lawyer, first and foremost. Claude's man.

Mayer had sought him out at the funeral, where he accepted his condolences before quietly asking him when his brother's will and testament would be read.

'When the mourning period is over, Mayer,' he had said.

Mayer had grabbed both of the lawyer's wrists and staring into his eyes he said, 'Listen to me, Emanuel. Please. This is a volatile and dangerous period for the bank. Decisions must be made.

Capital allocated. Strategies set in motion. I need to know with certainty how I must approach the future. No one respects our traditions as much as I do but I cannot wait for the mourning period to lapse.'

'Then you must come by my office at your convenience. I will endeavor to be of assistance.'

The lawyer entered the anteroom and escorted Mayer to his inner chamber.

'Difficult times, so difficult,' Spiegelman said. 'Tell me, what are the police telling you?'

Mayer took a seat and crossed his legs. 'They seem to know nothing. If the bank were as incompetent as the police we should be in liquidation.'

'And I must ask you, Mayer, as your lawyer and your friend. What do you think happened to Claude?'

'He was murdered, Emanuel. He was cut down as Jean was cut down. I cannot say by whom.'

Although they were alone in the office, the lawyer nevertheless lowered his voice and leaned forward in an expression of privacy.

'Yes, but surely you have an opinion. Surely you must suspect that this sorry business bears a relation in some direct or indirect fashion to the Vatican loan.'

Mayer and the lawyer had not spoken of the loan in years. When Jean Sassoon had been held hostage in Gaeta, he and Spiegelman had tried to persuade Claude not to bow to the pressure and agree to the Vatican's unfavorable terms. But the distraught father had overruled them and Spiegelman had been pressed into service to draft the loan contracts.

'You spoke with Claude after he received news of Jean's death, did you not?' Mayer asked.

'Of course I did. I called on him that very day.'

'And what was his opinion of a connection between Jean's death and the debt?'

'Indeed he believed there was a connection.'

Mayer sighed pitifully. 'And so do I.'

'What is your intention with respect to the obligation?' the lawyer asked.

'For the sake of the bank, my son, my nephew, I will not pursue repayment. It is a fatal business. I will not ask you to send a demand letter to Rome. I will not raise the matter. It is over.'

'They never intended to pay,' the lawyer clucked.

'I fear not.'

'Well, you and your brother did much these past years to place the firm on strong footings. I believe you are positioned to weather the storm.'

'And that is why I am here, Emanuel. I need to know where I stand. For many, many years, Claude has promised me that he intended to rectify our partnership inequalities for the sake of the next generation. I will not ask you to enumerate all the provisions in Claude's last will and testament. I can wait for the details. However, I cannot wait for this: please tell me once and for all if Claude abided by his promise to transfer the requisite shares to my side of the family so that we may be equals in the management of the enterprise.'

The lawyer stood, and in a gesture not lost upon Mayer, peered out of his window at the crush of horse-drawn carriages rolling down Threadneedle Street. In doing so, he turned his back on the banker.

'I will tell you this, Mayer. Your brother loved you very much. Over the years we discussed the issue of his majority on multiple occasions. He knew the day would come when you or your son, Edouard, would sit in this office to learn of his legacy. His love for you was strong but his love for the bank was even stronger.'

Spiegelman turned toward the sound of sobbing.

'For God's sake, man,' Mayer cried, 'look me in the eye when you deliver this death blow.'

The lawyer took his chair again. 'I'm sorry, Mayer, although it is hardly a death blow. Nothing will change. Fifty-two percent of the shares will reside with Claude's sole surviving son, Andre, and you will hold forty-eight percent. In the end, Claude felt that a majority was necessary to assure the efficiency of making critical business decisions. Resolving disputes in an equal partnership can be devilish and decremental to the firm. Furthermore . . .'

The lawyer's words trailed off when Mayer pushed himself from his chair and slowly walked out of the room.

'Mayer, please,' the lawyer said, chasing after him and catching him in the anteroom with a hand to the shoulder.

Mayer wheeled around and said, 'So, Andre, a fourteen-year-old boy, is the majority owner of the Sassoon Bank. Am I not to be his guardian? Not even this?'

'He has had his bar mitzvah,' the lawyer said. 'By Jewish law he is a man and does not require guardianship.'

'Goodbye, Emanuel,' Mayer said. 'I do not believe we need to speak again.'

Monsignor Raffaello Parizo was so ancient that no one, including himself, quite knew precisely how old he was.

'I'm an eighteenth-century man,' he would tell his colleagues. 'This modern age confuses me. I don't understand anything anymore. If I simply stick to my work and my prayers I can just about get through the day.'

He puttered around the corridors of the Apostolic Palace, shifting papers through ecclesiastical offices, gathering required signatures from high officials, and occasionally making tea for his boss, Cardinal Antonelli. Antonelli had inherited him from a now-deceased Vatican cardinal, whom he had served as an aide for decades, because, in Parizo's own words, 'he knew where all the bodies were buried'. Given that cardinal's bruising style, some took him quite literally.

Stooped and shuffling, the old priest rapped on Antonelli's door and entered when permission was given.

The cardinal, busily writing, didn't look up from his paperwork. 'Yes, what is it?'

Parizo had a thick envelope in his arthritic hand. 'A courier delivered this today. It is from Tizziani.'

Antonelli put his pen back into its holder and stared at the envelope. 'Have you opened it?'

'I believe it is intended for your eyes.'

The cardinal opened the envelope with a small knife and pulled out the papers. There was a short letter and two contracts.

> *Eminence,*
> *By this letter I give you my personal assurance that the vexing problem of your debt is resolved. You do not need to know how this was accomplished. I return your copies of the contracts to do with as you see fit. An offer was extended to grant me an audience with the Holy Father and I will call upon your good offices when next I travel to Rome.*
> *Tizziani*

Antonelli breathed hard and nodded.

'It is done,' he told the priest, his relief palpable.

Returning the papers to the envelope, he told Parizo to take them away and burn them. Then he rose and adjusted his zucchetto.

'I'm off to tell the Holy Father,' he said. 'All too frequently it has fallen on me to deliver bad news to him. Mercifully today is different. Join me for supper tonight, Raffaello. I will open a good bottle of wine.'

The old priest had painstakingly made his way to his tiny office, clutching the fat envelope under his arm. By the time he settled behind his desk he was short of breath and feeling chesty. He attributed the burning sensation in his chest to the rebellion of a luncheon sausage.

When another priest, a young functionary at the beginning of his bureaucratic career, amiably poked his head in to see how his venerable colleague was doing, he found a frustrated Parizo trying to reach a metal waste bin under his desk.

'Here, let my help you, monsignor,' he said, rushing in.

'Thank you. That's very kind. Please place it on my desk.'

'As you like,' the priest said. 'Is there anything else I can do for you?'

'Matches. I can't remember where I put my matches.'

The young priest searched around and found a box tucked away behind a picture on the mantelpiece.

'What are you going to do?' the young man asked.

Parizo chortled. 'I am going to make something disappear. Like a conjuror.'

When Parizo was alone he laid the three documents – a letter, a contract, and its annex – on his desk and started with the duke's letter, striking a match and setting the corner alight. Holding it over the bin until the last moment, he waited a second too long and had to drop it in pain. He thrust his inflamed thumb and forefinger into his mouth but just then his chest began to burn more fiercely. He pulled his fingers out and rubbed his hand on his sternum. When his discomfort ebbed he turned his attention to the large annex. He would take care of it first then finish with the contract. He began to burn one page at a time but his chest started aching again so he decided to speed up the process to get back to his dormitory and rest. He hurriedly applied a match to the corner of all the remaining pages and the sheaf erupted strongly. When he dropped the pages into the bin they blazed fiercely and threw a cloud of thick smoke straight into his face.

Parizo inhaled one full breath of the noxious vapor and began to cough. He felt his throat tighten. His chest felt like someone had placed a millstone on it. In a panic he tried to get up from his chair but he could not. Instead, he felt himself helplessly pitching forward.

An hour later, the young priest happened by again, and seeing the old man slumped on his desk, his sooty head half in and half out of the toppled bin, at first he thought he had simply fallen asleep. But it didn't take him long to realize that Monsignor Parizo was dead.

A bevy of monsignors and even a couple of bishops answered the young priest's calls for help and proceeded to debate the administration of last rites, finally deciding that there might still be at least a small last breath inside the old man's breast. When the sacraments were delivered, his body was carried away.

'Do you know what he was burning?' a bishop asked the young priest.

'Only some papers.'

Just then a grave-looking Cardinal Antonelli entered. Seemingly relieved that the body was gone, he sniffed at the sooty air and asked whether they had found any burned documents.

The priest, in some awe at being in the presence of the cardinal secretary, volunteered that he had been with Parizo when he was about to burn some papers.

'Where? Show me?' the cardinal asked.

He was shown the metal waste bin and the pile of ashes inside. Satisfied, Antonelli made a rather generic statement about the fragility of life and the need to always maintain a devout attitude, then left.

'What would you like me to do with all the rest of his papers and correspondence?' the priest asked the bishop.

'You should do what we always do in these circumstances. You attended to Monsignor Moreno upon his passing, I believe. Do the same and see to it immediately. This is a good office. I have a monsignor I would like to take occupancy tomorrow.'

*   *   *

The next morning, the chief archivist at the Vatican Secret Archive sighed when he saw the two large crates of documents that had been left on his desk the previous evening with a paper marking them as the contents of the office of M. Parizo. It was clear that his day would be consumed with an unexpected filing job. Reaching into the first box he took out an envelope containing something that looked like a contract. He put it back, glancing at the name on the envelope: Duke Tizziani of Romagna.

He tossed the envelope on to his large table. He did not know who this duke was and he wondered if it would be necessary to make a new file box in the section of the archive reserved for the minor nobility of the Vatican States. The archivist yawned. Probably no one would ever look at it again once it was consigned to one of his shelves.

SEVENTEEN

C al returned from the small basement toilet where he had doused his face with a handful of cold water. Returning to the stacks he read *The Times* of London article one more time.

Fire at the Sassoon Bank
Proprietor Dead in Blaze

Shortly before midnight a passerby on Cannon Street saw flames leaping from the windows of the merchant bank Sassoon's and notified the fire brigade. Thanks to a rapid response that included a large engine, a hand engine and a leathern pipe sufficient water was delivered to save the building and the nearby residences. However, on inspection of the smoldering premises the charred remains of the proprietor of the bank, Mr Claude Sassoon, the prominent Jewish banker, were discovered. Apparently, Mr Sassoon was in his office late at work when the fire erupted, perhaps caused by an unattended candle. Superintendent Wheeler of the Metropolitan Police has stated that there was no indication of arson. The bank houses an abundance of documents which, with certainty, provided fuel to the blaze. Mr Sassoon is survived by a wife and a son, Andre. Tragically, he had recently been informed of the death of his eldest son in the city of Venice.

So, they killed Mayer Sassoon and started a fire. The thoughts raced around Cal's brain. The Vatican *had* to be in some way responsible for these murders. The loan *had* been made under duress. There had *never* been an intention to repay it.

Then he checked himself. These weren't conclusions a professional historian ought to be making. These were working hypotheses at best. But in his gut he knew where the truth lay.

The giddy excitement of discovery rapidly gave way to a gloomy sense that those responsible for the fire had probably either stolen the loan contracts or torched them. What were his chances of finding them now?

Again, that faint rustling at the rear of the basement interrupted his thoughts. A foraging rodent, no doubt, but just in case he called for Mrs Gomes again. It was getting too late for her to come. He wondered if he ought to give her a call or better yet, a text, to let her know he'd be staying on, possibly until morning.

The business card with her mobile number was on her desk. He sat in her chair to compose the text. A few moments after he sent it he thought he heard a faint high-pitched sound from somewhere in the basement.

'Hello?'

He rose, ready to dismiss the sound as a product of his imagination, but when he heard it again he couldn't ignore it.

'Hello? Mrs Gomes, are you there?'

He began to head toward the elevator through a corridor of stacked file boxes from the 1890s when he noticed an entire shelf labeled in bold calligraphy.

Mr Wilkins – Materials for Restoration

The faint smell of smoke tickled his nostrils.

He was torn. Should he investigate the high-pitched sounds or the Wilkins shelf?

He chose the latter, pulling down a box at random. As soon as he opened it the nature of these materials became clear enough. There were batches of papers, all of them significantly more fire-damaged than the ones he'd encountered in the chronological stacks. Each document was protectively encased in its own acetate folder. Some pages were practically destroyed, some looked to be so brittle they might turn to dust with handling, others were more lightly affected. The archivist, Wilkins, had probably done a sort in the 1920s, triaging the damaged documents and filling several shelves with boxes of papers that were too fragile to remain in the stacks. But restoration work was time-consuming and expensive and he could well imagine that the Sassoons of Wilkin's era might have balked at the cost.

He delicately flipped through the acetates, looking to date the papers.

1827, 1838, 1852, 1858.

None were later than 1858, consistent with the account in *The Times*.

The papers weren't in strict chronological order but the shelf was ripe for exploration. Parking away any thoughts of the faint noises, he got a chair and began a systematic search.

It was eleven o'clock. He thought it would take an hour or two, to make it through the section. At twelve thirty he was still going when there was that rustling again. This time he completely ignored it and opened a new file box, this one positively reeking of old smoke.

And there it was, visible through the yellowing acetate, written in English in a thickly lettered script. He'd seen a copy of this document before, the loan contract he'd found in the Vatican Secret Archives.

Agreement between the Sassoon Bank of Rome and London and the Sancta Sedes for a Loan with a Face Value of Three Hundred Thousand Pounds Sterling

He couldn't contain his excitement.
'Yes!'
The triumphant shout filled the basement.

He hurried back to Gomes's desk with the folder and found a pair of tweezers in her desk drawer. When he extracted the first scorched page of the brittle contract from the acetate about an eighth of it crumbled away. The next page was only half-intact. He laid it next to the first page and read what he could. Then he extracted the third page. Two inches were missing from its bottom. The signatures of Claude Sassoon and Cardinal Antonelli were burned away.

This was worrisome but it wasn't a problem. He had already found an intact copy of the contract, complete with signatures.

But what of the annex?

The next page in the folder was only partially readable through the discolored acetate; he couldn't be sure what it was. Holding his breath, he tweezered it out. The bottom of this sheet was also scorched, and to his horror another inch disintegrated in front of his eyes as he set it upon the desk. But the upper parts of the paper were fine.

Then he read the bold header.

Setting Forward the Terms and Conditions of a Loan Between the Sassoon Bank and the Sancta Sedes

Cal would have pounded the desk in triumph if the brittle papers hadn't been there.

The annex was much longer than the underlying contract. He removed the sheets one by one; the state of damage varied significantly from page to page. One of the middle pages was all but destroyed with only a fragment intact. The penultimate page was also in terrible shape so he used the tweezers to take both remaining sheets out of the plastic together.

The make or break moment was here.

Peeling away the frail upper sheet he saw them.

Two pristine signatures: Claude Sassoon for the Sassoon Bank and Cardinal Giacomo Antonelli for the Holy See.

'Got you!' he exclaimed. 'Hell yes!'

It was nearly one fifteen in the morning, seven fifteen in Italy. From what he knew of the pope's habits, Celestine would be up and about but he decided to wait to break the news until a more businesslike hour.

It took several heart-stopping minutes to maneuver the brittle pages back into the folder but he needed more padding before transporting them. A quick rummage through Gomes's desk unearthed an old faculty directory from New York University of the right size to swallow the folder. He slipped it inside the directory and made his way to the elevator with a vision dancing in his head of the chilled half-bottle of vodka in the hotel mini-fridge.

It was the strangest sensation.

He always kept his hair on the longish side, over ears, over the collar. It was as if an intense jet of air parted the hair at his left temple. He instinctively raised his left hand to inspect the spot right after something slammed into the shelf just over his shoulder.

Confused, he wheeled around and saw a small black hole in a file box.

In his rebellious youth, Cal had found what he thought was a damn good way to irritate his parents and assert his independence. Instead of going straight to college after high school he joined the army, an experiment that had gone wrong almost from the first day. Even the army it seemed couldn't purge his fierce individuality. He stubbornly dug in and lasted for two years and might have made it longer had he not slugged a sergeant over his treatment of a vulnerable private. If Cal's father hadn't been friendly with a very influential Massachusetts senator, Cal would have earned a dishonorable discharge. That fate avoided, his next stop was Harvard College.

Even though his army days were twenty-five years in the past, some things stayed with him, like those vivid memories of live-fire drills and the terrifying sensation of rounds impacting all over the drill zone.

He hit the floor like he'd been trained all those years ago and when he was on his belly he slid the telephone directory under a bookshelf.

He was a sitting duck. Whoever was on the business end of the firearm had only to march over and this time he wouldn't miss.

So he sprang up and ran toward the front of the basement just as another round came from the direction of the elevator and thwocked into a stack of ledger books. He lost his traction trying to navigate a sharp turn at the end of a row of shelving and his shoulder hit a bookcase on the next row. The case rocked slightly and a book on a top shelf tumbled off. He kept running but his shoes, noisily slapping the floor, were a dead giveaway. He paused only long enough to kick them off before taking off on stockinged feet, doing a controlled slide at each turn.

There were gaps in the shelves every ten meters to allow for easy passage from one section to another. He used these gaps, zigging and zagging through the archive, trying to be unpredict-able, all the while listening for the chirp of the attacker's crepe soles. There were only two ways out – the elevator and the emer-gency stairs – both at the rear. He needed to get to the stairs but the shooter would know that. Could he make a 911 call while running? He brushed over his trousers pocket and didn't feel his phone.

He silently swore. He'd left it on the archivist's desk.

So he ran and slid, ran and slid.

From the sound of the shooter's squealing soles, Cal could tell the guy was a calculating bastard. He was sticking toward the rear of the building to block his exit, probably roaming the ends of the rows to try to catch a line of sight. Each time Cal slid into a new row he glanced toward the rear. If he saw the attacker he'd have to dive through a gap to the next row.

He was on autonomic overdrive. His heart was thumping. He was panting like a hot dog. It was only a matter of time before he picked the wrong row at the wrong time and a chunk of lead took him down. Playing defense wouldn't save his skin.

He had to shift to offense.

He came to a sliding halt and listened for the chirping shoes. He heard nothing for several seconds; the shooter was probably listening too. Then there was a squeak to his left so he shot the gap to his right.

His feet caught on something.

He was flying.

Picking himself up he looked back to see what tripped him.

It was an outstretched arm.

Gomes was lying in a puddle of blood, her mobile phone among the spilled contents of her handbag

There was no point in checking her. Her head wound was catastrophic.

He didn't panic.

He got angry.

All this poor woman had done was go out of her way to be helpful to a colleague and for that her life had been snuffed out.

Ever since he was a boy, when someone crossed him he didn't stop until he got even. Pity the schoolyard bully. Cal was the vigilante kid protecting the pipsqueak, sending the bully off with a split lip. He'd never outgrown it. Maybe it wasn't professorial. Maybe it wasn't Christian. But in his book, assholes had to pay.

There was a new sound.

Books hitting the floor.

The guy was pushing them off shelves to make himself shooting windows.

But these sounds were easier to localize than his squealing shoes.

Cal took off in a run, heading straight for him.

The thudding stopped as he got closer.

He slowed and hesitantly passed through a gap. There was no shooter but a pile of books on the floor under a partially cleared out shoulder-high shelf.

Then Cal coughed.

Not an involuntary cough, a purposeful one.

He edged closer to the shooting window and coughed again.

Two points made a line. He was declaring the direction of his movement.

There was a soft chirp from the man's shoes, then another coming from the other side of the bookcases. He was going to set up at the window he'd created and when Cal moved past it he'd be a fat target at a shooting gallery.

Cal stopped dead and listened, trying to pinpoint the attacker's exact position. When he thought he had it, he moved as far away from the bookcase as the narrow corridor would allow then charged the case with the blind anger of a skewered bull going for a matador. He possessed a fraction of the mass as a bull but just as much rage.

The tall bookcase was firmly grounded but he kept pressing forward well after his shoulder made contact, getting the case up on to its rear set of feet. At the tipping point, the contents of the shelves began to rain down until the case lightened enough for Cal to be able to finish the job.

It fell with a crash that intermingled with another sound.

A high-pitched shout and then a low *ugghhh*.

Cal ran to the end of the row and circled around to get a look at the toppled case and the mound of books underneath it.

He began digging through the pile, trying to get to the shooter before he could free himself.

The pistol, a semiautomatic with a long suppressor threaded on to the barrel, was lying under a pile of ledger books. He picked it up and backed away when he saw the pile begin to move.

'Stay down,' Cal shouted. 'I've got your gun. I swear I'll use it.'

The pile kept shifting, books and file boxes falling away as the man tried to stand.

With a final push, a bald head emerged through the toppled shelving, then a shoulder, then an arm, then a hand clutching another pistol, this one a snub-nosed revolver.

Cal fired until the clip was empty, a long run of muffled eighth notes, turning the man's head into pulp.

EIGHTEEN

A t five a.m. Cal was still waiting for that chilled vodka but he had moved on and he was now fixated on coffee instead. One of the crime-scene investigators told him that the nearest Starbucks opened in half an hour.

Dawn wouldn't break for two hours on the day he'd killed someone. It wasn't the most glorious of feelings.

He'd been consigned to the archivist's desk as detectives, uniformed officers, and forensics people buzzed around. The lead homicide detective from the 19th precinct, a sleepy-looking guy with a drooping moustache and a cigarette voice named Gonzalez, stopped by every so often asking follow-on questions to his initial interview.

Gail Sassoon had arrived on the heels of the police. Cal hadn't thought to call her; she was on file as the bank's official contact in the case of an emergency. He had been impressed by a couple of things, first that she'd sobered up so efficiently considering how smashed she'd been, and second, how well-put-together she looked for someone yanked out of bed at two in the morning. When she arrived she went into full lawyer mode, hovering over Cal protec-tively, zealously representing the bank's interests, and personally calling Consuela Gomes's husband to offer support and arranging for a bank employee to stay with the children so he could come to the scene.

After a prolonged absence Gail reappeared with two cups of coffee from the office machine. 'Hanging in there?' she asked him.

He thanked her and took a long, grateful sip. 'Better now. Any idea how much longer they want me here?'

'Shouldn't be long,' she said. 'One of our people finally came in and unlocked the security closet. The detectives are upstairs reviewing the closed-circuit cameras. Once that's done, I'm sure they'll have everything they need.'

'To prove I'm not a murderer?'

'I think what happened is pretty clear even without the cameras. The police know this was self-defense.'

'The why it happened isn't so clear,' he said.

'Once they've identified the body hopefully a motive should come into focus.' She sipped at her cup and said, 'You know, I didn't ask you. Did you find it? The contract?'

He opened Gomes's upper desk drawer and gently removed the acetate folder from the university directory.

She smiled for the first time since arriving. 'You *did* find it!'

'It was in a shelf of material for restoration. There was a fire in the mid-nineteenth century, when the bank was based in London. In the 1920s your first archivist, Conrad Wilkins, set aside partially burned documents for a conservator. That's where I found the annex. It was damaged.'

'What about the signature page?'

'It's readable.'

'Show me.'

'Now?'

'Please.'

He tweezered out the pages for her inspection.

'Look, Cal, I can't speak to the validity of a contract of this age with these kinds of jurisdictional, provenance, and I expect, myriad legal issues, but purely from the viewpoint of its complete-ness with a clear execution by lender and lendee, it's got a shot at being valid and enforceable.'

Detective Gonzalez appeared. It looked like he had found the same coffee machine upstairs.

'OK, Mr Donovan, it looks like the security cameras support your version,' he said, dragging out his words so slowly it drove Cal crazy. 'You're either lucky to be alive or you're one smart cookie, the way you ran through the place under fire.'

'Mostly lucky,' Cal said.

'So there won't be any charges?' Gail asked.

'Open and shut. Self-defense,' Gonzalez said. 'That's what I'll put in my report. The district attorney will have a look but I wouldn't lose any sleep. The cameras tell the story.'

Cal nodded in weary relief. 'Still, I've got to live with what I did.'

'Get over it, is my advice,' Gonzalez said, bluntly. 'This prick walked right up to Mrs Gomes and shot her in the face. Then he takes her watch and her wallet.'

'The poor woman,' Gail gasped.

'What time did it happen?' Cal asked.

'Just before ten according to the time log. You returned at a quarter past ten so you just missed it.'

'But that means he waited almost three hours,' Cal said. 'What the hell was he doing?'

'Not a lot from what I could see on the footage. He was hanging out by the elevator mostly, biding his time by the looks of it.'

'But whatever did he want?' Gail asked. 'There's nothing of any intrinsic value down here.'

'Let me tell you folks something: not all criminals are brainy. This guy probably saw Mrs Gomes coming in late. He sees the word bank on your plaque. He thinks to himself, banks have money. Maybe she didn't close the front door properly. Maybe he just pushed in after her. The front door closes real slow. Did you know that? And you should also know that there's something wrong with the camera on that door. You should have it fixed. Anyway, he follows her into the basement where he kills her. We see him looking around until he hears you returning after your dinner and then he hides, waiting to see what's what. All he knows is that the place is full of papers, not the green folding kind. Eventually he gets tired of waiting and decides to do to you what he did to her.'

'Who is he, do you know?' Cal asked.

'No ID, none whatsoever. We'll have to wait on fingerprints. A guy like this is bound to have priors.'

'So you think it was just a crime of opportunity and he was just a petty thief?' Cal asked.

'Unless something else surfaces, yeah, I do.'

'He had a suppressor on his pistol,' Cal said. 'What kind of petty thief walks around with that kind of gear?'

'This is New York. I've been working homicides for a long time. Nothing amazes me anymore. Well almost nothing. Ninety-nine times out of a hundred, a civilian's going to call it a silencer. How come you know the correct terminology?'

'I was in the army.'

'Oh yeah? See any action?'

'Only in the bars around Fort Campbell.'

'Shit, I was in the Airborne too, man,' the detective said, extending his arm.

'You might not want to shake my hand,' Cal said. 'I got tossed out for punching my sergeant.'

Gonzalez shook it anyway.

'Shit, I could tell from the cameras you were a brawler. I didn't think professors were tough guys.'

'Depends on their department.'

'Oh yeah? What's yours?'

'Religion.'

Cal slept through the afternoon and well into the evening. When he awoke, his hotel suite was already dark. Momentarily disoriented, the events of the night came back to him fast and hard. Standing in front of the coffee station and mini-bar, he considered his options and went for the vodka.

By the time he'd showered, a note had been slipped under his door. He had turned his mobile off and put the hotel phone on do not disturb so Gail had resorted to a hand-delivered message. The message was an invitation to a dinner at her apartment. Marcus would be there. They had a lot to discuss, she wrote.

He texted her. That's when he saw he had a bunch of voicemails.

Switching to coffee, he made a few calls then dressed for dinner. Before he left he opened the room safe one more time to lay eyes on the contract.

At least something good had come out of this awful day.

He walked to the Sassoons through the first snow showers of the season, cutting over to Park Avenue through residential streets, their townhouses decorated with strings of lights and wreaths in a last, post-Christmas gasp before January broke the spell and winter became just winter.

A butler greeted the private elevator that stopped inside the residence and took Cal's snow-dusted coat and scarf. The dinner party of five was dwarfed by the grand sitting room that was designed for huge gatherings. Henry looked spent and droopy in his wheelchair, laboring over every sentence. Marcus kept his conversation to the bare minimum. Marcus's wife, one of those women who had spoiled her natural good looks with too much surgery, said nothing at all beyond her initial 'Oh hello.' It fell upon Gail and Cal to keep things flowing. Over a white burgundy they recapped the traumas of the previous night.

'Did the police contact you today?' Gail asked.

'I had a message from Detective Gonzalez. I got his voicemail when I returned it,' Cal replied.

'They only finished up at the bank a few hours ago. I spoke with him when he left.'

'What did he say?' Cal asked.

She had a perplexed expression. 'Apparently, the killer's fingerprints weren't in any state or federal database. Also, all his clothes appeared to be brand new.'

'That doesn't make me feel warm and fuzzy,' Cal said. 'When I talk to him I'm going to suggest he check the fingerprints with Interpol.'

'Why?' Henry asked.

'Just to be thorough. In case this wasn't a crime of opportunity, as Gonzalez called it.'

'You? You think he was – after you?' Henry rasped. 'Why?'

'Isn't it obvious?' Gail said. 'The contract. Who else knows about it, Cal?'

'From what I understand, very few, but the Vatican's never been good at keeping secrets. It's more like a colander than a pot.'

Gail noticed that her husband was crying and asked what was wrong.

It was hard for him to get it out. 'I can't stop – thinking about her. Consuela Gomes was – a lovely woman,' he said. 'We must take care of – her family.'

Gail got up to dab at his eyes. 'Of course we will.'

'What will we do without her?' Henry asked.

'I don't know why we needed an archivist in the first place,' Marcus said, his tone as cold as the winter night. Cal caught his silent wife flinching.

Henry breathed the word, 'Legacy.'

'I don't know what kind of return on investment you're expecting by keeping ledger books from 1899 and paying someone to catalogue more paper than the regulators require,' Marcus said.

Gail asked if Cal would answer as a historian.

He took the bait. 'I've found that sometimes the most mundane documents are the ones that shed the brightest light on key moments in history. So you never know. It's a mistake to preserve documents selectively and it's a disaster to not preserve them at all. Carefully archive them all and you serve the future best. I applaud your efforts.'

'Well said,' Henry puffed. 'Thank you.'

Gail thanked him too and Marcus grunted something unintelligible. 'Cal, before we go through to dinner,' she said, 'could you tell us about the marvelous discoveries you made before you were attacked?'

His glass of wine had been refilled; he hadn't seen the butler sneaking up on it. He sipped at it and said, 'Other than that, how did you enjoy the play, Mrs Lincoln?'

Henry laughed and began to choke. Everything came to a halt while the nurse who was on call, waiting in the kitchen, was summoned to wheel him away for suctioning.

Henry's color restored, to its baseline gray, he returned and begged to be spared further humor.

'I do better with grief – than mirth,' he said.

'You have my word,' Cal said. 'What happened last night was awful and what happened a hundred sixty years ago was awful too. What I'm piecing together is a depressing story that went well beyond the kidnapping and extortion at the heart of the loan. Your ancestors were murdered; their property was set on fire. My best guess – and it's only a guess – is that this was a concerted effort to erase all knowledge of the loan. When the perpetrators were done with their dirty work, it was as if the loan never existed.'

When Cal finished describing the body of evidence, Gail asked, 'Was the Vatican behind these atrocities?'

'I found nothing directly implicating Vatican officials. But we have a letter from Cardinal Lambruschini to Cardinal Antonelli, proposing that this duke, Duke Tizziani, help them, quote-unquote, deal with these bankers in Venice and in their foreign offices. So the presumption has to be that the Vatican did play at least some role in orchestrating the affair.'

'But even so,' Gail said, 'the contract was sitting in the archive all along.'

'Fire-damaged but largely intact,' Cal said. 'We don't know how it survived and why Claude Sassoon's successor didn't pursue a claim for payment. But here we are. I would have brought it over tonight to show everybody but it's in a fragile state.'

'It's our property, goddamn it!' Marcus shouted.

His wife finally spoke. 'Marcus, please!'

Gail jumped in. 'I asked Cal to hold on to it,' she said. 'He's going to recommend a restoration expert.'

'I've got an appointment with someone tomorrow morning, at a company that does a lot of work for the Met,' he said. 'They'll photograph it and keep it in their safe. I'll provide you with an estimate for the work.'

Marcus fidgeted in his chair, looking like he wanted to get up and leave.

Henry adjusted his oxygen prongs and said, 'Marcus, what the hell's – bugging you. You look mightily – pissed off.'

'I'll tell you what's the matter,' his cousin fumed. 'We're all sitting here seriously contemplating doing business with these bastards at the Vatican, the same gang of thieves that killed our relatives and stole our money.'

'It was a long time ago,' Gail said.

'That's no excuse,' Marcus said. 'I say we get a copy of the contract to our lawyers and send these bastards a demand letter.'

Henry hit the arm of his wheelchair with the heel of his hand and labored to spit this out. 'No. We're going to – talk to them. Gail will be the point person. You can participate – in the process or you can choose – not to. I have the majority. We're going to do this – my way.'

It was like throwing a match into a barrel of gunpowder. Marcus flew out of his chair and demanded his wife come with him.

'Always your damn majority,' he shouted. 'It was the same thing in 1858. You saw the letter. My side of the family was supposed to have an equal say in things. That never happened, did it? You've never known what it feels like to play second fiddle, Henry. I'll tell you what it feels like. It stinks.'

Henry began to cough and barely managed to tell his cousin to calm down before the nurse had to be called again. By the time she'd finished attending to his secretions and brought him back in, Marcus and his wife had left.

Cal had been squirming as the family drama played out but he brushed off Gail's apologies.

'I think everyone's been under stress,' he said.

'You were the one who was almost killed,' she said. 'Marcus's behavior was unacceptable.'

'I agree,' Henry said.

'I'm glad you're still willing to talk to the Vatican,' Cal said. 'I was able to speak with the pope's private secretary. Celestine has invited us to meet with him to discuss his ideas for a foundation.'

'When?' Gail asked.

'Ideally, in the next day or two. He's very concerned about leaks.'

The butler whispered to Gail that dinner was served and that he had reduced the number of place settings.

She rose to push her husband's chair and said to Cal, 'Unless you're right and there's already been a leak.'

Henry told them that his private jet was at their disposal. 'But see if you can get Marcus – back in the fold,' he said. 'I wish I hadn't – pulled rank on him again. Smooth it over with him, Gail. Smooth it over.'

Marcus Sassoon lived on the Upper West Side, on the opposite side of Central Park from his cousin, with high, sweeping views over the treetops. He could stand in his living room with a glass of scotch in his hand and see his cousin's building. There was a fine brass telescope on a wooden tripod in one corner of the living room. Personally, he had never used it to get a bead on Henry's windows, although his son had used it to spy in the past and was doing so now.

'I wish you wouldn't do that,' Marcus said. 'You're acting like a peeping Tom.'

Albert persisted. 'Wouldn't you like to know if Gail is having it off with Donovan?'

'She *was* giving him the eye,' his father allowed. 'Henry's no use to her anymore.'

'Was she drunk?'

'Not when we left but the night was young.'

Albert tired of looking at pulled curtains. He flopped on a sofa. 'So what are you going to do?' he asked.

'I'll probably go to Rome with them, if only to look after our interests as best I can. I'll be searching for ways to scuttle a deal, of course. But as long as Henry owns fifty-two percent, there's nothing I *can* do.'

'He's not a well man,' Albert said, amused at the understatement.

'Don't go there. He's still my cousin.'

'Touching. I wonder if he's got the same soft spot you have. I wonder if he's going to come through with a transfer of shares in his will.'

Marcus knocked back his scotch. 'He's been promising it for

years. Our side and his, you and Julian – equal partners going forward.'

'Steven will be pissed.'

'I've taken care of your brother in my estate. But he's going to have to work for you or make his way at another firm. You hit the firstborn lottery.'

'I'm happy you're a traditionalist.'

'You should be.'

Albert reached for a handful of potato chips and stuffed them in his mouth. 'I think we should send the contract to a good lawyer. Not Bob Stein. He'll tell Gail. Someone we haven't used before so it won't get back to her.'

'What's the point?'

'If this foundation idea gets shit-canned, like you just said, then the Vatican's going to get an army of lawyers to say the contract isn't worth crap. We need to be ready with our own lawyers to say it's pure gold.'

'That's not a stupid idea,' Marcus said.

Albert snorted. 'High praise coming from you.'

'It's a good thing you got in touch with me,' Cal's mother said. 'Gail Sassoon sent me a message on Facebook that she'd met you the day before yesterday. I would have been cross if you'd given me the slip.'

Cal had taken her to one of her usual luncheon haunts in midtown; it was no use hauling her off to somewhere new. She would have complained about the food or the service or the taste of her cocktail and he would have been miserable.

'It was an unplanned visit,' he said.

'Well, I was delighted you've connected with her. She's a fabulous lady. Very charitable. Her husband's ill, you know.'

'I met him.'

Bess took the cocktail straw from her mouth. Her drink was a green concoction that looked unappealing. 'Really?' she said. 'He's a recluse, especially now. How did you manage to see him?'

'Over dinner at their place last night.'

'Well, aren't you the anointed one? What's the connection? You're not exactly into high finance.'

'Unfortunately I can't talk about it.'

'Well, that makes me very, very curious. I won't pry but I do expect to get a full accounting of the story one fine day.'

She seemed to be in a cheery mood. Whatever was in her cocktail was making her giddy. It was a shame he had to bring her down.

'You haven't seen the news today, have you?' he asked.

'I read the paper, why?'

By the paper, he knew she meant her bible, the *New York Times*, her breakfast companion since the beginning of time. The story had broken too late for the print edition.

He steeled himself with a sip of his straightforward vodka on the rocks. 'I wanted to see you in person before I went back to Rome tonight.'

'You were just there!'

'And now I'm going back. I'll be going with Gail.'

'My, my, how mysterious can you get?'

'In this case, pretty damn mysterious. But here's the thing. You're going to read a story about me, or a friend of yours is going to call you about it.'

She finally seemed to notice that he was looking deathly serious. Her smile evaporated. 'Cal, what's going on?'

'I killed a man the night before last.'

They played telephone tag right up to the point that he was about to board the Sassoon Gulfstream jet at Teterboro Airport.

'I hear you're leaving the country,' Detective Gonzalez said.

'In a few minutes. That's not a problem, is it?'

'No, you can go about your business. I just wanted to have a quick word with you about the dead guy.'

'I heard from the Sassoons that you couldn't identify him.'

'That's right. So far, we haven't.'

'Have you checked with Interpol?'

'You're a detective too?'

'I've seen a lot of movies.'

'Well, as a matter of fact, we have checked with Interpol, Europol, you name it. Nothing yet. But what I wanted to ask you was this: besides the Sassoons, who else knew you were going to be at the archives?'

'Mrs Gomes, of course.'

'Yeah. Anyone else?'

'Not specifically.'

'OK, who knew you were in New York?'

'That's a longer list. Several people at the university, a few people at the Vatican.'

'I'm going to need names and contact numbers.'

'It sounds like you're coming off your theory that it was a crime of opportunity,' Cal said.

'Just trying to be thorough. Like in the movies.'

'I'll email you a list of people from the plane. Are you going to be calling all of them?'

The tone was borderline sarcastic. 'That's a fair assumption.'

'Well, when you speak to Pope Celestine, give him my regards.'

NINETEEN

'**D**o you like it?' Gail asked Cal.

She was talking about the airplane. The Gulfstream G550 was one of the bank's toys, as she would call it before becoming self-conscious and justifying it as an essential business tool. It was configured for thirteen passengers but there were only three in the cabin plus an attendant, a fresh-faced young man seated by the galley with a magazine, patiently awaiting a summons.

Cal and Gail sat side by side on a white leather sofa in the rear. Marcus Sassoon was in a front-facing seat by the cabin nursing a soda. The only way he could have set himself farther away would have been to sit on the pilot's lap.

'It's pretty sweet,' Cal said. 'Beats flying commercial.'

They were cruising over a darkening Atlantic through a pastel, twilight sky. She was wearing a clingy skirt that kept her occupied pulling on the hem every time it took a ride. Cal noticed but pretended he didn't.

'I understand you like the finer things in life,' she said.

The comment floored him. 'Now how would you know that?'

'I did my research,' she said, waving her empty fluted glass to catch the attention of the steward. He promptly poured more champagne and asked Cal if he wanted another vodka.

'I won't say no.'

She took a sip of champagne. 'I found an interview you did with the *Times* for the launch of one of your books.'

'Oh, God, I remember that one. I was goaded into giving a list of the creature comforts I enjoyed. The book was on asceticism in the medieval Catholic Church. Get the angle? Once that stuff goes online it's there forever.'

She had memorized the list. 'Great hotels, great restaurants, first-class travel, a fine home library, a few nice pieces of art.'

'You saw the article's title,' he said. '*A Harvard Professor's Tour-de-Force on Ascetics*, and it's subtitle: *Guess what? He Isn't One*. I was toast with my colleagues.'

'I'll bet you were, especially those who couldn't begin to afford your lifestyle.'

'Jesus, Gail, did you get hold of my bank statements too?'

She laughed. 'No, that's from your mother. She told me you inherited a sizable trust fund when your father died.'

'Wonderful,' he said ruefully. 'Consider me an open book.'

She was getting tipsy and the flight was in its infancy. 'Oh, don't be mad. My only intent was to try to understand you.'

'Understand what?'

'Your motivation in all of this. What do you expect to get out of it?'

He thought for a few moments before speaking. It was a fair enough question. He expected that in the world she came from, money was the great motivator. His comfortable financial position must have confused her.

'Let me tell you what I don't expect,' he began. 'I don't expect any financial reward. None whatsoever.'

'I hardly thought you did.'

'Good. Just wanted to make that clear. I'll be frank with you. My reasons for getting involved with this are twofold. The history of the Vatican's borrowing and usury laws interest me. I've written about it and one day I'd like to write about the history of the Sassoon debt. I think it would make a terrific book. That's what I do. I write books that pretty much no one reads.'

'I'd read it.'

He smiled. 'One guaranteed pre-order. The other reason is that I consider Pope Celestine to be a friend. He asked for my help. You help friends whether they're popes or drinking buddies.'

'Now that would be an even more interesting book.'

'What's that?'

'The pope and the professor.'

'Don't hold your breath on that one.'

Marcus unbuckled his seatbelt and was making his way to the rear lavatory when he clearly succumbed to an urge to be snarky.

'Your glass is full, Gail,' he said. 'That's not like you.'

'Charming as ever, Marcus.'

'My middle name.'

She waited for the lavatory door to close before apologizing to Cal for having to bear captive witness to their family dynamics.

'What family doesn't have its issues?' he said. 'I don't think he's a happy camper.'

She polished off her drink in three gulps and asked for a refill. 'I imagine it hasn't been easy being a thin-skinned asshole who's been Henry's butt-boy his entire life.'

Cal wished he could retreat to one of the oversized chairs in the middle of the cabin and pull out a book from his bag. But he'd probably have to wait until Gail drank herself to sleep.

'Blessedly, I was an only child,' he said.

'I was too,' she said. 'That makes us quite the brats if you didn't know.'

As they waited in the reception area of the Sanctae Marthae guesthouse, Cal could see the look of confusion on Marcus Sassoon's face.

'What's the matter?' Cal asked.

'This is where he lives?' Marcus said. 'It's pretty damned basic.'

'He's a humble man,' Cal said.

'Or a con man putting on a show.'

Gail angrily shushed him. 'Marcus, please. Someone will hear.'

'I'm just stating the obvious,' Marcus said defensively.

They had spent the morning at the hotel the Sassoons had booked. Cal wasn't surprised at the choice. The Excelsior on the Via Veneto had been a go-to place for visiting executives and celebrities for a century. It wasn't exactly his cup of tea but he went along for solidarity and besides, they were picking up the tab.

After a morning rest the three of them had met in the lobby. Before leaving New York, Cal had picked up one of the suits he kept stashed at his mother's place. Gail, dressed in a conservative suit herself, had whispered to Cal that he cleaned up good.

'I hope Celestine recognizes me,' Cal had said. 'I'm not usually this done-up when I visit.'

Now, sitting in reception, Cal was loosening the knot of his necktie, his least favorite and least-worn item of clothing.

'You'll be able to judge the man for yourself,' Cal told Marcus. 'And if you want to see some of the more salubrious places in the Vatican, I can give you a tour later.'

'Been there, done it,' Marcus replied.

'When was that?'

'I took a year off between college and business school, got a Eurorail ticket. You know the drill.'

The drill. Saw the Vatican once. Check. Cal held his tongue. The decision-makers were Gail and her husband. At worst, Marcus needed to be neutralized, not antagonized.

'Well, the offer's on the table,' Cal said.

The pope's man, Monsignor Moller, arrived to escort the group to the pontiff's office. Along the way, he whispered to Cal that the Holy Father had been told about the violence that had occurred at the Sassoon archive and wished to speak with him privately after the meeting. Inside his office, a smiling Celestine was standing in front of his desk, awaiting them.

'Greetings,' he said. 'So good of you to come. I hope your journey was pleasant.'

Gail genuflected and said, 'Holy Father,' somewhat in awe. Marcus coolly shook his hand as he would any business adversary. The pope took both of Cal's hands, made a small joke about the frequent-flier miles he must be accumulating, then quietly told him he was glad he was safe.

The pope took a padded, high-backed chair and the others sat in a semi-circle around him. Monsignor Moller, clutching his ubiquitous notebook, was making his way toward the corner when the pope informed him that he didn't need to attend the meeting. With a flash of surprise and a small bow of his head, Moller retreated.

Cal had wondered how the pope would begin the discussion. The answer was with humility.

'I must tell you,' Celestine said, 'few things surprise me. The papacy is an old institution, the Vatican is a well-worn bureaucracy, and human nature is older still. And yet, Professor Donovan succeeded in unearthing this great surprise about the unpaid debt to your family. I want to begin with a heartfelt apology for the actions of the Vatican nearly two centuries ago that brought tragedy to your ancestors.'

Gail was visibly moved and had to pull a tissue from her bag. Even Marcus seemed affected on some level, his lower lip trembling, although his emotion might have been anger.

Gail said she spoke for the entire family. 'On behalf of the chairman of the bank, my husband Henry, who was too ill to fly to Rome, we are grateful for your kind words, Your Holiness.'

'Please pass my blessings to Mr Sassoon. The professor has told me about his illness. I will pray for him.' The pope paused as if to consider how he would broach the essence of the discussion. 'With accumulated interest, the debt to your bank is now a great sum of money,' he said. 'Now, one might imagine, as the head of the Vatican, that I would have a fiduciary responsibility to act in the best financial interest of the institution. My lawyers have advised me that there are many persuasive legal arguments that may be put forward that would have the effect of rendering the collection of this debt highly improbable. Probably long after all of us in this room are gone, the case would remain under litigation in the courts. But as you know, I regard this debt as providential. I do not wish to dispute it. I wish to embrace it. I see it as a tool to move the Church closer to its charitable roots as articulated in the Gospels.'

'With all due respect,' Marcus said, 'twenty-five billion euros is a great deal of money. Do you have twenty-five billion euros in cash and marketable securities? How would you make payment?'

The pope sighed loudly, likely for effect. 'The Church as a whole is a wealthy institution, although much of its wealth lies within individual dioceses of which the Vatican has no ownership. The Vatican itself is wealthy but not as cash-rich as many believe. Even I cannot get an accurate picture of exactly how much liquidity the Vatican possesses but it is certainly less than the magnitude of the debt we are discussing today. And in any event, I cannot drain us dry. We have important work to do on the international stage, we have employees, pension obligations. Well, I don't have to tell the Sassoons anything about the ongoing needs of complex organizations. So, should I elect to satisfy this debt it would require raising substantial additional funds.'

'How?' Marcus asked.

'I apologize for Marcus,' Gail said, her face flushed with embarrassment. 'He can be quite direct.'

'It's quite all right,' Celestine said. 'I appreciate the quality of directness and candor. I believe, Mr Sassoon, that we have the means to satisfy the obligation to your family.'

'A Jewish family,' Marcus said, tartly.

'A Jewish family,' Celestine said. 'You are not mistaken. Your faith is not immaterial given the history of your people and mine. Even as pope I would lack the moral authority to satisfy this debt as a purely commercial transaction with a transfer of funds from the Vatican to your firm. But if the funds were to go to charity to satisfy the core principles upon which the Church was built, then I believe I could persuade my colleagues and more importantly, my flock. What do you think?'

Gail agreed, saying, 'Through my own foundation work I've found that altruism is a quality that can bring us together. Giving nurtures the soul and makes people feel better about themselves.'

'Yes, yes,' the pope said, gently rocking forward and back in his seat. 'Professor, what is your opinion?'

'As long as the charitable work isn't deemed to be overtly political, I think most people – certainly not all, but most – will rally behind the venture. One could argue that politics, not the Devil, is the root of all evil.'

Celestine laughed. 'Of course this is completely true,' he said. 'The Devil could learn from politicians. That is why the foundation I am contemplating, and which I would like to discuss with you, would serve all the peoples of the world without respect to their religion, ethnicity, or nationality. Catholics do not live in a vacuum. They are citizens of the world. If the world becomes a better, more humane place, their lives will be enriched even if many of them will not be among the direct beneficiaries. As I see it, the common denominators for the goals of this foundation would be the alleviation of poverty, strife, and desperation. We should wish to lift people from their despair and deliver kindness and charity.'

'Not to mention twenty-five billion euros,' Marcus added.

'True, Mr Sassoon,' the pope said. 'Good intentions alone do not put food in people's stomachs, roofs over their heads, medicines in their bodies. Ideally, this well-funded foundation would sow seeds that would keep bearing fruit long into the future to change lives for the better not only today but also tomorrow. But surely, Mrs Sassoon, you are an expert in these matters.' He reached for the stack of papers on his desk. Celestine showed the sheaf to Gail – printouts of press releases and news articles about the Sassoon Foundation. 'I've done my research,' he said. 'You seem to do excellent work. I believe that as a lawyer and a philanthropist you would be an ideal partner.'

Her cheeks were already flushed but pride made them even redder. She told him she had always wished she could do more.

'I imagine you could do a lot more with twenty-five billion euros,' Cal said helpfully.

'We have done some research. This would be the third-best endowed foundation in the world,' the pope said, 'closely behind the Bill and Melinda Gates Foundation and the INGKA Foundation established by the Swedish family that owns IKEA stores. We could do some marvelous good, in my opinion.'

Marcus grimaced as a way of previewing his concerns. 'Assuming we went along with this, how would the governance work? Who'd control what? Who'd choose the trustees and the administrators? Where would it be based? How would the investment decisions be made?'

The pope, who had been leaning forward, sat back and folded his hands over his cassock. 'These are all relevant technical questions, Mr Sassoon. I am ignorant in the mechanics of foundations but I am sure we can find experts who might assist us in creating a strong framework. All decisions would have to be reached mutually. The purpose of this meeting is to see if the Vatican and the Sassoon family might agree on a broad concept of cooperation. If so, we can decide on next steps.'

Gail nodded vigorously. 'In the brief time since Professor Donovan reached out to us, my husband and I have talked at length. Henry and I are in agreement. We want to proceed and take the conversation forward. We are enthusiastic.'

'Marvelous news,' the pope said, 'truly marvelous. In that case I would like to share with you the name that I thought we might call this foundation, subject to your approval, of course. I thought the Interfaith Fund for Humanity captures the essence of the credo.'

Gail warmly endorsed it, letting 'the IFH' trip off her tongue.

Marcus, however, clearly felt the pope needed to know that all was not sweetness and light in Sassoon land. 'My cousin is the chairman of the firm and he has a controlling interest but I would be remiss if I didn't express some concerns.'

'Please, Mr Sassoon,' the pope said. 'I value your input.'

'I am deeply concerned about anti-Semitism,' Marcus said. 'Many will say that it's the Jews' fault that the Vatican had to sell off assets. They'll say that we could have forgiven the debt. Personally, I think this could get very ugly.'

'I am not naive,' the pope said. 'There will be plenty of criticism to go around but I will make it known that I was the one to insist on repayment provided that a foundation was the beneficiary. Surely my fellow Catholics will be divided in their opinions. Some will agree with my intentions. Others will see this as a betrayal of our traditions. But let me say this: I am prepared for the slings and arrows. I will gladly martyr myself on the altar of charity and mercy.'

When the meeting was over, Monsignor Moller was summoned to lead Gail and Marcus back to the reception area so Cal and the pope could have a chat.

'I wanted to express my concern, Professor,' Celestine said. 'Moller passed along what happened to you the other evening. To take a life is a horrible event but if you had not, I would have lost my friend. God has already forgiven you.'

Cal thanked him and admitted that he remained shaken.

'Tell me,' the pope asked. 'Do you share my concern that this attack upon your life might have been related to your search for the loan contract?'

'I'm afraid I do.'

'Then you must be very careful, Professor. I would never be able to forgive myself if you came to harm because of your kindness in assisting me.'

'I promise I'll be careful, Your Holiness.'

'Please reinforce with the Sassoons the necessity of keeping our conversations private. There will be elements inside the Church and outside who will not want us to succeed. I will try to confine the knowledge of our plans to the smallest possible circle of confidants.'

'The Vatican has never been leak-proof,' Cal said.

'Indeed not. Tell me, what are your plans? Will you finally be able to return home?'

'Tomorrow morning. The Sassoons are going to drop me in Boston on their way back to New York. I've got a new semester coming up, lectures to prepare, papers to write.' He noticed the pope's mouth open at the last item on his to-do-list. 'Don't worry, I won't be writing a paper about the Sassoon debt just yet.'

Marcus blew off dinner plans in favor of room service but Cal agreed to join Gail in the restaurant at the Excelsior. She was buoyant about meeting the pope and hadn't come down from her cloud. Sampling the champagne the sommelier had recommended, she told him the only thing that would have made the day even better would have been posting a photo of her with the pope on her Facebook page.

Cal repeated the admonitions about confidentiality but added, 'If this deal closes, you're going to have more publicity than you'll know how to handle. This is going to be big, Gail. You sure you're going to enjoy the hot light of celebrity?'

'I guess I'll find out but I think I'll be fine. Of course Marcus believes it will be bad for the family and bad for business.'

'It's possible he may be right, no?'

'We'll see. Marcus is a difficult man but he's smart. But the way I look at it, the IFH is bigger than the bank. It would be a chance to do philanthropy on a truly global scale. Hopefully the positives will outweigh the negatives. Henry won't live forever. It will be his legacy.'

'And yours.'

'And mine.'

'What about your son? What's his take likely to be?'

'Julian will support his father, even if the bank's business suffers in the short term. I'm not even certain he's going to want to join the firm when he graduates. He's more of a Silicon Valley than a Wall Street type of kid. Hopefully you'll meet him one day.'

'Hopefully.'

'So, Cal,' she said, after putting a dent in her drink. 'Will I be seeing you again soon?'

He knew this was coming. 'You know, I think my work here is done, as they say. I was happy to facilitate this, despite what happened the other night. But I've got a day job and it's time to get stuck back into it.'

She reached across the table and touched his hand. 'No time for your personal life?'

He didn't exactly pull his hand away. It was more like a gentle retreat.

'I think it's best if we kept this professional.'

She found another use for her hand, curling it around her champagne glass.

'Oh well,' she sighed. 'I wanted to meet the pope, I wanted this foundation to get off the ground, and I wanted you. Two out of three isn't bad. Will you do something for me?'

'What's that?'

'Come to the bar with me. I don't want to drink alone tonight.'

Marcus was seated at a table in his suite, eating chicken and watching CNN, when the doorbell rang.

'I don't want housekeeping,' he shouted.

The bell rang again.

'Can't you see my do not disturb sign?'

There was a third ring.

Disgusted he got up and opened the door, ready to give the housekeeper a good dressing-down.

The thin, distinguished man standing there was dressed in black clerical robes accented by red trim and a red sash.

'I am terribly sorry to disturb you, Mr Sassoon, but I think we need to talk. My name is Cardinal Pascal Lauriat. I am the Vatican secretary of state.'

Cal lost track of several things. The number of vodkas he put away at the hotel bar. How he made it through the lobby to the elevator. Whether he offered any resistance. The time.

When he opened his eyes the first thing he saw were three glowing numbers from the bedside clock: 4:04.

His mouth was dry as hell.

It was dark but there was a sliver of light shining below the bathroom door. Except that he was sure it was on the wrong side of his room.

Unless. Unless it wasn't his room.

He moved his hand around the bed until he came upon an expanse of naked flesh.

Gail stirred.

'Oh shit,' he said.

'Cal?' She sounded hoarse and far away. 'What time is it?'

'It's late. Or it's early. I'm going back to my room now.'

'Do you have to?'

'Yeah, I do.'

She was snoring as he crawled around the floor looking for his clothes.

Damn you, Cal, he thought. So much for being professional.

TWENTY

No one could remember the last time the pope had visited the Palace of the Governorate. It was an imposing symmetrical building located behind St Peter's Basilica on the edge of the Vatican gardens, a short walk from Celestine's guesthouse residence. Although visitors passed it by without a thought, it was the nerve center of administration for the City State. Moller had reserved a small, nondescript conference room in one of the wings, across the hall from the Vatican motor vehicle registration department, of all places.

Awaiting the pontiff was a small group of individuals who, with one exception, either knew each other in passing or were close colleagues. The most senior figure, Cardinal Sandro Portolano, was the president of the Pontifical Council for Culture, the organization that presided over the guardianship of the historical and artistic patrimony of the Church – all the works of art, historical documents, books, everything kept in the museums, libraries, and archives. One of his direct reports, Professor Daniele Boni, the director of the Vatican Museums, sat to his left, busily answering correspondence on his phone. Another direct report, Archbishop Gabriel Thorn, the Luxembourgian archivist and librarian of the Holy Roman Church, sat quietly to his right, bridging his fingers. The Pontifical Commission for Sacred Archaeology was also part of Cardinal Portolano's brief. Ordinarily, inviting the secretary of the Pontifical Commission rather than its president to a papal meeting would have caused something of a political earthquake, but everyone knew that Sister Elisabetta Celestino was the pope's favorite. Her special status harkened back to the extraordinary services she had provided to the Vatican during the stormy time of Celestine's conclave. The one person who was a stranger to the others was a Canadian, Monsignor Trevor Joseph, the secretary of APSA, the Administration of the Patrimony of the Apostolic See, the department within the Secretariat for the Economy tasked, among other functions, with controlling the Holy See's real-estate portfolio.

After a while, Professor Boni looked up from his phone and asked if anyone knew the purpose of the meeting.

There were headshakes around the table and even Cardinal Portolano admitted he had no idea.

'And we're sure the pope is personally attending?' Joseph asked.

'That's what Moller said,' the cardinal replied.

'I don't think I've ever been to a meeting in this palace,' Elisabetta said. She had come from her archeology office located outside the Vatican on the Via Napoleone.

'It's a strange venue for a meeting with the pope,' Boni said. 'It's where I come for my parking stickers. It's almost like he doesn't want to be seen with us.'

'Well, I've never personally met the Holy Father,' Joseph said. 'I must admit, I've got butterflies, but I can't imagine what I have in common with the rest of you.'

'All will be revealed, I expect,' the cardinal grumbled.

When the door to the room finally opened, a plain-clothed member of the Vatican Gendarmerie entered first and glanced around the room. When he exited, Moller came in followed by Celestine, who warmly greeted everyone by name, spending the most time with Elisabetta, inquiring about the health of her family. When everyone settled back down, Moller pulled out his ubiquitous notebook and recorded the names of the attendees.

'Thank you for taking the time from your busy schedules,' the pope began modestly. 'I am in need of your expert service. But I must ask you to hold this meeting in confidence. May I count on your discretion?'

Whispered assents floated around the table.

The pope thanked them and said, 'I'm sure you've all read in the papers rumors about my displeasure with the state of Vatican finances, about the lack of data for certain departments, the failure of transparency. That is why I wanted to solicit your help.'

Cardinal Portolano waited until Celestine paused to take a sip of water before saying, 'But, Holy Father, what can we do to assist you in this endeavor?'

'Something that has troubled me is that we seem to have no idea about the value of many of our assets. What I have learned from the accountants is that any organization, whether a business or a not-for-profit, needs to have a clear understanding of its liabilities and its assets. With our recent initiatives we are making some progress in learning more about our liabilities. As to our assets, we have no idea, no idea whatsoever. For example, do you know the value we carry on our books for all the artwork in the Vatican Museum?'

When no one replied, the pope answered himself. 'One euro! How ridiculous is that? Today, I want us to begin the exercise of correctly valuing our assets – our buildings, our land holdings, our paintings, our sculptures, our manuscripts. You are the ones who can do this. What do you think about this exercise?'

Again, no one seemed to want to offer an opinion.

Celestine laughed and said, 'Never mind. Let us start somewhere. What about real estate? Tell me about the value of our real estate, Monsignor Joseph.'

The monsignor, an energetic fellow from Toronto who had been an accountant before entering the priesthood, nervously scratched his thinning blond hair and wondered out loud where to start.

'Wherever you like,' the pope replied.

'Well, Holy Father, as you know, the bulk of our properties are within Italy although we do have significant assets throughout Europe. Each diocese around the world is an independent legal entity and their real-estate assets are on their books, not ours. It is no easy thing pegging a value to the Holy See's real-estate holdings as market conditions may fluctuate. If pressed, I would say that the value would be well in excess of ten billion euros. At last count, we own over one hundred thousand properties in Italy alone, although the great majority are churches, convents, and monasteries.'

'I see, good,' the pope said. 'What about non-religious properties?'

'We own hotels, office buildings, apartment blocks, buildings housing retail tenants, banks, insurance companies, and the like. Some of them in capital cities like London and Paris would be considered trophy properties owing to their prestige value. And we own a good deal of agricultural land that we lease to individual farmers and collectives.'

'And the value of these properties?' the pope asked.

'I would have to do some work, Holy Father, but I would say several billion euros.'

'I see. That was very helpful. Now, let us turn to other categories. Who would like to go next to hazard an opinion about the value of assets in their departments?'

Archbishop Thorn tentatively raised his hand and said, 'Holy Father, I have to tell you that the Vatican Library and Vatican Secret Archives have never undertaken an exercise of placing a value on our collections. Most of our books, codices, manuscripts, maps, letters, papal bulls, pronouncements, and concordats are unique items of the sort that never go under an auction hammer. How can one put a value on the Concordat of Worms? The Pax Veneta? A letter from Genghis Khan to Pope Innocent IV? A scroll that transcribes the trial of the Knights Templar? The tract from the English Parliament to Clement VII regarding the "Great Matter" of King Henry VIII?' He stopped there but his exasperation lingered.

The pope said, 'Of course I see your point but surely there are experts who are able to appraise unique pieces. I won't hold you to any figures but what does your gut tell you about value?'

'I don't know, Holy Father,' he sputtered. 'Of the most important historical pieces? Tens of millions? Hundreds of millions? I'm at a loss.'

'Don't worry,' the pope said, 'this is only the beginning of a process. Let's keep going around the table.'

Although Sister Elisabetta's face was turned downward, the pope seemed to notice a small smile. He smiled back and said, 'Sister Elisabetta, tell me what you think about our antiquities.'

Professor Boni stiffened as a show of his annoyance. Her organization, the Pontifical Commission for Sacred Archaeology, was the group responsible for directing excavations in the catacombs of Rome and other sites of Christian antiquarian interest and of safeguarding artifacts found during digs, not curating and maintaining them for exhibition. That was the job of the Vatican Museums. But there was little he could do or say. Everyone knew she was the pope's fair-haired girl.

Elisabetta, aware of the sensitivity, prefaced her remarks with an acknowledgement that the staff of the museum was best positioned to give an opinion on value but that she would tentatively weigh in.

'From what I've read,' she said, 'the auction market for important works of antiquity has been quite strong. This would be particularly true for works with the kind of provenance as pieces within the Vatican collections. Unless there is a clear chain of ownership, most museums won't bid on ancient artifacts because they won't risk trafficking in looted goods. My personal view is that our Greek, Roman, Etruscan, early Christian, and Egyptian collections of statuary and art are unparalleled in their excellence and significance. Add to this our amazing ethnological collection of regional antiquities. I would be happy to work with Professor Boni's people to do valuation exercises but I would think the value is in the hundreds of millions if not considerably more.'

Celestine thanked her and turned to Boni. 'So, Professor, it is your turn. What about the value of our art collections?'

Boni began, 'Holy Father, as others have said, it is not so easy to put a value on objects that have long been considered priceless. Works such as ours have rarely, if ever, gone to auction. Having said that, the art market is quite strong of late, particularly for modern art, although this is less relevant to our discussion. The highest price ever paid for a classical painting was in 2015 – three hundred million dollars for Gauguin's *When Will You Marry?*, followed by the 2011 sale of Cézanne's *The Card Players* for some two hundred sixty million dollars. I believe any museum curator in the world would say that we have many, many paintings and sculptures that would easily exceed these figures.'

The pope scrunched his face and a question followed. 'Can you explain something for me? I have never understood the concept of a work of art being priceless. Surely if there is a willing seller and a willing buyer a price may be negotiated.'

'It is a loosely used term, Holy Father. I believe it relates to the fact that for some pieces there are very few museums or individuals with the capacity to pay an astronomical price, even if it is a fair price. But you are correct. If our collection were to ever come to the market, there would certainly be major museums – the Louvre, the Metropolitan in New York, the Getty, the Tate and National Galleries in London, among others, as well as assorted billionaires who would pull out their checkbooks.'

'Do you have any impressions of the overall value of our holdings?' the pope asked.

Boni sighed, 'Many, many billions.'

Celestine clapped his hands together once and rubbed them. 'Well then, I wish to thank you all for your kind attention and trenchant observations. This has been an excellent start. Please begin work on a comprehensive valuation exercise but do not involve outside experts at this time. Please respect my desire for secrecy. Outsiders to this process may not understand the intent of your work. Until then, no leaks. Is that clear?'

He collected their nods and yeses like a nosegay of daisies and stood to leave.

'Sister, a moment if you will,' he said. 'Moller, it's OK, go on without me. The bodyguards will see to it I don't get lost.'

When alone he said, 'So, Sister, I have taken note of this smile you can't seem to get rid of. What's on your mind?'

She looked like a child caught passing notes in class. 'Nothing really, Holy Father.'

'Don't lie to the pope,' he said lightly.

'Am I that obvious?'

'I'm afraid so.'

'It's only that I was thinking you might have another motive for this exercise.'

'And what might that be?'

'It's hard to sell treasure if you don't know its value.'

Celestine nodded. 'You're a wise one, Elisabetta. You always have been. Do you know Matthew 19:21?'

She closed her eyes for a few seconds before answering. 'If you want to be perfect go sell your possessions and give to the poor and you will have treasure in heaven.'

He beamed like a proud father. 'You and those like you are the true treasure of the Church and always have been.'

TWENTY-ONE

I t wasn't unusual for cardinals to gather after business hours for social gatherings but out of an abundance of caution the three of them purposely metered out their arrivals to Cardinal Leoncino's apartment. The last to show up at the Palazzo San Carlo was Cardinal Lauriat. The residential building was within the Vatican grounds next door to the pope's quarters at the Domus Sanctae Marthae and it was this proximity that contributed to their conspiratorial anxiety.

Lauriat took the elevator to the third floor and entered Leoncino's spacious flat to find the others sipping wine and sampling finger food. It was dark but he knew full well its glorious views over the Vatican grounds and the Eternal City beyond.

'Sit, Pascal, sit,' Leoncino said, sending an elderly nun to bring the cardinal secretary a glass of Prosecco. In the intimate lighting, Leoncino's vitiligo looked positively Day-Glo.

Cardinal Malucchi, a man with a physique worthy of his prodigious appetite, was buried in a soft sofa, with an overflowing plate of food balanced on his lap.

'Save some room for supper, Domenico,' Leoncino told the vicar-general. 'The sisters have outdone themselves.'

'I was busy. I skipped lunch,' Malucchi groused.

'I find that difficult to believe,' Cardinal Cassar said, popping a piece of bruschetta into his mouth.

'Well, only a small sandwich,' Malucchi said.

Lauriat settled in with them and asked Leoncino if he could ask the nuns to give them privacy.

'They hear nothing, they see nothing,' Leoncino said.

'Please, Mario, humor me,' Lauriat said.

The nuns dispatched to the kitchen, Lauriat took a sip of wine and put down the glass. His host knew he wasn't much of a drinker and would likely not touch it again. Leoncino lived lavishly but couldn't shake his frugality. If it hadn't been a sparkling wine he might have had it poured back into the bottle at the end of the evening.

'So tell us, Pascal,' Leoncino said. 'How did your meeting go with Sassoon?'

'As you might expect, he was cautious. I don't know that he trusted me at first.'

'But you're a persuasive man,' Malucchi said, his eyes dancing.

'I try to be,' Lauriat said. 'Let's just say that he came to realize that our interests were aligned.'

'What did you tell him?' Leoncino asked.

'I told him that Celestine's proposed foundation would never get off the ground. The blowback from within the Church would be too great especially when it became apparent that the legal framework for the validity of the loan was fatally weak.'

'And how did he respond?'

'He said he had commissioned his own legal analysis and that the preliminary view was that the loan appeared to be enforceable.'

'Of course he'd say that,' Cassar said.

'It did not surprise me in the least,' Lauriat said. 'He's a businessman. Lawyers are hired hands. They will say whatever their client wants them to say. But as to common ground, he also made it clear that he thinks the idea for a foundation is ludicrous.'

'What does *he* want?' Malucchi asked.

'If it were his decision, and his alone, he would want the loan to be repaid. To the bank.'

'But surely you told him that wasn't going to happen,' Cassar spat.

'Of course I did, Joseph. I took his proposal calmly, as a negotiating position. After all, this, as many things in life, is nothing more than a negotiation. I told him we were confident in our legal position and that the bank was free to sue the Vatican. He replied that he'd happily do so.'

'And what did you say?' Leoncino said, clearly enjoying the conversation.

'I asked him how old he was.'

'You didn't!' Leoncino said.

'I most certainly did. I pointed out to him that it was highly unlikely that the matter would resolve itself in Italian courts during his lifetime. So would you like to know how he replied?'

The three cardinals nodded eagerly.

'He said, "All right. My number is twenty-seven billion dollars and yours is zero. What's it going to take to make both of us happy?"'

Malucchi appeared spellbound, a wedge of salami hovering near his mouth. 'And?'

'Well, I didn't want to make the first offer, did I?' Lauriat said. 'I asked him, given the circumstances, what would make him happy. He quickly threw out a number as if he'd already thought it through. Two billion. That was his number.'

Leoncino sputtered something unintelligible amid a clamor of groans.

'Don't worry,' Lauriat said. 'I told him that number could never be acceptable. His reply surprised me. He said he was concerned about an anti-Semitic backlash in any scenario where the bank received a payment from the Vatican for such an old loan.'

'As well he should be,' Cassar said.

'He said that in his proposal, the bank would only net one billion. To mitigate the backlash, one billion would go to charity by way of Henry Sassoon's charitable foundation. That way, his cousin would be induced to support the settlement.'

'Clever fellow,' Malucchi said.

'Isn't he?' Lauriat said. 'I told him the charity notion was sound but that I had in mind a figure significantly below one billion. However, I was not authorized to complete a negotiation at this time.'

'I say, we pay no more than ten million to make this go away,' Leoncino huffed.

'I think we'll probably have to go higher,' Lauriat said. 'He'll know that if we have to defend ourselves in court, our legal fees will be enormous. In any event, I didn't want to keep tossing numbers on to the table. We ended on amicable terms. He knows there's likely a deal to be done provided, as he put it, "we're able to get control of the situation on our end."'

'Is that what he said?' Cassar asked.

'That's precisely what he said. He also said this: the current situation is that Henry Sassoon is the majority owner of the bank. When his cousin dies, he expects this to change per an agreement reached between them. At that time, Marcus Sassoon will have equal voting rights with Henry Sassoon's side of the family. Eventually, he will be in a position to veto any debt-repayment deal he doesn't endorse.'

'How ill is the cousin?' Cassar asked.

'Quite ill, as I understand it, but I have no insight into his prognosis.'

'Did he bring up the shooting at the bank?' Malucchi asked.

'We talked about it briefly. He told me the police believe it was a random crime of opportunity. The man thought he was robbing a bank and wound up inside an archive instead. They can find no evidence of a connection to Donovan's document search.'

All of them seemed shocked when Malucchi asked, 'But tell us, Pascal, *was* there a connection?'

Lauriat frowned and surprised Leoncino by reaching for his wine glass. He took another sip before answering, 'I really don't know why you are asking me this question, Domenico. Surely you don't think that I was involved.'

Malucchi was contrite. 'I had to ask and now you've answered. End of story.'

An awkward silence followed until Leoncino leaned forward a bit and said, 'It's my turn to ask you a difficult question, Pascal. Where are you getting your insights into Celestine's recent activities? Who gave you the number for the C8 call?'

Lauriat thrust out his jaw in a show of defiance. 'Do you really want to know how the sausage is made? Isn't it better if you don't?'

Leoncino used his eyes to seek Cassar's help, a gesture not lost on Lauriat; the others had clearly been fussing behind the cardinal secretary's back.

'Go ahead, Joseph,' Lauriat said. 'It seems you've been called to action.'

Cassar cleared his throat and said, 'As I see it, Pascal, this fellow, Marcus Sassoon, has it right. It is up to us to get control of the situation. We have to get the pope to change his mind or at least delay any of his damaging actions long enough for nature to take its course. It may take a conclave to put an end to this nonsense. If we are to be your full partners in this – what shall I call it? – defensive strategy, then we feel we should know your sources of information.'

Lauriat nodded while he thought and with a sigh he opened his kimono. 'Room 206.'

It was Leoncino who came to it first. 'That's Moller's office at the Sanctae Marthae!'

'However did you get him to be your pope whisperer?' Malucchi asked.

'The good monsignor was indiscreet,' Lauriat said. 'A gentleman within the Gendarmerie Corps received a photo of Moller deep in the bowels of an underground club in Rome. He's a very fit man, our Moller. And quite flexible, as was the man he was – well, you get the idea. I kept the photo until I needed it. There you have it.'

'Moller knows everything,' Malucchi said, admiringly. 'He writes it all down in his little notebook.'

'Not everything,' Lauriat said. 'In recent days he's been excluded from a few conversations. Celestine is being especially cautious with this loan business.'

'For example?' Leoncino asked.

'Moller attended a meeting between the pope and Donovan in the early stages of Donovan's document search. In Moller's presence Celestine encouraged the professor to make further searches to ensure the loan documents were found by a friendly party.'

'This is what Celestine told the C10,' Leoncino said.

'But then Moller was asked to leave so that the pope could speak to Donovan about a private manner. My guess is that this was the moment when the pope revealed his true intentions.'

'You believe that he confided in Donovan first?' Cassar asked.

'I do,' Lauriat said. 'I think that's why the professor was so determined in his efforts. There's more. I'm also told that Celestine met privately with the nun, Elisabetta Celestino.'

'He's always taken a shine to her,' Malucchi said wickedly.

'Where was this meeting?' Cassar asked.

'I've saved the worst for last,' Lauriat said. 'The pope called for a meeting of several department heads including Cardinal Portolano, Boni from the museum, Thorn from the archives, Trevor Joseph from APSA, and the nun, representing her archeology commission. The meeting was held at the Palace of the Governorate, a venue about as clandestine as one can find within the Vatican.'

'I can't see what these people have in common and what Celestine would want from them,' Cassar said.

'Can't you?' Lauriat said. 'Think about it. These are the officials tasked with managing the patrimony of the Church. They are the stewards of the true wealth of the Vatican.'

'You can't mean it!' Malucchi exclaimed. 'This is how he intends to pay the debt? It's unthinkable. Was it discussed explicitly?'

'No, he was more discreet than that,' Lauriat said. 'He set them off on what seemed on the surface to be a dry exercise to properly assess and record our assets' values. Perhaps it was after the meeting when he confided his true intentions to the nun.'

'What is wrong with him?' Malucchi said. 'Does the pope need a psychiatrist? We have to stop him.'

Lauriat stood and brushed a few crumbs from his cassock.

'Are you not staying for supper?' Leoncino asked.

'Unfortunately no. I'm meeting someone who might be able to help us put a stop to this.'

'Who?' Malucchi asked.

Lauriat shook his head. 'This is one bit of sausage-making you certainly don't want to know about.'

A man was waiting for Lauriat at the entrance to the cardinal's apartment in the Apostolic Palace.

'Come inside,' Lauriat said, unlocking the ornate door.

The man didn't expect small talk and none was given.

'Do you have it?' Lauriat asked.

The man nodded and produced a folder from his briefcase.

'There's a statement from her sister and a photograph of the girl when she was eighteen,' he said. 'She was pretty.'

Lauriat opened the folder and inspected the photo. 'How much did you have to pay?'

'It was manageable. Short money for something like this. Who will publish it?' the man asked.

'Don't worry about that.'

'Will you need anything more from me?'

'It's difficult to say. I know how to find you.'

The man had a good laugh.

TWENTY-TWO

'**A** dozen books. Three hundred fourteen papers.'

Cal wasn't sure why he was here. He had a look around President Clarke's Massachusetts Hall office while she flipped through his curriculum vitae. When he arrived for the meeting she had invited him over to the conversation area by an unlit colonial-era fireplace.

Faculty members usually received an out-of-the-blue summons to the Harvard president's office only when they had done something rather spectacularly wrong. He hadn't been back in Cambridge for a full day when he'd gotten the call. He was certain he'd recall committing a recent horrible act but one never knew. He tried to think back to the last time he was very drunk in public. My God, he thought. Had he said something despicable to a grad student or a junior faculty member at the anthropology department Christmas party? He'd been relatively sober at the more staid Divinity School affair.

'Every one of them has its own small war story.'

'Sorry?' Clarke said, looking up. She'd been elevated to the presidency, by way of university provost, from the ranks of the English department. An Emily Dickinson scholar, she looked passably like her subject.

'The papers and books,' Cal said. 'There was somewhat of a struggle behind each one.'

She smiled. 'I know what you mean. Nature of the beast. So, Cal, I'm sure you're wondering why I wanted to see you.'

'I was trying to imagine what I'd done.'

'It's not that sort of meeting.'

'Good, I'm relieved.'

'Not that sort of meeting at all. In fact, quite the opposite. We've had our eye on you, Cal.'

'You have?'

'Oh, yes. Your scholarship and the quality of your teaching place you in the upper echelon of our faculty. You've demonstrated an ability to cross the boundaries of multiple disciplines and pursue all your endeavors with excellence. You know what that means, don't you?'

He didn't.

'You've been named a University Professor, Cal. Congratulations. We have two thousand faculty members, nine hundred with tenure, and only twenty-four – excuse me – twenty-five university professorships. It's a rarified club, as you know.'

So that's why his pal Frank Epstein at the business school had been prematurely congratulating him. Within the university, the appointment was a big deal. University Professors had the right to do research and teach courses in any department. There was probably a pay raise involved too, but he wasn't going to ask about that. Bad form.

'Wow, thank you, Evelyn.'

'Don't thank me. This bubbled up from your peers. I understand your father was also a university professor.'

He actually remembered attending the honors ceremony as a very young boy.

'I'm quite sure this is our first example of a father-son honor,' Clarke added.

It probably wasn't the first thing a newly minted University Professor ought to do but he couldn't help himself. He needed to fix his Joe Murphy problem.

'I wonder if this could help me solve a problem,' he said. 'I've got a very talented grad student from Ireland, a Catholic priest actually, who's just received his doctorate. It was an excellent piece of work. He's top-of-the heap, a very good academic, a medievalist, who wants to teach here. I tried to get Gil Daniels to take him on at the Divinity School but he didn't go for it.'

'Why?'

'There was one slot and he opted for one of his own students.'

'Ah. Would you like me to have a word with him?'

'I don't think it would be good for anyone to have my guy crammed down Gil's throat. What if I presented his credentials to the History Department? His work would fit in there too.'

'I'll give Mary Schott a call,' Clarke said. 'Grease the skids for you. Maybe I could pitch it as a package. You could work up a proposal for a new undergraduate course within the history department to complement your priest's area of expertise.'

'That's terrific, really great. Thanks, Evelyn.'

'So I understand you're just back from Rome. Anything interesting going on there?'

He wished he could tell her the story but that wasn't going to happen. 'Maybe paper number three hundred fifteen,' he said. 'We'll see.'

'Mr Sassoon – he's in bed,' his nurse told Marcus answering the door to the apartment.

Marcus Sassoon had come unannounced, hoping for a word. Henry didn't go to the office anymore. It was too arduous for him and he had an aversion to revealing his frailty to his employees.

'Is he sleeping?' Marcus asked.

'I don't think so,' the nurse said. 'He's watching TV.'

'Is Gail in?'

'She went shopping. She'll be back after lunch.'

Marcus asked the woman, a thin Latina in an agency uniform, if she was new. She replied that she had taken care of Henry on and off over the past year at home and before that, in his office when he was still working.

'I recognize you,' she said. 'You're his cousin. You don't remember me?'

'Sorry, no.'

She showed her displeasure with a shrug. 'I'm Maria. Next time I see you maybe you'll remember. You need me to show you where his room is?'

'I know where it is, thank you.'

He found Henry lying on a made bed with a thin comforter over his trouser legs. The TV was tuned to a financial channel.

Henry removed the oxygen prongs from his nose and put the TV on mute. His skin looked particularly dusky and his hands shook. 'I wasn't expecting you,' he said. 'Come. Sit.'

Marcus settled into a small armchair on Henry's side of the bed.

'I wanted to speak with you about this Vatican business.'

'OK, of course.' He paused to pant. 'It's a great thing, isn't it?'

'I don't think it's so great, actually.'

Henry grimaced. 'Gail was – enthusiastic. You were there. I wasn't.' His chest was heaving and he had to put the oxygen prongs back in his nose.

'If Gail wants to be a do-gooder with your money, more power to her,' Marcus said. 'I'm more concerned about the bank. The Vatican stole our money a hundred seventy years ago and they murdered our family. This is the bank's money, Henry. They owe us the money. Now this pope wants to score some points by giving our money away.'

'It's for charity. Anyway, if the Vatican – gave the money to the bank – we'd see anti-Semitism like – nobody's business. To raise that kind of money – he's going to have to – sell the store. That'll piss off the Catholics – big time.'

'Look, Henry. A very important cardinal reached out to me directly and told me a lot of bigwigs are opposed to Celestine's plan. There's a win-win proposition on the table. If we play ball with this group and reject the pope's foundation idea, they'll drop legal opposition and give us a sizable settlement – an amount to be negotiated – and we can give some portion of it to your foundation to do whatever you and Gail see fit.'

'How much?'

Marcus smiled at the question. His cousin was still in the game.

'I asked for two billion. This fellow's eyes popped out of his head. We won't get that. I'd say maybe they'd settle for a half a billion or so. With your blessing I'll start negotiating like a son-of-a-bitch.'

Henry began to shake his head. Marcus looked with disdain at the Yankees cap as it moved from left to right and back. As far as he knew Henry hadn't watched a baseball game in decades.

'This fund for humanity – the IFH – would be the third biggest charity in the world. Third. Gates. IKEA. Sassoon. This is my – legacy, Marcus. The Sassoon Foundation is – small. If we took even most – of your settlement – we'd be bigger but still small. The IFH would be my legacy. When you've got – lungs like mine – you think about these things.'

Marcus leaned back and rubbed his eyes with the heels of his hands. When he was ready to speak again he said, 'For God's sake, Henry, the bank is your legacy. Our ancestors founded it over two hundred years ago. You want Julian to go into the business. I've got Albert and Steven. Think about them, not your goddamn foundation all the time.'

'The bank is strong.'

Marcus let the comment pass. 'Think of what we could do to expand the business with all that extra working capital.'

'My mind's made up,' Henry puffed.

'For God's sake, Henry. I want you to reconsider.'

'I won't!' he said as loudly as his thickened lungs would allow. 'I've got majority control. I'm sorry.'

Those words – majority control – were like a provocation. Marcus stood up, his mouth trembling. The cousins locked eyes. From past bouts, both men knew that Marcus wasn't going to push back. Whenever Marcus crossed the line in the past, Henry retaliated by telling him to watch it or else. The *or else* was the threat that he'd reverse his decision to equalize voting rights upon his death. After two centuries favoring Henry's lineage, both sides of the family would finally have parity.

Marcus went to the edge of the bed and towered over his frail relative. When they were growing up, Henry was the taller and the stronger of the two, dominating his younger cousin in every possible way. The roles were reversed now.

'Let me tell you something,' Marcus seethed. 'The bank isn't as strong as you think. We need the capital or we've got a big fucking problem. We've got a two-hundred-million-dollar donut hole you don't know about. Nobody knows about it except for Albert and me. We had some trading losses on our own account. It was Albert's fault. He can be an idiot. He got in a hole and kept digging. We can't paper them over forever. If the regulators find out before we can fix it then it could all come crashing down.'

Henry's chest began to heave. 'What – have you – done?' He began to cough.

'We can fix this, Henry. All you need to do is say yes to my plan.'

'I'll *fix* you! You'll never – have equal – ownership.'

There was more coughing. A full-blown spasm. Henry reached for his call button to bring the nurse.

Marcus brushed it away beyond his cousin's reach, turned up the TV volume with the remote, and went to close the door.

'What – are you – doing?' Henry managed to say through his coughing fit. His face was turning purple.

'I'm doing what's best for the bank,' he said with surprising calm.

'Nurse,' Henry rasped.

Marcus bent over and removed the oxygen prongs.

'What—?' Henry couldn't finish the sentence.

The coughing intensified and Marcus turned up the volume some more. He stood there, his arms hanging to the sides of his baggy suit jacket, watching his Henry choke on his own secretions. Henry's eyes begged for a while and then became unfocused as the coughing stopped. His chest rose and fell in increasingly shallow motions until there were none at all.

Marcus became aware of just how loudly the TV was blaring and he turned it way down. He put the nasal prongs back in place and felt around a purple neck for a pulse. To be sure he waited a few minutes before opening the door and shouting for the nurse.

'Maria? Come quickly!'

The nurse came running down the hall and looked in with horror.

'Mr Sassoon? Mr Sassoon!'

She grabbed a stethoscope from the nightstand and slapped it on his chest.

'There's no heartbeat! What happened?' she cried.

'He just stopped breathing.'

'Just like that?'

'In mid-sentence.'

'When?'

'Just now.'

She shone a penlight into his eyes. The pupils were wide and fixed.

'That's not true. He's been dead for longer. Tell me what you did.'

'I didn't do anything.'

She stiffened. 'This is for the police. It's not for me. I'm calling them.'

Marcus sat down on the armchair in a move designed to be non-threatening. 'How much?' he asked.

She moved to the other side of the bed. She didn't play dumb; she knew exactly what he meant.

Hands on bony hips she replied, 'One million dollars.'

He laughed. 'You've got balls. I'll give you a hundred thousand. Tonight.'

'Two. Two hundred thousand. It needs to be cash. I got a divorce, and I don't want my husband to know.'

He seemed to enjoy the negotiation even though it was taking place over his cousin's dead body. 'We've got a deal. I like you, Maria. I won't be forgetting your name anytime soon. But after tonight I never want to hear from you again. I won't be blackmailed. If you try you'll seriously regret it. Understand?'

She nodded once. 'He would have died soon anyway, I think.'

TWENTY-THREE

'I read the announcement in *The Crimson*,' Father Murphy said the moment he entered Cal's office. 'Heartfelt congratulations.'

'I wasn't expecting it,' Cal said. 'It's pretty cool, but have a seat, Joe, I've got some more news.'

'Uh-oh. Do I need to book my flight to Dublin?'

'Not unless you want to take a quick vacation before starting your new job.'

Murphy wasn't the grinning sort but he began to grin as he unwrapped his wooly scarf.

'Tell me more.'

'One of the perks of being a University Professor is having the ability to teach in any department. I'm not going to be developing a lecture series in mathematics anytime soon but the History Department's another matter. I've pitched an idea for a course on the medieval Church to Professor Schott and she loved it. I committed to giving a few anchor lectures but I can't carry the full load. I suggested a new talent who could lead the charge. She's reviewed your faculty application and I'm happy to say she's taking you on. You're going to be offered a position as assistant professor of history, Joe. Mary thinks it's going to be cool having a priest in her department.'

Murphy shook his head in disbelief and half-rose from his chair to shake Cal's hand. 'I can't believe it. It's a dream come true. I was kind of a shit parish priest, if you must know. There's that deficit of mine – in the empathy department. You've saved a parish back home from a terrible fate.'

Cal dropped Murphy's hand as Gil Daniels appeared at the threshold apologizing for the interruption.

'Nonsense, come on in, Gil.'

Daniels delivered his felicitations through a forced smile. 'Congratulations are in order, Cal. University Professor! Wow. It's a coup for the Divinity School. Our first one. I looked it up. Should be excellent for fundraising.'

'Well, it was a big surprise, that's for sure.'

Daniels' face returned to its normal pucker and he told Murphy he was sorry that things didn't work out for his faculty appointment. The priest left it to Cal to deliver the news.

'Really?' Daniels said, doing a poor job of hiding his discomfort. 'Mary took you on? I suppose the History Department has a different set of criteria.'

Cal picked up on Murphy's flickering wince.

'Well, this is a red-letter day, all around, isn't it?' Daniels said. He quickly changed the subject. 'So, thanks for letting me have that brief chat with Pope Celestine, Cal. Made my day. I thought you were having me on at first. I'm glad I didn't say anything I'd live to regret.'

'He's got a pretty good sense of humor,' Cal said. 'He would have laughed off almost anything.'

'Except for blasphemy.'

'Yeah, blasphemy probably excluded.'

'How was the rest of your trip?' Daniels asked, edging for the door. 'Golden library card pay off for you?'

It was a little cruel but Cal couldn't resist getting in a retaliatory elbow. 'Gil, you have no idea. Absolutely no idea.'

Cal was wrapping up with Murphy when his mobile rang, showing Gail Sassoon's number. From the way she breathed Cal's name, he knew there was a problem.

'What's wrong, Gail?'

'It's Henry. He's dead.'

The funeral was a private, family affair, hastily arranged per Jewish tradition for the day after Henry Sassoon's death. There had been some concern, felt most acutely by Marcus, that the New York City Medical Examiner would put a hold on the release of his body pending an autopsy, but Henry's doctor certified the death as the natural result of his pulmonary condition and there was no official push-back. Gail sent the jet to Boston to pick up Henry's son, Julian, and the young man gave one of the three eulogies. Marcus talked about Henry's business life, Gail discussed her husband's philanthropic nature, and Julian, tasked with speaking about Henry's paternal side, seemed to struggle to come up with all that many humanizing anecdotes.

'Let's face it,' Julian began, 'for Dad, the bank came first but family was a reasonably close second.'

When the procession returned to the city from the cemetery on

Long Island, family, employees, and friends gathered to sit shiva at Henry's apartment. Julian, movie-star handsome in a dark suit, found himself the center of attention, fielding questions about his post-school intentions.

None was more curious than his cousin, Albert.

'That was pretty cool, what you said about Henry,' Albert said.

'Was it? I didn't know what to say.'

'Hard to believe he's gone.'

'Not really. I mean there wasn't going to be a cure.'

'True, true. So last semester at the B-School, huh?'

'Yeah, final stretch.'

Albert and he had never been close even though they'd been thrust together at family events since childhood. As Julian sipped his beer he seemed to know where the conversation was going and he visibly stiffened.

'So, have you given any thought to what you're going to do when you're done?' Albert asked.

'I haven't actually. Just trying to finish strong.'

'Well, obviously there's always going to be a place for you at the firm.'

'Obviously.'

Albert wasn't oblivious to Julian's shirty attitude, but Albert clearly had an agenda and seemed determined to play his cards.

'Of course, we're all expecting the governance changes your dad and my dad have been discussing. Equal partnership going forward, well you know the score.'

'I was never involved with that,' Julian said, finishing his beer, shaking the empty bottle to signal his intent to head to the kitchen for another. 'Just going with the flow.'

'Well, if you decide you want to join the bank, all of us can sit down and work out the parameters. Of course, if it's not your thing, our side of the family can always run the firm for your benefit. Passive income's a great thing.'

Julian gave his cousin a faux-friendly pat on the back. 'You're a prince, Albert,' he said, walking off.

'You know about the crazy Vatican shit, right?' Albert called after him.

'I don't have a clue what you're talking about.'

'Ask Gail.'

* * *

Ludwig Moller was in a panic.

The pope was conducting Mass in the chapel at the Sanctae Marthae guesthouse and Moller could do nothing but wait for the conclusion. He had slipped the printout into a folder to hide it from view but everyone he encountered that morning was whispering behind his back.

It wasn't a newspaper that Moller typically read. He'd been awakened by a pre-dawn call from the agitated Vatican director of communications who in turn had been called by a well-known journalist seeking a comment. The director told the journalist he'd ring him back, and in the darkness he opened his browser to inspect the tabloid, *Il Fatto Quotidiano*. The bold headline sent him into a frenzy.

A Love Child, an Abortion, a Suicide, and a Future Pope: Celestine's Darkest Days Revealed

When Mass was over, the pope caught sight of Moller's fraught expression. Walking to his office, Celestine asked him what was wrong.

'An inflammatory newspaper story, Holy Father.'

'Concerning?'

'You.'

The pope sat at his desk and read Moller's printout, his expression betraying not a hint of emotion. When he was done he carefully folded his reading glasses and passed the pages back to the priest.

'First the news of Henry Sassoon's death,' Celestine said. 'Now this. It seems our fortitude is being challenged.'

'We must respond to this story, Holy Father.'

'Must we?' he said, wistfully. 'I suppose we must. This woman, Lidia, what happened to her was a tragedy. This account in the paper of what happened to her, well, it's largely true. The part about me is false, of course. I don't know why her sister is saying these things. Perhaps someone has paid her money. One must be suspicious that it is an attempt to discredit me at a critical moment. Perhaps it relates to my attempts to root out corruption. What do you think, Ludwig?'

Moller shook his head. 'I don't know what to think about motivation, Holy Father. It is incumbent upon this office that we work with the communications department to tell our side of the story and nip this in the bud quickly before more damage is done.'

'This girl and I, we went to the same high school in Naples. We were friends. More than friends, actually, but I wasn't always a priest, was I? When I entered the seminary our lives diverged. I was ordained and took up duties in a parish just outside the city. She found a job, a government job of some sort, and had a series of boyfriends. One of them got her pregnant. Believe me, it wasn't me. Her mother knew my mother and the two of them conspired to have me speak to Lidia because she had decided to get an abortion. She and the father didn't want to get married. She found some local doctor who agreed to perform it. I visited her. She was in bad shape. Very emotionally fragile. I counseled her strongly to have the baby, to put it up for adoption, that I would help arrange it. She refused. There was only so much I could do. Anyway, after she had the abortion, she became desperately depressed and attempted suicide twice. She received competent care and we thought she would recover her emotional balance but a year later she stepped in front of a train. My life continued. Hers didn't.'

Moller, as usual, was taking notes. 'I assume Lidia's mother is no longer living.'

'I presided over her funeral Mass in the eighties.'

'Do you recall the name of the baby's father?'

'I don't believe I ever knew it.'

'Other than this sister who was the source of the story, did she have any other siblings?'

'So long ago,' the pope said. 'I seem to recall she had a brother who moved to America after the mother died.'

'Do you remember his name? The city he went to live?'

'It might be in one of my old address books. I could have a look.'

Moller tapped his pen against his page.

'What?' the pope asked.

'Might you have a look now?'

'I seem to be spending more time with priests than rabbis these days.'

Marcus Sassoon had sent a car and driver to pick up Joseph Cassar from JFK Airport and he and the cardinal were sitting down to cocktails in his study. Cassar was dressed as a simple priest, free of the trappings of his office.

'It really is good of you to see me in the present circumstances,' Cassar said, taking in the snowy vista of Central Park. 'The cardinal secretary wanted me to personally represent him. He wishes to express his condolences to the Sassoon family.'

'Tell Cardinal Lauriat I appreciate that but a phone call would have sufficed.'

'Perhaps, but he felt that the situation between us was quite dynamic and needed to be addressed with a face-to-face discussion.'

'Dynamic,' Marcus parroted. 'I'll say it's dynamic. I assume this planted story about the pope and the gal who had an abortion was your doing?'

'Ah, you've seen it. Given your bereavement we didn't know if you would have received the news. Actually I have no idea how the press came by this woman's story.'

'Fine. I'm sure you don't.'

Cassar let the sarcasm pass without further comment.

'But here's a newsflash for you,' Marcus said, tapping the rim of his whiskey glass with his index finger, 'if you're going to smear someone, make sure it sticks. A fat lot of good it does you if twenty-four hours later the gal's brother is found in San Diego and he identifies the real father who proceeds to torpedo the whole salacious story. And to top it off, the dead gal's sister is now saying she was misrepresented and that she didn't actually say that Celestine was the father.'

'You've been following the tale quite closely, I see,' Cassar said through an artificial smile.

'Yeah, I've been following it, all right. It's a big story over here. But now Celestine looks like the aggrieved party, not some hypocrite priest who forced his lover to get an abortion. Not smart. You can tell Cardinal Lauriat I said so. Your leverage is nonexistent.'

'Indeed. However, with respect to the debt, it seems that your cousin's untimely passing has presented us with an alternate path to achieve what both of us want. You indicated to Cardinal Lauriat that if he were to succumb to his illness, you would have effective veto power over the formation of the pope's foundation.'

'That's correct. It won't be official until my cousin's estate is settled and the shares are transferred but believe me, the foundation's dead on arrival.'

'Then it's incumbent upon us to finalize our negotiation so both sides can move forward with clarity.'

'Are you empowered to negotiate on Lauriat's behalf?'

'Subject to his final approval of terms, yes.'

'Then let me freshen your drink and let's have at it. I've got an hour before I've got to go across town to Henry's place. It's the fourth day of sitting shiva.'

'Such a lovely ritual,' Cassar said, holding out his glass for the pour. 'Very healing for family and friends, I imagine.'

Gail Sassoon waited for the seventh day of mourning to pass before asking to see Marcus at the bank. When she arrived, Marcus was surprised that Julian was with her.

'I thought you were heading back to Cambridge,' Marcus said.

'Gail asked me to stick around one more day.' Despite her best efforts to claim the title of mom and his father's exhortations, Julian had always insisted on calling his stepmother by name.

'I think Albert's around somewhere. Want me to find him for you, Julian?'

'No, Marcus,' Gail said, 'I wanted Julian to attend our meeting.'

'I didn't know it was a meeting,' Marcus said stiffly. 'Otherwise I'd have asked for an agenda.'

It was his idea of a joke but it fell flat.

'It's about Henry's will,' Gail said. 'I wanted you and Julian to both hear some details in advance of the formal estate process.'

Marcus didn't look happy. He took a chair at his conference table. Julian slouched beside Gail looking somewhat bored.

'Is this Gail the wife talking today or Gail the lawyer?' he asked.

'Both, I suppose.'

'Well, I don't know what Henry told you,' Marcus said, 'but the two of us had a firm understanding of what was going to happen in the event of his death. An equalization of voting rights has been a long time coming. It's my expectation that his estate plan will provide for that.'

Her response was icy and brutish, prompting Julian to sit bolt upright and stare at her in wide-eyed admiration.

'Then your expectations are wrong, Marcus.'

Marcus gulped, not a silent one but a loud, hollow gulp redolent of a pneumatic valve closing. 'Excuse me?'

'Henry and I discussed his estate plan extensively,' Gail said. 'It's true there was a time when he thought about making an even distribution in voting shares. But two years ago his thinking changed.'

'His thinking or yours?' Marcus said, his voice cracking.

'His,' she said, emphatically, 'his. He always valued my opinion but Henry was very much his own man. His thinking changed when his condition worsened and he saw the handwriting on the wall. It also changed when Julian decided to go to business school.'

'He never talked to me about it,' Julian said.

'He wanted you to make your own decisions in life and make your own way. If you wanted to get involved with the bank, it was going to have to come from within. He forbade me to talk about his estate plan with you. So, Marcus, and so, Julian, here's what Henry decided to do with respect to the ownership of the bank. His fifty-two percent ownership is staying within our side of the family. Of that, forty-nine percent is bequeathed to Julian and three percent is bequeathed to me.'

Julian shook his head. 'Gail, I'm not interested in the bank. I never was.'

'Please let me finish,' she said. While she talked, Marcus looked out the window with a blank, unfocused expression, his mouth slightly agape. 'Henry devised this structure to encourage you and me to work together to achieve majority control. He always wanted us to get along, Julian. You know that. Following a recent development, Henry was especially happy with the arrangement.'

'The Vatican thing?' Julian asked.

'How do you know about that?' Gail asked.

'I don't,' he said. 'Albert mentioned something the other day. He said to ask you about it.'

'I'll tell you about it in a minute,' she said. 'But first, hear the other parameters of the ownership plan. When I die, Julian will inherit my shares. You'll have the absolute majority at that time, Julian. If you die childless, your shares pass to the Sassoon Foundation to be managed by the foundation trustees.'

It was too much for Marcus to bear. He got up and yelled, 'So that's it? And my side of the family? Perpetually disadvantaged? Always second-class citizens?'

'It's a structure that's served the bank for generations,' she said. 'Henry felt the weight of history. And now that we have this Vatican business, a clear majority structure will enable us to render a clear decision. So, Marcus, would you like to tell Julian about the Vatican debt or shall I?'

Marcus walked out without saying another word.

'Then it's up to me to tell you, Julian,' Gail said. 'I think Marcus is letting us use his office.'

TWENTY-FOUR

Cal recognized Julian from photos on Gail's Facebook page and he approached the young man at the bar. Julian had suggested the Russell House Tavern, a popular spot for business-school students, which was fine with him. He hadn't been there in years but he assumed they still served vodka.

'Hey, Professor,' Julian said, extending a hand. 'I'm Julian.'

'Cal works better in a bar.'

Julian was drinking a beer, a scarf wrapped rakishly around his neck, Frye boots dug into the barstool cross-brace. He had black curly hair that fell over his forehead in corkscrews.

Cal delivered his condolences and ordered his usual vodka on the rocks.

'Good basic drink,' Julian observed.

'It does the job. So your mother wanted us to meet.'

'She's not my mother. She's my stepmother.'

Cal treated the remark lightly and revised the sentence to: Gail had wanted them to meet.

'Gail usually gets her way. How long've you known her?'

'We only just met.'

'She made it seem like it was longer. Something about your mother?'

'I think they're both card-carrying members of the New York ladies who lunch.'

'Lunch and drink,' Julian said, tilting his wrist to his mouth. 'Mind if I just ask you something to clear the air?'

'Shoot.'

'Do you and Gail have something going on? I mean I don't give a shit what she does but it would've been a rotten thing to do with my dad on his sick bed.'

Cal took a good pull on his just-served vodka. He hoped he had his poker face going. 'I'm not sure why you're asking me this.'

'Because she's like that.'

He didn't give it a second thought. He'd have to lie, of course.

'I usually wouldn't dignify that kind of a question with an answer but I'm going to make an exception. No. Nothing's going on. Strictly business.'

'OK, cool. Then here's my next question. What are you getting out of brokering the deal? Is there a commission at the end of the rainbow?'

'You know, I do believe I like you, Julian. You're direct. No BS. When I was your age I was like that.'

'You're not anymore?'

'When you work at a university you learn to be a little more political. It's a survival skill. Keeping the latches on the frontal lobes. Even so I'm way more direct than some of my colleagues would like. But no, I'm not getting anything financial out of this. I like the pope. I think he's a good man and I'm trying to help. That's the long and the short of it.'

'Just trying to figure out what's going on.'

'That's fine. Gail tells me you haven't decided whether you want to join the bank when you graduate.'

'A week ago I would have said, no fucking way. I grew up hating it. I hated Gail because she pulled my father away from my mom. I hated my cousins. I hated that the bank sucked my father dry – all he did was work and make money. He never had any time for me.'

'I thought he devoted energy to collecting art and the family foundation.'

'The art was more of an investment thing, a diversification. I don't think he really liked the shit hanging on our walls. The foundation? You may have a point there. I think he got some pleasure in it. To give Gail some credit, she was the prime mover there. But my dad's death? Has that changed the equation? Maybe. I don't know. Did Gail tell you about his diabolical plan to force her and me to work together?'

Cal shook his head and Julian explained the new ownership structure. Then he added, 'Under the firm's charter, no capital allocation decisions can be made without an affirmative vote of fifty-one percent. So my dad's pulling me in from the grave. I don't know how I can make rational voting decisions as an outsider. As much as I have a problem with Gail I completely hate Marcus's guts. You met him, right?'

'I did.'

'Come on, Cal, be direct with me.'

'He's not someone I'd care to hang out with.'

At that, Julian initiated on a fist-bump. 'The only way I can screw Marcus is to get involved. But that kind of screws me too. I was thinking about doing a tech startup with a buddy of mine from college who's a fabulous coder but shit-for-brains as a business guy. Now I don't know.'

'Gail told me you know about the Vatican debt. Does it make joining the bank more or less palatable?'

Julian called the bartender over and ordered a round for the both of them.

'I know it's got to make Marcus and Albert crazy that funds would wind up in a foundation instead of their bank accounts. So, it makes it more palatable, much more. I'm keen on the idea of philanthropy too. I'm a little young for the philanthropy game but I always wanted to give back eventually, not be one of these bratty rich kids who post their bling on Instagram. What's the foundation name the pope suggested – the IFH? Gail wants me to be on its board.'

'Would you?'

'Sure, I'd go for that. Twenty-five billion euros is a lot of money to put into play.'

'It boggles the mind.'

'Do you think the Vatican has those kind of liquid assets?'

'I really don't know. I think it's a stretch.'

'They can't donate what they don't have.'

'Pope Celestine strikes me as a man with a plan.'

'He's an interesting guy from what I've read,' Julian said. 'I'd like to meet him one day.'

'How about Wednesday?'

'Are you serious?'

'He and I talked this morning. I passed along what Gail told me, that with your father's death you'd be involved in decision-making about the foundation. He regretted not meeting your father and he wants to meet you.'

'Classes start again on Monday,' Julian said.

'For me too,' Cal said.

Julian gave a thumb's up. 'Fuck it, I'm in.'

Cal raised his glass. 'Me too.'

*   *   *

Cardinal Malucchi concluded Sunday Mass at the church of San Salvatore in Lauro where he served as cardinal-deacon. Afterwards, Cardinal Lauriat joined him in the sacristy while he slowly shed his vestments.

'You honored me with your presence today, Pascal.'

'It's been too long since I prayed here,' Lauriat said. 'After all, it is the spiritual center for the diffusion of the word of our venerated saint, Padre Pio.'

Malucchi dismissed the young priest who was assisting his disrobing.

'Perhaps you also wished to discuss some things with me?' Malucchi asked.

'You know me too well, Domenico,' Lauriat said, pulling up a chair. 'Would you like some help?'

Malucchi was struggling a bit with his cincture that was looped around his considerable girth. But he managed to untie it and waved it triumphantly at the cardinal secretary.

'Cassar stopped by to see me yesterday on the way back to Malta. He met with Marcus Sassoon and wanted to report back in person. I think we're all hesitant to discuss these matters on the telephone.'

'Can't be too careful,' Malucchi agreed. 'How did he get on?'

'Initially well. He arrived at a settlement number that could, in principle, work for us.'

'Well, what was it?'

'As it happens there is no point in discussing it. When Joseph arrived back in Rome he found a message to call Sassoon. It seems that Mr Sassoon is no longer in a position to make a deal.'

'What happened?'

'An age-old story, that's what happened. One relative dominates another for control of the family fortune. The terms of Henry Sassoon's will have become known. Marcus Sassoon is not getting what he thought he would. The ownership structure will remain in favor of Henry's son, Julian, and the wife. It is quite useless for us to negotiate with him any further.'

Malucchi abandoned his efforts to remove his long white alb and sat down heavily. 'First the business with that woman in Naples backfires, now Sassoon. What are we to do?'

'I've discussed my proposed plan of action with Cassar and with Leoncino. I'm here to discuss it with you. If you concur, it's time for an escalation.'

TWENTY-FIVE

On the day before he was scheduled to return to Rome with Julian, Cal was giving a graduate seminar on the origins of the First Crusade, aware that his mobile phone in his pocket was buzzing incessantly. He resisted the urge to see what was going on, and when the last student had filtered out of the seminar room, he had a look.

His notification screen was filled with different versions of the same news story along with several texts and missed calls.

'Holy shit,' he mumbled, trying to decide whom to call first.

Ludwig Moller hovered over the pope's shoulder as the pontiff read the newspaper article on his iPad. Celestine couldn't see that the priest was trembling and that he had to steady himself by gripping the chair back.

'It is a betrayal,' the pope finally said, sliding the tablet away. 'The Vatican is a nest of vipers and I have been bitten.'

'Is the story true?' Moller asked.

Celestine swiveled the chair to face him. He seemed to be studying the priest's face as a policeman might study a suspect before launching an interrogation.

'What do you think, Ludwig? Do you think it's true?'

'I would have no way of knowing, Holy Father. The story about Lidia, the young woman from Naples, was a fabrication.'

'Well, this story is different. It is accurate up to a point but quite inaccurate in one significant regard. The question is who leaked the story to the press?'

'May I ask who knew about it?'

'Professor Donovan knew but I trust him completely. Sister Elisabetta Celestino knew but I trust her completely. The C8 knew. I discussed the matter with them on the last teleconference. You set up that call, Ludwig. You didn't listen in, did you?'

'Holy Father! I would never do that.'

Celestine grunted. 'I thought I could trust each and every member of the C8 but maybe I am mistaken. It could have been one of them.'

'I believe these men are loyal to you, Holy Father.'

'Perhaps seven are. One may not be.'

'Have you considered parties outside the Vatican?'

'I have complete trust in Professor Donovan. Could it be one of the Sassoons, particularly Marcus Sassoon? Yes, it's a possibility. But now what am I to do? Conduct a witch-hunt? Let it lie? There is so much important work to do and now I must busy myself with fighting a rearguard action. It is a betrayal, Ludwig. A deliberate act of sabotage.'

'What would you like me to do, Holy Father? The press office is overwhelmed with inquiries. The staff is frantic.'

'Leave it to me. I will draft a statement. Set up an emergency call with the C8 for this evening.'

Moller hurried to his office and sat at his desk. His hands were shaking so badly he almost fumbled the handset of the ringing phone.

'Moller here.'

'Moller, it's Cardinal Lauriat.'

The priest couldn't speak.

'Are you still there?'

'Yes, I'm here.'

'I want you to come to my office immediately.'

'I'm sorry, Your Eminence, but I am extremely busy, as you can imagine.'

'This isn't a request, Ludwig. It is an order.'

When Moller appeared at Lauriat's suite within the Apostolic Palace, Lauriat kept him standing.

'How has he reacted?'

'Perhaps you should ask him?' Moller answered.

Lauriat's voice thickened. 'Don't you dare take that tone with me.'

'He is upset.'

'Who does he believe leaked the story?'

'He suspects someone on the C8.'

'Good. And what does he intend to do about it?'

'He is calling a telephonic meeting of the C8 for tonight.'

'I want to listen in again. Bring the phone number and the code to me when you have it.'

Moller shook his head defiantly. 'I'm sorry but I will not.'

Lauriat unfolded his arms and pointed at the priest. 'Have you lost your mind? Do you want to see those photos again? Do you want to see how you'll look in all the magazines and newspapers? You mother and father are still alive, aren't they? How proud they'll be of their son!'

'Do what you must, cardinal secretary. I will no longer be your spy.'

'Cal, I've been desperate to reach you. Have you seen the news?'

She did sound desperate but also a little angry, as if she expected Cal to be instantly available to her.

'I was teaching, Gail, but yes, I've seen it. It's lit up the Internet like a Christmas tree. You're the first person I called.'

'What are we supposed to do?'

'I wouldn't think you'd be obligated to do anything at this point.'

'But we've got to correct the record. The account in the press was dangerously wrong.'

'I know that, but you can't pick and choose what parts to refute.'

'Reporters are already making inquiries to the bank.'

'I think you need to let the Vatican take the lead on this. A no comment from your end ought to suffice if someone corners you or an employee.'

'This is going to explode, Cal. It's not going to be a tempest in a teapot. It's not going away.'

'I'm sure you're right, but again, the Vatican's got to run point on it. If you like I can place a call or two to see which way the wind's blowing over there. If I don't get a quick response then Julian and I can talk to Celestine in person.'

'I think you should postpone. I'm concerned for Julian's safety. He's going to be in the eye of the storm. You were right about the Vatican being leaky as a sieve. Someone tried to kill you, remember?'

'That was before. Now that the loan contract's in hand, the game has changed. It's all about political pressure now. Look, I'll call to confirm that the meeting is still on but assuming it is, I suggest we move forward and get this done so it becomes a fait accompli.'

'Then I'm going to arrange for a personal security detail. The bank has used a private company before. They'll be able to provide armed guards in Rome.'

'If that makes you feel safer, then go ahead. But I suggest you let Julian know in advance.'

'Why?'

'Because in case you haven't realized it, Julian's a grown man.'

Gil Daniels was not giving Cal an easy time. Cal was loath to hand him the ammunition to be a jerk, but it was proper protocol to talk to your department chairman when teaching slots were going to be missed. So, hat in hand, he humbly presented himself to Daniels' office.

'It's the first week of a new semester and you're leaving town? It's really not good form, Cal, is it?'

He hated it when Daniels went into his starchy full-on Brit mode, saying things like good form and sticky wicket.

'Believe me, it's not my choice, Gil. The trip just came up and it's mandatory.'

'Where to?'

'Back to Rome.'

'Again?'

'Afraid so.'

'It's nothing to do with the story I read in *The Globe* about the pope's alleged plan to give away billions of dollars, does it?'

'Actually, Gil, it does.'

Daniels arched an eyebrow theatrically. He reminded Cal of a character in a period British parlor-room drama whose monocle had just popped out.

'I think you owe me a full account,' Daniels said.

'I will if you let me sit down rather than standing in front of your desk like a naughty schoolboy.'

'Yes, sit, sit. The article in the paper suggests that evidence of a previously unknown nineteenth-century loan between the Vatican and the Sassoon Bank was recently discovered in the Vatican Secret Archives. Was that your doing?'

'It wasn't what I was originally looking for but I stumbled across a letter and kept following my nose. The actual loan contracts were in archives elsewhere in Rome and in New York.'

'And the loan is valued at twenty-five billion euros? Did the article get that right?'

'With interest that's what it's worth today.'

'And is it true the pope intends to repay the debt to the bank?'

'That part isn't technically correct, Gil, but I'm not at liberty to go into details.'

'Not technically correct? But essentially correct? It's inconceivable that the Vatican would willingly bankrupt itself or sell cultural assets to pay off an ancient debt. And to a Jewish bank? I'm not Catholic but it even sets me off.'

'Again, Gil, I can't say anymore. I'm sure the full story will come out sooner rather than later. That's why I've got to get over to the Vatican and work through some of the issues.'

'But you're an academic, not an international financier! What role could you possibly play at this juncture?'

'Again, I can't go into it. Sorry.'

'Well, what about your classes? What are we going to do about them?'

'I've got it covered. Pete Manning's agreed to fill in for my undergrad course, Spiritualism in the Middle Ages. He's got a light load this semester. And Joe Murphy's going to take my grad seminar on the Crusades. He was my TA on it last year.'

'Murphy,' Daniels sniffed. 'I'm getting a little sick of him, you know.'

Celestine concluded his telecon with the C8 and rang Moller's office to ask the priest to come see him.

'During my call, I thought I heard some shouts coming from the piazza. What's going on?'

'There was a small protest,' Moller said. 'Some people came with a bullhorn and some signs. The gendarmes moved them along. As a precaution your security detail inside and around the guesthouse has been increased.'

'What were they saying, these protesters?'

'They were praying to God, rather loudly, asking Him to prevent the Vatican from destroying the Church.'

'The Vatican or me?'

'In truth, you, Holy Father.'

'I see.'

'Could I ask if you have drafted a statement?' the priest asked. 'The press office remains on standby.'

'I have a draft. I'll make a few changes based on the suggestions of the C8. You look tired, Ludwig. You should go home. I will ring the press office to collect the statement when it is ready.'

'Thank you, Holy Father,' he said, about to leave. But he hesitated and added, 'I wanted to say that I am sorry.'

'Sorry for what?'

'I – I am sorry you have had such a difficult day.'

Gail Sassoon's housekeeper found her in her bedroom to tell her that Marcus Sassoon was on the phone.

'Do you know what just happened to me, Gail?' Marcus said.

'No, but I'm sure you're going to tell me,' she answered acidly.

'I was leaving work tonight and someone swore at me for what I was doing to the Catholics. The jerk called me a kike. Then he spit on me.'

She briefly closed her eyes. 'Actually, I'm quite sorry to hear that. Did you call the police?'

'Didn't have to. We've had media outside all day and the police were there keeping the traffic moving. They nabbed the son-of-a-bitch. I'm pressing charges. Who knows if the filthy bastard's carrying a disease?'

'You should press charges.'

Gail waited for it and it came.

'I told you so, didn't I?'

'Told me what, Marcus?'

'That this Vatican business would unleash a shitstorm of anti-Semitism.'

'All the articles got it wrong. The money isn't going to the bank. There was no mention of a foundation. When the record gets corrected people will come around.'

'Well, who's correcting it?'

'Hopefully the Vatican and hopefully soon.'

'I'm telling you again, Gail, this is going to end badly. You're going to wind up destroying the bank.'

He made sure he had the last word by hanging up on her.

Cal was at his home packing for the early-morning flight when his phone rang. He wasn't surprised by who was calling. Cardinal Da Silva was his usual apologetic self for imposing on Cal so late in the evening.

'I carry a message from the pope,' he said. 'He hopes you will still be coming tomorrow.'

'I'll be there with Julian Sassoon.'

'Good. He also wants you to hear the statement he has written for the media and to pass it along, if you could, to the Sassoon family. Would you care to take it down? It's fairly short.'

Cal got a pen and wrote as Da Silva read it.

'The Vatican takes note of the article published earlier today in the Italian press. While the Holy See does not typically comment on rumor and speculation, in this instance it is deemed necessary to clarify the record. It is true that there has been a recent discovery of a previously unknown financial debt between the Vatican and a certain banking institution. However, experts have not yet determined the validity of the debt and there has been no decision with respect to Vatican repayment of the debt. There will be no further statements until the matter is resolved.'

Cal arrived at the private aviation terminal at Logan Airport and was informed that the Sassoon jet had arrived from Teterboro. Julian Sassoon had already boarded.

Julian rose from a forward seat to greet Cal. 'I've got a little surprise for you,' he said.

The rear lavatory door opened and the surprise emerged. Gail Sassoon gave Cal a smile and a wave.

'Mommie Dearest decided to come along,' Julian said. 'She either wants to spend more time with me, the pope or with you. My money's on you.'

TWENTY-SIX

At Fiumicino Airport the Sassoon Gulfstream was met by a group of Italian security guards who'd been hired by the bank. They were an elite crew, ex-special forces, all of them from the 9th Parachute Assault Regiment. The squad leader, an intimidating fellow with a shaved head and a neck tattoo that crept just above his dress shirt, boarded the plane. He identified himself and asked to speak with the woman who had hired them, Gail Sassoon.

Julian and Cal exchanged glances and Cal let Julian do the talking.

'I'm Julian Sassoon,' he said. 'Mr Scotto, I believe your first assignment is helping Mrs Sassoon off the plane.'

Gail wasn't exactly passed out. Cal figured she was equal parts asleep and drunk. She had started drinking during the New York to Boston leg and had continued at a steady clip. Somewhere mid-Atlantic she had said something to Cal resembling a pass, prompting Julian to change seats to get as far away from her as he could. The first time Julian used the lavatory, Cal had urgently engaged her.

'Look, Gail. Like I told you the morning after our thing in Rome, it was a mistake on my part. You got drunk, I got drunk, but it's never, ever going to happen again. It can't. Especially now I've met Julian. Understand?'

She had slurred her words, 'Of course I understand, Cal. Never, ever.'

The three passengers had spent the rest of the journey spaced evenly throughout the cabin.

Scotto bundled Gail into a black people-mover and the three protectees and their security detail were driven to the Excelsior Hotel where the Sassoons were checked in under assumed names. Scotto was insistent – Gail and Julian were told to stay in and order room service. Cal was cut loose. His threat level was low according to the Italian, which suited him just fine. He happily went for a walk in the wintry chill.

Cal had observed the phenomenon before: by the following morning, Gail was bright as a new penny. Scotto had protected his share of sloshed celebrities. In the lobby he discreetly reintroduced himself and escorted her to the van where Julian and Cal were waiting.

Julian scowled at her and when she asked him why he was being so moody, he said sarcastically, 'I don't know, no reason in particular.'

'And you, Cal? You're awfully quiet. Are you also in a funk?'

'Me? Couldn't be better,' he said, slipping on sunglasses. 'The sun is shining and we're off to see the pope.'

The people-mover stopped at the entrance to St Peter's Square. Scotto explained that they were not permitted to bring weapons into Vatican City. He and two of his men left their pistols in a lock box and after doing a threat assessment outside the van, he led the three of them surrounded by a phalanx into the square.

'This is so lame,' Julian said to Cal. 'No one knows who the hell we are.'

Gail overheard and said something to the effect of better to be safe than sorry.

If anything, having bodyguards with earpieces attracted more attention than if they'd blended in, unprotected, among the tourists.

As they waited in the lobby of the Sanctae Marthae guesthouse, the guards stationed outside, Cal marveled at Julian's demeanor. The kid was a cool customer, seemingly unfazed at the prospect of meeting a pope. Gail, on the other hand, kept checking her face with her compact, nervously touching up her makeup.

The monsignor who came for them was someone Cal had never met. When the priest introduced himself Cal asked after Moller and he was informed that the monsignor was off duty today.

The pope greeted them with a frowning expression.

'Mrs Sassoon, Mr Sassoon, I was so very sorry to hear of the loss of your husband and your father. As you know, I never met him but from the way, Mrs Sassoon, you spoke about his spirit and his vision, I nevertheless felt a certain closeness to him. I have prayed for you and I have prayed for him.'

Something about the greeting seemed to get to Julian and Cal saw one of his knees buckle. Maybe the kid wasn't so cool after all.

Perhaps Celestine noticed too because he took Julian's hands and said, 'I have seen photos of your father and you look so like him. He lives on through his son. Such are the blessings of the family.'

He asked everyone to sit and turned his attention to Cal.

'And Professor Donovan. What else can I say about your friendship? This is your third trip to visit us within a short period. I thank you from the bottom of my heart.'

'It's my pleasure, Holy Father.'

'And congratulations are in order. I was informed by Monsignor Moller that Harvard has awarded you a prestigious professorship.'

Cal laughed. 'How did he find out?'

'Our Moller seems to know everything. I don't know what I would do without him.

'So,' the pope began, 'you see the cat is partially out of the bag. I had a sense we would need to proceed quickly with our new foundation and my fears have proven to have a basis. There are elements within the Church, perhaps within the Curia, who will oppose us. They have planted false and half-true stories with the media. This is only the beginning of what will certainly become a larger and louder campaign.'

'Do you have any idea where the leak came from?' Cal asked.

'I have no idea,' Celestine said wearily. 'Very few people know the facts. I am convinced that my most trusted advisors and confidants are blameless.' He looked toward Gail and asked, 'What do you think, Mrs Sassoon?'

His penetrating gaze seemed to unnerve her. 'I would never speak to anyone about this! I'm a huge supporter of the notion of the IFH.'

'I only found out about this a couple of days ago,' Julian added, pushing aside a curly lock that had fallen over one eye. 'I've spoken to no one other than Gail and Professor Donovan.'

The pope nodded. 'I have no doubt that the three of you have been discreet, but there is another party.'

'You mean Marcus?' Gail said.

The pope turned a palm upward. 'He did strike me as unsupportive.'

'I can't believe Marcus would do such a thing,' Gail said but she didn't sound like she was totally convinced.

'I think he's perfectly capable of doing it,' Julian said.

'I don't know Marcus Sassoon very well,' Cal said, 'so I'm not the one to comment but I'd like to point out that there was likely an earlier leak before anyone in the Sassoon family was even aware of the loan.'

'You speak of the attempt on your life,' the pope said.

'That's right. It suggests a Vatican source. Where there's one leak others might follow.'

'Well, this is troubling,' Celestine said, 'but we must not be diverted from the task at hand. I understand, Mr Sassoon, that your father in his wisdom has made you a significant beneficiary of his interest in the bank. You are therefore in a position to have a great deal of influence in the establishment of the foundation. That is why I wanted to meet you, to answer any questions you might have and to see if you are supportive.'

Julian leaned in and said, 'As you can see, I'm fairly young. I haven't had all that much so-called real-world experience. I went from college to business school with only a year in between where I traveled and had a good time. Other than doing some part-time work at the bank I've never held down a job. But here's what I do have. I have my father's genes and I spent my life watching how he conducted himself. He was an honest, honorable man and I'd like to think that I am too.'

'Wonderful, wonderful,' the pope murmured.

'He was a great fan of what you wanted to accomplish and so am I. You have my full support. I'll be voting to accept your settlement terms for the debt and with my stepmother's shares we'll have the majority. My cousins may not like it but they'll have no choice but to accept it.'

Gail reached for a tissue to blot her eyes. Cal couldn't tell whether she was proud of him or rueful of the stepmother tag.

'What a mature young man you are,' the pope said beaming his first smile of the day. 'You deserve credit for the man you have become, although your parents and your teachers are owed some too.'

'Thank you,' Gail said.

'Let me tell you a small personal anecdote,' the pope continued. 'When I was a young man, about your age, I too had little in the way of real-world experience. But I had a sense, an overpowering sense, that I had a calling to the priesthood. My parents and my friends argued that I should experience more of a secular life before making this spiritual commitment but I knew who I was. So I tell you, keep following your instincts, keep following your heart and your path in life will be a smooth one.'

'I never thought a pope would be offering me life-coaching,' Julian joked, 'but I appreciate the advice. Here's what my instincts are telling me. I need to move fast to take control of the bank so that, along with my stepmother's shares, I can intelligently exercise my majority control. At the same time, I want to be intimately involved with setting up and governing the IFH, if that's acceptable with you.'

'It would be a pleasure to have your intimate involvement.'

'What about school?' Gail blurted out.

'I don't need the degree. It's only a piece of paper. It's time for me to step up and enter the ring.'

The pope smiled again. 'I would have thought that a degree from Harvard had a certain value, wouldn't you say so, Professor?'

'Maybe one from the Divinity School,' he deadpanned.

'You said I could ask you some questions?' Julian said.

'Of course.'

'OK, here's the big one. I've been doing some research on the state of Vatican finances. Two things jumped out at me. First, you guys – sorry, I probably shouldn't be referring to you as a guy – you gentlemen probably don't have a good handle on the precise magnitude of your assets and liabilities. It looks like you've been fairly public about your frustrations on lack of financial transparency among some of your departments.'

'Indeed I have. Go on.'

'Second, from publicly available data, I'd be amazed if you have even a tenth of the liquid assets to satisfy a twenty-five-billion-euro debt. So here's my question: how are you going to raise the money?'

The kid's a force of nature, Cal thought.

'Mr Sassoon,' the pope said, 'if you hadn't decided to work for your own bank I would have been pleased to offer you a position as a consultant to help us work through our financial issues. It seems you have – what do the Americans call it – the right stuff. Now, to the issue of funding the IFH. As you correctly surmise, we do not have the necessary cash on hand – nowhere near it. We will be obliged to sell certain assets.'

'Which assets?' Julian asked.

Gail intervened. 'For heaven's sake, Julian! Marcus sat here two weeks ago and asked the same question. Isn't that up to the Vatican? It seems to me it's none of our business.'

'I'm afraid I don't agree, Gail,' Julian said. 'It's an important question.'

Cal thought he caught Celestine looking slightly startled at Julian's use of her first name.

Julian pressed on. 'The Sassoon Bank – a Jewish bank – is going to have to deal with the public fallout over this arrangement. It's one thing if the Vatican is going to be liquidating mutual funds and selling commercial real estate. It's something very different if you've got to sell off art.'

Cal never had the temerity to ask specifically how Celestine intended to raise the funds. But the kid was right. He'd certainly thought about it. Liquidating artwork was going to be a tough pill for the faithful to swallow.

The pope folded his arms across his cassock and said, 'In the Gospel of Luke, Jesus said, "Sell all that you possess and distribute it to the poor, and you shall have treasure in heaven." We do have assets we can sell to acquire treasure in heaven. Some of them, including real estate and land, are not so controversial. Others are more so.'

'Paintings,' Gail said quietly. 'Sculptures.'

'Yes, these things,' the pope said. 'How much of it, I do not yet know. A valuation exercise is in progress.'

'This could get ugly,' Julian said, shaking his curly head.

'Professor, do you agree?' the pope asked.

'I'm afraid I do but I'm sure Your Holiness has given the matter extensive thought.'

'More than thought. Prayer as well.'

'So where do we go from here?' Cal asked. 'How are you intending to correct the media representation that the Vatican intends to pay billions directly to the Sassoons?'

'We must correct the record swiftly,' the pope said, 'before the misperceptions of the public harden. This means we have to quickly work behind the scenes to work through the parameters by which the IFH will function. We need to thrash out a foundation charter and recruit a nucleus of trustees. Then and only then can we offer full transparency as to our intention to satisfy the debt via the IFH.'

Julian nodded vigorously. 'My stepmother and I are both willing to serve as trustees.'

'Excellent,' the pope said. 'Might I suggest two gentlemen to represent the Vatican, Cardinals Da Silva of Boston and Vargas of Toledo, Spain. This nucleus of four can help recruit future trustees with the necessary expertise along with the staff to manage a large foundation.'

'I'm willing to roll up my sleeves and stay here until the job is done,' Julian said.

'I am too,' Gail said.

'Wonderful,' the pope declared. 'I will summon these cardinals to the Vatican.'

'It looks like my work here is done,' Cal said lightly.

'Actually, Professor,' Celestine said, 'I would like to request your help with a necessary task to help us move forward.'

Ever since her mother died there had been a tradition in Elisabetta Celestino's family to come together once a week for supper at her father's apartment in Rome. On this evening, she was the last to arrive and had to endure the taunts of her siblings for being late.

Her sister, Micaela, laid it on thick. 'I'm a doctor with a ward full of patients, Zazo's the number two man in the Vatican Gendarmerie, which is up to its ass with protesters if you haven't heard, and my sister, the archeologist, is the late one. What happened, did a skeleton try and escape from the catacombs?'

Their father told Micaela to be more respectful to a woman of God then laughed at his own comment since no one was as irreverent as he. Carlo Celestino had been appalled when Elisabetta decided to throw in the towel on a promising career in archeology to become a nun, but ever since the pope had chosen her for a prominent position at the Pontifical Commission for Sacred Archaeology and she had moved from her communal residence to her own apartment, he had calmed down considerably.

'At least she's essentially back in academia again,' he had said.

For him, academics had been his whole life. His mandatory retirement from the Department of Theoretical Mathematics at La Sapienza hadn't gone down particularly easily. The family night was one way his children kept tabs on his mental and physical well being.

'I'm starving,' Zazo said. 'If you were another minute longer

I'd have passed out.' Zazo couldn't escape his childhood nickname around the supper table but his men knew him as Colonel Emilio Celestino.

'Who cooked?' Elisabetta asked, sitting down at the table.

'Papa,' Micaela said, rolling her eyes. 'I was too busy.'

'What's with the attitude?' Carlo asked. 'I can cook.'

'When you're all clutching your stomachs later, just be grateful I'm a gastroenterologist,' she said.

'So, Papa,' Elisabetta said, 'how's Goldbach?'

It was a running joke. Carlo had been trying his whole career to solve the Goldbach conjecture, one of the thorniest problems in theoretical mathematics for over two centuries. His children were convinced that old Goldbach was one of the few things keeping Carlo ticking. If he ever solved it, or worse still, if someone else solved it, it might be a happy day for mathematics but a sad day for the Celestino siblings.

'Goldbach is fine,' Carlo said, 'he says hello.'

As Micaela was passing the platter, her brother's mobile phone started ringing from his uniform jacket in the hall.

'Leave it,' Carlo said.

'I can't. It's my work phone,' he said, rising to grab it from the coat rack.

'How can you tell?'

'Different ring. If you couldn't figure that out how do you expect to solve your Goldbach?'

'That was so cruel!' Elisabetta laughed.

He came back in looking glum. 'Looks like I'm going to be the only one who won't need a stomach pump tonight.'

'What's the matter?' Micaela asked.

'One of my guys is waiting out front to pick me up. The pope's private secretary, Monsignor Moller, seems to be missing. We've been asked to find him.'

Micaela perked up. 'Which one of your guys?'

'She's hoping it's Vittorio,' Elisabetta teased.

'I am not,' her sister said. 'Well, is it?'

'Yes, it's Vittorio,' her brother said, rolling his eyes.

'You'd better ask him up,' Carlo said, 'or she'll be impossible for the rest of the evening.'

Major Vittorio Pinotti was a bit on the young side but Micaela didn't view his age as disqualifying. From her perspective he had a lot going for him. He was quite good looking, although he wasn't a genius, he wasn't a dunce either, he was unattached, heterosexual, and most importantly, her brother vouched for him. Pinotti had been on the receiving end of Celestino's promotions, backfilling the vacant slot.

'*Ciao*, everyone,' Pinotti said. 'Sorry to break up a family meal.'

'*Ciao*, Vittorio,' Micaela purred.

Pinotti seemed to get the hint. 'I should give you a call sometime,' he said. 'Do I have your number? Is it OK if I call her, Colonel?'

'What is this, the Middle Ages?' Micaela said. 'You need to get the permission of my brother?' She gave him a business card and said, 'This is maybe the fifth card I've given you. I'm running out of them.'

'Come on, let's go,' Celestino said, pulling on his coat.

Pinotti said, 'I'll call you.'

Ludwig Moller lived in an unassuming apartment block on the Via Aurelia, a short distance from Vatican City. Since it was outside his jurisdiction, Colonel Celestino was obligated to work with the Roman Municipal Police to effect entry if necessary. From the street the apartment had its lights on.

'We'll try his number again,' Celestino said to his fresh-faced municipal colleagues.

'Hopefully he answers and we can go back to our warm car,' the male officer said.

'Call him, Vittorio.'

There was no reply and Celestino said, 'OK, let's go.'

Pinotti rang the doorbell of the first-floor flat and banged on the door a few times before Celestino declared that it was necessary to force entry for a wellness check.

'Are you sure he didn't just take a vacation?' the female officer asked.

'Look, his boss is concerned about him and we can't leave until I know.'

'Who's his boss?'

'Pope Celestine.'

'Then you'd better break the lock,' the male officer said.

Celestino corrected him. 'No, *you'd* better break it. First off, it's your jurisdiction. Second, I outrank you. By a lot.'

The female officer gave her colleague a 'well, don't look at me' glance and he reluctantly put his boot to it until wood splintered around the lock.

The hallway was dark but a light was coming from the lounge.

Pinotti called out, 'Hello? Monsignor Moller? It's the Vatican Gendarmes.'

The lounge was empty. Everything was tidy and in place. The small adjoining kitchen was immaculate.

'I'll check the bedroom,' Celestino said.

It was dark and when he switched on the light, there was a sealed envelope on the perfectly made bed. It was addressed to His Holiness, Pope Celestine.

The male officer came in and began to reach for it before Pinotti warned him off. 'Hey, get your gloves on,' he said.

The bathroom door was closed but a light was shining underneath it.

Pushing the door open, Celestino saw its reflection in the mirror above the sink.

A bloated head the color of blueberries, dangling from the shower head by an electrical cord.

To Cal, it seemed that the pontiff might have hardly slept; he appeared to have aged overnight, the flesh of his face loosened by grief.

'It was a suicide,' the pope said. 'He was found last night but the authorities say he probably took his life the previous night. Here is the letter he left for me.'

> *Holy Father,*
> *Please know that it has been the joy of my life to serve you. I have never known a man with so much wisdom, compassion, and spiritual grace. I have failed you and for this I offer my abject apology and my life,*
> *Yours in Christ,*
> *Ludwig Moller*

'How did he fail you?' Cal asked.

'My interpretation is that he was taking responsibility for the leak to the press. However, I have no idea how he learned about the debt or with whom he communicated. I excluded him from meetings where I discussed it. These may be secrets that poor Ludwig has taken to his grave.'

'There must have been something else,' Cal said. 'Something else in his life.'

The pope's sadness was heartbreaking. 'Perhaps. I saw him almost every day for two years yet I hardly knew him. Whose fault is that but mine? I understand he played the violin very well. I wish I had asked him to play for me.'

'I'm sorry, Holy Father.'

'Life must go on. We still have work to do, important work, before we are called to Christ's kingdom – me, well before you. I wanted to talk to you about the assignment you agreed to undertake even before you knew what it was! You are indeed a dear friend. Remind me that I need to know you better, Professor – when we have more time, of course.'

'I will.'

'Now, the work. When we formally announce the debt repayment and the formation of the IFH we will need to issue a formal declaration of ecclesiastical principles, the foundation upon which we have made our decision.'

'Historically, that could range anywhere from an ecclesiastical letter to a papal bull,' Cal said.

'Given the immensity of the actions and the attendant controversy likely to be engendered, I was considering a papal bull.'

'I would tend to agree.'

'Ordinarily, I would assign Vatican personnel to undertake the appropriate research and drafting but given the secrecy involved, I cannot do so. Is this something you might be able to help me with? I understand you have a facility with the subject matter.'

Cal leapt at the opportunity. He'd studied papal proclamations and had written papers on papal bulls including his oft-quoted one, *Papal Bulls – Alpha to Omega*. In it he summarized the form and content of bulls from the first one, issued in 1059 by Pope Nicholas II, to the most modern one at the time of writing, released in 1998 by John Paul II. It would mean staying several more days in Rome but his teaching obligations were covered for a while and more importantly, he had Gil Daniels on his heels.

'It would be a rare honor and a great pleasure, Holy Father.'

*   *   *

'Can you believe the bastard killed himself?' Cardinal Malucchi asked, popping an olive into his mouth.

'He was obviously mentally unstable as evidenced by his deviant behavior. Do we have a problem, Pascal?' Cardinal Leoncino asked.

Upon hearing the news they had hurriedly assembled in Lauriat's apartment hoping for the measure of reassurance that the cardinal secretary smoothly delivered.

'I personally saw a copy of his suicide note,' he said. 'It was blessedly vague. He offered an apology to Celestine, though he failed to mention his transgressions. There was certainly nothing pointing to us.'

Leoncino jabbed back. 'You mean to *you.*'

'Yes, Mario, to me.'

'Then we're in the clear,' Malucchi said.

'As to Moller, apparently so,' Lauriat said. 'However, our problems continue elsewhere. The press bulletin that Celestine had the Vatican issue blunted the public outcry somewhat.'

'Only somewhat,' Malucchi observed. 'Coming here just now I walked through a fairly large protest in the piazza. They had all sorts of signs and some of them carried empty picture frames.'

'Did they?' Lauriat said, smiling. 'I'm glad that people are coming to the conclusion that the only way to satisfy this enormous debt is to sell our artistic patrimony.'

'But how much?' Leoncino winced.

'How much indeed? Lauriat said. 'There is more to consider. I also have troubling news. The pope has had visitors. Gail Sassoon and her son, Julian, are in Rome along with Calvin Donovan.'

'So, Celestine is pressing forward,' Malucchi said.

'It appears so,' Lauriat said. 'For the sake of the Church, we must press forward too.'

TWENTY-SEVEN

The atmosphere was often combustible whenever the Inspector General of the Vatican Gendarmerie Corps and the Commander of the Swiss Guards were in the same room. Although they lived and worked within the tight confines of Vatican City the two men had a relationship that lay somewhere in the netherworld between friendship and animosity. The Gendarmerie, a civil organization, was responsible for general police duties within the Vatican City while the Swiss Guards were tasked by ancient charter with the protection of the pope and the Apostolic Palace. Arturo Viola, the IG, had been a Roman police detective before moving to the Vatican Gendarmerie some twenty years earlier. Now in his sixties, with carefully dyed hair to maintain a semblance of youthfulness, his gut had begun to overhang his belt, but he still seemed fit for a man of his age. He was much shorter than his Swiss Guards counterpart, Kaspar Meyer, who used his height to lord over him. Meyer, like all the Guards, was a Swiss national, a thin imperious sort, who never seemed to crack a smile or launch a joke. The Guards were a military organization and the level of discipline within the organization reflected that. The Gendarmerie was a looser bunch, more like cops anywhere around the world. The conflicts between the two forces, such as they existed, arose from obvious cultural differences – Italian versus Swiss – but also from an overlap in duties. In practice, the pope received close protection in public places by a split-contingent of plain-clothes Gendarmes and Guards. Yet to the consternation of Meyer, Celestine had chosen Viola as his chief bodyguard, a coveted role. The pope enjoyed bantering with him in Italian and felt more at ease with his flexible style. He was, as Celestine once said, like a comfortable pair of shoes.

Cardinal Lauriat brought the meeting to order, thanking Viola, his Deputy Inspector, Colonel Celestino, Meyer and his Deputy Commander, Klaus Zeller, for coming.

'Gentleman, the agenda is simple: in this environment, how do you propose to increase the security of the pope and the residents of Vatican City and how do you intend to deal with the rash of demonstrations we are seeing on a daily basis?'

As usual, there was a competition between Viola and Meyer to be the first to answer. The both began speaking at the same time and it was left to Lauriat to offer Meyer the floor.

'We regard the current situation as business as usual,' he said. 'We have our robust practices and procedures and they are scalable to meet extraordinary threats. In a way, the threat of Islamic terrorism and our responses to it have tempered our capabilities. I have no doubt we can meet the present challenges. Zeller can speak to the details. As to the demonstrations, this is the responsibility of the Gendarmerie.'

Viola seemed irritated. 'We prefer to be proactive and not merely reactive. Plots against the pope and the Vatican are not spontaneous. Plotters plot. They talk among themselves.' He paused to cough a few times, covering his mouth with a handkerchief. 'Sorry, a bad cold. Yes, they talk among themselves. Their electronic conversations may be picked up by intelligence agencies. That is why we place a premium on our relations with external security services. Colonel Celestino can elaborate as he is in charge of these liaisons. He is also the point man for dealing with demonstrations in St Peter's Square.'

Meyer, who had been scowling, spoke before Celestino could. 'I must object to the notion that we are not proactive. Of course we are.'

'No one is doubting the capabilities of the Guards,' Lauriat said patiently. 'Colonel Celestino?'

Celestino began by reminding the cardinal of the close ties between his department and Interpol. 'Our Interpol National Central Bureau for Vatican City is tasked with collecting and sharing relevant information on crime and security with Interpol. Of course we also obtain data directly from the Italian intelligence agencies, but Interpol is a great clearinghouse of intelligence. I can tell you that as of this morning, we have no credible evidence of a plot against the Vatican. I do, however, have an officer who is fluent in several languages who is dedicated to scouring Internet chat groups regarding Vatican controversies. I regard it as an early-warning system. It is quite clear that the revelations about this debt and the speculation about the intentions of the Vatican regarding repayment have sparked tremendous debate and even vitriol but no specific threats have emerged at this time. Obviously the situation could change at any moment so our monitoring is continuous. Our operations and control room is staffed twenty-four hours a day.'

'And the demonstrations?' Lauriat asked.

'As you know, the pope has instructed us to be more tolerant of freedom of expression in the piazza than some of his predecessors,' Celestino said. 'However, there are clear red lines that trigger action. We don't tolerate hate speech or signage or any expressions considered blasphemous. We don't allow megaphones. We don't allow the rights of religious or touristic visitors to free passage and general enjoyment to become infringed. We don't allow any nudity. We don't allow large crowds to form. We will allow small, respectful demonstrators to congregate for a while before encouraging them to move along.'

'I must say,' Meyer said, 'if it were up to the Swiss Guards, we would not permit any organized protests within the Vatican, even though we might sympathize with some of their attitudes.'

'What is that supposed to mean?' Viola asked.

'It means that we always do our job as professionals even when we might have the personal opinions that the Vatican is straying from its course.'

Viola's hacking cough flared again before he managed to say, 'Our personal beliefs must never enter into the conversation.'

'No, I must correct you,' Meyer said. 'They must never enter into our work decisions but in a private setting, among colleagues, I see no harm in expressing an opinion when appropriate. Who among us can really say they support the dismantling of the heritage of the Church for the advantage of foreign bankers? It is somewhat horrifying, no?'

Everyone around Lauriat's conference table stiffened. It was left to the cardinal secretary to break the silence.

'With all due respect, Herr Meyer, this is not the purpose of today's meeting.'

'Fine,' Meyer said, stiffly sitting back in his chair, 'what else can we do for you, Eminence?'

Lauriat replied, 'I would like to go over the schedule of the Holy Father's public appearances for the next week so that we might anticipate all circumstances.'

'I would ask the Holy Father to limit his public appearances,'

Meyer said. 'I feel he is safest within the guesthouse with a cordon of Guards around it.'

'The Holy Father has told me he has no intention of reducing his schedule,' Lauriat said.

Viola stifled a cough and said, 'I for one am confident in the precautions we have taken. Besides, the pope has said that the Vatican is watched over by the Archangel Michael. Couple that with our collective expertise and I would say there can be no greater protection than that.'

Cal was so immersed in the language and cadence of papal bulls that he almost didn't pick up the call. When he glanced at the number, an unknown one from Manhattan, he reluctantly decided to answer. For all he knew, something was up with his mother. The molasses-slow growl of Detective Gonzalez brought him uncomfortably back to the real world.

'How're you doing, Professor?' the detective said. 'You still in New York or back in Boston?'

'Neither. I'm in Rome.'

'As in Italy?'

'The very place.'

'You get around, don't you?'

'How can I help you?'

'I'm not sure you can, but seeing where you're at, maybe I can help you. We've got an ID on the guy you popped. Europol had his prints. He's from where you're at. More specifically from some place called Catanzaro. You near there?'

'It's a few hundred miles south.'

'OK. Well, once we had him ID'd we were able to find his hotel in New York and his passport and belongings. Seems he flew into JFK three days before the shootings. He's a member of a mob. Shit, I can't pronounce it. Don't these people use vowels? N-D-something.'

''Ndrangheta?'

'Bingo. You heard of them.'

Suddenly Cal felt chilly despite the heat pumping into his hotel room. 'They're big in that region of Italy. Calabria.'

'Yeah. Apparently they've got some associates in our fair city too. That's probably how he got the guns though the serial numbers were filed so we might not know for sure. Anyway, I thought you'd like to know. It was an Italian job, like the movie. We've asked Europol to help run down known associates over in Italy to see if we can get a handle on motive, but this isn't smelling like an ordinary robbery no more.'

'Didn't think it was,' Cal said.

'Well, you were right. Anyway, stay safe, Professor, and duck if you see any of them Ndra-whatevers over there. If I know more, I'll fill you in.'

Cal put down the phone and was about to open the mini-bar for something clear and cold to settle his nerves when he remembered he had an appointment. He needed to stay sober for a while.

'This is excellent work, Professor, an ambitious and successful draft. And so fast! It would have taken my people very much longer.'

Cal wasn't used to having his work evaluated in real-time. That's what he did for his students. And when the evaluator was the pope, the exercise took on a rather unique dimension.

'I'm glad you're pleased.'

The draft papal bull ran to almost twenty double-spaced pages including references. A useful template had proven to be John Paul II's bull *Incarnationis Mysterium*, 'The Mystery of the Incarnation', issued upon the occasion of the Great Jubilee of 2000. While papal bulls always had a certain audience among academics and the faithful, Cal was fairly certain that this one would be the most widely read in history. It was the document that had to lay down the theological rationale and argument for a monumental act of institutional charity and as such he had labored over every word.

'I must say,' Celestine noted, 'that I am particularly pleased you gave prominence to Luke 11:41: "But give that which is within as charity, and then all things are clean for you." For this will surely be a cleansing act for the Church and its followers, will it not?'

'There will be many who take it that way, Holy Father. And realistically, there will be others who won't.'

'You are correct, of course. This will anger those who are willfully blind to the simple logic and beauty of the act. For the sake of the poor, we must have a poor Church. I will endeavor to explain my decision in essays, in interviews, in any way I can, but the bedrock principles we espouse will be present in this bull. Professor

Donovan, I wish to ask you a question because your views are uniquely interesting. You were born to a Jewish mother and a Catholic father. You chose to become a Catholic. You are also a scholar of religion. What is your opinion of the manner in which I am choosing to repay this debt?'

Cal took a full breath to give himself a moment to collect his thoughts. 'I have qualms, I must admit, but fundamentally I support it. The Church has always been proud of the way it glorified Christ, the Virgin Mary, and the saints through art and architecture. Losing elements of the Vatican's central repository of this work saddens me. However, the humanistic principles embodied by your action are far more important. Also, I must say that establishing a foundation that serves the poor of all faiths is heartening. It's a far more powerful statement than limiting it to a single faith. The last thing I'd say, Holy Father, is that it's politically enlightened to use the moral obligation of a debt repayment, particularly a debt that was brutally coerced, as an instrument to achieve the moral restructuring of the Church. That said, I do share the concerns of the Sassoons about triggering a tsunami of anti-Semitism.'

'Thank you for your candor. I would like to explore these subjects with you in greater depth. Please give me a day to go over your draft in greater detail. Perhaps I might suggest a revision or two.'

'I hope you will.'

'It occurs to me that apart from one very meager breakfast, the two of us have never dined. What about tomorrow night? Are you available? I can do a little better than the cafeteria.'

'That would be wonderful. There is something else I wanted to mention. I've received some information about the man who tried to kill me in New York. He was 'Ndrangheta, sent from Calabria.'

Cal saw the pontiff's Adam's apple rise and fall within his fleshy neck. 'I feared as much,' he said. 'The plotters will stop at nothing.'

Julian had let Cal know earlier in the day that he wanted to have dinner with him and had made it clear he had no interest in going anywhere with Scotto's bodyguards in tow. So Julian told Gail he'd be taking room service and turning in early. When it was time to leave, he slipped out of the Excelsior Hotel through the restaurant, avoiding Scotto's night detail in the lobby.

He'd told Cal he really craved a juicy burger so they met at the Hard Rock Café, where he got his wish.

'Where're your bodyguards?' Cal asked.

'I blew them off,' Julian said, ordering a beer.

'I don't think that was a great idea.'

'Don't tell me you're buying into Gail's paranoia.'

'It's not paranoia. She's got it right.'

Even after Cal told him about the 'Ndrangheta connection, Julian was cavalier.

'I don't know, Professor. Some shadowy guys sending a mob goon from Italy to prevent you from finding the loan? I think maybe you've been watching too many movies.'

'It didn't feel like a movie when I shot the guy,' Cal said, before draining his vodka.

'I'm sure it was traumatic but the papers said it was a robbery gone bad.'

'Don't believe everything you read in the papers.'

Julian shrugged and steered the conversation away from conspiracies to politics. He and Gail were scheduled to see the pope's proposed representatives to the IFH board in the morning and Julian wanted to find out as much as he could about the two cardinals who had flown in earlier that day. Over the din of loud music Cal sang Cardinal Da Silva's praises but confessed to knowing less about the Spanish cardinal, although he was quite sure that Vargas would share Celestine's views on the core mission of the Church.

'I think you can assume he's picked two of his most trusted brothers,' Cal said. 'You won't find any daylight between their positions and his.'

'Glad to hear it. They'll be plenty of organizational bullshit and infighting to come. No sense starting out with it. One voice and all that.'

Cal smiled. 'You're a pretty . . . confident guy for someone your age. Know that?'

'You were going to say cocky.'

'That was one of the other adjectives I was batting around.'

'I'm my father's son, I guess. My mother – my real mother – used to tell me that Henry was a cocky bastard when he was young.'

'Did you always want to go into business like him?'

'It was the last thing I wanted until I was a sophomore in college. I took a finance class for a lark and a bell went off. Of course I wasn't interested in the family biz. Anything but, preferably something in tech, and preferably as far as I could get from New York. Until – well, all this shit. How about you? I read your father was a professor at Harvard. Did you always want to go into the family biz?'

'I was like you, I suppose. Anything but until somehow it was something I wanted badly. You got a girlfriend, Julian?'

'I've got two actually. One from college who's in med school at Stanford, and a classmate at the B-School. They don't know about each other. Gotta watch Facebook and Instagram like a hawk to keep from getting busted.'

Cal raised his glass for a clink. 'Christ, man, it's scary how alike we are.'

When they got back to the Excelsior, both of them tipsy, they had to deal with a pair of very upset bodyguards who couldn't believe their eyes when Julian marched past.

'Calm down,' Julian said. 'You work for *me*, remember?'

'No, signor, we work for your mother.'

'One: she's not my mother. Two: bitch to her about it, not me.'

The guards turned their ire toward Cal who told them in Italian, 'Don't look at me like I'm the bad guy. If you haven't noticed he's not a boy.'

In the elevator Julian asked him what he'd said.

'I told them I took full responsibility.'

'You did not. You're such a bullshitter.'

They both melted in a fit of drunken laughter until the door opened to their common floor.

Cal's room was at the end of the long hall and when they got a bit closer they saw a woman camped outside his door.

'Looks like you've got company,' Julian snorted. 'No rest for the wicked.'

Closer still, Julian stopped and swore.

She saw them and began to walk, sloppily veering from one side of the corridor to the other.

'Cal! Julian!' Gail said. 'I was knocking on your door, Cal. I wanted to see you. Where were you?'

She was shoeless and very drunk.

Julian lit into her. 'For fuck's sake, Gail. What the hell's the matter with you?'

'I'll take care of it,' Cal told him. 'I'll bring her back to her room.'

'What's wrong?' she said. 'I just wanted to talk to Cal. What's wrong with that? Why are you so judgmental?'

'Henry just died, Gail. Remember?'

She began to cry. 'And that's why I'm so sad. I wanted to talk to someone, that's all.'

Julian seethed at her. 'You're a drunk, Gail. You know that? Here's the deal. If you're sober enough to come to the meeting tomorrow morning then come. But then you're going to get on the goddamn plane and fly back to New York and you're going to get yourself some help. If you don't, forget about my cooperation. I'll vote my shares with Marcus and you can kiss your precious foundation goodbye.'

TWENTY-EIGHT

T rue to form, Gail emerged from her room the next morning looking energetic and no worse for wear.

She met Julian in the lobby, completely ignoring the nighttime episode, glibly spouting platitudes about how excited she was about their meeting.

'You do remember what happened last night,' Julian said.

'It was nothing, Julian. One cocktail too many and an Ambien for jet lag. It's not a good combination. Won't happen again.'

'You're going home today,' he said.

'Oh, Julian, please,' she said dismissively.

'In case you forgot what I said last night . . .'

'Of course I remember. You were angry. I understand.'

'I meant it, Gail! I'll stay on a few days to work with these people but you're leaving. Either agree right now or I'm ditching this meeting and voting my shares with Marcus.'

'Julian, don't make a scene in public.'

He clapped once. 'All right, I'm done. I'm going back to my room.'

As Scotto and the bodyguard team watched impassively, inured to the mercurial behavior of celebrity clients, Julian turned toward the elevators.

Gail called after him. 'All right, you win. I agree. You know something? You've got a lot of Henry in you.'

In the people-mover, Scotto took the occasion to chide Julian for evading his protection last night but Julian would hear none of it.

'Look, Mr Scotto, you work for me now. Mrs Sassoon is leaving this afternoon. You'll do things the way I want or I'll cancel your contract.'

Scotto looked to Gail who smiled bravely and said, 'It appears there's a new sheriff in town.'

'OK, Mr Sassoon, you're the client. We'll advise you the best we can and then it's for you. We take our reputation seriously. If we think it will be in jeopardy, we may suggest you use another security company.'

The meeting took place in a small conference room on the ground floor of the Apostolic Palace, attended only by Gail and Julian and the two cardinals. Cardinal Da Silva was his warm and jovial self, chit-chatting over coffee and biscuits about Boston weather, sports teams, and, of course, Cal Donovan. Vargas was more reserved, a small, cerebral man who had risen to the College of Cardinals not by dint of personality but by the power of intellect. He was widely considered by his peers to be the best writer among them; his books and essays were widely published in translation. He was one of Celestine's most ardent philosophical soulmates. When the pope was cardinal secretary, Vargas was perhaps the only cardinal who had known the fullness of his theological views, positions that would only bloom after the conclave.

Absent a chairman and an agenda, the group of four initially drifted, spending time discussing the kinds of grants made by Gail's small foundation.

Then Julian impatiently asserted himself. 'With all due respect, it seems to me that we need to settle on a few key tasks today, go off and implement them, then meet again to discuss next steps.'

'Very sensible,' Da Silva said.

'Do you have a notion what these key tasks should be?' Vargas asked.

'I do,' Julian said, pulling out an agenda of sorts he'd prepared. 'I've printed copies.'

Gail smiled a little sheepishly as she reviewed the task list. It was the embodiment of the kind of proactive approach she would have undertaken as a young lawyer. Today, she was unprepared. She looked up and hid her embarrassment with a sip of water.

Vargas nodded repeatedly while reading it then said, 'I greatly admire the clarity of your thinking on this matter, Mr Sassoon. You seem well suited to be our partner in the Holy Father's initiative.'

For his part, Da Silva decided to begin to read the list out loud. 'One: Agree upon statement of mission and philosophy of investment.' He removed his glasses and added, 'As an aside, I do believe that describing our proposed donations as investments is the correct thinking. We should be investing in the well-being of the beneficiaries.'

'I think we should have a goal of sustainability,' Gail said.

'Giving food in the middle of a famine or bottled water in a drought saves lives which is so very vital but we need to do more. It seems to me that we need to have a focus on long-term infrastructure projects. That's been the philosophy of our family foundation.'

Vargas said, 'Give a man a fish, you feed him for a day. Teach him to fish, you feed him for life.'

'Matthew 4:19,' Julian said, prompting the cardinals to stare in admiration. 'Jesus said, "Come, follow me and I will make you fishers of men."'

'You know your Bible, young man,' Vargas marveled.

Julian grinned. 'I looked it up. I thought it might come in handy, you know, a Jew quoting the New Testament to break the ice.'

There was a moment of silence until Da Silva broke out laughing. 'It is certainly going to be a pleasure working with you.'

Da Silva, once recovered, read out the rest of Julian's list. Draft a foundation charter. Analyze investment practices of several notable philanthropic foundations. Hire a search firm to identify candidates for IFH executive director and additional board members. Hire a public relations firm to shape message to media.

At a break in their discussions, Gail sidled up to Julian and quietly said, 'I know you're angry at me and I know you don't particularly like me right now. But I am very, very proud of you.'

Cal was working at the hotel on a revision to the papal bull when Gail phoned his room.

'I'm mortified about last night,' she said.

'If I had ten cents for every time I made a damn fool of myself by drinking too much – well, you know the expression.'

'Julian is insisting that I leave.'

'He told me.'

'So I'm leaving. I'll send the jet back for you and Julian.'

'That's fine. I'll be done with my work day after tomorrow. I think that's Julian's timeframe too.'

'Will you do something for me, Cal?'

'Anything I can.'

'Look after him.'

'He's got bodyguards.'

'Not that way. I'm concerned about his mental state too. He hasn't grieved, at least not openly. He bottles up his emotions. He always has. Henry's death is going to hit him and when it does it's going to hit him hard. If it happens on your watch, please help him as best you can.'

'I'll try.'

'And Cal?'

'Yes?'

'Please put in a good word for me. I'm not a bad person, at least I don't think I am.'

The table was set with linen and fine china. There were flickering candles on the sideboard and Renaissance paintings on the wall – moody and dark: saints in prayer, saints in agony. Some diners might have been put off by visions of half-naked, pierced, and bleeding men but Cal was not one of them. He was in the dining room of the formal papal apartments in the Apostolic Palace and he was having the time of his life.

His dinner companion ate sparingly, the strain of recent events weighing upon him. Three Sicilian nuns had been laboring half the day in the kitchen and the food was excellent home-cooked fare. It was meant to be a social dinner, an opportunity to solidify a budding friendship, but the pontiff couldn't get away from the work at hand.

'Your new draft,' he said. 'I believe we are getting closer.'

Cal was drinking a good Sangiovese. Vodka did not appear to be on the menu. 'Thank you. Your notes were very clear.'

'I have a name for the bull. *A Tempore Ad Caritas*. What do you think?'

'A Time for Charity. I think it says it all.'

'Then we shall use it. The group of four met this morning. I've been told the meeting was highly productive. Da Silva and Vargas were impressed with both of the Sassoons and were pleasantly surprised by the maturity and judgment of Julian.'

'He's an impressive young man.'

'For me, this was a critical hurdle,' the pope said. 'Without a common vision the success of the IFH would be in jeopardy. I can feel more comfortable now.'

Cal could feel something consequential coming.

'Given the furor over the leak and the deliberate ambiguity of the initial Vatican statement I have decided to accelerate the announcement of our plans.'

'To when?'

'Tomorrow.'

Cal had expected to be back in the cloisters of university life when the bomb dropped. Instead he'd have a front-row seat at ground zero.

'I'm a bit surprised,' he said. 'The bull still needs some work.'

'We can issue it in a few days. However, I drew from it for the announcement tomorrow. I should have said we. Da Silva and Vargas collaborated on the draft. Would you like to see it?'

Cal put down his utensils to read the press bulletin. It was all there, nothing held back. Including the elephant in the room.

'You mention the art,' Cal said quietly.

'How could we not?'

'Are you prepared for the storm, Your Holiness?'

'Hardly a storm, Professor. More like a typhoon. But yes, I am ready. There will be an outcry. There will be anger. The pope will be accused of this and that. If our Lord and Savior could willfully die for our sins then I, mere man, can sacrifice my comfortable existence for the sake of human dignity.'

'I'll do anything I can to help.'

'There will be interest, I am sure, in how the existence of the debt became known. Are you willing to be named? Are you willing to be interviewed?'

'I've never been shy.'

'Good. We will make you available to the press. I have granted an exclusive papal interview with a journalist from *Corriere Della Sera*. It will be a busy day.'

Two nuns came to clear the first course. The women were so diminutive that at a distance they could have been mistaken for children.

'Could I ask you something, Holy Father?' Cal said when the nuns had left. 'Do your museum people, your curators know of your plans?'

'Ah, the keepers of the treasure. They know of my interest in assigning a value to our collections but I don't think they suspect. No, that is not entirely true. One of them more than suspects. She knows because she is unusually perceptive. Have you met the nun, Elisabetta Celestino?'

'Yes and no. I ran into her in the Vatican Secret Archives but we didn't speak.'

'I would like you to meet her properly,' the pope said, 'perhaps before your first interview. You will certainly be asked about your views on the art. You may express yourself freely but it might be helpful to have the perspective of someone in the Vatican with a curatorial type of role. She is quite articulate.'

'I've been told she has an interesting background.'

Plates of ravioli arrived. The pope asked if it was, perhaps, his favorite, with ricotta and nutmeg, and when informed that it was, he brightened and told Cal he was in for a treat.

When the nuns returned to the kitchen he told Cal that Sister Elisabetta did indeed have an interesting past and an important association with his papacy.

Celestine sampled the ravioli then said, 'Years ago she was a graduate student in archeology at the University of Rome, where her father was an eminent mathematician. Unfortunately she was the victim of a violent crime during which her boyfriend was killed. She was left grievously wounded. During her arduous recovery she made the life-changing decision to become a nun. Years later the Vatican called upon her for assistance to help it understand a sensitive and provocative discovery made at the Catacombs of Callixtus, her prior area of study. She agreed to help and became embroiled in a dangerous episode involving a plot to decimate the Church during the last convocation – my convocation.'

'The bombing. Yes, I know,' Cal said. 'It was a tragedy but I had no idea she was involved.'

'She was more than involved. Her actions and the actions of her brother, a member of the Vatican Gendarmerie Corps, saved many lives and saved the Church from an era of chaos and despair. It was a feeling of gratitude and joy that led me to choose my papal name based on hers.'

Cal stared across the table in fascination. 'I had no idea.'

'So will you speak to my dear Elisabetta?'

TWENTY-NINE

E arly the next morning the Vatican press bulletin hit with the force of an atomic blast. For Cal it was one thing to read the draft and quite another to see it embedded in breaking-news stories on his laptop.

Celestine Announces Formation of New
International Humanitarian Foundation in
Cooperation with the Sassoon Bank

Vatican City – The Holy Father wishes it to be known that the Holy See and the Sassoon Bank of New York have reached an agreement in principle to create a charitable foundation for the benefit of people around the world suffering from poverty, malnutrition, disease, lack of education, and conflict. The Interfaith Fund for Humanity will administer grants without respect to geography, race, or religious affiliation with an aim to lift needy people up from misery and strife via lifesaving and sustainable initiatives.

The origin of this new foundation lies with the recent discovery of a hitherto unknown nineteenth-century debt owed to the Sassoon Bank by the Holy See. The loan documents, properly executed in 1858, were discovered by an academic researcher in the Vatican Secret Archives and in the private archives of the Sassoon Bank. With accrued interest the present value of the debt is 25 billion euros.

The Holy See is of the opinion that it has a moral and legal obligation to satisfy this loan, which was obtained in a violent and coercive manner that has saddened the Holy Father. However, the Holy See and the Sassoon Bank have agreed that payment of the debt would be made, not to the bank, but to this new foundation. Representatives of the Sassoon family will serve on the board of trustees along with representatives of the Holy See and a distinguished group of international aid experts.

In order to satisfy the repayment of this debt without

compromising the financial stability of the Holy See and the Vatican Governorate or any of its administrative functions and obligations, it will be necessary to monetize certain assets under Vatican control. These include a carefully selected portfolio of real-estate holdings and works of art. None of the existing charitable initiatives of the Holy See will be impacted. The funds raised by the annual Peter's Pence donations that go to support Catholics in need will not be diverted to the new foundation.

The Holy Father states, 'The mission of the Church is to provide for the spiritual wellbeing of its flock according to the beautiful and timeless principles laid down in the Gospels. Remember that in the Book of Matthew Jesus said, "If you want to be perfect, go sell your possessions and give to the poor, and you will have treasure in heaven." In repayment of this old debt we are evoking Christ's proclamation mindful that people of the Catholic faith do not live in a vacuum. What affects one child of one faith in one part of the world affects all people in all parts of the world. To bow down with compassionate love to the weak and the needy is a fundamental part of the authentic spirit of the Catholic faith.'

Cal reached for the remote and turned on the TV and began flipping channels. The only ones not carrying the news were the cartoon and home-shopping networks. The coverage was urgent and breathless. He imagined that talking heads were being rushed to TV studios around the world to opine on the significance of the announcement.

His phone rang.

'So the news just hit,' Julian said.

'I'm watching it. What do you think?'

'I think it's a big fucking deal.'

'That it is. Your life isn't going to be the same.'

'That's OK. I'm ready.'

'You sure?'

'I guess we'll see.'

'Who's handling media for the bank?'

'I got a text from Gail. She's back and possibly sober – at least the text made sense. She's going to be doing interviews in New York today. I'm making myself available at the hotel for a press conference tomorrow morning. I made nice with Scotto and he's handling the prep. I'll be tied up for the rest of the day working on a mission statement and interviewing search firms to flesh out the IFH. What about you?'

'Celestine is going to be disclosing my involvement this afternoon in his interview with an Italian paper. The Vatican press office is going to sort through requests from journalists and send a minder over to the hotel to monitor my interviews. In the meantime I'll be finalizing the papal bull. It could be released as early as tomorrow.'

'Rocking and rolling,' Julian said.

'That's one way to put it.'

They were back in the Palace of the Governorate in the same drab conference room across the hall from the parking office. At their last meeting, while awaiting the pope, they had been quizzical and a bit restless. This time they were tense, coiled like tight springs, a few of them monitoring Twitter feeds on their phones.

'The pope is definitely coming?' Boni, the director of the Vatican Museums, asked Cardinal Portolano, the president of the Pontifical Council for Culture.

'That's what I was told.'

'The last time I saw Monsignor Moller was in this room,' Archbishop Thorn, the Vatican archivist and librarian, said to no one in particular. 'Such a tragedy. Do you think it had something to do with all of this?'

'Who knows?' Portolano said. 'May his soul rest in peace.'

Monsignor Joseph, the real-estate supervisor from APSA, whispered to Elisabetta Celestino, 'I had no idea the valuation exercise was meant for this purpose, did you?'

'I didn't know what to think,' she replied enigmatically.

His bodyguards came in first to check on the room, then Celestine entered, accompanied by a young Vietnamese monsignor, who held a notebook remarkably similar to the one Moller used to carry. The pope sat beside Portolano, smiled at Elisabetta, then turned serious.

'So, gentlemen and lady, here we are once again,' the pope said. 'I must apologize for my inability to have been fully candid with you at our first meeting. It would have been premature to do so. Following the announcement this morning you will understand the reasons for the exercise you have undertaken. We do intend to liquidate some assets to satisfy this debt of ours to fund this new foundation. Today I am keen to hear about your progress. My second private secretary, Monsignor Dinh, will be taking notes.'

The young priest shyly nodded and opened his book.

Celestine took stock of the many glum stares around the table and perhaps for this reason he began with something of a homily about world poverty and strife and the need for the Church to do more to help alleviate suffering. He spoke fluidly and passionately about the Vatican setting an example for other Catholic dioceses, international non-government organizations, and nation states by committing meaningful sums to combat the great injustices affecting peoples of all faiths.

'We can be a beacon, illuminating the darkest corners, showing unfortunate men, women, and children the bright light of our love,' he said. 'Even if others don't follow our lead, perhaps Catholics will be proud of the actions of their Church and elevate further the traditions of charity within their own communities.'

The museums' director was becoming visibly agitated, his tension building until it found its release in the form of an outburst.

'But Holy Father,' Boni said, 'to me, our cultural heritage *is* the Church! Well, at least its material embodiment. Our predecessors began commissioning and procuring Christian art centuries ago, not for the sake of being collectors but to create a tangible representation of our faith and our values. Our art is a statement of the ideals of Christian humanism, of the harmonious development of the faculties of the human mind on natural and spiritual planes, all for the greater glory of God.' He began to sob. 'I simply cannot bear the thought of cleaving off the beloved heritage of the Church, *my* Church.'

'Professor Boni,' Cardinal Portolano said sharply. 'We serve at the Holy Father's pleasure. We must put aside our personal views. This applies to me, it applies to you, it applies to all of us. The contents of the museums do not belong to you. They belong to the Church and the pontiff may decide what becomes of them. If you cannot assist the Holy Father in this endeavor, however painful it may be, we can find others who can.'

Boni composed himself and apologized for his outburst. When he was done, Celestine, who had been patiently taking it in, got up to put a hand on his shoulder.

'Professor, I understand your state of mind and I empathize with your feelings about the artwork under your care. I too appreciate the immense cultural meaning of our paintings and sculptures. Yet imagine, if you will, a giant scale. On one side we have a magnificent Renaissance painting. On the other, a starving child. Which way do you suppose the scale tilts? What is more important to God – a sheet of painted canvas, a piece of marble, or a human life?' Returning to his seat he said, 'You are a good man, Professor. You know the answer. And consider this: we are not discussing the destruction of masterpieces, merely the sale and transfer to other museums and galleries where the public may still enjoy them. I also wish to say emphatically that our art is not *the* heritage of the Church. It is but one of its heritages, the least important in my opinion. The Gospels of Christ are more important. Our liturgical traditions are more important. Our body of canon law is more important. Our people are more important. I say we can and should sacrifice some of our cultural heritage for the sake of humanity.'

Boni closed his folder containing his notes for the meeting. It was his turn to stand. His lower lip was trembling. 'I'm sorry, Holy Father, I cannot participate in this. You have my resignation. I won't be remembered as the curator who oversaw the dismantling of the Vatican Museums.'

Celestine replied sternly, 'Very well, Professor, I accept your resignation effective immediately. Be so good as to hand over your folder to Sister Elisabetta. She will be in charge of the tasks ahead on behalf of the museums.'

Boni left the folder in its place and headed for the door but before he left he turned and spat out, 'At least you can't peddle the frescoes and painted ceilings. Or maybe you can. Sell the walls, why don't you?'

The slamming of the door was the last sound for many uncomfortable moments. No one but Celestine was going to break the ice.

'I feel for the professor,' the pope finally said. 'The artwork is his life. A bear protects its cubs, a mother protects her child. He is following his conscience although I believe he is misguided. Now we must get to work. Archbishop, could you please pass the folder to Sister Elisabetta?'

Thorn did so and Elisabetta opened it and began thumbing through Boni's spreadsheets.

Celestine suggested they start with the least emotive portfolio of assets and called upon Monsignor Joseph to give his report.

The Canadian crisply delivered his assessment. 'Following our last meeting I concentrated on the non-ecclesiastical real estate and agricultural land throughout Italy and the rest of Europe under the direct control of the Vatican. Much of it is highly desirable, particularly the commercial retail space in major cities and the apartment blocks. For the purposes of the exercise I assumed that we would liquidate assets in a controlled manner so that we would not be seen as entering into fire sales, as it were. If we were to take a disciplined approach, I believe the fair market value of our portfolio is approximately five billion euros. Of course, these are rent-bearing properties so there would be a loss of revenues of several million euros per annum.'

Celestine thanked him and noted that although the loss of revenues was no small issue, there were budget initiatives he was championing for other departments that would alleviate shortfalls. He turned to Archbishop Thorn and asked him to go next.

Thorn nervously cleared his throat. 'Thank you, Holy Father. With respect to the materials in our archives and libraries, I thought long and hard about the approach I would take on the valuation exercise. Clearly, with thousands upon thousands of books, manuscripts, letters, ledgers, et cetera, it was not possible to individually assess value. Nor would there be a significant market for the vast proportion of our holdings. Therefore I confined my analysis to certain high-profile documents that would likely attract bids from archives, museums, and wealthy collectors. For example, I put a value of ten million euros on the letter sent to Pope Clement concerning the divorce of Henry VIII and Anne Boleyn. In aggregate the fifty or so most marketable items in our archives would achieve an auction value of approximately thirty million euros.'

'Is that all?' the pope asked. 'A drop in the proverbial bucket.'

'I have a confidence in my projections. The market for manuscripts is not of the same magnitude as art. Of course, if we were to sell our entire archive or entire library to one of the great libraries in Britain or America, perhaps we could make considerably more.'

The archbishop exhaled in relief when Celestine said that a wholesale sale was out of the question. 'So,' the pope said, 'the burden falls upon the museums. Sister, I hate to put you on the spot, but can you make anything out of Boni's paperwork?'

Elisabetta had been urgently studying the contents of the museum director's folder but her time had run out. She closed the leather portfolio and composed herself.

'I have an intimate knowledge of part of our collections since you asked me to work on valuing the antiquities and artifacts. For example, our ancient statue collection is quite magnificent, containing a great number of highly desirable pieces that many great museums would love to own. *The Venus of Knidos*. *Apollo Belvedere*. Our *Augustus*. The *Athena Giustiniani*. The *Deity of the River Nile*. I could go on and on. I estimate that we have well over one billion euros of statuary. If one adds in our extensive Etruscan and Egyptian collections, I would put the total antiquities value at two billion.'

'I see, I see,' Celestine said. 'What of Boni's estimates?'

She smiled. 'My cursory review, Holy Father, is that Professor Boni did his typically thorough work. It seems he has assigned a low value, a high value and a mid-point value to hundreds of paintings, classical statues, decorative arts, and tapestries. Some of the notable works are indeed famous. Raphael's *Coronation of the Virgin* and his *Transfiguration*. Caravaggio's *Deposition*. Leonardo's *St Jerome*. Bellini's *Burial of Christ*. Titian's *Madonna de San Niccolo dei Frari*. Boni values for each of these a low value of three hundred million, a high value of four hundred million. I think he doesn't even hazard a guess at Michelangelo's *Pietà* because there are only question marks next to it. Give me a moment to check the totals.' She opened the folder again, found the summary page and looked up, blinking, as if a bright light had been shone into her eyes. 'The grand total, choosing the mid-point valuation, is twenty-four billion euros, Holy Father.'

Celestine's barrel chest heaved out a sigh. 'And there we have it,' he said.

Cardinal Portolano cleared his throat to get the pope's attention. 'Excuse me, Holy Father, but I would like to point out that we derive approximately one hundred million euros per year in museum admission fees from visiting tourists. Who knows how much of this we would lose if our collections were seriously diminished?'

'An excellent point, Sandro. Perhaps we could restructure our galleries and exhibition halls to show the results of our charitable works. We might also have empty frames for contemplation or perhaps some excellent photographic replicas of the originals. Don't you think this would interest our tourists?'

'Perhaps not as much,' the cardinal said as diplomatically as possible. 'But I could be mistaken.'

'Well, we will have to make up budgetary deficits elsewhere,' Celestine said impatiently, bringing the meeting to a close. 'Again, I ask you to keep our discussion private, although I imagine that Professor Boni's tongue will wag enough for all of you.'

Boni left the palace and wandered around St Peter's Square in a daze. There was a generous crowd, far more visitors than usual for the time of day and many were demonstrators. He stopped and watched a group of twenty or so, holding signs lettered by the same hand. SAVE OUR CHURCH. SAVE OUR HERITAGE. SAY NO TO LOOTING. PLEASE CELESTINE – DO NOT DO THIS. He felt like shaking hands, joining the protest, but he kept walking. Should he go to the museum and empty out his desk? Write an open letter to the Holy See? Go home?

Two middle-aged women caught his eye. They had just entered the square and were walking purposefully toward the Vatican obelisk. Once there they unrolled two signs and held them defiantly over their heads. WE SUPPORT CELESTINE. FOR GOD'S SAKE: HELP THE POOR. Boni was outraged. He considered challenging them, asking whether they had any notion of the importance of culture, but then a curious thing happened – at least curious to him. A few people, then more and more came up to the women and began clapping and before long a spontaneous chant began. 'Help the poor. Help the poor.'

Disgusted, he turned away and faced the Apostolic Palace.

A monsignor knocked on Cardinal Lauriat's door and saw that Cardinal Leoncino was in with Lauriat.

'I'm sorry to bother you, Eminences, but Professor Boni wished to see you. He says it's urgent.'

'The museum director? Do you know what he wants?' Lauriat asked.

'Shall I inquire?'

'We should see him, Pascal,' Leoncino said. 'It could be interesting.'

Boni was given a chair and a glass of water. The cardinals could see his obvious state of distress.

He told them about the meeting he had fled, about his horror, about his resignation.

'Perhaps Your Eminences support this, this initiative,' Boni said. 'If so, I will leave.'

'Stay,' Leoncino said. 'You are among friends.'

At that, Boni calmed down. He realized his tie was too tight and he eased it.

'How did this happen?' Boni asked despondently.

'How indeed? Lauriat said. 'The Church confers ultimate authority upon the pope. The Curia shapes that authority. Usually there is a satisfactory balance. For the moment, that balance is off. For the moment.'

'But doesn't Celestine understand what will happen?' Boni said. 'This money, all these billions. Look at the problems in the world. I'm not blind to them. I have empathy. But these billions are only a drop in the bucket. They'll disappear like water poured into sand until there won't be any money left and still there will be poverty and suffering. But our museum walls will be bare and the Vatican will be diminished, less spiritual.'

While he spoke, both cardinals nodded vigorously and when he was done, Lauriat said, 'Professor, do something for me and your Church. Send the Holy Father a letter rescinding your resignation. Tell him you were upset but now you are more serene. Tell him you will faithfully serve at his pleasure. Once this storm passes, our paintings and statues will still be there and your job will remain as important as it always has.'

They met in one of the reception rooms at the official papal apartments. There were ten identical wing chairs in a large circle around a small decorative table. It was a space intended for larger gatherings but there were just the two of them. Their first order of business was figuring out where to sit.

'If we don't sit next to each other, we're going to have to shout,' Cal said.

Elisabetta smiled and selected a chair. Cal took an adjoining one. She smoothed her habit so that it flowed nicely to her ankles.

'The Holy Father suggested we meet – more formally,' she said.

Cal couldn't get over her perfect face, framed like a portrait by her starched veil. He considered himself a feminist – not exactly a shocker for a liberal professor from the university dubbed Kremlin-on-the-Charles – but he had a decidedly sexist thought: what had brought a woman that beautiful and that academically accomplished to become a nun? He reproached himself; he would probably never have a similar thought about a handsome, accomplished priest. He searched for something neutral to say.

'Thanks for making the time today. I imagine you're busy.'

That prompted a musical laugh. 'An understatement,' she said.

He noticed something then that accompanied her smile, a rather deep look into his eyes that lasted a second or two longer than needed. He knew what it meant – he'd gotten that look from countless women. She found him attractive too.

'Well, I won't keep you long,' he said, shaking off the distraction. 'I wanted to talk to you about my interviews this afternoon. Celestine outed me this morning in his interview. I don't know if you know my role in this.'

'The Holy Father told me. I congratulate you.'

'It doesn't feel like a celebration just yet. It feels like all hell's breaking loose. I had to turn off my phone.'

'Mercifully, I am still anonymous,' she said. 'I hope it stays so but here in Italy the journalists are very persistent. I think I'll also be outed for what I've been asked to do.'

'That's what I wanted to talk about. It's inevitable that I'm going to be asked this afternoon about the art. I understand that's partially your department.'

She scrunched her mouth which dimpled her cheeks. 'More than partially, I'm afraid. I was working on the antiquities but as of this morning, all of it has landed in my lap.'

'What happened?'

'A personnel change. I shouldn't say more.'

He backed off. 'I was hoping you could give me some insight into the process for valuing and selecting the pieces to be sold?'

'First of all, it's not just art,' she said emphatically. 'It starts with buildings and land holdings. The more money that can be raised there, the less art will need to be sold. Some valuable and historically noteworthy letters and manuscripts from the Vatican Secret Archives may be sold. The remainder will then come from the museums. Carefully selected pieces will be auctioned. I advocate covenants that require the sold work to be available for public display but this is a discussion item.'

She described the internal valuation process and he asked about a few famous works – whether they might be included. She responded with a small, deliberate nod of her veiled head to each query.

'It's sobering,' Cal said. 'I come down in favor of what Celestine is doing but it's not a slam dunk for me.'

'Slam dunk?'

'Sorry. American basketball slang. It means an easy call, an easy decision.'

'It's painful, of course,' she said, 'but nowhere as painful as what a starving child or a landmine victim who can't get a prosthesis must endure. For me, it's a slam dunk.'

He was embarrassed by the simple power of her argument. 'When you put it that way,' he said.

Her eyes seemed to glow, not with anger but intensity. 'I believe it's the only way to put it.'

The sound of a demonstration from the piazza grew louder. To change the subject Cal said, 'I understand your brother is a command officer with the Gendarmerie. This must be a challenging time for him.'

'He's quite busy, that's for sure. How do you know about him?'

'The pope told me.'

Again, the smile and the look into his eyes. 'Did he tell you about me too?'

'Enough to understand that you have a special relationship with him.'

'And he told me enough to say the same about you.' She paused and seemed to weigh her next words. 'The Holy Father is a wonderful man. Even though there are always people around him, I think it's a very lonely job. So many in the Curia have their own agendas. It must be difficult for him to know whom to trust. It's good that he has you as a friend, Professor. Thank you for this. I pray for him several times a day.'

Cal couldn't stop himself from saying what was on his mind. On later reflection it was damned if he did, damned if he didn't.

'I'm going to kick myself hard when I leave here but I've got to open up about something.'

'I hope you don't bruise yourself,' she said, seemingly preparing herself to hear something provocative.

'The pope told me something of your story, how you came to a religious life following a career in academia. It's quite inspirational but—'

'But what, Professor?'

'But it can't stop me from telling you that I find you incredibly attractive and intellectually stimulating.'

She pressed her lips into a thin smile, deepening her dimples. 'And being a nun can't stop me from telling you that I share your feelings. Perhaps if we had met – well, before. When you take your orders and put on your habit, it doesn't stop you from being a woman with all manner of feelings. I'm not a machine. But I cherish the life I've chosen to live and I've found it empowering to pour all the human emotions I feel into my love of God. Can you understand that, Professor?'

'I can, absolutely. I hope I haven't ruined our ability to work together.'

'Certainly not. You may have enhanced it. And now I have someone else to pray for.'

'Me?'

She nodded and stood. 'Now I will pray for you too.'

THIRTY

I t took a day for the full impact of the Vatican announcement to be felt. Over breakfast in his hotel suite Cal clicked through his newsfeed of American and Italian newspapers and marveled at the polarization of opinion. There didn't seem to be much of a middle ground; just about all the editorials came down hard in one camp or another. Celestine's idea was either the stuff of the angels or the work of the Devil.

Pro- and anti-IFH demonstrations were cropping up around the globe. Crowds were biggest in New York City and Rome, where tensions among opposing groups boiled over with several arrests. The most violent scene was outside the Sassoon Bank in New York, where some neo-Nazis bussed themselves in from Pennsylvania and unfurled predictably venomous Christ-killer signs. When members of the radical Jewish Defense League arrived from Brooklyn to take them on, mayhem ensued.

Petitions were being circulated online, some begging the Vatican to preserve its cultural history, others supporting the humanitarian initiative. One enterprising sort started a GoFundMe campaign to raise twenty-seven billion dollars so the Church wouldn't have to sell its art. Overnight it raised $11,513.12.

Cal called over to Julian's room to take his temperature. The kid was resolute. He was going to have his press conference in the hotel ballroom come hell or high water. Cal wished him luck and hopped into the shower.

Cal checked out of the hotel, toting his shoulder bag, and took a taxi to the Vatican. The entrance to St Peter's Square was tightly controlled by the Gendarmerie, who had set up metal detectors at the far end of the Via della Conciliazione. It took him almost an hour to get through and he was grateful he'd left enough time. It wasn't good form to be late for a papal meeting.

The piazza was thick with the faithful, the curious, the demonstrators, all under the watchful eye of more gendarmes than he'd ever seen in one place. He noticed a pair of smartly dressed plainclothes officers with earpieces and wondered whether one of them might be Elisabetta's brother.

There was another bottleneck, a queue trying to get close to the Casa Sanctae Marthae guesthouse. Members of the press and visiting prelates had to present themselves to the Swiss Guards manning the barriers and show identification and passes. When Cal got to the gate he told them about his appointment. A radio call was made and he was allowed through.

At the front door of the guesthouse he was stopped again, this time by another well-dressed man with a dark suit and an earpiece.

'Excuse me, who are you here to see?' he asked.

'I have an appointment with Pope Celestine,' Cal answered.

'Your name, please?'

'Calvin Donovan.'

The man asked for his ID, checked a list, and told him he could enter.

'Thank you,' Cal said. 'You wouldn't be Emilio Celestino, would you?'

'Sorry, no. I'm his boss, Arturo Viola. Do you know Colonel Celestino?'

'I know his sister.'

'He has two sisters.'

'The nun.'

'Well, I'll tell him you asked after him.'

Although he was a few minutes late, the pontiff kept him waiting for over an hour. As he sat, a steady stream of cardinals, many with granite expressions, exited the papal suite. Cal suspected that Celestine was getting an earful.

The second private secretary, Monsignor Dinh, apologized profusely when he finally came for him. Cal said he understood and followed the small man down the corridor, imagining Ludwig Moller in his place.

Celestine looked like he hadn't slept. His fleshy face drooped more than usual, his eyes, typically bright, were dull. Yet in typical fashion, the pope expressed concern for Cal's wellbeing.

'You look tired, Professor.'

'I had a somewhat restless night, Holy Father.'

'Sleep did not come easily for me either. On the other hand there was much time for prayer and meditation. I received a report that your interviews were successful. Alas, I haven't had the chance to read any of them this morning.'

'I think they went well enough. Some better than others. Most of the journalists wanted to hear about the archive searches. Only one of them did enough work to discover the shooting at the Sassoon Bank. I expressed the opinion that it was unrelated, a robbery. In other words, I lied.'

'When one says something untruthful to a reporter, is it a lie or a survival skill?' the pope asked, pleased at his joke. At least the laughter brought some color to his face. 'So, you leave today?'

'I'm heading from here to the airport. I have what I hope is the final draft of *A Tempore Ad Caritas.*'

'Splendid. If possible, I'd like to have it released today. I'm mindful of the bitterly divided reaction around the world, within the Church, within our very Curia. This bull gives the decision an intellectual backbone and hopefully will sway some of those whose opinions have not yet solidified.'

'It might even change the minds of some doubters,' Cal said with a touch of faux optimism.

Celestine took the draft bull and began reading it while Cal looked on, wondering whether Celestine had the fortitude to weather a storm that wouldn't be breaking up anytime soon.

At the Excelsior Hotel a narrow table with microphones had been set up on a raised platform at one end of the Winter Garden banquet hall. The rows upon rows of red chairs set on blue and gold carpeting made something of a regal statement. The hall was filling up, which surprised the events staff since the room was set up for several hundred.

Julian waited in a small adjoining room, chatting with his translator. An event planner hovered, speaking to someone inside the hall via her headset.

'It's almost time,' she said. 'We're going to be cutting people off from entering soon. We're at capacity.'

Julian smiled nervously. 'Big crowd,' he jested. 'I wonder who's speaking?'

Scotto too was working his headset, communicating with his men who were deployed throughout the Winter Garden. The space was too large to cover with the usual detail of four bodyguards so he had arranged to double the number.

'We're ready for you, Mr Sassoon,' the event planner said.

'Wait,' Scotto said. He barked some instructions into his mic and listened to the replies from his earpiece. 'OK, we can go.'

Scotto led the way to the stage, Julian and the interpreter following.

The young man sat, and surveyed the crowd of print journalists, bloggers, and videographers. He took a couple of handwritten pages from his sport coat and tapped the microphone to see if it was on.

'Hello, good morning,' he said in English. 'My name is Julian Sassoon. I'd like to read a brief statement then I'll be happy to take your questions.'

He was about to start reading when his translator reminded him that he needed to give him a chance.

'Sorry,' he whispered. 'I've clearly never done this before.'

When the translation was finished Julian began to read.

'When I first heard about Pope Celestine's idea of establishing an important new humanitarian foundation to satisfy an old debt between the Vatican and my family my first reaction was surprise, followed by skepticism. However, the more I learned about . . .'

One of the videographers at the front of the room who was hunched over his LCD monitor rose up and shouted, 'Jew bastard!'

Julian stopped reading.

There was a handgun.

Pop. Pop. Pop. Pop.

The pope removed his spectacles and told Cal, 'Yes, I think we are there. Perhaps one very small change to the second to last paragraph. It's more of a matter of syntax than substance.'

Cal listened to the suggestion and agreed with it.

'Then, Professor, I believe we can say that you have written your first papal bull. You know what we shall do? When it has been issued by the press office on official letterhead I shall sign a copy for you and perhaps you will wish to keep it as a memento of this rather extraordinary week.'

'It will be my proudest possession, Holy . . .'

Inspector General Viola burst into the room without knocking. He was breathing hard, his face twisted in alarm.

'I'm sorry, Holy Father. You must come with me. There's been a shooting on the Via Veneto. Julian Sassoon.' A coughing fit prevented him from continuing for a few seconds. He managed to clear his throat. 'We've received an indication of a threat on your person. There's no time.'

Celestine didn't react quickly enough for his chief bodyguard. He seemed slack in his chair. Viola began lifting him by his shoulders but the large man was like jelly. Viola shouted for Cal to help. Cal took one shoulder, Viola the other until the pontiff was upright.

Coming to his senses, the pope asked, 'How is he? Julian?'

'I don't know,' Viola said, moving him toward the door, 'but he was hit.'

Scotto was standing at one side of the stage behind Julian and the translator.

His instincts were razor-sharp. Before the word bastard finished echoing in the hall, he had drawn his own gun from its shoulder holster. But such was the speed of the attack that four shots rang out before Scotto could return fire.

Two of Scotto's men had been standing in front of the stage, facing the crowd. The one closest to the fake videographer squeezed off a quick volley at the assailant.

Everyone in the hall dove for the floor. When the gunfire stopped, the only ones standing or sitting were the bodyguards and Julian. The assassin was bleeding out on the magnificent carpet.

Julian was still in his seat, perfectly immobile, staring ahead.

Then slowly, he raised his right hand to feel at his chest.

'Holy Father,' Viola said urgently, 'we are going to go out the back entrance. We don't have to run but I want you to walk as quickly as possible. Mr Donovan, will you assist me, please?'

Cal took a forearm for stability. Monsignor Dinh was in the hallway, scared and flustered by Viola's galloping intrusion. Celestine told him that everything was all right, that he was not to worry.

'But, Holy Father, where are they taking you?'

'Where are we going, Inspector General?' the pope asked.

'Somewhere safe,' Viola said.

'I'll call when I get there,' Celestine told the priest. 'Pray for me.'

Viola led them through the dining room and into the kitchen where the staff stopped chopping and stirring to stare at the unexpected sight. Outside, at the service entrance, a black American-made SUV was idling. The driver, a Gendarmerie officer, leapt out and opened the rear door for the pontiff and Cal helped him in.

Cal was mumbling some kind of farewell when Viola pulled him aside and said, 'Mr Donovan, please accompany us.'

'Me? Why?'

'This intervention. It will be hard for him. He's an old man. I'm told you're a friend. It will only be for a few hours until it's safe to return.'

Cal thought about his flight but when he looked at the pope's distraught face he went around and climbed in beside him.

'You're coming too?' Celestine asked.

'To keep you company,' Cal said.

The pope touched his arm. 'Bless you, Professor.'

Julian's forefinger found a hole in his dress shirt and moved on to a second one in the lapel of his sport coat.

There was blood on the table.

His translator's head was resting on his stenography notebook, oozing red.

Julian was aware of shouting. One of the bodyguards was screaming for an ambulance. Scotto was standing over him shouting too.

'Are you hit? Are you hit?'

'My chest,' he croaked.

Scotto pulled him backwards, gently toppling the chair until he was lying on the floor.

He violently ripped open Julian's shirt, popping the buttons.

The ballistic vest had two impact points, one of them directly over the heart.

Scotto undid the Velcro straps and lifted the vest off. There were two angry red marks on his chest. He probed them.

'Ow!'

'You'll have big bruises. Maybe there's a cracked rib. This is why I insisted on the vest.'

'Help him,' Julian said. 'The translator.'

'He's dead,' Scotto said. 'We've got to go now. Let's get you up.'

'Go where?'

'The airport. Your plane. We're getting you out of Italy.'

*   *   *

The SUV with its blackened rear windows sped off heading out of the Vatican and into the congestion of Rome. Viola coughed and scanned the streets from the front passenger seat, giving directions to the driver, looking for the fastest route.

'Can you find out if Julian Sassoon is all right?' the pope asked.

'I'll call soon, Holy Father,' Viola said. 'Let me just concentrate on the cars around us in case we were followed.'

Celestine closed his heavy eyelids and said he was going to pray for Julian.

Cal wasn't as complacent. He pulled out his phone and was about to call Julian's mobile when Viola shouted at him.

'Please, Mr Donovan. You need to turn off your phone. These plotters are sophisticated, I think. They have eyes everywhere. They will know you were with the Holy Father and they might track us with your phone.'

Cal agreed to turn it off but that wasn't enough for Viola.

'Even if it's off it can be tracked. Give it to me. I need to remove the SIM card.'

Cal was hesitant but Viola insisted.

The SUV finally broke free of traffic and entered the A1 highway heading north.

'Now can you tell us where we are going?' Celestine asked.

'We have a safe house in Nazzano. We'll be there shortly.'

'A safe house?' the pope asked, annoyed. 'Another asset I didn't know about?'

Cal was glad that Celestine was returning to form.

'It's on the books in my department,' Viola said. 'Don't worry, it's not much money.'

'Who's behind this?' Cal asked.

'That I don't know, but believe me, we'll find out and they'll pay the price. Common sense tells me that it's people who oppose your plan to give away this fortune.'

The pope said, 'It pains me greatly to think that I am responsible for harm coming to Julian Sassoon.'

'You're not, Holy Father,' Cal said. 'The plotters are the ones responsible.'

'Yes, but it is I who set all this in motion,' the pope said mournfully.

Cal thought back to the first letter he found in the archives from

Cardinal Antonelli: *nothing is more important to him than the safety of the banker.*

No, Cal thought, swallowing hard. I'm the one who set it in motion.

THIRTY-ONE

I t took about half an hour for them to reach the turnoff at Nazzano.

'Almost there,' Viola said. He coughed some more into a handkerchief.

Viola was giving directions to the driver, who clearly had never been there before.

They snaked through the small town to its outskirts where Viola had the man turn into a small industrial park comprised of a few medium-sized warehouses.

'The safe house is here?' Cal asked, peering through the darkened window.

'I should better call it a safe warehouse,' Viola said, 'but don't worry, it's quite comfortable inside.'

At the warehouse at the farthest edge, Viola hit the button of a garage-door opener. It lifted and Viola had his man drive inside.

Inside it was dimly lit. Cal couldn't make out much more than the shapes of a few more men, standing by.

'Ours?' Cal asked.

'Of course,' Viola said. 'Give me a moment then I'll let you out and escort you to the lounge.'

Viola stepped out and told the driver to come with him. The young officer unclicked his seatbelt and climbed down.

A loud percussion boomed and reverberated inside the steel building.

Cal saw the driver fall.

'My God!' the pope cried.

Cal tried to open his door but it was locked. He reached over the pope to the other door but it was also locked. He was trying to climb over the front seats when Viola opened the driver's side door and tossed in a hissing canister. The door slammed and the cabin filled with gray-green gas.

Cal began to choke. He heard Celestine coughing and moaning.

Cal made one last effort to scale the seats but it might as well have been Mount Everest.

Colonel Celestino grilled the Vietnamese priest. 'Again, I ask: did he say where he was taking the Holy Father?'

Dinh was seated in a room with senior officers of the Swiss Guards and the Vatican Gendarmerie, uncomfortably sipping a bottle of water to lubricate his mouth.

'I've told you, he only said somewhere safe.'

'And he didn't say why he was taking this action?' Meyer, the commander of the Swiss Guards, asked.

'Not to me. Perhaps he told the Holy Father in his office.'

'Did Donovan say anything?' Meyer asked.

'Not that I recall. He was helping the Holy Father walk quickly.'

'And he left his travel bag behind.'

'I found it in the office.'

'You mentioned the pope said he'd call when he got to this safe place,' Celestino said.

'He said that, yes.'

'Which number would he call?' Major Pinotti of the Gendarmerie asked.

'My office line.'

'Is someone monitoring that line now?' Celestino asked.

'Yes. One of the monsignors is there waiting by the phone.'

'You can return to your office,' Celestino said. 'Call immediately if the Holy Father rings. And don't discuss this with a soul.'

When the door closed behind him Klaus Zeller, the deputy commander of the Swiss Guards, said, 'What the hell is going on here? Has Viola gone mad? How can he do something like this without informing the Guards?'

'He didn't inform his own organization, either,' Celestino said. 'We're totally in the dark too.'

'Is it possible he had a legitimate reason?' Pinotti asked.

Celestino shook his head. 'Vittorio, it's not possible. It's a complete violation of protocol. Plus, they've been gone for over an hour. Even if it were some kind of emergency that only he knew about, he would have called from the car.'

'But there was an emergency, wasn't there?' Zeller said. 'The shooting at the Excelsior. Maybe Viola heard about it and was worried about an imminent attack.'

'Yes, but the timeline is off,' Celestino said. 'Vittorio, tell them what you found out.'

'Shots were fired at the hotel at exactly nine forty-seven. Viola's SUV was picked up on cameras leaving the Vatican just before nine forty-eight.'

'That's not enough time for Viola to have gotten a call and responded,' Meyer said. 'This looks terrible.'

'Because it is terrible,' Celestino said.

'Could Donovan be part of this?' Zeller asked.

Celestino pointed to Cal's shoulder bag. 'We searched his bag. There was nothing to incriminate him. He had airline tickets for a flight to Boston via London leaving this afternoon. His passport was there too. From what I've heard he's a reliable friend to the pontiff.'

'No one is ruled out,' Meyer said harshly. 'And what about your man at the wheel?'

Celestino shrugged. 'Corporal Ambrosini's a good officer. That's all I can say right now. We'll do more checks on him, of course.'

'No,' Zeller insisted. '*We* should do the checks on him. And on Inspector General Viola. Something is rotten in the Gendarmerie. You can't be trusted to police yourselves.'

'I'll choose to ignore that, Kaspar,' Celestino said, working to keep his cool. 'The pope is missing and we're going to need to work together to get to the bottom of this.'

'Celestino is right,' Meyer said. 'We've got no choice but to pool resources. Our timeline is short. We won't be able to keep a lid on this for long. We need to immediately liaise with the city police to find out what we can about the hotel shooter and get access to CCTV from around Rome looking for Viola's car. The Guards can't make those inquiries. It's out of protocol. The Gendarmerie's got to do it.'

'We're already working on it,' Celestino said. 'I need to get back to my command center.'

The curtains were closed but Cal could see that it was no longer daytime. A dusky gray light was leaking around the edges.

His head throbbed and his stomach was queasy, pretty much the way he felt after a particularly heavy night on the bottle. He was flat on his back and when he tried to lift his head, the pounding only got worse.

Then he realized there was a sound in the room.

Snoring.

He turned his head. There was a second bed. The white cassock almost glowed in the semi-darkness.

'Holy Father,' he said, his throat as coarse as sandpaper.

The snoring continued unabated.

Cal forced himself to a seated position and tried to stand. He made it up on the second try but dizziness sent him down again. The next time upright he held on to the nearest nightstand and let his balance harden before taking a few steps. His body hurt all over. He couldn't make out a light switch but there was an open doorway. He went for it and discovered a bathroom. Turning on the light there were toiletries and towels laid out and in the mirror he saw that his shirt was stained with secretions.

Then he remembered the gas.

He quickly drank from the tap, used the toilet, and found the light switch in the bedroom.

The pope was lying on his back. His cassock and the top of his sash were stained the same as Cal's shirt. He let him sleep and tried the bedroom door. It was dead-bolted and there was no key. When he parted the curtains he saw an iron grate screwed on to the window frame. There were no lights outside, just shapes of large trees moving in the evening gloom.

At the sound of a shuddering moan, Cal kneeled at the side of the pope's bed and put a hand to his shoulder. 'Your Holiness, are you all right?'

There were a few rumbles from deep inside his large body coming from a place where words were formed.

'Holy Father, can you hear me? It's Cal Donovan.'

Both eyes opened a slant. 'Where . . . where . . .'

'I don't know where we are. We were taken. Can you remember?'

'In a car. Couldn't breathe.'

'He gassed us.'

'Who did?'

'Viola.'

'Yes, yes, Viola,' the pope said, trying to sit up.

Cal helped him to swing his legs over on to the floor. He coughed a few times, still in a daze.

'My cassock. Goodness.'

'Let me get a towel.'

Cal wet a towel and cleaned off his garment as best he could. Then he filled a water glass from the tap. Celestine drank thirstily.

'Is that a bathroom?' the pope asked.

Cal helped him up and made sure he was steady enough to make his way. Through the closed door he heard him brush his teeth and use the toilet. When he emerged he looked more composed.

'So, it seems we are alive,' the pope said. 'That is a blessing. We must presume that Inspector General Viola has some plan for us.'

'He's got to be part of something bigger,' Cal said. 'He's not acting alone.'

Celestine sat back on to the bed. 'I understand my plan for the IFH is controversial, even radical to some. But why must men object to ideas with violence? Why not civilized discourse?'

'Fear of change,' Cal said. 'Some will resort to extreme measures to protect the status quo, entrenched interests.'

'It was this mentality on the part of the Romans that led to the crucifixion of Christ. Destroy what you fear. What do you suppose they want from us, Professor?'

'Let's find out.'

He went to the door and began banging on it with his fist, shouting for someone to open it.

The Gulfstream was midway across the Atlantic when Julian received yet another call from Gail Sassoon on the satellite phone.

'What now?' he answered. He was alone in the cabin. There hadn't been time to arrange crew beyond the pilots.

'I just sent you an email with a file. Did you get it?' she asked. She sounded less frantic than on the previous calls.

'What is it?' he asked.

'Just look at it, please. I'll hold the line.'

He got his laptop and logged on to the plane's WiFi. Gail's email was headed, Open Immediately.

The attachment was a MOV file. When he clicked on it, the face of Viola's filled the frame.

'My name is Inspector General Arturo Viola of the Vatican Gendarmerie. This message is for the Sassoon Bank. I am the one who took the Holy Father and Mr Calvin Donovan. I am the one who ordered the killing of Mr Julian Sassoon. I sincerely regret that he escaped. I took these actions on my own behalf. No one else at the Vatican was in any way involved. I took these actions to . . .' He began to cough and at that point the recording clearly stopped then started up again when he had ceased coughing. 'I took these actions to protest and to foil this diabolical plot to destroy the heritage of the Church and its financial integrity by giving away an obscene sum of money in a confused attempt to satisfy an illegal and invalid debt that is almost two hundred years old. Here is my demand. The Sassoon Bank and the Sassoon family must legally remove any claim to the Vatican debt and refuse to participate in the International Fund of Humanity or any such foundation. Your written declaration to that effect must be made publicly available for legal experts to validate its proper form and substance. Only then will the Holy Father and Donovan be released. Please be aware that your family will never be safe unless you agree. Likewise if you rescind or renege on your agreement you will be targeted for assassination. Even when I am dead a dedicated army of Catholic sons will carry on and they will exact a terrible revenge. You have forty-eight hours.'

'Julian, are you there?' Gail asked.

'I'm here.'

'Marcus has seen this too.'

'What did he say?'

'Several variants of I told you so. He wants out, of course.'

'And you?' Julian asked.

'I think we have to withdraw from this. They almost killed you. This is a nightmare.'

'What's the Vatican saying?'

'Nothing! Nothing at all. There's no news of a kidnapping.'

'Maybe it didn't happen.'

'I tried calling Cal. There was no answer.'

'Did you try calling Celestine?'

'No, I should try that,' she said.

Julian gripped the phone tightly. 'Here's the thing, Gail. Whether or not it's true, I'm not backing down. They're not going to intimidate me. My reply to them is a big fuck you. And don't you dare get soft on me. If you want my respect you're going to have to suck it up and vote your shares with me. Understand?'

Cardinal Leoncino joined Lauriat in his office to initiate the international conference call with the other members of the C10. When everyone had announced his presence Lauriat asked if they were all aware of the assassination attempt on Julian Sassoon. All responded in the affirmative. He then astounded them with the news that Celestine had been abducted along with his visitor, Professor Donovan.

Cardinals Da Silva and Vargas were still in Rome continuing to work on the formation of the IFH. From his room at the Sanctae Marthae guesthouse, a short distance from the site of the kidnapping, Da Silva asked who had done such a thing and how was it possible.

'I regret to say, but it was the pope's chief bodyguard, Arturo Viola. I have received an email from him admitting responsibility. He claims he did it to protest the repayment of the debt and that the Holy Father will be held until the plans he announced have been withdrawn.'

'But surely,' the bishop of Mainz said, 'only the Holy Father can do that.'

Leoncino leaned closer to the speakerphone. 'Or the Sassoons.'

'Where is Julian Sassoon?' Cardinal Vargas asked.

'We understand he is on a private plane heading back to America,' Lauriat said. 'If it weren't for a bulletproof vest he surely would have been gravely injured.'

'Was Viola involved with the shooting too?' Da Silva asked.

'Presumably.'

'Are there other conspirators?' the archbishop of Lima asked. 'Within the Vatican,' he added almost in a whisper.

'Not to our knowledge,' Lauriat said.

'What are the police saying?' the archbishop of Manila asked.

'Nothing yet. They're at an early stage of their investigation. However, they want to enlist the help of the public in finding the official vehicle that Viola used for the abduction. That means that we shall have to announce the kidnapping. Inevitably the news will leak soon anyway. I am preparing a press bulletin that we will release within the hour.'

'What can we do?' the Nigerian cardinal asked.

Leoncino leaned toward the speaker. 'We should do what we do best. We should pray.'

THIRTY-TWO

Someone came to the door and unlocked it.
'Back away,' the voice commanded through the door.
Cal obeyed and retreated toward his bed.

A young man with a sleeve of tattoos on one arm and an unshaven face entered, pistol first.

He glowered at Cal but when he saw the pope, he partially lowered his gun arm and seemed overwhelmed to be in his presence.

'Holy Father,' the man said. 'I apologize for your treatment.'

'Tell me, young man,' Celestine said gently, 'who are you?'

'I'm Antonio. I am a good Catholic, I promise. This is a job for me. They only told me it was you when I was here.'

'And where is here?' the pope asked.

'I'm not allowed to say. It's a villa. It's in a remote place.'

'Is it just you, Antonio?' the pope asked.

'There are others.'

'Is Viola here?' Cal answered.

Cal didn't garner the same respect. Antonio raised his pistol again and pointed it at him.

'Please lower your weapon, Antonio,' Celestine said calmly and when he did so, the pontiff repeated Cal's question.

'Yes, he's downstairs. He's sleeping.'

'Kindly ask him to come and speak with me when he awakens.'

'I will, Holy Father. Are you hungry? I can get you food.'

The pope looked to Cal who shook his head. He was still churning inside from the gas and he suspected Celestine was too.

'Not at this time,' Celestine told the young man but he added, 'Does this villa have a coffee machine?'

'I'll bring you some.'

'Two cups. Don't forget the professor. And Antonio?'

'Yes, Holy Father?'

'I'll pray for you.'

Antonio nodded in astonishment and left them.

*   *   *

When the call with the C10 was over, Lauriat told Leoncino that he was going to get Malucchi and Cassar on the line.

'I thought you didn't want calls with the four of us showing up on your telephone records?'

'In the wake of a papal kidnapping, I think it's plausible that groups of cardinals can be expected to communicate.'

Cassar sounded agitated although the reception on his mobile phone was poor.

'Where are you?' Lauriat said. 'I tried your office number.'

'I just got on the golf course. I'm walking now. Is that better?'

'Golf, in the winter?' Malucchi said.

'In Malta it's sunny and warm enough with a sweater. Are you calling with news on Celestine?'

'The police are working on it. That's all I know,' Lauriat said. 'The press office is releasing a bulletin shortly acknowledging the abduction. We couldn't hold off any longer.'

'That's the end of my game, I suppose,' Cassar said. 'I'll have to go back to my diocese to deal with the local fallout.'

'Such sacrifice,' Leoncino mumbled under his breath.

'Tell me, Pascal,' Cassar said, 'I didn't ask when you called me before but I'm asking now. Did you have anything to do with this?'

'Don't ask me questions like that,' Lauriat replied angrily. 'Don't ever ask me.'

The next time the bedroom door opened it was Viola holding a small tray with two cups of coffee. Antonio was behind him, his gun-arm slack, hanging at his side.

'I have your coffee the way you like it, Holy Father,' Viola said. 'Mr Donovan, I didn't know your preference. I put milk in it.'

Celestine and Cal sat on their beds and received the cups politely, suspending reality, as if they were guests in the man's house.

Viola looked as tired as his captors. He helped himself to a wooden chair against a wall. Antonio remained by the door.

'I don't ask for your forgiveness, Holy Father,' Viola said, 'but I must express my sorrow for treating you so roughly. I felt I had no choice. It was necessary to bring you here in – well, a clandestine manner.'

From his aching back, Cal put two and two together. 'You put us in the trunk of a car,' he said.

'I don't wish to speak of this,' Viola said, his expression pained.

Celestine pointedly used his first name. 'Why, Arturo, why did you feel it was necessary to commit this violence upon the pope which is also a form of violence upon the Church? And why did you commit violence against this innocent young man, Julian Sassoon?'

'Isn't it obvious, Holy Father?'

'It is not so obvious to me, Arturo, how you could take a difference in opinion as a justification for violence,' the pope said. 'Tell me, have you taken his life?'

'He survived,' Viola said. 'Apparently he was unhurt.'

Celestine closed his eyes and murmured his thanks to God.

'You see, this is more than a difference in opinion, Holy Father,' Viola said. 'There's no doubt that you are a good man but men of conscience cannot stand by and allow you to destroy the Church we love.'

'We?' Celestine said. 'Who else has done this, Arturo? It wasn't just you, acting alone. Who are the plotters and schemers? Who among the Curia? Which cardinals are among your confederation?'

'I alone,' he replied defiantly.

'And was it you, alone, who tried to kill Professor Donovan in New York?'

'It was nothing personal, Mr Donovan. If we had succeeded, none of this would have been necessary.'

Cal had a few angry things he wanted to say about that but this was the pope's dialogue.

'There's the we again,' the pope said. 'You could not have known about the loan, Arturo. Someone must have told you. Who was it?'

'Moller,' he spat. 'He was a degenerate. I blackmailed him.'

'Moller didn't know either.'

'Your conference call with the C8. He gave me the code. I listened.'

Celestine shook his head and put his coffee aside. 'All right,' he said wearily. 'I won't press you further on this but I must press you on your motivations. Do you read the Bible, Arturo?'

'When I was young. Not now.'

'Do you go to Mass?'

'Only when you are giving it, Holy Father.'

'Do you listen on these occasions?'

'I have to concentrate on the crowds. That's my job.'

'If there is a Bible in this house, I want you to read the Gospels,' the pope said. 'I want you to read the word of Jesus Christ, our savior, and what he has to say about Christian charity and goodness. Then come to me to discuss the mission of the Church, for I say to you, Arturo, alleviating poverty and suffering *is* our mission, not operating a museum. Our business is caring for people in this life and saving souls for the next. What about your soul, Arturo? What will become of it?'

'I will face my fate with serenity,' he answered.

'Then tell me,' Celestine said. 'What is the point of this abduction? What is its purpose?'

'For the good of all I hold dear, we – I want you to abandon your plan to poison the well of the Church and reverse your decision to give away our fortune and our treasure. Say this publicly. Describe a change of heart.'

'You know I will not do that.'

Viola rose and coughed a few times into his handkerchief. 'I'll leave you to think about it,' he said. 'This young man will bring you food.'

It was dark when the leaders of the Swiss Guard joined Colonel Celestino and his team in the Gendarmerie operations center for a telephonic briefing with officials from the Carabinieri. A Carabinieri lieutenant general was passing along news from their review of CCTV recordings from Rome highways. They had just found an image of Viola's official SUV on the A1, just north of the A90 orbital. A team of officers was reviewing additional camera files to the north and would report findings in real time. He moved on to the identity of the gunman at the Excelsior. He was a resident of Crotone in Calabria with a long arrest record and ties to the 'Ndrangheta. More information was expected from the local authorities. Finally, the public hotline was inundated with calls but so far none were credible leads.

Celestino thanked the lieutenant general but said, 'Excuse me, sir, but we specifically requested that Lieutenant Colonel Cecchi from the ROS assist the Vatican on this matter.'

Tommaso Cecchi, the deputy head of the special ops group within the Carabinieri, the Raggruppamento Operativo Speciale, was well known to Celestino and the Gendarmerie, having helped the Vatican in the affair involving Berardini, the stigmatic priest. Pope Celestine had personally bestowed on him a medal, the Order of Saint Gregory the Great, for his services to the Holy See.

'Cecchi is out on leave,' the lieutenant general said.

A voice interrupted the officer. 'This is Cecchi. I'm here at the ROS. I cancelled my own leave. One doesn't take a vacation when the pope is kidnapped.'

'Very well, Cecchi,' the lieutenant general said, 'consider yourself in charge of the Carabinieri's efforts.'

'Emilio Celestino here. I look forward to working with you, lieutenant colonel.'

'Let's find the Holy Father,' Cecchi said.

Cardinal Lauriat was in his bedchamber when his prepaid phone rang, the one given to him by Viola only a fortnight ago. He'd left it in his briefcase, so he had to push away his bedclothes and pad across the polished floor in bare feet to retrieve it.

'We need to talk,' Viola said.

'I can hardly hear you. The reception is bad.'

'It's the mountains,' Viola said, trying another part of the room. 'How's that?'

'A little better. Is there a problem?' Lauriat said, taking the phone back to his bed. 'Did he not recover?'

'He recovered from the gas. He's fine. We talked.'

'And?'

'He wanted to know who else was involved in this.'

'And what did you tell him?'

'That I acted alone. That Moller was my source of information.'

'As we discussed, but that's not the reason for your call, is it?'

'No. I don't think he's going to relent.'

'He's been a prisoner for less than a day.'

'Believe me, Eminence, he won't change his mind.'

'And what do you suggest?'

'It pains me to say it but I think that the Holy Father and Donovan will have to be eliminated.'

'Viola, that is a terrible idea. Have you no concept of the awesome power of martyrdom? If Celestine were sacrificed at the altar of his liberalism, what do you think would happen?'

'I don't know, Eminence, but I imagine you're going to tell me.'

'What would happen is this: the next conclave will see a tidal wave of sympathy and a coalescence around some cardinal from South America perhaps, maybe even Da Silva from Boston, someone who is even more liberal than Celestine. We will be worse off.'

'Then what can we do if he's intransigent?'

'Talk to him again tomorrow. If there is no softening of his position then give him a deadline. Tell him if he has not drafted and recorded a public repudiation of the debt repayment then Calvin Donovan will be executed.'

THIRTY-THREE

As soon as Cal awoke the next morning he made a beeline to the barred window, dressed only in his boxer shorts, to check on their surroundings.

'And what can you see, Professor?'

'I hope I didn't wake you, Holy Father.'

'I've been awake for a while, thinking, meditating, however one might prefer to characterize it. I didn't rise to pray because I didn't want to disturb you. You seemed quite peaceful. So what is outside our sunny window?'

'Trees and a very nice hillside. I can't see anything. Oh, there's snow on the ground.'

'Well, it's warm in here,' the pope said, placing his bare feet on the floor. 'They do not seem to be trying to freeze us to death.'

He had laid his vestments on a chair the night before.

'I'll quickly use the bathroom, if that works for you,' Cal said.

Cal did his ablutions and dressed inside the bathroom to preserve the pontiff's modesty. As roommate scenarios went, this one was well off the charts.

When he got out, Celestine was working on his sash. When Cal asked if he needed help, the pope assured him that he did these chores himself. When the pontiff emerged from the bathroom, his hair neatly combed, he commented that Viola had taken the care to buy his usual brand of toothpaste.

'That was thoughtful, don't you think?' he said.

'Thoughtful would have been not kidnapping and gassing you,' Cal said.

'I suppose you are right, but still, it does show a touch of humanity. Would you care to join me in morning prayers?'

'I'm a little rusty,' Cal said, 'but it would be an honor.'

The large man's knees creaked and popped when he lowered himself to the floor. Cal joined him at the altar of the pope's bed.

Celestine closed his eyes tightly and said, 'In the name of our Lord Jesus Christ I will begin this day. I thank you, Lord, for having preserved us during the night. I will do my best to make

all I do today pleasing to You and in accordance with Your will.
My dear mother Mary, watch over us this day. My Guardian Angel,
take care of us. St Joseph and all you saints of God, pray for me
and for my dear friend, Calvin.'

Downstairs in the kitchen of the villa, Viola was instructing a
fellow named Giaccomo how to prepare the pope's breakfast.

'Light toast, no browner than your skin, assorted fruit, cut nicely
– please don't be sloppy – and coffee with two sugars and milk.'

'What about the other guy?'

'Who cares about the other guy?' Viola said. 'Give him the same!'

He went into the lounge where Antonio and two other young
men were watching the morning news. The prime minister was
giving a live statement.

'What's that jackass saying?' Viola asked.

'That they're looking for him,' Antonio said.

'Well, they haven't found him yet,' another one cracked.

Viola spilled some coffee when he suddenly began to cough.
When it subsided he looked at his handkerchief. It was streaked
with blood.

'You OK, boss?' Antonio asked.

'I'm not your boss. This is a one-time job. I'll never see you
again, you'll never see me again.'

'Hell with you,' Antonio said, leaving for the kitchen in a lather.
'I was just asking if you were all right.'

The newscast went on to highlight international reaction to the
kidnapping and after a minute of watching, Viola got up, lit a
cigarette, and went outside for a walk in the snowy garden.

Celestine munched on his dry toast and told Cal, who was doing
the same, that it was a shame he had to suffer for the pope's sins.

'It could become my new breakfast,' Cal joked. 'A lot healthier
than Pop Tarts.'

Celestine inquired as to what those were and Cal told him he
really didn't want to know. When he was finished with his tray
Cal got up and walked the length of the small room back and forth
a few times, disguising his mounting agitation by pretending to
look out of the window each time.

'Is something the matter?' the pope asked. 'I mean beyond the
obvious?'

Cal returned to his bed.

'I guess I'm a little jittery,' he said quietly.

'Why is that?'

'You're going to make me confess something I haven't confessed to myself.'

Celestine said nothing but the receptivity of Celestine's body language spurred Cal on.

He took a deep, smooth breath before saying, 'Last night was the first time in I don't remember how long that I didn't have a drink. I'm feeling it this morning.'

'I see,' the pope said. 'You're a big drinker?'

'I suppose I am.'

'I intended our dinner the other night to learn more about you but I spent too much time talking about work. I still don't really know you, Professor.'

'Why would you?'

'You're right. We've had a wonderful friendship that has been the source of some pleasure for me but it's been a friendship based upon your work and our mutual interests. I have never asked about you as a person. We certainly have not been – what's the American expression – drinking buddies.'

'I wouldn't have expected you to engage with me beyond professional interests. I mean, you're the pope!'

Celestine gestured expansively at the room. 'But here we are. Bound together by our captivity. A perfect time to talk, don't you think?'

Cal took the bait. The version of his life that flowed out with a fluidity that frankly surprised him was more intimate and psychologically shaded than he'd revealed to any friend or lover. A brittle, distant mother. An imperious father whose archeology digs took him away for extended stretches. A lonely boy, raised in privilege, who became a wild adolescent, a hell-raiser. The big professor's house in Cambridge, all his when his lonely mother decamped for her haunts in Manhattan, that became the hub of wild parties, big-time drinking, and girls, girls, girls. His rebellious decision – a thumb in the eye to his parents – to enlist in the army instead of going to college. Washing out after only two years the moment his fist landed on his sergeant's jaw. His father pulling strings to get him into Harvard despite his ignominious discharge. Getting his life on some sort of even keel only to be upended when his father died in mysterious circumstances on a Middle Eastern dig. Fighting the gravitational pull of this man he disliked and feared, but eventually succumbing to it and embarking on a strikingly similar academic career. Coming to grips with the religious ambiguity of his childhood and choosing his father's Catholicism over his mother's Judaism. Despite his best intentions, becoming too much like his father the older he got. His old man was a drinker and a womanizer. He was too. In spades. At least Cal had the decency of never marrying or even subjecting a partner to some shaky version of long-term commitment. He knew himself too well. He'd only stray off the reservation.

The pontiff listened without interrupting, nodding at times, furrowing his brow, frowning, smiling. When he did speak, this was his question: 'You say you feared your father, even disliked him, but did you love him?'

Cal looked toward the cold, sunlit window before answering. 'I respected him. He was a legend in his field. I've got a joint appointment in the archeology department and I walk past the Hiram Donovan Laboratory to get to my office. I never got to really know him. I wish I had.'

'That wasn't my question.'

'I think I did. Deep down.'

'Losing a parent, particularly at a time of important transition in life, particularly a dominant kind of parent like your father – this can be terribly difficult and something you have to carry like a heavy weight.'

Cal wouldn't let himself get teary. He hadn't cried since childhood and even this conversation wasn't going to turn on the waterworks. 'It does feel like that sometimes.'

'Professor, I'm not a psychologist, I'm a priest who, for reasons that are mysterious to me, kept getting promoted to fancier and fancier jobs. As a priest I ask you: do you think this burden you carry causes your drinking?'

At that, Cal got up again, drawn to the window. 'Maybe,' was the best he could do. 'I mean, who knows if I'm a single-issue kind of drinker? These things can be more complicated, I'm sure.'

'Have you tried to stop drinking?'

'It's part of who I am and it's never interfered with my work, so no. I think the term is functional alcoholic.' He thought of Gail

Sassoon, a sloppy, dysfunctional drunk if ever there was one. 'If I ever crossed the line I'd have to deal with it.'

Celestine bent the curve of the conversation. 'Tell me about your faith. What did your mother think about your choice to embrace your father's religion?'

'She was bitter and resentful at the time and twenty years later she's still bitter and resentful.'

That made the pope laugh. 'She wouldn't be a Jewish mother if she thought otherwise. And what about your faith, Professor? Is it strong?'

'Is it strong?' Cal repeated. 'To be honest, it could be a lot stronger. I don't attend Mass except when I happen upon a ceremony at a church I'm visiting for academic interest. The last time I prayed like I did with you this morning was when I was undergoing my conversion.'

'No, your faith.'

'I don't *not* believe in God.'

'That's a starting point. Why did you become a Catholic? Can you remember?'

Cal gulped at the question. His nose got stuffy though his eyes remained dry. 'I think I did it to be closer to my father.'

'That is a fine reason, Professor, a fine reason.'

There was a polite knock on the door before it was unlocked and opened. Viola and his shadow, Antonio, came in.

'Was your breakfast satisfactory, Your Holiness?'

'It was fine, Arturo, thank you.'

The inspector general coughed a few times and asked whether he had thought about the demand to reverse his decision.

'I had a restless night which gave me much time to think about what you want. My answer is the same as yesterday. I cannot change what I believe to be a fundamentally correct and decent choice.'

It couldn't have come as much of a surprise but Viola nevertheless looked shaken. 'I'm very sorry you feel this way, Holy Father. I too cannot change my views. You force me to make an ultimatum. You have until the day after tomorrow to alter your position and make a public declaration via a video message or I will have no choice but to take drastic measures.'

'Arturo,' the pope said in a gently scolding manner, 'how can you threaten the pope? How will you live with yourself?'

'I don't have to worry about such a thing, Holy Father. I have an advanced lung cancer. I am dying. I don't have a lot of time. And I will tell you this: I am not threatening you. It's Mr Donovan. If you don't do what I ask I'll have to execute him. His blood will be on my hands but it will be on your hands too.'

With that, Viola turned away to spare himself looking into the pope's incredulous eyes and left with Antonio.

After a pregnant pause, Cal broke the tension by saying, 'Well, that'll get me focused on my faith.'

'Your humor masks your bravery, Professor.'

'I don't feel very brave.'

'Well, on the positive side of this distressing situation we find ourselves in, it seems we have at least two days to continue our dialogue. I'll tell you what. Let me take my turn. Let me bare my soul to you as you have done to me.'

Thus, the head of the Church, the Vicar of Christ, began a rendition of his life, more candid than any contained in any of his several authorized or even unauthorized biographies.

'We were quite poor, Professor, a typical working-class family from a not-so-terrific part of Naples. My mother wore herself out prematurely having eight children. Her health was never strong, though she lived into her seventies, thanks to God. One of my brothers died of a fever very young, the rest survived and mainly thrived. I was the youngest and because I am now an old man, I am the last. Naples then, as Naples now, is a wonderful city, full of vitality and history, so picturesque. I miss it so. It is a much-misunderstood city, Professor, as I'm sure you know. Tourists hear talk of pickpockets or the Camorra or trash-collection strikes but that is not Naples. If a pope could ever retire, in my retirement, I would write a book about my Naples, my misunderstood beauty. My father was a draftsman, a real master of the pencil. When you were talking about your father I saw my father in my mind's eye. He was a distant one, I'd say. He wasn't so quick to anger but he was very slow to praise. It's not a good thing for a child. Praise is like mother's milk. It nurtures and strengthens. Fortunately my mother had plenty of the milk of human kindness. My father died when I was in my thirties, already a priest, so not as young as your situation but difficult in the same way as he and I never had important conversations. You can never find a perfect substitute for father-and-son conversations that never occurred. I tell you this to show you that you and I have some similarities. Let me tell you another similarity. I was very much a lady's man when I was young, also something of a hell-raiser. I wasn't like a lot of the young men I would meet in the seminary, fellows who became celibate without knowing much about carnal pleasures. It's easier to give up something you never knew about and more of a sacrifice if you have known certain delights. Anyway, that's the way I look at it. One of the reasons this recent story about the young lady, Lidia, who took her own life after having an abortion, the reason it was so painful to me was that she was my girlfriend in high school. Let me be clear, I wasn't the one who got her pregnant years later – I took my vows as a priest as seriously then as I do now – but I felt great tenderness for her. When she came to me for help as a friend I treated her like a priest. When I felt I wasn't getting through to her, that I wasn't changing her mind about having an abortion, I got angry and judgmental. Who knows if the guilt I made her feel carried over afterwards and led to her suicide. This has stayed with me, Professor, and I have tried to use this failing of mine as a priest to more compassionately serve my flock, a flock that has grown in size to over a billion souls.'

'When did you decide on the priesthood?' Cal asked.

'It was in my last year of university. Do you want to hear something amusing, or at least ironic? I attended the Naples Academy of Fine Arts. You see, I inherited from my father the ability to draw. I studied Italian Renaissance art and I suppose that staring at wonderful ecclesiastical imagery for three years stoked my religious feelings. Anyway, I wasn't a good enough artist to expect to get a decent job, so there's that too. So here you have the pope that wishes to sell Vatican art – he is a failed art student.'

Cal smiled at that. 'Can I ask about your faith? Did it ever waiver?'

'I have to say that that was never an issue in my life. We were raised to go to church and believe in God. There was never a moment of doubt. Whenever I became challenged, after Lidia, for example, and at other times, even now, even during this long night we just had, I may have doubted my abilities as a servant of God and as his messenger, but I never once doubted my faith. Until my last breath, that is the one thing that will never leave me.'

THIRTY-FOUR

Although Celestino knew all about Cecchi's previous work on the Berardini case, they had never met. Now that they were face-to-face in the Gendarmerie operations center, he instantly took a liking to the ROS officer. He was an athletic man in his fifties with a military bearing – up to a point. Once he was comfortable with the competency and temperament of a colleague, Cecchi became more like a detective in the trenches. Within a short while, he and Celestino were working together seamlessly.

'A lot of your tech is similar to what we have at the Piazza del Popolo,' Cecchi said. 'Let's put the IT guys on the phone and we'll be able to send our CCTV data to your server.'

The two men had a coffee in the Gendarmerie cafeteria while the data transfer was being sorted out.

'So it must be pretty rough, the situation you're in,' Cecchi said.

Celestino knew immediately what he was talking about.

'It's inconceivable to me,' Celestino said. 'A betrayal on the highest order. I've known Arturo Viola for a long time. I've admired him as a leader. To think that he's the one behind this plot – I can't get my head around it. It's a stain – maybe a permanent stain – on the Gendarmerie.'

'We're going to help you remove the stain by catching Viola and getting the pope back safely,' Cecchi said. 'Between you and me, the optics are going to be important. The ROS and the entire Carabinieri has elevated this affair to the highest priority and we'll do everything possible to succeed, but when the hammer drops on Viola, it's important that you guys in the Gendarmerie, and you personally, be the one seen to be holding that hammer.'

'Look, I appreciate your attitude more than I can say,' Celestino said. 'Let's hope there's an endgame that makes us all smell like roses.'

Cecchi made a face at the bad coffee and added more sugar to his espresso. 'The FBI gave us the video that Viola sent to the Sassoon Bank.'

'We got it too.'

'And there's been nothing similar to the Vatican?'

'Nothing. He hasn't communicated at all.'

'Don't you find that odd? He takes the pope and makes no demands?'

'I can only assume that he's putting the pressure directly on Celestine,' Celestino said. 'He's the only one who can modify his decision on the debt.'

'He's the only one right now,' Cecchi said, swallowing the rest of his espresso like medicine. 'If it becomes necessary to have another conclave, the next pope will decide.'

Celestino looked down at the table then met Cecchi's gaze. 'Of course, I've thought about this too.'

Cecchi looked around to see who was close. A few officers were at the vending machine against the wall. 'Do you think Viola's acting alone?' he whispered. 'Is there a larger conspiracy?'

'I hope not but I wouldn't be a good cop if I closed my mind to the possibility.'

Cecchi received a text from his IT man. The data transfer was successful. He told Celestino they were ready and said, 'I think we're going to get along fine, Emilio,' he said. 'Let's go watch some videos.'

In the ops center there was a paused video from a highway camera on the main monitor. Celestino told Major Pinotti to let it play.

Cecchi narrated, 'This is the view from the A1 exit to Firenze, about fifty kilometers north of the Vatican. We can clearly see the Vatican City plates with the SCV prefix on this black Yukon SUV. Note the time stamp. Given the amount of traffic that day it's consistent with a direct route from Vatican City to this point. We can see the SUV exiting here. Next video, please. OK, here we are on Strada Provinciale 20b heading toward Nazzano and here is Viola's car ten minutes later. Last video, please. This is six minutes later on the Via Dante Alighieri in the center of Nazzano. Here is the SUV passing the camera. That's the last image we have.'

'What makes you think that Nazzano was their destination?' Celestino asked. 'Vittorio, pull up a map of the area.'

Pinotti projected a map of Rome and followed the A1 to Nazzano.

'There are plenty of small villages in the area along the Tiber,' Celestino said.

'For sure,' Cecchi said, 'but to get to them you've got to go on SP40b.' He got up and pointed to an intersection on the road just northeast of Nazzano. 'There's a camera here. We reviewed the feed from that camera for a full twenty-four hours beyond the kidnapping. Nothing. They never went past.'

'So it's Nazzano,' Celestino said. 'We've got to search it.'

'The Polizia di Stato are already mobilizing. On our orders they'll swarm the town. An ROS chopper can pick us up from the Vatican heliport and have us there in twenty minutes.'

'Tell them it's a go,' Celestino said, buttoning his jacket. 'Let's get up to Nazzano.'

'You want me to go with you, boss?' Pinotti asked.

'You stay here and man the fort, Vittorio, and keep pressing on Viola's background.'

The Sassoon family arrived at the bank before dawn, having to talk themselves through rings of security to get inside the building. NYPD patrolmen manned the outermost ring of temporary wooden barricades and FBI agents from the Manhattan south office watched the entrances. Julian had his own private bodyguards providing close support. They went inside with him and waited outside the boardroom.

'Your security guys, they're ripped. I recognize one of them from my gym,' Albert Sassoon said, arriving last.

Julian ignored him, taking his father's chair at the head of the table. When he sat down he had to adjust the protective vest under his shirt. He'd become a believer.

Gail sat to his left, Marcus to his right, and Albert picked a place several chairs away from the others.

'Why don't you join us, Albert,' his father said gruffly. He obeyed but showed his defiance childishly by sliding his coffee mug across the polished surface to a closer spot.

'You wanted to meet, Marcus,' Julian said. 'Here we are.'

'Of course I wanted to meet. How could I not want to meet? We're in a crisis that was one hundred percent foreseeable. The bank is under siege by the media, by bigots, by kooks, and cranks. The shooter in the archive is looking more and more like a hitman. Someone tried to kill you in Rome. Your translator's brains got splattered on a table. The pope's been kidnapped. Donovan's been kidnapped. It's early days but our business looks like it's going to suffer. How many meetings have been cancelled, Albert?'

'The French underwriters postponed Project Mercury. The Belgians at LavaCal want to reassess.'

'So what's your point, Marcus?' Julian said.

'My point is that this is madness. You're putting lives at risk and the bank at risk on the altar of your own goddamn ego. This foundation bullshit is going to kill us.'

Julian clenched and unclenched a fist under the table. Gail saw him doing it. 'Only the weak back down under pressure,' he said. 'Only the strong stand up and fight for what they believe in. Do you think I'm weak, Marcus?'

'Oh, I think you're a strong young fellow,' Marcus said contemptuously. 'Headstrong. Do you think your father would have sat in that chair and presided over the demise of the Sassoon Bank?'

Gail jumped in. 'Henry would have been brave and he would have been stubborn as hell. He always was when he believed in something.'

'He wouldn't do this,' Marcus shouted. 'I say, stop this madness and stop this deal.'

'I'm going to say something I heard my father say on more than one occasion,' Julian said. 'I have the majority.'

'But you don't,' Marcus countered. 'You've got forty-nine percent. Gail, this is going to be up to you.'

'Here's my position,' Gail said, fixing him with her best lawyer's gaze. 'I'm with Julian. I'm with my son.'

The police were scouring Nazzano, going door-to-door, searching every garage, and showing residents pictures of the black Yukon with Vatican plates. Celestino and Cecchi took to the ROS helicopter to search by air. Both of them pointed at the same time to the small industrial park at the northern edge of the town.

'We should check there,' Celestino said.

The pilot put down in a corner of the car park and when the pair of them disembarked they approached a couple of workers having a smoke outside the nearest warehouse.

'Carabinieri,' Cecchi said, producing a photo. 'Have you seen this car?'

The men shook their heads.

'What do you do here?' Cecchi asked.

'Machine parts.'

'We need to look inside.'

One of the men opened the door and bellowed for the manager, who talked to them and let them have a look inside the workshop.

'Three of the buildings are like this,' the manager said, escorting them back outside. 'The one at the far end, that one's been empty for almost a year. It's for rent.'

The two officers jogged up the small hill and went around the building until they got to a door with a small, dirty window. Celestino tried it but it was locked. He used his sleeve to clean the window but it was dark inside and he couldn't see a thing.

'Do you have a torch?' he asked Cecchi.

The ROS officer produced a small tactical light from one of his jacket pockets and Celestino shone it through. There was a black SUV parked in the cavernous space.

He whispered to his colleague and drew his Glock. Cecchi's Beretta Cougar was already in his hand.

'We should call for back-up,' Celestino said.

'I'm your back-up and you're mine,' Cecchi replied, chambering a round. 'I don't want to wait for a big operation. Let's do this.'

'OK. I'll go around to the other door,' Celestino said. 'When I shout a go command, I'll shoot the lock and enter.'

'I'll do the same,' Cecchi said. 'And Emilio, try not to shoot me.'

When he was in position, Celestino shouted and two shots went off simultaneously.

Celestino shouted in the dark, 'Armed police, show yourselves!' Cecchi must have found a light switch because suddenly the place was bright as day. The SUV was on its own near a wall but there didn't seem to be anyone in the warehouse space. Celestino kicked open the door of a small office with a desk and a few chairs. Fast-food debris littered the room.

Cecchi was already slowly approaching the car and Celestino joined him.

'Carabinieri!' Cecchi shouted, opening one of the rear doors with his free hand.

'Shit!' he shouted. 'Emilio!'

Celestino came running. Cecchi was opening the rear hatch and shining his torch inside.

'Body. Driver's seat,' Cecchi said to him. 'It's not the pope.'

Celestino stared at the dead man.

'He's one of mine,' he said mechanically. 'Ambrosini.' Then he turned away and said, 'I swear I'm going to kill Viola.'

An hour later, the forensics team arrived at the warehouse. Celestino had already done the hard work of calling Ambrosini's wife, telling her that her husband died a hero and that his killers would be brought to justice.

His phone rang. It was Cardinal Lauriat returning his call.

'Cardinal secretary,' Celestino said. 'We found Viola's SUV abandoned in Nazzano inside a vacant warehouse. One of my men, the driver, was shot, execution-style. I suspect he was an unwitting member of the plot. There's no sign of the Holy Father and no blood in the car other than the driver's.'

'Do you have any idea where they might have taken him?' Lauriat asked.

'None whatsoever. I'll keep you informed if any clues turn up here. Otherwise we're continuing with our investigation into Viola.'

'I want to be updated on every detail, Celestino, every single detail.'

THIRTY-FIVE

Celestino pulled down the blinds of his glass office door and sat alone in the dark for several minutes. A rap on the glass brought him back to the moment.

He allowed Pinotti to enter and asked him if he had anything new.

'We talked to Viola's sister in Trieste. Did you know he has cancer?'

Celestino turned on his desk lamp. 'No, what kind? What's his condition?'

'She said it's in the lungs and it's spread. He's a big smoker, as we know. She says he doesn't have long.'

'So he figures he's got nothing to lose,' Celestino said, rubbing his temples to ease his headache. 'You can't kill a dead man. Is the search of his apartment done?'

'There was nothing. We took it apart.'

'How are we doing with his telephone and financial records?'

'I've got men going through them.'

Celestino wanted to see the paperwork for himself so he went over to the room where the officers were working. Viola had a Vatican-owned mobile phone and landline and had his checking, savings, and credit-card accounts at the Vatican Bank so searching his records was a simple matter not requiring a court order. One officer was sorting through his mobile-phone records, another, records from the phone line in his apartment, and two officers were wading through his banking statements.

Celestino and Pinotti approached the officer with a stack of mobile-phone data and Celestino asked him what he was finding.

'We didn't know how far to go back,' the fellow said, 'so we made the decision to look at the past six months.'

'I think that's probably a waste of effort,' Celestino said. 'Unless we're missing something, this affair started in December when Donovan began looking for the loan.'

'The idea was to define a baseline of his calling practices to see if there was a deviation during the critical time period,' Pinotti said.

'OK, Vittorio,' Celestino said, 'I'll buy that.'

Pinotti ran his thumb over the edge of the stack and said, 'Viola made and received a lot of calls, which isn't unusual given his responsibilities. You're number one on the list, actually.'

Celestino clucked, 'He kept me on a short leash. Who else?'

'Lots of calls to various Governorate departments, the cardinal secretary and staff, various police and security departments in Rome. His sister in Trieste, a brother in Puglia. A lot of calls to a medical clinic in Rome. A lot of one-off and miscellaneous numbers I've yet to identify. So far I don't see any obvious pattern changes during December or January.'

Celestino picked up the stack and spent a minute rummaging.

'What about the texts?'

'He didn't text as much.'

'He texted me all the time,' Celestino said.

'You're number one, for sure,' the officer said.

The stack of text records was smaller and Celestino looked at a random page.

'It's only numbers sent and received,' he said. 'What about the actual messages?'

'We can get those,' Pinotti said. 'It'll take a while to pull them off the server.'

'Get them,' Celestino said, 'we have to have them.'

'Will do,' Pinotti said.

Celestino leafed through the pages of texts, slowing down when he got to the month of December and then January. Something clicked and he took a chair, flipping back to the late-December sheets.

'What's up, boss?' Pinotti asked.

'Something's not right.'

'What?' Pinotti asked.

'Christ, give me a second to think!'

Celestino whipped out his own mobile phone and went to the SMS app.

'There! Look at this,' he said, pointing to his screen. 'I knew there was something. I remember he texted me half a dozen times on Christmas Eve about security for the pope's midnight Mass. Here are the messages. Where are they in these records?'

Pinotti took the pages and examined them. 'You're right. The twenty-fifth of December is missing.'

'What's up with that, Luigi?' Celestino asked the reviewing officer.

'You've got what I've got,' the officer said. 'I didn't lose a sheet.'

'Who'd we get these from?'

'The Vatican Telephone Service. Major Pinotti picked them up personally.'

'This is what they gave me,' Pinotti said.

'We need to get to the bottom of this. Luigi, get over to the Governorate Palace double-time and bring me another set of messages. OK, let me see the bank records.'

Celestino took a personal interest in Viola's bank accounts and was in his office examining a copy of the last several weeks of his banking and credit-card transactions. He had just circled a 31 December purchase for about sixty-five euros at a shop at the Rome Termini railway station when his sister, Elisabetta, called to see how he was doing.

'I'm all right, considering,' he said.

'Any news on the Holy Father and the professor?'

'Nothing yet. We're working it hard as you can imagine.'

'I shouldn't bother you but Papa offered to help. He told me to tell you he could analyze data, help look for connections.'

'He needs a break from Goldbach?'

'Don't be mean. You know how clever he is.'

'Tell him I appreciate it.'

'I'm paralyzed with fear,' she said. 'All I can do is pray.'

'That's not a bad strategy.'

His officer, Luigi, knocked on the door with the new set of phone records and he signed off with Elisabetta.

'Was the page for Christmas Eve there?' Celestino asked.

'Right here. You've got to take a look at it, Colonel.'

At the same moment, Julian Sassoon was sitting in his father's chair at his father's desk in his father's office. Henry Sassoon hadn't gone into his work office during the last six months of his life and it was dusty and untouched from his last day. There were a couple of oxygen cylinders standing in the corner and some unused suction catheters coiled in the bathroom. Outside on the street, one protester with a bullhorn made his life miserable for a while until the police ticketed the shrill lady for a noise violation and things got more peaceful.

He'd decided that it had been time to jump in with both feet and put his fancy business-school education to work. If he was going to sit in the big chair and not get steamrolled by Marcus and members of his staff he needed to get up to speed and learn the operations. So, he approached it as if he'd been assigned a case study at the B-School and he had piled the desk with spreadsheets and audit reports – the guts of the business – and had begun his own analysis. On day three of the exercise, he was trying to figure out some balance-sheet entries that on the surface looked mundane, but that had niggled at him overnight.

Equity position in Plowshares Master Fund IV, LLP:
$203,387,290

Plowshares had first appeared in the books two years earlier at approximately the sixty-million-dollar level. A year later it was over two hundred million. It wasn't unusual for the bank to carry an equity investment on its books for a quarter or two until it unwound its position but he hadn't seen one of this magnitude and duration. The audit reports were fairly mute on Plowshares, describing it as a Cayman Islands diversified hedge fund with a five-year annualized rate of return of fourteen percent.

He phoned the bank's chief financial officer, Mike Ritter.

'Mike, what can you tell me about Plowshares IV?'

'It's a Cayman hedge fund we invested in a couple of years ago. The investment got upped last year.'

'Upped? It quadrupled.'

'Yeah, a big up.'

'Who are they?'

'I never met the management. West coast guys I understand. It's Marcus's deal. They're supposed to be studs.'

'Since when do we hold a position this long?'

'It's unusual, I'll give you that. But you should talk to Marcus.'

His next call was to the bank's external auditors. He'd never met the audit partner who spent a little while giving his condolences.

'So I understand you're the new sheriff in town,' the auditor said. 'We should meet.'

'Yeah, I'll set something up,' Julian said. 'Look, I wanted to see what you guys know about our investment in Plowshares IV, a Cayman hedge fund.'

'I'm glad you called about that. It's been a concern of ours.'

'Tell me more.'

'Well, when the bank put sixty-odd million into it two years ago, it wasn't particularly material, since past practice was to roll out of these things pretty fast. At two hundred mill it's become a lot more material. We wanted to dig into it but Marcus assured us that he was in the process of liquidating it.'

'What do you know about it?'

'We have their Cayman filings but if you've ever seen those, they're on the minimalist side.'

'Do you think you could get more forensic? I want to understand what makes them tick.'

'More than happy to.'

'And do me a favor. Don't talk to Marcus about this.'

Celestino strode over to Vittorio Pinotti's office with a single sheet of paper in his hand. The office was empty.

'Anyone seen the major?' he called out to the duty room.

One of the clerks looked up from her computer and told him she'd seen him leave a half-hour earlier.

'Go see if his car is in the lot,' he told the clerk.

He sat down at Pinotti's desk and looked at the sheet again.

On 24 December there was an 8:14 p.m. text to the mobile phone of Cardinal Pascal Lauriat and at 9:02 p.m. there was a text to Vittorio Pinotti, the one and only text in six months between Viola and Pinotti.

Celestino's mobile phone rang. His officer sounded out of breath.

'What do you have, Luigi?'

'I've got the texts off the server, Colonel. The one to Cardinal Lauriat was "Consider it done."'

'And to Vittorio?'

'It was, "See me at ten."'

'That's it?'

'That's it.'

'OK, look, get me all of Vittorio's records. Everything – phone, bank, credit cards – the works. And do the same for Pascal Lauriat.'

'The cardinal secretary?'

'Yes, the cardinal secretary.'

He tried calling Pinotti's mobile a couple of times and on the last try he left a simple voicemail: 'We need to talk, Vittorio. We need to talk now.'

His next call was to Cecchi. He told him what he'd found out and asked for his help in finding Pinotti. Cecchi took down the make, model, and plate number of the major's car and his home address. Celestino also asked if he could send the Carabinieri over to the Rome Termini station to find out what Viola had purchased there. After he hung up he emailed over the information on Viola's credit-card transaction and began rifling through Pinotti's desk.

Forty-five minutes later, Cecchi rang Celestino back.

'We found your man,' Cecchi said. 'We put out a bulletin on his car to the Municipal and State Police and a cop spotted it in the south, near the Laurentina subway station. It's a few blocks away from his flat.'

'Is he in custody?'

'They have him boxed in but he's waving them off. He's got a gun.'

'We need him alive, Tommaso.'

'Understood. I'm on my way over there. I'll call you back.'

Celestino tried Pinotti's number again. He was startled when he picked up.

'Emilio.'

'Vittorio,' he said as calmly as he could, 'you need to throw down your gun and give yourself up.'

'I can't do that.'

'Of course you can. Whatever it is, we can work this out.'

'I don't think we can.'

'Where is the pope, Vittorio?'

'I don't know.'

'Please.'

'Believe me, I don't know.'

'Who else is involved?'

He replied in an insistent, childlike whine. 'I don't know.'

'Then tell me why you did it.'

'Because it's my Church too.'

'Listen to me, Vittorio . . .'

Pinotti didn't let him finish. 'Tell your sister, Micaela, something for me, will you? Tell her I'm sorry we never went out together.'

'Vittorio . . .'

The gunshot was so loud, Celestino dropped his phone.

THIRTY-SIX

The next few hours sped by but to Emilio Celestino it seemed as if each hour was merely minutes.

Pieces of data flowed into the ops center like flotsam floating along the strong current of the Tiber.

On 6 January, Pascal Lauriat made a cash withdrawal of ten thousand euros from his personal Vatican bank account. On 7 January, Vittorio Pinotti sent a postal money order of ten thousand euros to a company called Alpha Epsilon Ltd. The money order was cashed at a post office in Reggio Calabria in southern Italy but the company appeared to be fictitious with no incorporation or trading records according to the Italian financial police, the Guardia di Finanza. Then, as evening fell, the Carabinieri, working with the manager of the Hudson News store at the underground level of the Rome Termini station, located Viola's credit card purchase on 31 December, a pair of prepaid Vodafones. With the bar codes of the phones in hand, Cecchi applied for an emergency court order to compel Vodafone to provide the mobile numbers. The managing director of Vodafone, Italy was tracked down at a restaurant and an hour later, Cecchi had the numbers and the call logs of both phones.

'The two numbers only call each other,' Cecchi told Celestino over the phone. 'Two times before the kidnapping, four times since, the last two hours ago.'

'Can you trace them?'

'One of them. The other signal is too weak. Guess where the strong signal is coming from?'

'Vatican City.'

'Bullseye.'

'Lauriat, for sure.'

'Are you going to question him?'

'He's not going to admit his role so easily,' Celestino said, 'and we've only got a few small pieces of circumstantial evidence. We can't arrest the second most powerful official at the Vatican based on crumbs.'

'If the two Vodafones call each other again we'll be more likely to pick up the signal of the other one as it bounces off the nearest towers. We'll have to wait and see.'

'Maybe we don't have to be so passive.'

The policeman in him made Celestino want to do this in person. He could have picked up the phone but he wanted to get a measure of the man, to see the small movements of facial muscles, to peer into the soul of a liar.

Cardinal Lauriat received him in his apartment in the Apostolic Palace, dressed for the evening in slacks and a sweater.

'You have some news, Colonel?'

'I do, Your Eminence. It's our first good news. We know where they've taken the pope.'

Lauriat arched a brow and reached for his glass of hot lemon water.

'Where? Where is he?'

'The Carabinieri won't tell me. Because of Viola and Pinotti they're making the painful assumption that the Gendarmerie is riddled with conspirators. All they say is that they are planning an operation.'

Celestino saw the cardinal's jaw ripple. 'When?'

'They won't even tell me that. But I thought you should know what I know.'

'Thank you for that, Colonel. I will be retiring for the night but do not hesitate to wake me with updates. Now, if you'll excuse me, I will pray for the Holy Father.'

Viola had assumed a fetal position in his narrow bed to deal with the acute pain in his belly. When the mobile phone chimed from the dresser he was forced to uncurl himself.

'What's the matter?' he asked.

'Hello?' Lauriat said. 'I can't hear you.'

Viola had to walk across the room, doubled-over. 'I said, what's the matter.'

'That's better. You don't sound well.'

'I'm fine. Why are you calling?'

'Celestino came to see me. The Carabinieri are saying they know where you are and that they're coming for you.'

'Oh yes? Where is that?'

'They won't tell him. After you and Pinotti they think the Gendarmerie is rotten.'

'They don't know anything,' Viola said. 'Vittorio didn't know where we are. Even you don't know.'

'What about the ones you brought with you?'

'None of these 'Ndrangheta boys knew where we were going before we got here. I didn't allow any of them to bring their phones. I had Vittorio rent the villa in cash through a false company.'

'Why are the Carabinieri saying it?'

'I don't know.'

'I'd feel better if you could get Celestine to renounce the foundation now.'

'Tomorrow morning is the deadline. When I put a gun to Donovan's head, he'll come around.'

'Do it tonight. Make a video. We can't wait any longer.'

'Very well, I'll do it but not for your reason.'

'What reason then?'

'You were right. I'm not well. I might not be alive tomorrow.'

He was businesslike, not triumphant. 'We've got him,' Cecchi told Celestino. 'Come to the ROS headquarters immediately.'

The traffic was light but Celestino fired up his blue lights and gunned his car to the limits of safety.

He parked on the Piazza del Popolo and flew into the ROS building where he was escorted to the operations center. Cecchi had been kind when he had said the two departments had similar technology. The ROS command post looked to Celestino like something he'd only seen on TV shows – super-high-tech with multiple satellite, infrared, and CCTV feeds projected on a wall of monitors.

'Good, you're here,' Cecchi said. 'This is the screen you need to be looking at.'

It was one of the infrared images, the one on the central monitor. It was all shades of green and black, a shifting view of a roof in the middle of nowhere.

'Where is it?' Celestino asked.

'Campania. A mountain near Sanza.'

'South? We thought they were heading north.'

'A sleight of hand, I think,' Cecchi said. 'They switch cars north of Rome and go south instead.'

'Is this real-time?' Celestino asked.

'It's a live feed. We got the air force to scramble an MQ-9 Reaper drone, one of the ones we use in Libya, from the Amendola Airbase in Foggia.'

'You sure it's the right location?'

'The cell signal wasn't strong but there's nothing else nearby. The house is isolated as hell. See there? There's a couple of cars in the driveway so it's occupied. And get this. The villa is a rental. We're trying to contact the owner but we've got some very useful photos of the interior from the rental website.'

'How do you want to play this?' Celestino asked.

'I have an ROS tactical team assembling at our helipad as we speak. I assume you want to take part.'

'You assume correctly.'

'Good. We leave in ten minutes, at nine on the dot. We'll get you a vest.'

It was a little past ten o'clock. The pope had fallen asleep but Cal was awake, doing some thinking about his life and wishing he had a bottle of vodka to go along with the exercise. He'd been gradually resigning himself to an unhappy endgame and he was a little surprised at his phlegmatic state of mind. It wasn't as if he was content to say goodbye to the earthly world; there was a lot to like about being Cal Donovan. After all, he'd just been made a University Professor and he'd hardly been able to exercise any bragging rights with his colleagues. But what had really surprised him was this realization: when faced with the final curtain and all that, most men, he assumed, would look back on life and regret this and regret that. But he wasn't having any of it. No revisionist history for me, he thought. I did things the way I wanted to, I treated good people well and bad people poorly, I left a paper trail of my accomplishments, I slept with some great ladies, and I drank some pretty good booze along the way. Besides, how many people were in a position to have a pope say a prayer over their dead body?

Celestine stirred at the sound of the door bolt sliding open.

Viola came in and his shadow, Antonio, assumed his usual position by the door.

The pope sat up and Viola hit the light switch.

'I'm sorry to wake you, Holy Father. Believe me, I am.'

'Arturo, what is the matter?' Celestine said. 'You look like you're in great pain.'

There was no hiding it. Viola had waited for over an hour, hoping the pain would subside. He couldn't stand straight. He couldn't think straight. It didn't seem that the problem was going to spontaneously resolve. He had to act while he could.

'Please don't worry about me, Holy Father,' he said through twisted lips. 'I told you that I would wait until tomorrow for your answer but I need to know tonight.'

'But, Arturo, surely you know what my answer must be.'

A severe cramp hit Viola. He put a hand hard against his stomach and managed to say, 'I'll have no choice but to kill Donovan. I'm going to have to do it. I'm going to have to do it now.'

The pope pushed himself off his bed and stood. He was clad only in his underwear but he didn't pay any heed to modesty.

Cal got up too. Being shot in bed wasn't the way he pictured it.

The pope looked to Viola's pain-squinted and then to Antonio's fearful eyes and said, 'No, Arturo, no, Antonio. Do not do this. A life is too precious. It is not for you to take. Do not put yourself in the position of God. It is forbidden. I forbid it.'

Viola opened his mouth. The words, 'Holy Father,' came out, followed by a pailful of bright red blood.

THIRTY-SEVEN

Viola collapsed to his knees and to Cal, everything seemed to be in slow motion.

The pope almost slipped on vomited blood as he laboriously stooped to help Viola.

Viola retched another gusher of blood.

Antonio made what seemed to be the most languid of movements of his gun hand as Cal commenced his leap.

And nothing seemed real until the moment Cal's shoulder rammed into Antonio's chest.

Then everything sped up considerably.

The amateur boxer in Cal came out of the ring punching and punching hard. Antonio tried to shout for help but a right to the jaw shut the kid up. He still had his gun but he seemed more interested in using his hands to block Cal's punches than putting the weapon to its intended purpose. The second he got it raised higher than his own waist, Cal hit him so hard in his thin gut that his grip failed and the gun dropped to the floor. They both looked at the pistol. When Antonio bent to pick it up, Cal delivered a cracking roundhouse to the kid's chin that was so fierce, it left Cal with an unbearable pain in his knuckles. God knows how Antonio felt because he went down like a toppled statue, his face splashing into Viola's bloody effluent.

Cal couldn't pick up the gun with his busted right hand. He had to settle for his left. The safety was off. He couldn't tell if there was a round in the chamber and one-handed as he was, he couldn't pull the slide back. There was only one way to tell and that was going to be by pulling the trigger.

Antonio got up on all fours. He wasn't finished.

Cal pointed the gun at his head.

'Professor, no!' the pope cried. 'For God's sake, don't shoot the boy.'

Cal nodded and brought the butt of the pistol down on the dome of Antonio's head.

'I'm going for help,' was all Cal said before creeping into the hall.

'Don't do a flyover,' Cecchi told the pilot of the AgustaWestland Merlin. 'We need to surprise them.'

The helicopter pilot found a relatively flat piece of land to put down on about one and a half kilometers below the villa as the crow flies but more like three kilometers of winding road up the mountain. A dozen ROS SWAT officers jumped out of the chopper along with Cecchi and Celestino and were met by an arctic blast of wind.

'Ready for a nice little jog?' Cecchi asked, sprinting to catch up with his men.

Celestino, glad to be wearing rubber-soled boots, took off after him up the snowy road.

Celestine cradled Viola's head on his lap.

'Just try to breathe normally, Arturo.'

Viola opened his eyes. 'The pain is less,' he croaked. 'Something let loose and now it's better.'

'That's good. It's a blessing,' the pope said.

'Let me try to get up,' Viola said.

'Easy. Go easy, my son.'

He sat himself against a wall and looked at a bottle of water on the nearest nightstand.

'Are you thirsty?'

Viola nodded but said he was afraid to drink in case he vomited again.

'Just a small sip, perhaps,' the pope said, rising to his own feet on the slippery floor with a fair bit of difficulty.

He handed the bottle to Viola, who managed to hold down a small amount. He thanked the pope and said, 'The cancer. It's spread to my liver and intestine. I think – no I know – this is my last night on the earth.'

'Then you must confess your sins, Arturo. Are you prepared to do this?'

Cal edged down the stairs, barefoot and shirtless, in his boxer shorts, gripping Antonio's gun in his off hand. His right hand, broken for sure, alternated between stabbing and throbbing pain.

A voice came from somewhere on the ground level. 'Antonio? Everything OK up there?'

Cal kept coming. There was no other choice. He didn't know how many other men were in the house but he couldn't deal with them upstairs. He didn't want bullets flying around near the pope. A young man appeared in the hall. They saw each other at the same moment. Cal was about to find out if a round was seated in the chamber. He aimed the best he could with his left hand and squeezed the trigger.

The gun fired; a bullet creased the wall and sent the man diving back into a lower bedroom. The fellow was shouting now, calling his companions to action.

Cal couldn't stay put. The staircase felt like a lane in a shooting range and he felt like a man-sized bullseye target. He started eating up steps, moving as fast as he could, and when he got to the downstairs hall and the open door where the man had retreated, he blindly fired twice into the room as he moved past it.

He heard a shout behind him, a different voice, and then an explosion. In the confined space it sounded more like a cannon than a pistol and he knew instantly he'd been hit. The spray of blood from his grazed deltoid muscle spattered the right side of his face and the pain registered an instant later. He kept running. Cocking back his left arm and without looking let alone aiming, he fired three more times at whomever was behind him.

The front door was coming up fast. The doorknob was going to be a problem. He could either toss his gun or try to use a broken fist attached to a shot arm. The gun seemed too important so his snap decision was to opt for agony. He bellowed as he clamped down on the knob and gave it a twist. If he hadn't had so much adrenaline pumping around he might have passed out.

Thankfully, the door wasn't locked.

He blew out into the freezing cold just as someone fired at him again.

It was sleeting and the driveway was slick.

His bare feet gave him no traction and he slipped and fell immediately. He found himself by one of the parked cars and put the gun on the ground for a moment to use a door handle to get up.

There were more shouts from behind and zero time to look for keys inside the vehicle. He kept running but the flat upper driveway gave way to a slope. His feet went out from under him again and this time he landed squarely on his bleeding upper arm.

An involuntary scream pierced the thin mountain air.

Pain wasn't his only problem.

His gun hand was empty now and he kept on sliding downhill on mostly bare skin. His body became a toboggan, picking up speed. Eventually the roadway curved but he kept going straight until he crashed into a snow bank.

Momentarily stunned, he heard the urgent sounds of men coming after him, and he willed himself back on his feet. The only way he was going to get traction was by moving alongside the road in deeper snow and he took off running again, all his pain melting together into something hot and bright.

At least two men were following him on foot. He heard them shouting to one another, asking if they saw where he went.

Another shot rang out, the sound echoing off the next mountain peak. He had no way of knowing if it was aimed or just intended to keep him ensnared by fear. But then he heard a more terrifying noise, a car starting up and tires rolling and skidding on the snowy drive.

He thought of running at a sharp angle to the road but where there was impenetrable blackness there might be a blind drop into nothingness. The car was getting closer and headlights began to dance around a curve.

There was no other way.

He'd have to turn away from the road and take the plunge toward an ink-black fate.

Suddenly his eyes hurt.

Beams of light made him squint then clamp his lids shut. He stumbled into a knee-high drift.

The car was almost on him.

There were shots, lots of them, but they were throatier and louder than the pistol fire.

The car kept coming but it was sliding past him now, moving fast into the abyss, disappearing from the road entirely, followed seconds later by a fearsome grinding of metal against stone.

Gloved hands were pulling him out of the snow bank, carrying him on to the road.

An ROS officer was speaking loudly at him while others shone their torches in his face.

'Are you Donovan? Where is the pope?'

Cal answered numbly. His lips felt thick. 'He's up at the house.'

Cecchi arrived, followed by Celestino.

'Is the Holy Father safe?' Cecchi asked.

'I – I think so.'

Celestino peeled off his jacket and threw it over Cal. 'Who's there with him?'

'Viola. Others.'

'Stay with him,' Cecchi ordered one of his men. 'He's bleeding badly.'

Cal was watching the officer pull a first-aid kit out of his pack when mercifully he slipped out of consciousness.

The pope winced at the sound of every distant gunshot.

'Please, Arturo, can you make your people stop shooting at the professor? He's a good man. He's my friend.'

Viola was still propped up against the wall, sipping from the bottle of water, his chin and shirt stained with his own blood.

'There's nothing I can do.'

'I beg of you, Arturo. Call to them.'

The pope turned his attention to Antonio, motionless on the floor.

'Thank God,' he said. 'He's still breathing. Antonio, can you wake up?'

A man called up the stairs. 'Antonio? Viola?'

Viola tried to yell but it came out weakly. 'Up here.'

Two men appeared. They were young and scared and seemed unnerved at the sight of Celestine, his underclothes smeared in blood.

'Young men,' the pope said, 'I beg you to put down your weapons. I beg you not to harm Professor Donovan.'

'Where is he?' Viola asked.

'He ran away,' one of them answered. 'Two guys went after him.'

'Is Antonio dead?' the other man asked.

'He's knocked out, that's all,' Viola said.

From a short distance they heard a volley of automatic weapons.

'We've got company!' one of the men shouted. 'Come on, Marco!'

Viola managed to rise to his feet by hugging the wall. Celestine watched as he pulled a small pistol from his trouser pocket.

'I don't think we have time for my confession, Holy Father.'

'You should put away your gun,' the pope scolded. Perhaps most men would have backed away when a gun was pointed at them but Celestine did the opposite. He extended his arms in a gesture of peace and began slowly walking toward his adversary.

'But that I can't do,' Viola said. 'You see, we've come to the end of this affair, Holy Father. There's only one way to stop you from destroying the Church. It won't hurt, I promise. I'll follow along shortly but we may not be arriving at the same destination.'

Ear-piercing volleys of automatic gunfire filled the lower level of the villa and the smell of gunpowder drifted up into the bedroom.

There was a rush of footsteps up the stairs.

Before Viola could react, Celestino was at the threshold with Cecchi only a step behind.

They both saw Viola's pistol but it was Cecchi who yelled, 'Gun!'

Viola pointed his gun at the pope's head as Celestino raised his Glock.

The pope was still moving forward; he was close enough to brush Viola's cheek with his hand when the pope looked at Celestino and shouted, 'No, don't!'

Celestino fired first but the pope was intentionally thrusting his body between Viola and the colonel.

A red circle appeared on the pope's undershirt over his belly button and he slowly slumped to the floor.

Viola had the presence of mind to adjust his aim for a coup-de-grace to the pope's head but a single shot from Cecchi's Beretta stopped him dead.

Celestino rushed to the pope's side and began putting pressure on the wound.

'Radio the chopper,' Cecchi screamed down the stairs. 'Tell him he's got to land up here now!'

THIRTY-EIGHT

The nurse tried to dress him but he waved her off. Five minutes later Cal sheepishly rang his call bell for help after trying and failing to get his shirt on over the cast on his hand and the bandage on his shoulder. The nurse chided him while doing up his buttons.

'Can I go now?' he asked.

'You have to wait for the doctor. She needs to write your discharge paper.'

His room at Rome's Gemelli Hospital was overheated so he cracked the window with his good hand. That allowed him to hear the hubbub from the omnipresent crowd below.

His mobile rang. It was his mother. Again. He understood her anxiety but her confusion about time zones meant she was calling at all hours including the middle of the night.

'Yes, it's still happening today,' he said. 'I'm just waiting for the doctor to discharge me.'

'Are you in much pain, dear?'

'I'm OK.'

'And you're coming right home?'

'Tomorrow morning. The Sassoons were nice enough to send their airplane.'

'Gail's a dear. Why don't you come to New York instead of Boston? You can stay with me. I can get you a private duty nurse.'

Cal laughed it off. 'I have a broken hand and a flesh wound in my shoulder. What exactly would a nurse do?'

'Sponge baths?'

The newspaper came while he was waiting. He glanced at the banner headline: THE WORLD PRAYS.

At midday he was free to go. Armed with prescriptions for antibiotics and pain relief he looked for the pharmacy but saw the sign for the ICU first. Stepping off the elevator he didn't get far. A cordon of plain-clothes Swiss Guards and Vatican Gendarmes blocked the corridor.

'Your business, please?' he was asked.

'I wonder if I might see him?' Cal asked.

'See who?'

'The pope.'

'Who are you?'

'Calvin Donovan.'

'Are you on the list?'

'I don't know.'

The guard checked a clipboard and told him to get back on the elevator.

A gendarme close by overheard the exchange.

'Professor Donovan?' he asked.

'Yes.'

'Please wait one minute.'

He returned after a while and told Cal to come with him. The doors to the ICU slid open and they entered the cool antisepsis of the ward. The nursing station was crowded with hospital personnel – nurses, doctors, respiratory therapists, and technicians – but all the patient cubicles were empty.

Except for one.

There was a single chair beside the elevated bed.

'Do you know her?' the gendarme whispered to Cal. 'She hasn't left his side.'

'I know her.'

Elisabetta stood when she saw Cal. She tenderly touched him on the arm, asked how he was feeling, and apologized for not coming to see him.

'I was worried that he might wake and I wouldn't be there,' she said.

There was nothing to show that the patient was a pope. He simply looked like an old, overweight, and critically ill man with tubes in his arms, a catheter running to a collection system, and a breathing tube connected by hoses to a respirator. The incessant beeping from a monitor might have been a small irritation were it not indicative of a steady heartbeat.

'How is he?' Cal asked.

She had been present for all the doctors' bedside conferences.

'He lost a lot of blood before he got to the hospital in Sanza. They don't know if it affected his brain. He hasn't woken up. The surgery went well but they had to remove several feet of his small intestine. There's an infection. Peritonitis. Today they're worried about pneumonia. He's seventy-eight, you know. That makes it especially difficult. He's in God's hands.'

'May I touch his hand?'

'Of course. I've been holding it a lot.'

She watched him as he gently squeezed a few fingertips with his uninjured hand.

'I think your friendship means a lot to him,' she said.

He swallowed and nodded.

'My brother is suffering,' she said. 'It was his bullet.'

'I wasn't in the room but I spoke to Lieutenant Colonel Cecchi. It wasn't his fault. Celestine took the bullet for Viola.'

'Still, he has to live with it. People are saying he's the one who shot the pope. And with Arturo Viola and Vittorio Pinotti's involvement, the Gendarmerie Corps is under a big cloud.'

'Your brother is a good and honorable man.'

She was grateful for his kind words. 'What are your plans?'

'I've got to get back home. I'm missing in action from my teaching duties.'

'I'm sure it will be hard adjusting to your usual routine,' she said.

It wouldn't be hard, it would be impossible.

'And you?' he asked.

She turned that lovely face to him and said, 'I will be sitting here until – until he wakes up. And Professor?'

'Yes.'

'I'm still praying for you every day.'

The external auditor sat across the desk from Julian and looked over his shoulder through the glass panels on both sides of the door.

'Marcus saw me on the way in,' he said. 'He asked me why I was here.'

'What did you tell him?'

'Courtesy call. To introduce myself to you. Know what he said?'

'That he didn't want you showing up without informing him first?' Julian asked.

'How'd you know?'

'Because I know Marcus.'

'Rough news from Italy.'

Julian nodded. He'd been trying to reach Donovan. 'What did you find out?'

Even though they were alone and the door was shut he lowered his voice. 'Plowshares Master Fund IV was incorporated as a Cayman fund only a month before it recorded the initial sixty-million-dollar investment from the bank.'

'Tell me there are other investors . . .'

'Apparently not.'

Julian's face darkened.

'There's more,' the auditor said. 'Plowshares' resident manager is a lawyer down in the Caymans. That's not atypical. But it turns out that Plowshares IV is a wholly owned subsidiary of another Cayman entity, Mount Laurentian LLC, managed by the same George Town lawyer, and Mount Laurentian is, in turn wholly owned by an Isle of Man LLC called Angle Iron Enterprises.'

'And who might the manager of Angle Iron be?' Julian asked.

'Marcus Sassoon.'

Julian swiveled his chair. A steady snowfall was accumulating on the windowpanes. 'Go on.'

'We can't be sure without conducting an audit of Plowshares – and I imagine we'd need a subpoena to get access to them – but I suspect we're going to find that there's no money in it. The two hundred million on its books is going to be a sham.'

'You think it's a vehicle to paper over bank losses elsewhere?'

'I do.'

'From where?'

'Hard to know. Nothing turned up on our bank audits so we'd have to go with the assumption that if there's one set of fraudulent paperwork there are going to be others. I think we need to get forensic, Julian. Personally I'd recommend starting with the trading desk.'

Julian sneered. 'Which cousin Albert runs.'

'If I were a betting man I'd say that we're going to find two hundred million in papered-over trading losses.'

'Are you a betting man?'

'I've been known to place a bet or two.'

'Then go ahead. Get forensic.'

'There's something we've got to do first. I'm obligated to make some calls.'

'To whom?'

'The SEC, the New York State Banking Department, and the US Attorney's office.'

Julian smiled. 'Do it.'

Back at his hotel suite, Cal's things were untouched. There had been some reporters in the lobby but he'd blown past them without comment. He sat for a while staring into space, thinking about the cold vodka lurking behind the little door.

He pushed off the chair to get his ringing phone.

'There you are,' the Irish voice said. 'I'm blue in the face calling you.'

He hadn't been purposely avoiding Murphy's calls. He just hadn't been ready to speak to friends and colleagues.

'Hey, Joe. And here I am . . .'

'Look, Professor, I don't want to bug you. I really just wanted to hear your voice. We've all been so worried and concerned.'

'I'm OK. Just got out of the hospital. Coming home tomorrow.'

'Well that's excellent. Any news on the pope? The Vatican hasn't been a font of information.'

'He's in rough shape. Touch and go.'

'Well, we're all praying for him. I imagine he's a tough old boy.'

'He is that.'

Hanging up, he popped a pain pill and laid himself down. Before long he was drifting off and probably would have slept well into the evening had his phone not rung again.

'Cal, it's Gil Daniels. How the hell are you?'

'Feel like a truck ran over me.'

'Well, you're all over the news. A real hero.'

'I'm not a hero, Gil. I was a victim.'

'Heroes always say that. So look, we've been fielding media requests. *Sixty Minutes* wants you for this Sunday. They're willing to come to Rome.'

'I'll be in Cambridge tomorrow.'

'Well, that's good news. I'll have Jean compile all the media calls and email them to you so you can sort them out yourself. When do you think you'll be back in the classroom?'

'Don't worry, Gil,' he said with an edge. 'I'll be back in the saddle by the end of the week.'

'Actually, there's no rush. I sat in on one of Joe Murphy's

substitute lectures. You were right about him, Cal. He's good.
I think I made the wrong call.'

Cal put the phone down and got out of bed. It was getting dark.
There were church bells tolling in the distance. He wondered if
there was a reason for them but he really didn't want to know.
With his good hand he opened the door to the mini-bar.

At the sound of the buzzer, Cardinal Leoncino put his cheek against
his apartment door to look through the peephole.

He opened it a crack and said, 'You shouldn't have come, Pascal.
We shouldn't be seen together.'

'Thank you, Mario. Yes, I will come in.'

Lauriat made tracks to the drinks cabinet and helped himself
to Leoncino's best brandy.

'What's the matter?' Leoncino asked. 'Is there news about the pope?'

'Nothing.'

'Then what brings you here at this hour?'

'I've always liked this apartment, Mario.'

'Fine, fine, but what reason is that?'

'A friendly monsignor at the Vatican Bank told me that the
Gendarmerie examined my accounts.'

Leoncino sat down hard, his face a study in worry. 'So what?
What will they find?'

'I did something quite silly. I withdrew a good sum of money
from my savings. Viola and Pinotti needed it to pay for . . .'

Leoncino leapt up and shouted, 'Stop it! Stop talking! I don't want
to hear anything about this. This is your affair, Pascal, not mine.'

'You're right, Mario. It's my problem. Do you mind if I take
my brandy out on to your balcony? It's such a clear night.'

'Sure, sure. That's a lot of brandy. For you, I mean. I won't
join you. It's too cold for me.'

Lauriat closed the balcony doors behind him and went to the
railing. The lights of Rome were beckoning and cheerful and
looking out, he sipped at the liquor.

Leoncino yawned impatiently. He wanted his guest to leave
and he wanted to sleep.

'Pascal? Could you come in now? It's getting late,' he called
through the door.

When he finally got up and braved the icy chill, the balcony
was vacant, an empty glass on the railing.

THIRTY-NINE

Three months later

The office manager barged into his office without knocking
or apologizing.
'Julian! The FBI are here!'
His feet had been up on his desk, his computer on his lap. She
expected shock. Instead he calmly smiled at her.
'Are they?' he said. 'I'd better come and see what they want.'
'We've got media outside too. Lots of them.'
A posse of men and women in blue and white windbreakers
came marching down the hall.
'Federal agents!' one of them said. 'Please remain at your work
stations.'
'I'm Mr Sassoon,' Julian said.
'Marcus or Albert?' the lead special agent asked.
'Julian.'
'We don't want you. We want them.'
'I'm sure you do.'
'We're executing their federal arrest warrants for securities
fraud.'
'Three offices down is Albert,' Julian said, merrily pointing.
'The one in the corner is Marcus.'

'This is Detective Gonzalez.' As usual, Gonzalez sounded sleepy.
'Yeah, my name is Leon Soto. I want to report a crime. At least
I think it's a crime.'
'You think you've got a crime,' Gonzalez said wearily.
'No, I'm pretty sure. My ex-wife, Maria – well, she's still my
wife but we're supposed to be signing our divorce papers – I'm
pretty sure she's covering for a guy.'
'Covering what?'
'Murder.'
'You think your wife is covering up for a murder?'
'Yeah.'

'Illuminate me.'

'She's a nurse. One of her patients died a few months ago.'

'I assume he was sick,' Gonzalez said, preparing to hang up on the guy.

'Sure he was. But she came into a lot of money all of a sudden she tried to hide from me. I mean a lot of money. She told a girlfriend who happens to be my friend, if you know what I mean, that a guy named Marcus paid her because he might have helped this patient shuffle down the road.'

'Shuffle down the road?'

'You know, kill him. I didn't have a clue who this guy was but I think I just saw him on the TV.'

'Oh yeah? Where's that?'

'In front of his office. The FBI was arresting him for something. I recognized the building. Maria used to go there to take care of the dead guy before he had to stay home. I picked her up there once.'

'And this guy. You just saw him on TV.'

'Yeah, just now. They got his name on the screen.'

'What is it? His name.'

'Sassoon. Marcus Sassoon.'

The ceremony was being held at a grand reception hall in the Apostolic Palace and the visitors were assembling, taking their places in the rows of gold chairs.

'Where do we sit?' Carlo Celestino asked his daughter.

Elisabetta pointed to their assigned chairs in the first row.

'Best seats in the house,' he said, sitting down and taking his little notebook from his suit pocket.

'Papa,' Micaela Celestino said, sitting beside him, 'do you have to do Goldbach now?'

'Why not? We're early. Why shouldn't I do some work while we're waiting for the show to start?'

'Let him,' Elisabetta said, leaning over her father to whisper. 'It's like giving a child a coloring book to keep him quiet.'

'I'm right here,' Carlo said. 'I can hear you.'

The rest of the reserved seating filled with senior members of the Vatican Gendarmerie, the Swiss Guards, including Commander Meyer and Deputy Commander Zeller, and an assortment of cardinals and bishops. As the top of the hour approached, the rest of the chairs filled with Vatican employees.

A door opened behind the podium and Emilio Celestino emerged, dressed in his best black suit with a new silk tie his sisters had bought him as a gift. There was a chair for him beside the podium.

Then the door opened again and two Swiss Guards emerged in full ceremonial regalia, carrying their traditional halberds.

'Ladies and gentlemen,' they called out in unison, 'please rise for His Holiness, Pope Celestine VI.'

The pope came through the door, walking slowly with mincing steps, his body slightly bowed at the waist. He still used a cane much of the day but for this occasion he had left it in the anteroom. For those who hadn't seen him since his hospital discharge, his weight loss was noticeable, enough that a tailor had to alter his vestments. He had joked to colleagues that there were perhaps healthier ways to slim down.

He gripped the podium for stability and asked the assembly to sit.

'Few things give me greater pleasure,' he began, 'than to reward a deserving man or woman. Emilio Celestino is such a person. He is a dedicated professional who adheres to the highest standards of ethics. He came to the Gendarmerie Corps of the Vatican City State as a younger man – and look at him – he is still a young man! He has ascended the ranks because of his abilities and today he arrives at the summit for his installation as Inspector General of the Gendarmerie. Because of the unfortunate events of our recent past, the reputation of the Corps has suffered. But I will tell you this: the Corps was not rotten. It was only a couple of its members. The new inspector general is the man to restore the reputation and the dignity of this fine organization.'

Celestino looked straight ahead, his jaw fixed, betraying none of the emotions brewing inside.

'I am going to betray a confidence,' the pope said, 'because it needs to be said. This young man said to me, "Holy Father, I am devastated that it was I who shot you and caused you great harm." But I said to him, "No, Emilio, you did not harm me. You saved me, and that is why you will be the Inspector General of the Corps and my new chief bodyguard."'

After the ceremony, Celestine lingered for a while chatting with the Celestino family, particularly Carlo. He had been briefed on the mathematician's Goldbach quest and innocently asked about it. Two minutes into Carlo's effervescent discourse on prime numbers and number theory, Elisabetta rescued the pontiff and reminded him of his next appointment.

Cardinal Da Silva came over to offer an arm and the pope gladly took it.

'Thank you,' the pope said. 'Tell me how my new Cardinal Secretary of State is faring.'

'I am settling in, Holy Father.'

'And what of Leoncino, Malucchi, and Cassar?'

'I have sent them into quiet retirement. I don't believe we will be seeing much of them around the Vatican.'

'Well, God be with them,' Celestine said, 'for I am not.'

'There is one matter I should like to discuss with you.'

'Of course.'

'I'm a bit uncomfortable with the lavishness of Pascal Lauriat's apartment. I wonder if I might find more suitable accommodation at the Sanctae Marthae guesthouse.'

'That would be splendid,' Celestine said. 'I would welcome the company. Please see my new first private secretary, Sister Elisabetta, to sort out the details.'

Cal hopped out of the London taxi and made his way into the packed hall. He found her standing at the rear. As the only nun in the room she was easy to spot. He couldn't hide his pleasure in seeing her again.

'Congratulations on your new post,' he said. 'I was excited to hear about it.'

She turned at his voice and smiled. 'I appreciate that very much. It's an interesting job with a steep learning curve. I'm afraid I've never mastered the art of Vatican politics.'

'I'm sure you'll excel at it.'

'To date, I've been relying on confusing the Curia by dint of being a woman. They don't know quite what to make of the situation.'

'I'm sure they don't.'

'Of course you know what my position means?'

'Do I?'

'It means we shall be seeing more of each other. The pope asked me to tell you that he hopes you will visit him with regularity.'

'Well, please tell him that I will.'

She reached into her habit and pulled out a new business card. 'There,' she said. 'You have my private number now.' She lowered her voice. 'I think about you often, if you must know.'

The lump in his throat made him swallow. Its saltiness tasted of longing and the sadness of inevitability. 'I think about you too.'

He felt a tap on his shoulder. It was Julian Sassoon with Gail. Cal had flown over with them and was staying on the same floor at the Langham Hotel. He had found Gail's complete sobriety to be utterly remarkable. All that the new Gail had been knocking back were sparkling waters with slices of lemon.

Cal introduced them to Elisabetta and asked if they wanted to find seats.

'I'd rather stand,' Julian said. 'Gives you a perspective on the room.'

'Then we'll stand,' Cal said. 'How're you feeling about this, Gail?'

'Excited. Nervous. I hardly slept. Can you believe the crowd?'

'I talked to someone on the way in,' Cal said. 'He told me this was the most people they've ever had.'

The house lights dipped and the last of the stragglers made their way inside.

Cal opened his catalogue and turned to the page after the preface. It was a beautiful printing job. The papal bull, *A Tempore Ad Caritas*, filled several pages in a clean typeface. As he read his own words his chest swelled with a melancholy-tinged pride.

A dapper-looking gentleman in a bold pinstripe suit and a rather large bow tie climbed the stage and settled behind the podium.

'A warm welcome to everyone who has turned out for this special, indeed historical event this morning at Christie's. My name is Harris Farquhar. In addition to the overflow crowd with us in London, we have multitudinous attendees by telephone and on the Internet. I believe we all know why we are here. You haven't come to listen to me prattle on, so we're going to launch in with Lot Number 1. May I have the curtain, please?'

The curtain behind him parted and a collective gasp filled the room.

Farquhar waited a full minute for the reality to sink in and for the crowd to settle down. The huge, creamy statue, illuminated in soft spotlight, towered over him. Armed guards formed a semicircle around it.

'Since its creation in 1499, Michelangelo's magnificent Renaissance masterpiece in marble, *Pietà*, has inspired the highest emotions of faith and emotion through its elegant depiction of the body of Jesus Christ brought down from the cross and lying on the lap of the Virgin Mary. *Pietà* is the only work Michelangelo ever signed. For all but two hundred of its years the statue has been housed at St Peter's Basilica at the Vatican. We're going to be opening the bidding on the *Pietà* with a telephone bid.'

Christie's telephone representatives, each holding a red phone, finished their transmittal of Farquhar's remarks. On the lines were sheikhs from Saudi Arabia, the United Arab Emirates, and Qatar, Chinese billionaires, Russian oligarchs, the CEOs of an American casino and a social media company, and the directors of a number of important museums.

The auctioneer paused for effect and leaned over the podium.

'Ladies and gentlemen, we have an opening bid of one billion euros. Do I hear one billion one hundred million?'

AUTHOR'S NOTE

Sister Elisabetta Celestino is mentioned in the book as being the pope's favorite. She had provided extraordinary services to the Vatican during the turbulent time of Celestine's conclave, which led to her special status. Her incredible story features in one of my earlier novels, *The Devil Will Come*.